Holy Fire

Holy Fire

Paul W. Lentz, Jr.

Ty Ty Press, Peachtree City, Georgia, USA

www.stuff-of-life.org

Copyright 2016 as "Where Were You When the World Ended?"
by Paul W. Lentz, Jr.

ISBN 978-0692679500
ISBN 10: 0692679502

10 9 8 7 6 5 4 3 2

Table of Contents

Part I-Today

"It is the absolute right of the state
to manage the formation of public opinion."
Josef Goebbels, Nazi Propaganda Minister, 1939 C.E.

"If Hitler and Goebbels had the internet,
we'd be speaking German today.
The potential for tyranny
is greater than ever before."
Oregon Governor Susan Kennedy,
Democratic Candidate for President

Those who do not remember history may not be doomed
to repeat it, but they are doomed to be taken advantage of
by those who do remember history.
Anonymous

"And I saw when the Lamb opened the seals, four horses and
upon them four riders, and the riders were Pestilence, War,
Famine, and Death. And they were given power, and rode forth."
Pastor Russell Fallow, at the One True Christian Church
Washington Cathedral on Cable Channel *God's Word for You.*

CHAPTER 1: MICHAEL COOKSON

With freedom comes responsibility. Freedom of Speech comes
with the responsibility to speak out against injustice.
Azisa Beman

"Squirt Your Message!" (Internet ad posted on several
popular search engines and social networks.) "Darknet to
Internet; absolute anonymity, privacy, security. Post on darknet
and we'll put it on the Internet. *B* 1.00 per 200 messages. Prices
subject to change. End-to-end encryption available."

~~~~~

NSA Headquarters, Ft. Meade, Maryland

"In less than 24 hours, more than 1,400,000 people in
this country have signed up for this new *Squirt* site," a senior
analyst reported. "We've not been able to penetrate it or find
who runs it. It mimics one of the popular social networking sites
but uses the ampersand for hashtags. This one is on the darknet,
but promises to put posts—that they call *squirts*—on the Internet,
and they're charging for the service in one of the
cryptocurrencies—Bitcoin."

The civilian Deputy Director of the NSA didn't hesitate.
"I want our credit card database updated. Add a field. Mark
everyone who purchases bitcoins after the site went live. And
run correlation algorithms. We should be able to identify most of
the users that way."

"What do we do with the data?" a senior analyst asked.

"For the moment, nothing," the Deputy Director said. "But if things go as expected, we'll need it."

The Director said nothing. He was a political appointee, despite his military grade. He'd first learned about computers when Hollerith punch cards input programs and data, and he had trouble understanding what his staff was talking about.

Condominium of Michael Cookson, Arlington, Virginia

A call from the front desk interrupted my writing.

"Mr. Cookson, two men are on the way up. They had badges and demanded access."

I pressed the F5 key and an image from the webcam above the front door replaced the report I had been reading. One man raised his hand to knock. I pressed another function key and hoped that the computer would have enough time to encrypt and close the files that had been open.

I answered the door.

"Mr. Tom Paine?" one of the men asked.

"I write under that pen name, yes. My name is Michael Cookson. And who might you be?"

The men flipped open badge holders. They probably thought it looked impressive, but I thought they looked like Dr. Who showing someone his psychic paper. I had no time to read the information nor did I have any way of knowing if they were legitimate.

"You use that name on the internet?" The taller man asked.

"Occasionally."

"You know it's against the law to use an alias on the internet?"

"Only if I intend to defraud or defame someone or commit a crime using that alias."

"You talk like a lawyer."

4

"I am. Graduate of UVA, admitted to the bar in Virginia, Maryland, the District of Columbia, and before the Supreme Court." That didn't slow the men. Probably didn't impress them, either.

"You did internet research on Bitcoins. How to buy, what they were worth. You planning a crime?" one asked.

"No, I am writing a book about a dystopian future in which the US government sends agents to harass people for doing things that are legal. Ring any bells, gentlemen?"

The two men exchanged looks that said more than I could understand.

"You should be more careful. We have our eye on you," the taller man said. They both turned and left.

You are right. I will be more careful, I thought. I switched to the wifi signal from the pizza place across the street and opened the darknet browser.

Internet Crash

New York Afterword. The two largest social networking sites went dark at 3:00 AM and remained unavailable until early afternoon. When the sites were restored, the flood of traffic took both down for a short time until flow control could be established. Spokespersons for both sites blame problems at the root-name computers, and renewed calls for implementation of the Anycast software to allow the root-name function to operate from multiple geographic locations. The Federal Communication Commission did not respond to our calls by press time.

Condominium of Michael Cookson, Arlington, Virginia

A young man and a young woman, both dressed in black, entered the foyer. The man's hair was tied in a ponytail; the woman's hair had short, bright red tips that stood out from her head. Both had piercings in nose and ears.

"Are you sure this is the right place? Pretty high-class for a hacker," the woman said.

"Yeah, this is it for sure. We saw the pizza place . . . I traced him that far, before he caught me and blew me off the 'net. And we passed the bank. He uses their wifi, too," the man said.

"He hacked a bank? No wonder he's living in Crystal City."

"Don't think that, Maelwen. He wouldn't. At least, I don't think he would. Come on." The man made a call on his cell phone. Moments later, the inner door buzzed open.

Michael Cookson was standing in the doorway when they reached his condo.

"I'm Dark Knight," the young man said. "This is Maelwen. We're in the right place. I hope?"

"Yes, I'm Red Dragon," Michael said. "Come in. And thank you for trusting me. Want something to drink?"

After everyone was seated, Michael explained. "I don't think what happened to the 'net was an accident. I think someone in the government—Defense, NSA, FCC, I don't know—tested their ability to take down critical parts of the internet. They probably thought it would be justified to fight terrorism. At least, that's the excuse they're using to scare people into accepting a lot of things they're doing."

"Red, you've never been a conspiracy nut," Dark Knight said. "But you're sounding like one, now."

"That's right out of *Where Were You*," Maelwen said, naming a popular multi-player, on-line game set in a dystopian fantasy world of the future.

"If you will follow me into the inner sanctum, I will show you things few mortals have seen," Red Dragon said, quoting a line from the role-playing game in which the three had met.

"Whoa, dude!" Dark Knight said, falling out of character. "This is seriously high tech!" He looked at six large-screen iMacs.

"I never knew anyone who had his own server, before," Maelwen said. "Will you marry me?" She didn't specify whether in real life or in an on-line game.

"Maybe we can talk about that later," Red Dragon said. "For now, watch and learn."

He sat at a keyboard and called up data. As each screen appeared, he explained it in a few words. "Internet backbone. Root computers highlighted. Sub-network among root computers. Watch the traffic. Watch the clock. Traffic count on the backbone. Watch it and watch the clock."

"The message went from the Arlington node to the others. Then *bam* traffic drops," Dark Knight said.

"Can you isolate just the two social sites that went down?" Maelwen asked.

"Glad you asked. Watch."

The data were clear: the two sites went down seconds after the message from the Arlington node to the other root-name computers.

"Correlation is not causation," Maelwen cautioned.

"But it's damn suspicious," Dark Knight said. "And it means we need to watch this."

"More than watch," Maelwen said. "We need to find a way to do without them . . . the root computers, I mean."

"Without the internet, itself," Red Dragon said. "And that's the real reason I asked you to come here. In the early days of wifi, people were making antennas by wrapping wire around Pringles potato chip cans. FM radio stations have this thing called RDS—radio data service—that puts the name of the song and the artist on people's car radio displays. Do you know—"

"Hold on, dude. You want to build a new internet with potato chip cans and hijacked signals?"

"An *alternet*," Red Dragon said. "And yes—potato chip cans, unused parts of the radio spectrum, forgotten copper wire circuits, and more." He paused. "Are you in?"

"Right on, dude, and you can forget about Maelwen. I want to marry you!" Dark Knight said.

Home of hackattack, Omaha, Nebraska

What the heck! the young man thought. He had checked his home wifi system; he had tested connectivity six different ways. The internet was still there, just not all of it. He swung his chair in a quarter circle and typed on a different keyboard. *No joy,* he thought. *Time for chip cans.*

At the urging of a hacker known only as Red Dragon, hackers and geeks were creating a potato-chip net. The network was cooperative. Guest accounts allowed access to carefully vetted friends. *Chipcan,* texted to a cell phone, was the signal to activate the net. At least, that was the theory. Kevin Stewart opened his cell phone and texted *chipcan* to his friends list. Then, he turned on his computer and switched to the antenna pointed at his best friend's house.

It worked! he thought, and exchanged messages with others on what they called the *alternet*. The chatter was from as far away as Alaska and Ecuador. *How do we connect with Ecuador?* Kevin wondered, but lost that thought in the immediacy of the moment.

~~~~~

Condominium of Representative Thomas Stanley (R-OK), Arlington, Virginia

—high flyer from red dragon your signal leaks like titanic what you using for antenna

George Stanley nearly peed his pants when the message appeared on his screen. It was using a chat program he knew he hadn't opened. He'd heard of Red Dragon. He was said to be a good guy. George debated for a moment before replying.

—one built into router
—that's your problem not directional try pringles can

Before High Flyer could ask, Red Dragon had sent a file with specs and a diagram

—pulls more energy but more directional you in condo 1501 point toward middle fifth floor

George watched the chat screen disappear and went to the kitchen. *Pringles,* he thought. *Who'd have guessed? Now, where am I going to get bare copper wire?*

CHAPTER 2: TIM KARUS

Archbishop Isaac Trucido's Estate, Shenandoah Mountains, Virginia

"Your Eminence, the Council is assembled," I said.

"Thank you, Tim. You know that ten years ago, you might have helped me put on seven layers of robes, and then march into the meeting room ahead of me, carrying a cross on a stick."

"Actually, Isaac, ten years ago that's exactly what I did. And believe me, I'm just as happy as you that you wear business suits now."

Archbishop Isaac Trucido, absolute leader of the One True Christian Church, picked up not a crosier but an iPad. I took my own iPad and followed him into the meeting room. The Council stood when Isaac entered.

"Gentlemen, please be seated. Mr. Karus has the agenda."

I poked at my iPad and the agenda appeared on the screen.

The first item was a review of the recent elections, and the victories by Republicans and the ballooning American Freedom First Party. Super-Political Action Committee money, much of it from Isaac, supported the AFFP.

"How much did the election cost us?" Councilor Eleven asked.

I poked my iPad again and displayed a summary.

"The Kentucky Biblical Values people were big fund-raisers for Democrats in that state. They and the unions put about $7 million behind them. Our Super-PAC spent over $12 million, but it paid off. AFFP candidates swept the state."

"What are we doing to contain the Biblical Values people?"

Isaac took that question. "We sent missionaries into the state. They'll preach our message . . . and overwhelm the so-called *Biblical Values* group."

Those missionaries will do more than preach, I thought. *They will convince pastors to link their congregations with the One True Christian Church and will eliminate those who do not.* I didn't understand the Council's reasoning. The Biblical Values people believed the same things the OTCC professed to believe, the same things Isaac pretended to believe. Why were we attacking them? I decided it was because they had power and money that Isaac wanted.

"We put $18 million into New Jersey to counter liberal unions, and $10 million in Virginia to counter anti-gun propaganda. Half of that went through the firearms lobbies. Our total, including the other races on the screen, was $90,350,000." I didn't say we'd need over three billion dollars for the upcoming presidential election.

"None of it can be traced to us. Is that correct?" one of the Twelve asked.

"Yes, sir. That is correct. These Super-PACs are isolated from us. However, all officials of the S-PACs are members of the Church, vetted for—"

"And if someone figures that out?" Councilor Seven interrupted me.

"Although all are members, none are on the rolls of any affiliated congregation," Isaac said, saving me from having to answer. He didn't say that the men managing the S-PACs were all sworn members of the Soldiers of the Cross. The Councilors didn't need to know that.

12

"If there are no other questions," I said, "the next agenda item is a report from Councilor Six." He was the only one of the Twelve who was ordained. It had been easy for Isaac to recruit him to a more powerful pulpit.

"Gentlemen, *But of that day and that hour knoweth no man, no, not the angels which are in heaven, neither the Son, but the Father.* Or, so we teach. And so they believe. Five years ago, a Pew Research poll showed that nearly fifty percent of Christians in the US believed that Christ would return to Earth by the year 2050. Thanks to our work, that number is now thirty percent." He chuckled.

"We can't do long-term planning if our people are living in a short-term dream. Part of that planning includes penetration of the Department of the Treasury and the White House through control of the Secret Service. Forty-eight members of the Soldiers of the Cross have obtained employment with the Secret Service. Twenty are assigned to Treasury; twenty-seven are members of protective details for various officials and embassies. One is in administration."

The Councilor's smile at the mutters of disappointment was brief. "He is head of the personnel office, responsible for processing all applicants. Gentlemen, we are in."

I was surprised that we were trying to get into the White House. The Treasury part made sense. They investigated money laundering and Isaac's church was a bigger money launderer than the Mexican drug cartels. Having our people in Treasury would provide early warning of problems and perhaps prevent investigations. But the White House? The people who protect the president? What were we planning?

I almost missed Isaac's reply.

"Very good, Number Six. Superb."

Isaac turned to the man seated at his right. "Councilor One, what do we have on Senator March?"

"Warwick will put his top man on Senator March's staff. Mel Appleton will be March's chief political advisor. Given

Appleton's background, he'll be chief speechwriter, too. If anyone can scare up more Super-PAC money than we can, it is Richard Warwick. Our projections are that March will be elected."

"What will Warwick get out of this?"

"Access?" suggested Councilor Seven.

"Power, more likely," Isaac said. "Warwick wants to go public with his international connections. He'll need presidential support for trade agreements with South America. We've penetrated Warwick's shell companies. He owns half the mines in Chili and is buying up the largest companies in Brazil. He already owns most of the sugar cane—"

"Sugar cane? He's going into the rum business?" One of the councilors said. Isaac concealed his distaste at being interrupted.

"Not rum, biofuel. For when the oil runs out. Warwick plans for the long-term, just as we do. The real question is, what do we get out of it, and how can we trump Warwick?" Isaac said.

The Council debated, mostly squashing each other's ideas. I pretended to be fiddling with my iPad but was sending a position paper to Isaac. He read it and raised his eyebrow. Then, he spoke.

"Gentlemen, trumping Warwick will be simple. Bishop Fallow is the public face of the Church. To the public and the government he is the *de facto* head of the Church. Tim, summon him. Gentlemen, plan to remain overnight. We will meet with Bishop Fallow tomorrow, and I will explain our strategy."

~~~~~

"Tim, that was brilliant," Isaac said. We had returned to his private suite. He brushed my hair back from my forehead. "Truly brilliant."

After Isaac fell asleep, I slipped to my bedroom, but I could not sleep. I took the rosary from the bedside table and held it in my hands the way my grandmother taught me, but I could not say the words. The message I had sent to Isaac would begin a process that would turn the world upside down, and I was afraid.

Two days later, Isaac and I were reviewing his schedule when a phone rang. It was a private line, one I never answered. He said *yes*, listened for a few moments, and hung up.

"That was Councilor Six. We will receive a call from a Mr. Lewazi asking for a meeting. Six said it would be worthwhile to meet with him. Do you know who he is?" Isaac said.

I did not recognize Lewazi's name, but was already pressing keys on my computer. "It would help if I could spell Lewazi," I said, as combination after combination failed. Then, I got close enough that the Google search engine could fill in the blanks for me. *L'Wazi*. It took only seconds to read the first lines of his bio. This had to be the guy.

"Lobbyist for the National Association for the Advancement of Persons of Color," I said. "Usually just *NAAPC*. Graduate of Harvard Law *suma cum laude*. Clerked for Supreme Court Justice Clarence Thomas. Joined a Washington law firm and is now the senior partner."

Washington, DC. I thought. *In Councilor Six's territory. What's the connection?*

The call came less than an hour later on a line I was allowed to answer. I set up an appointment with Mr. L'Wazi.

CHAPTER 3: CASEY STEWART

"War is the continuation of politics
by other means."
Carl von Clausewitz 1780-1832 C.E.

US Air Force Academy

"For the Romans, it was Mars; for the Hindus, Kartikeye; for the Hittites, Wurrukatte; for the Greeks, Ares; for the Hebrews, Yahweh. These, among scores of others, were the gods of war. Every so-called civilization has had a god of war. But they were the gods of the rulers and the country. The soldiers' god was Mithras, from Zoroastrianism. Mithras was adopted by Greek soldiers and to a larger extent by the Roman legions, and then folded into the Christ myths of the New Testament."

Cadet Lieutenant Casey Stewart sat with twenty other members of his Senior Class. The lecture was one of a series billed as 'the philosophy of war.' It did not appear in the official curriculum. One could not sign up for the lectures. One had to be invited.

"Mithras did not grant victory," Captain Fall, the speaker, continued. "He would, if asked, grant strength and courage in the face of adversity and should death be inevitable, offer an easy death."

The captain explained further the differences between a god of war and a god of soldiers, and described the secret Mithras Brotherhood among members of the Roman Legions.

Six days before graduation, Casey and five of his classmates who had attended the first lecture were invited to join that secret brotherhood. By this time, they had attended dozens of lectures and discussions of the real military history of the world, and had determined for themselves that the brotherhood still existed.

~~~~~

Squadron Officers School, Maxwell Air Force Base, Alabama

Captain Casey Stewart sat in the auditorium called by generations of students, "the Blue Bedroom." Casey had studied military history, strategy, and tactics. Much of the information presented at the school was not new to him. He was looking forward to today's presentation. It would be a Top Secret discussion of the US nuclear arsenal and strategy. In the afternoon, an expert in the corresponding Soviet, now Russian, capabilities and plans would appear. Access to the Blue Bedroom required not only their official ID but also personal identification by their section's faculty advisor.

That night, Casey could not sleep. His mind dwelt on what he had heard. *MAD*, or *Mutually Assured Destruction* had always been more than that. *More like Mutual Annihilation, or Mutual Armageddon*, he thought. Even using today's reduced nuclear inventories, and even if one believed the Russians had really reduced theirs, a strike by the US or Russia would create a nuclear winter that would devastate the Northern Hemisphere, and likely end civilization.

No wonder the Brotherhood focuses on deterring war and avoiding fighting wherever possible, he thought.

~~~~~

Squadron Officers School Classroom Building

Casey had recognized a member of the faculty as one of the men who had been part of his initiation into the Brotherhood of Mithras. By custom, Casey could not make first contact. He was not surprised when the man spoke to him in the hallway. "Some of your friends are getting together tomorrow night," Lt. Colonel Fall said. "At the back of the dining room of the *Whatever* is a door marked 'private.' Be there."

Before Casey could acknowledge the order, the man turned and walked away.

"Whatever" Bar and Restaurant, Montgomery, Alabama

Casey entered the door marked 'Private.' It led to a short hallway. There was a button next to the door at the end of the hallway and a camera pointed at Casey. He pushed the button. The door buzzed, and he stepped in. Copper hardware cloth with metal bushings on the edges covered the inside of the door. *A screened facility in the back room of a bar?* he wondered. The Brotherhood of Mithras took on a new meaning, although he wasn't sure what it was.

Lt. Colonel Fall greeted Casey. He had seen Casey stare at the door. "More than you expected," he said.

Casey nodded. "Yes, sir. But, after what we heard recently, somehow I'm not surprised."

"I knew you were a good choice," Fall said. "Come, meet your brothers."

Before the evening was over, Casey had met members of the brotherhood from the other service academies, The Citadel, and VMI. He was not surprised to find women in the brotherhood, nor was he surprised that none of them seemed to find it odd to be a woman in a *brotherhood*.

~~~~~

Air Force Staffing Office, Old Executive Office Building, Washington, DC

Nor was Lt. Colonel Casey Stewart surprised that his commander on the White House Detail was General Fall. They had run into one another often since the day in November, 2000 when Casey had attended the first lecture on the philosophy of war.

"Casey," General Fall began. "It is no accident you are here. You are now one of five officers who will carry the president's *football*, the briefcase that carries the nuclear launch codes. You need to know a few things about that."

Their meeting took more than two hours after which Casey had a new understanding of his duties—and his responsibilities.

CHAPTER 4: LIAM MACLAUREN

You will never do anything in this world without courage.
It is the greatest quality of the mind next to honor.
Aristotle 384-322 BCE

Edmonton, Alberta

Liam MacLauren waited in the anteroom. He could not sit, but paced. His eighteenth birthday was only weeks away. He could no longer be a cadet in the Royal Canadian Air Cadet League. He knew what the board—adults, reservists and active duty officers—were doing in the next room. They were deciding his fate. There were few openings in the League for civilians or adults. Liam's felony record, even though sealed because he had been a minor, would prevent him from entering the Canadian military.

"Cadet Warrant Officer First Class MacLauren, please report to the board."

The voice interrupted Liam's reverie. He rose, pulled at the hem of his jacket, glanced at the shine on his boots, and entered the room. He halted, smartly at the table behind which sat his commander and four others whom he did not know. A man with three oak leaves on his epaulets returned Liam's salute. Liam knew then he was about to be led to the scaffold. He steeled himself, sat rigidly in the hard chair, and waited for the order of execution.

"Warrant Officer MacLauren, what is the first duty of a soldier in the Canadian Forces?"

Liam had been prepared for any question but that one. However, he answered quickly.

"To defend the Confederation against all enemies, whether external or internal, sir."

"Would you kill to perform that duty?"

Liam was taken aback. Never had he thought of killing as part of his duty to Queen and Country. However, "Yes, sir."

The next question was more surprising. It came from a woman in the uniform of an Air Forces colonel.

"Why?"

Liam thought. A small part of his mind saw that the people behind the table were not impatient with the delay.

"Ma'am, if one enemy death might save two innocents; if a dozen enemy deaths might save hundreds, I would do it, ma'am. I would kill. I hope you don't think I'd like it."

The people behind the table exchanged looks and nods. The woman spoke.

"You are the senior cadet in the Edmonton Wing. You have said you would kill if duty required. Would you at age eighteen agree to become a recruit-private again?"

The people behind the table gave Liam time to think.

"Yes, ma'am," he answered. "As long as there was a promise at the end."

The woman who had asked the question smiled. So did the senior officer.

"Tomorrow, you will leave for PQ, where you will become a recruit-private at Collège Militaire Royal de Saint-Jean."

CHAPTER 5: BIG BROTHER I

Big Brother is watching. Try to look busy.
Anonymous

Retirees & Dependents Must Submit to Biometric ID

The Department of Defense (DoD) announced that retirees and their families who have access to military installations must submit to the same biometric identification system used for active duty personnel, their dependents, and contractors. The system is crosschecked every 24 hours with the National Crime Information Center to determine whether any person registered with the system has active wants or warrants.

Department of Homeland Security, Deputy Director's Office

"So far, ma'am, eighteen states have adopted positive citizenship driver's licenses. They're all red states—the list is on your screen. Between them, they have about 20% of the US adult population registered. Not everyone is covered: children, the elderly who don't get the corresponding state ID card, and the illegals. We have people working on the other states and we continue to lobby Congress to make this a national requirement. So far, there's too much push-back to that from the libsymps."

"And we have that data base?" the Deputy Director asked.

"Yes, ma'am. And we're integrating it with the FBI databases. There are problems though. The FBI has millions of paper records that haven't been entered into their system. Mostly reports of non-prosecutions, releases, and acquittals."

"They would be the 'guilty until proven innocent' people," the Deputy Director said. "I'm not worried about them. It's always best to have something on people when we pick them up. Let them contest it. What does the Department of Defense say? Can we link this to their system?"

"They're still resisting, ma'am."

"We'll not get this president to overrule them. Maybe the next one."

The Deputy Director didn't worry about being replaced by a new administration. First, she was a career civil servant. Second, she was a member of the American Freedom First Party and of a Maryland congregation of the One True Christian Church. If a third reason were needed, she was ambitious, clever, and ruthless.

Biometrics, Inc., San Jose, CA

"Yes we're working Saturday—and Sunday. I'd better not see anyone the least bit buzzed. We're going global, and have reached the tipping point. The call from Interpol cinched the deal. We're going to provide one hundred thirty seven of our ID stations to them to register refugees. They're overwhelmed; no one else in the world has our technology. As soon as Germany and the rest of the EU countries see it in operation, we will get at least ten times that many orders.

"Get on the phone to China. They don't close on weekends and will be geared up. Make sure the chips we need are on the way by tomorrow—airfreight. Don't worry, Interpol will pay the difference."

Coffee Shop, Wheatly, Oklahoma

"Café Americano with an extra shot, and you got a burner I can rent?" The customer, one of many college-age customers, asked the barista.

"Café Americano high octane I can do. Burner's a no-go. They'd shut me down."

"Huh?"

"Homeland Security—something called the Bureau of Communication—came in last week, said we couldn't rent—not even lend—what they called *unregistered laptops*. I said, 'So, register them.' They warned me about getting smart with Federal Agents and said to get rid of the burners or they would shut me down. Can't afford that, man."

DHS Closes Terrorist Communications

God's Word for You. Terrorists' ability to communicate their plans against the Nation and the Lord God have been foiled by the Department of Homeland Security. Wifi hotspots around the nation have been ordered to destroy all unregistered laptop computers, the so-called *burners* that are used by terrorists, drug dealers, and other enemies of the state to communicate and coordinate their plans.

~~~~~

Biometrics, Inc., San Jose, CA

"Look, this is hot. It's our ticket to being part of the One Percent who control ninety-nine percent of the wealth of this country. Damn it, Leonard, if you can't see that . . . "

"I see it, all right. We have a chip that can be implanted in someone's breastbone—shot through the skin with an air gun. Cover the wound with a Band-Aid and the subject walks away. Can't be removed except by major surgery. No power until it's hit by a detector—at an airport, subway station, or in the hands of a DHS goon.

"Jim, you know I'm not a libsymp, but I'm not a mindless fundie, either. And I damn sure don't want that kind of power in the hands of the government."

"Leonard, don't forget that we have the ultimate control. We are the ones who provide the chips; we are the ones who program them—and all the detectors."

"Not we, Jim, the Chinese. They're the ones who make the chips, including the ones we put in the detectors. What if—"

"What if an asteroid from the Oort Cloud gets a tweak from Jupiter's gravity and decides to drop into Earth for a visit? What if the fundies are right, and the *rapture* is just around the corner?"

"Okay, Jim, I won't argue any more. Let's go with it, and see what happens."

CHAPTER 6: MEL APPLETON

One of the penalties for not voting
is that you end up being governed
by your inferiors.
Plato c. 428-348 BCE

Richard Warwick's Estate, Adirondack Mountains, New York

"A libsymp school teacher won the open seat on the Mt. Pleasant City Council. How did that happen?" Richard Warwick asked. He gestured for a butler to refill his coffee cup.

"Sir, the turnout was low," I answered after scanning the screen of my iPad. "Fewer than seven percent of registered voters showed at the polls, and only eighty percent of eligible voters are registered."

I hesitated before adding, "Sir, the American Freedom First Party swept the nation—governors' mansion and state legislatures. Louisiana is a given for Republicans—governor and legislature. Mount Pleasant is a town of only forty-five thousand people in the middle of a rural Georgia county. Why is it important?"

"Mel, that town has been a libsymp breeding ground for years," Warwick answered. He put down his coffee cup, stood, and paced. "The only time more than twenty percent of them voted was when there was a referendum on liquor sales on Sunday. Managed an eighty-five percent turnout for that.

"The black guy they elected to the state legislature is going to take on my man in the next congressional election. If the right people don't vote, I'll lose his seat. You ought to know this."

"I do, sir. I've filed the paperwork for an S-PAC to support your candidates in Georgia. I thought there might be something less obvious, something I was missing."

"Mel, keep an eye on Mt. Pleasant," Mr. Warwick said, and then changed the subject. "What have you got planned for Senator March?"

"An anti-immigration rally in Arizona. Officially, it's a state American Freedom First Party event, and officially, Senator March is still aligned with the Republican Party. He will announce at the rally that he is switching to the AFFP."

"Is your suitcase packed?"

"Always, sir."

"Transportation is waiting—helicopter to Frankfort-Highland airport and one of the Gulfstreams to Tempe. Senator March expects you. You will attend the rally in Arizona, and then hang on like a leech until he's elected and you get your own office in his White House. Keep this iPhone charged. It's got the same encryption and system override as the ones the Secret Service people carry."

Senator March's Hotel Suite, Tempe Arizona

"Senator March, I'm Mel Appleton. Thank you for this opportunity to work with you."

"You're not kidding me, Mr. Appleton, and I hope you're not kidding yourself. You're here because Richard Warwick wants you here, and you come with a lot of PAC dollars."

I wasn't prepared for so abrupt and frank a welcome. I was afraid that I would be kicked out of the room and blacklisted.

Then the senator said, "On the other hand, you also come with some impressive credentials. I got a call from Haley. He credits you with his win in 2003. Hell, you were still a teenager. As I said, impressive. You have a speech for me for tonight?"

"Yes, sir." I pulled a page from my briefcase. "I understand you don't want something written out for you, but just talking points and phrases."

The senator looked at my notes before folding them and putting them in his jacket pocket. "This will do. See Nick. He'll arrange your hotel room and give you the calendar, and make sure the rest of the team knows who you are."

I don't need the calendar, I thought. *I'm the one who made it up, and I'll be the one doing the scheduling from now until the inauguration—and, with luck and careful planning—for eight more years after that.*

Conference Center, Tempe Arizona

"Mel? What's going on? Did you forget to charge your phone?"

"No sir, Mr. Warwick."

"Mel, I didn't give you the phone for a paperweight. I expect to hear from you."

It's been less than a day, I thought. "Sir, I gave the notes for the speech to the Senator. I think he liked it. I've got a hotel room. Nothing else—"

"What did he say about the speech?"

"Just 'it will do,' sir."

"Pay attention to how he uses it. Which points he pounds, which ones he slides over, which ones he doesn't use. Remember who he talks to and what he says to them. You're his chief political advisor and speech writer, so you will be expected to stay close to him."

"Yes, sir." The phone beeped. Warwick had hung up.

March's advisor or Warwick's spy? I wondered. *The only political advice I will give will be what Warwick tells me to say. That wasn't necessarily bad. I will present Warwick's advice—orders—as if they were my own. To most of the staff, I will sound astute and clever. Only March will know I am no more than Warwick's echo.*

~~~~~

Since I was a new face on the March team, Nick Thackery got the Arizona State AFFP Chairman to stick to me while I stuck to Senator March. The Party Chairman knew names and faces including spouses and kids. He made sure I met everyone at the reception, in the green room, and afterwards at the Tex-Mex restaurant where we had beans, beer, ribs, pulled-pork, fry-bread, and green chili. I asked for a 5:00 AM wakeup call so I could get in a run, and took several of the antacids in my Dopp kit before I tried to sleep.

~~~~~

The core team, which now included me as March's second in command, took a Gulfstream to Washington. The Senator had to attend a quorum call for a critical vote on a budget supplement. Despite the historic push for a two-year budget agreement, no one was happy with all the compromises. Things were already being tweaked and twisted. This particular vote was on extra money for helium production for the aerostats deployed along the US borders to support the Department of Homeland Security. The only helium production facility was in Texas. And Senator March represented Texas. *Go figure,* I thought. *The helium balloons that kids used to have for their birthday parties were one of the first victims of the 'War on Terrorism.' But no one seemed to notice. It was the new normal.*

Senate Office Building, Washington, DC

"Mr. Appleton, this will be your office. I'll get my things out right away." Frank Hopkins, the man I was replacing on March's Washington staff wasn't too unhappy. He was going to run March's local offices in Texas. It wasn't a promotion, but it was better than being fired.

"We met before, Frank," I said. "At the Republican Governor's Convention a few years ago. You were working for Piyush. I was with Haley. We talked at the bar about the Pearl River reclamation project."

"I wasn't sure you'd remember," Frank said. "Too bad nothing came of that. The chemical runoff from the Stennis Space Center is as bad as ever. I don't think anyone has seen a fish or alligator in the river in years."

"Let's keep in touch," I said. "You know where Senator March is headed, and you know a lot about him. I could sure use your thoughts. We could work well, together."

I was making both a request and a promise. If Frank would help me during the campaign, I would push to get him on the transition team and then the White House staff. We were both betting our careers on Senator March. We'd rise or sink together. It didn't take him any time to agree.

"Sounds good, Mel. I won't have my special cell phone any more, but there's a secure phone in the Dallas and Houston offices. Nick Thackery can show you how to call them."

I put out my hand, and we shook. *Honor among thieves*, I thought, *has nothing on honor among political advisors and politicians' staff.*

CHAPTER 7: PORK PIE POLITICS

The World Citizen "Looks like at least one goobernor has found a way to take advantage of the current El Niño that has brought warmer and wetter winter weather to the Southeast. He's proposing more than three hundred million dollars for pork-barrel projects for *local reservoirs*, meaning lakes and dams in districts that supported him, plus some—in his words—'cutting edge' projects. Get this. He wants to pump surplus water into aquifers so it will be 'safe, saved, and stored' for future use. This guy is better at alliteration than I am, and I salute him for that.

"There are many other ways to deal with the state's chronic water shortage, most of them cheaper and more environmentally friendly. Preserving and restoring natural wetlands is the cheapest and simplest. That doesn't matter to the goobernor who is busy paying back campaign contributions with pork-barrel projects. This is Muldoon. Remember: all politics is about power, and all power is political. Think about it."

CHAPTER 8: SUSAN KENNEDY

"We receive as friendly
ideas that we find agreeable,
we resist with dislike
ideas that we find disagreeable."
Michael Faraday, 1821-1867 C.E.

WhatDrWho Blog: Bat Boy Endorses Kennedy

According to the *World of Weird,* after a lengthy and cordial meeting, Bat Boy has endorsed Governor Susan Kennedy to be the next President of the United States.

~~~~~

Rightly Sweeps 8:00 PM Slot

For Immediate Release—Ranogen Polling, Inc. Last night's edition of Bert Rightly's *Take 'Em to the Wire* garnered thirty-nine percent of the audience for his time slot.

~~~~~

Susan Kennedy's Hotel Room, Madison, Wisconsin

"And what about this *Bat Boy* report?" I asked Ruth.

"He does seem to have a thing for Democrats, doesn't he?" Ruth said. "He and Bill Clinton were buddies, according to the tabloids. Of course, the tabloids are written at the third grade level—right down there with foxprop. After what's happened to the public school system, it's probably reaching most of the population. Smile if someone asks and say you haven't seen that particular newspaper. It should shut off even the most persistent.

"On the serious side, Susan, National Radio Service has declared you the winner of the debate," Ruth said. "Ranogen agrees, but they're not saying much."

"Not too surprising," I said. "Have any of the right-wing press said anything?"

"Bert Rightly on *American Fire Network* said Mr. Stewart had 'a better grasp of economics,'" Ruth replied. "He said your message of rights for women, Blacks, Hispanics, and the LGBT community was *old style* Democratic rhetoric.

"He played and replayed this line," Ruth added, and pressed the play button on the TV remote.

Ruth, the rest of the staff, and I watched as my image said, "We have a genetic mandate to like those who are like us, and to fear, even hate, those who are not like us. But we also have a brain, a mind that can overcome our evolutionary past and break through those barriers."

"Susan, the right-wing press will have a field day with that."

"Let them," I said. "If we're going to break down the walls in people's minds, we're going to have to shock them with the truth."

Evolution a Plank in Kennedy's Platform?

God's Word for You. Oregon Governor Susan Kennedy's statement during last night's debate that "we can overcome our evolutionary past" raises again the specter that our children will be taught that humans are descended from monkeys, that we are only animals lacking a soul, and that the 'theory of evolution' must be taught to the exclusion of the Creation Story as told in the Inerrant Word of the Lord God.

Susan Kennedy's Campaign Bus

"How does Ranogen get their numbers so quickly?" I asked.

"They don't have to poll people," Ruth Gordon replied. "The cable TV people collect audience summaries and sell them to Ranogen. It's simply a report on the number of televisions tuned to each channel. There's no guarantee that anyone is watching. Still, it's useful data."

"You didn't say *information*; you said *data,*" I said.

"Big difference," Ruth said. "And Ranogen doesn't always understand that."

"Can we do anything?"

"Ignore them. Our own polling people will publish counter arguments. It may be hard to convince people, especially after they've seen Ranogen's numbers. It's hard to change someone's mind, even with the truth, once their mind is made up."

NAAPC Convention, Detroit, Michigan

The appearances at the convention of Governor Kennedy, Senator March, and the also-rans were carefully orchestrated so they would not encounter one another. Unscripted meetings between political opponents could prove awkward to both the speakers and the NAAPC. Historically, Democratic candidates were scheduled in the best time-slots. Mr. L'Wazi had played hardball with the leadership and scheduled March for prime time. The speeches would be carried on the *American Fire Network* and followed by the "Take 'Em to the Wire with Bert Rightly" show.

~~~~~

Mr. L'Wazi had made sure he was alone in the green room when Ruth and I were brought in.

"Mrs. Kennedy," L'Wazi said in greeting.

He ignored Ruth, and spoke directly to me. "Lots of folks looking forward to your speech, Mrs. Kennedy. You've brought up things that have only been whispered about."

"You mean my assertion that the so-called War on Drugs was deliberately designed to target black communities? I know that the righteous right says this is not true, but just rhetoric. You and I know that drugs and criminal prosecution for drug offenses have disproportionately affected Blacks."

L'Wazi brushed that off just as he had brushed off Ruth Gordon. I knew that powerful women were not part of his worldview. Women who served other women were even farther down the Great Chain of Being.

"Mrs. Kennedy, your speech will be delayed by thirty minutes. A diversion I arranged. We need time to talk about something important. Before this convention is over, there will be a split within this organization. A larger and more vibrant segment will align itself with the American Freedom First Party. The rest will continue to be the lukewarm, the old school, the sit-down-at-the-lunch-counter rather than stand-up-and-fight activists, the disinterested who were lulled into complacency by the Democratic Party, and who have sucked at the public teat for so long they can no longer produce milk." L'Wazi apparently thought his soft vulgarity would offend me, perhaps distract me.

"Why are you telling me this, Mr. L'Wazi?" I asked. *And what do you want in return?* I wondered.

"I will remain with the first group. I need to turn over power over the second group to someone . . . your boyfriend, Azisa Beman, Ms. Gordon?"

Ruth kept her composure. It was a closely held secret that she was dating a man who was one of the top lawyers for the Southern Freedom Law Center. The SFLC was too far to the left for most Democrats.

"Don't tell me you didn't know, Mrs. Kennedy," L'Wazi said.

"Of course I knew," I snapped. "You said we had thirty minutes. You've already wasted seven of them. Get to the point."

I watched L'Wazi's face as he tried not to show his surprise.

"Very well. I can ensure that Mr. Azisa Beman becomes not only the titular head of the left-leaning members of the NAAPC, but also its *de facto* leader. In return, I ask only access and information."

"You would have Ms. Gordon spy on her friend and on those who support him?"

"Not spy on, but exchange information, information that would benefit both of us."

"Your decision, Ruth," I said.

It took Ruth only a few moments of thought to answer. "I will tell Mr. Beman about this offer. If he agrees, it may be implemented. If I ever find that you are not being completely open and honest I will encourage him to terminate the arrangement."

"You have your answer from Ruth, Mr. L'Wazi," I said. "Fifteen minutes remain before my speech. Is there any bottled water?"

~~~~~

"It's a better hotel than the campaign can afford," I said.

"More of Mr. L'Wazi's doing, I suspect," Ruth said. "Is he for real? Should I trust him?"

"I could tell you my thoughts, but they might take you in the wrong direction. You must decide for yourself and for Azisa. I'm sorry you and he must be separated for so long."

"You are separated from your husband," Ruth said.

"True, but we've had many years to understand the need." I paused for a moment. Ruth waited.

"You'll want to talk to Azisa face-to-face," I said. "He's in Tennessee, at a trial. Do you suppose the campaign could manage a visit to . . . what's the name of the town? Dayton? That was where the Scopes trial was held, isn't it? What might we do there?"

"Susan, you're a genius!" Ruth said. "We need to comment on evolution, and to respond to the right's attack on you for using that word. Give me overnight to work it, and I'll have a schedule and a dynamite speech for you, tomorrow. And, thank you!"

Susan Kennedy, Dayton, Tennessee

I spent most campaign contributions on ads—mostly television. A few S-PACs were providing ad support, but their money couldn't be used for the campaign. These *Shadow* PACs were supposed to promote issues, not candidates, although that was a thin fiction. There was little money available for the luxury of a private plane or suites at the best hotels. My staff—Ruth and four aides—understood. The rooms at the Dayton Vacation Inn were Spartan. I surprised Ruth when I switched room keys with her.

"This key is to a room with a king-sized bed. I won't be needing that," I said.

The next morning, Ruth and Azisa met me for breakfast at a chain restaurant that featured pancakes. I stuck to yogurt and a flaky, nutty cereal, and smiled at the two young people's appetites.

"Ruth's told you?" I asked.

Azisa nodded. So did Ruth.

"And I have agreed to accept Mr. L'Wazi's offer," Azisa said. "With the conditions Ruth set and with others. I will not betray confidences or endanger people. And he is a dangerous man."

"I understand," I said. "You need not tell me anything more about it, but you always may ask me for help."

We finished our breakfast in silence.

I watched Ruth kiss her boyfriend goodbye. He would remain in Dayton while she traveled with me on the campaign trail. Ruth and Azisa's meetings were brief and secret. Even the most liberal party members were uncomfortable with mixed-race relationships, although few would admit it.

Kennedy Shocks the Nation *The World Citizen*

Governor Susan Kennedy, the leading Democratic candidate for the party's presidential nomination shocked party leaders and the nation when she asked her strongest rival, Arthur Stewart to be her running mate. Ms. Kennedy and Mr. Stewart individually have the support of more than 78% of likely Democratic voters. The poll has a margin of error of 3.7%. Pollsters are scurrying to find what the numbers will show if Mr. Stewart accepts the offer.

~~~~~

Susan Kennedy Motorcade

Ruth and I were alone in the back of a black Lincoln Town Car driven by a Secret Service agent. A sliding glass panel separated us from the driver. While not a limo, the stretched Town Car had extra legroom and a cooler stocked with water and protein bars. Black SUVs with aides and more Secret Service preceded and followed us.

"Susan, you know we have no chance of winning the election. The best we can do is show that there is opposition to the AFFP. The more votes we get, the easier will be your real job—after the election." Ruth said what we both knew to be true.

"I don't look forward to that. Speeches, travel, living out of a suitcase. It will be like the campaign, only worse."

"Susan, you've got to do it. Someone has to stand up to these fascists." Ruth paused before adding, "March is considering Representative Stanley as his running mate. There are rumors that Stanley's younger son, George, is gay. That could be useful—"

"No, absolutely not," I interrupted. "He's a child. This campaign, this party will not drag a child into the streets to be crucified on a cross of prejudice and the OTCC's version of Sharia Law." I spoke more firmly and sharply than I normally did.

"Susan, I was thinking of inclusion, not attack," Ruth said.

"I'm sorry, Ruth," I said. "The AFFP has taken the campaign into the gutter. I wasn't thinking. Inclusion, yes, but George Stanley, no."

~~~~~

Before he left the car, the driver removed a flash drive that held the recording of the two women's conversation and replaced it with a blank.

~~~~~

Headquarters, Soldiers of the Cross, Lynchburg, Virginia

"Director General, the transcription is ready to send to Archbishop Trucido." A young man in the uniform of a lieutenant of the Soldiers of the Cross spoke. "Kennedy is resigned to losing, but plans to be active after the election. Her aide believes Representative Thomas Stanley's younger son, George, is homosexual, but Kennedy refuses to pursue that. She spoke of Biblical Law as prejudicial and compared it to Sharia Law."

"Nothing more substantive than that?" the Director General asked.

"No, sir."

"Then send it."

~~~~~

Susan Kennedy-Arthur Stewart Campaign Bus

Ruth Gordon handed one copy of the *Banner* to me and another to Arthur. "Think we can swing 13% of the voters by November?" she asked.

"Unlikely, Ruth," I said. "But we will remain in the race and do our best. We're not fighting for the White House any more. We're fighting to keep enough of our people in office in enough states to stop March's plans."

"Do we know what the *righteous right* is planning?" Ruth asked.

"If they fulfill their campaign promises, they'll ban all abortions, even when medically necessary and overturn every civil-rights and gun-safety law we've passed since . . . since 1968." Arthur Stewart's voice was soft, but every word was bitten off. He spoke in a metronomic monotone, a stark contrast to his usual polished, Ivy-League diction.

"The AFFP and OTCC have proclaimed that they have the moral high ground. They've seized the flag, patriotism, and Bible-based Christianity as their own. They think they've left us nothing, but they're wrong. And we have to show them that."

CHAPTER 9: POLLY SINGER

A free press can, of course,
be good or bad, but,
most certainly without freedom,
the press can never be
anything but bad.
Albert Camus 1913-1960 C.E.

National Radio Service, Washington, DC

"Texas politics has pitted the state's economy against its universities, and Texas Senator March is in the middle.

"The Environmental Protection Agency has threatened to fine oil and gas drillers for releasing methane into the atmosphere. Cattle ranching is also being blamed for producing methane—not so much from the cows' flatulence but from waste produced in feedlots. Researchers at universities remind us that methane is a greenhouse gas. Although not as common as carbon dioxide, methane is a more powerful collector of solar energy and a significant contributor to global warming.

"Texas Senator March sits on the US Senate Committee on Energy and Natural Resources. One state away, Oklahoma Senator Markham Rivers chairs the Committee on the Environment. Senator March is being urged by Texas universities and the press to bring tighter controls on greenhouse gas emissions. Across the state line, Senator Rivers continues to deny that climate change is real, citing biblical authority. In his last speech he read into the Congressional Record a few lines from Psalm 46, 'God is our refuge and strength. Therefore we will not fear, though the mountains be carried into the midst of the sea; though the waters thereof roar and be troubled, though the mountains shake.' If you think about this, you will realize it doesn't really deny climate change, just tells people not to be afraid of it.

"What is perhaps more telling is Senator Rivers's statement to the press after the most recent committee hearing. 'While the earth remains, seedtime and harvest, cold and heat, summer and winter, day and night shall not cease.' Even that doesn't rule out extreme cold and extreme heat. Nor does it rule out the changes already seen in seedtime and harvest due to rising temperatures and drought.

"Senator Rivers is not alone. Half of Americans and three-fourths of Texans do not believe in climate change. Most of them rely on misinterpretations of the Bible, like those of Senator Rivers, for that belief, rather than on science.

"Senator March has announced a series of conferences hosted by the Texas State University System. The first will be at Sui Ross State University in Alpine. The Senator has invited the American Petroleum Institute, the Texas Cattleman's Association, university scientists, and federal agencies to attend.

"This is Polly Singer for National Radio Service."

~~~~~

"Good work, Polly. The Dallas affiliate called to say they're getting dozens of calls from listeners demanding that they cover the conferences. The Dallas station is planning a two-week series—radio and TV—on climate to kick off the conferences. I want you to fly to Dallas to work with them."

~~~~~

Dallas, Texas

A young woman was waiting for me at the DFW airport, holding a sign that read, "SINGER NRS." I felt very special, but wondered exactly what they would ask me to do. She drove me to a bed-and-breakfast that was less than a block from the station and within walking distance of a pedestrian mall with shops and restaurants. My room connected to the rest of the building, but had a separate entrance through a garden at the back of the house.

"It's a trade-off," the young woman said. "Nice accommodations but no rental car. Is that okay with you, Honey?"

"It's lovely," I said. I wasn't accustomed to being called *Honey*, especially by women. It was one of the Texas things I'd have to learn. "Probably a lot quieter than a regular hotel. And, after the drive here, I'm not sure I'd want to navigate Dallas traffic. Thank you."

"We should thank you. You stirred up a beehive, and it is dripping honey. We want to put you on the radio every morning the next two weeks. You up to that?"

"Pledge time?" I guessed.

"Yes, but since most of our morning listeners are stuck in their cars, we call it *drive time*. You freshen up. I'll take the car back to the station and then walk down here and show you around. Sam—she's the head of the Features Department—has scheduled a meeting at 4:00."

"Sounds good. I'll meet you in the lobby."

~~~~~

"Polly, you have a call. Frank Hopkins. He runs Senator March's local office." It was the intern. She had attached herself to me and become an unofficial personal assistant.

"Thank you," I pressed the button. "This is Polly Singer."

"Howdy, Ms. Singer. Frank Hopkins from Senator March's Dallas office. How are you today?"

"I'm well, Mr. Hopkins, but I have a deadline. I don't mean to be rude, but—"

"I understand, Ms. Singer. After you get finished, could we talk about the climate conferences? I think I can help you."

And you hope I can help you, I thought. *Tit-for-tat.* I didn't know then exactly what that would mean.

"It would have to be after 5:00, I'm afraid. Or at 7:00 tomorrow morning."

"Ms. Singer, please don't think me froward, but maybe a drink? There's a bar near the station where a lot of the NRS folks hang out . . . and my guess is that the staff has already shown you. We could meet, there."

Smart guy. Offering to meet on my home territory, or what passes for it in Dallas. And, he's right about the bar. The intern took me there yesterday. Except for the bartender, everyone there was from the station—or was with someone from the station.

"That's a fine idea, Mr. Hopkins. Five fifteen?"

He agreed and we exchanged cell numbers in case something came up.

~~~~~

I skipped out early, got to my room to freshen up, and reached the bar by 5:10. I realized that neither Hopkins nor I had any idea what the other looked like. *Oh, well, he can always call.* I chuckled, waved off the raised-eyebrow look I got from the bartender, and turned up the ringer of my cell phone.

I needn't have worried. Hopkins had done his homework. Or—more likely—had seen me on the TV segment two days ago. I watched a man come through the door, wait a moment for his eyes to adjust to the dimness, scan the room, and walk straight toward me.

"Ms. Singer?" He held out a business card. "I'm Frank Hopkins."

I took the card, looked at it long enough for him to think I took him seriously, and held out my hand to be shaken. It didn't get past me that he hadn't offered his hand first. One of those gentlemanly Texan things.

"Mr. Hopkins, please call me Polly."

"Then I must be Frank." I chuckled at a pun he must have used a million times—and caught a whiff of after-shave. *That son-of-a-bitch had shaved. So much for Southern charm. He's on the make!*

We ordered. I had a Tom Collins; he, vodka and tonic. Both of us ordered long drinks, a lesson from many DC cocktail parties. Folks from the station drifted in. A few I had met said a brief *hello* or *howdy* but no one imposed themselves. That was a perk of working with professionals. They knew the score.

Frank knew the score, too. He didn't push, but was smooth and charming. We talked about Dallas and DC, and played "do you know so-and-so" in Washington politics. The number of common acquaintances we shared did not surprise us. In fact, since I'd interned at C-SPAN and then worked for the DC NRS flagship station, the only surprise was that we'd never met.

"Well, NRS does tend to be a little left of center," Frank said. He laughed. It was an insider's joke.

"At least, not as far to the right of center as Senator March," I said. I laughed, but it was the signal to start the serious talking. We ordered our second drink.

Frank was not only smooth and charming, he was also clever. Rather than feed me information—which he knew I would suspect—he told me where to look for information. "Climate isn't a new topic. Lots of people have come and gone—politicians, professors, engineers, ranchers, consultants," he explained.

We'd reached a stopping point in our conversation. In spite of stretching out a second Tom Collins, I hadn't eaten since lunch and was feeling the alcohol.

"Frank, the bar serves burgers and chicken finger baskets, but I can get those in DC. There's a Mexican Restaurant just a block away. I'm dying to try it. They say it's authentic, and not just beans-and-cheese Tex-Mex."

"Good choice, and I've got to have something to eat before I have another drink."

That worked out well, I thought. *Or he's more perceptive than I realize.*

Frank insisted we split the check. "No perception of conflict of interest," he explained. I agreed. However he did not think my invitation to a nightcap would create the wrong perception, even after I told him about the garden entrance.

~~~~~

"The First Amendment prohibits the federal and state governments from passing laws that aid one religion, aid all religions, or prefer one religion over another . . .
No person can be punished for entertaining or professing religious beliefs or disbeliefs, for church attendance or nonattendance . . . "
Justice Hugo Black, United States Supreme Court, 1947 C.E.

Washington, DC

"It's the biggest secret in Washington since the Manhattan Project—or one of Clinton's affairs." Sugi was babbling. He had picked me up at Dulles Airport in one of the network's vans when I returned from Dallas.

"Clinton's affairs were never secret," I said. "What secret are you talking about?"

"That's what I want to know," Sugi said. "It's something about Senator March's campaign. He's called a press conference in two hours, in the capitol rotunda."

My cell rang. I fumbled it from my bag and looked at the caller ID. *The boss*, I thought. "Good morning, ma'am."

"Polly, you filed those stories on March from Dallas. Reckon you can get close to him, today?" the boss asked. I put the phone on speaker, lowered the visor, and checked my makeup.

"I'll try," I said.

"Good. Go straight to the capitol. Sugi's our best sound man, and he's big enough to run interference for you."

I put away the phone. "I guess we are invited to the press conference," I said.

"We'll have to walk at least two blocks from parking," Sugi said. "Sure glad it's not a cold winter. Us Alabama boys are warm-blooded."

Whether it was my looks or Sugi's size, or the residuum of respect the commercial media held for the National Radio Service, I was in front of the crowd of reporters, and the NRS logo was prominent among the forest of microphones on the lectern.

A door opened. A dozen men poured out and joined others already in position. All the men had curly wires leading from the collars of their shirts to their ears. Two men followed them.

"Senator March has just stepped into the rotunda and is walking this way," I said. I glanced at Sugi, who gave me a thumbs-up—his signal that I was getting through to the flagship station on M Street.

"There is a man beside him—" I nearly lost my composure. "It's Pastor Russell Fallow, the Bishop of Washington and spiritual leader of the One True Christian

Church. Senator March has reached the podium and is about to speak."

"Good morning, ladies and gentlemen of the press, and my fellow American patriots," March began. I glanced again at Sugi, who gave me another thumbs-up. The microphone on the lectern was also getting through.

"Thank you for joining us on this beautiful day. I will be brief. You know that I am a candidate for the American Freedom First Party's nomination for the office of President of the United States. With that, it is my great pleasure to turn the microphone over to Pastor Russell Fallow, the One True Christian Church's Bishop of Washington."

"Thank you, Senator. Folks, many of you understand that we the people have lost control of what is supposed to be the government of the people. Taxes take away more and more of the money we earn, money that should be ours. Money to provide for our children, money to make a future for them. This money is spent for immoral purposes—to support promiscuity, to support adultery, to support sex-change operations for felons incarcerated in our jails.

"Bureaucrats and antique laws tell us what we can and cannot do every waking moment.

"One of those antique laws says that a church may not engage in political activities and keep its tax-exempt status. This is wrong!

"The money that our people give to the church is not my money, it's not the church's money, it is the Lord God's money. No government has the right to tax the Lord God! The leaders of the church are stewards only, and spend that money on the Lord's work after consultation and prayer.

"Only our elected representatives can break us free of the bureaucrats, can break us free of antique laws, can break us free of the profligate spending of our money for immoral purposes.

"I know that Senator March is a God-fearing man. I and other leaders of the One True Christian Church have met with him and discussed his beliefs and his goals for this Great Nation.

"After much prayer, we have reached a decision.

"The One True Christian Church endorses Senator Edward March for the office of President of the United States, and we defy the unelected bureaucrats of the Internal Revenue Service to tell us we cannot do so."

I looked around. Most of the reporters stood with their mouths open. They, better than most, understood that this was not just the church's endorsement of a candidate. It was the amalgamation of the American Freedom First Party with the One True Christian Church. It heralded a transformation of American politics.

~~~~~

Before the crowd of reporters broke up enough for me to leave, my cell phone vibrated. I didn't recognize the number, but answered.

"Polly? This is Mel Appleton. Frank Hopkins gave me your name and number. I hope you don't mind."

Mind, I thought. There are at least 20 reporters standing here who would give their right arm to get a call from Mel Appleton.

"Not at all, Mr. Apple—"

"Please, call me Mel. Look, the Senator is holding a small reception. Can you join us? Just follow him and the Bishop down the hallway. Tell any of the Secret Service people who you are. Oh, just you. Not your sound man . . . this will be strictly background."

"Yes, Mel." I said. "Frank spoke of you. I'm looking forward to meeting you."

"Great. See you, soon."

"Sugi? You've got the keys to the van. I'll be staying. Please, tell the boss it's an off-the-record with Senator March.

Please ask someone . . . I don't know who, to edit the tape for *Afternoon Edition*. I'll miss that slot, but I'll be in later to prepare for tomorrow's *Morning Edition*."

"Got it, Miss Polly. And thank you."

"You're welcome, but for what?"

"For saying *please*. Most of the *talent* don't."

~~~~~

"Senator, this is Ms. Singer from National Radio Service."

"Ms. Singer, a pleasure to meet you. Welcome, and thank you for joining us."

"Thank you for the invitation, Senator. I'm looking forward to meeting these folks, too." There was a question in my raised eyebrows.

"My office staff, my campaign staff, Bishop Fallow's people, a few select members of the press. Do you suppose I should have had nametags?" Senator March's question, said so naïvely, put me at ease.

"My guess is that remembering names and faces is second nature to all of us, Senator."

He smiled what looked like a genuine smile. "Then you'll do okay."

Mel was at my elbow with someone I couldn't see. I returned the senator's smile and stepped aside. I didn't need to hear Mel's introduction to know who it was.

"Senator, you know Bert Rightly, of course."

I couldn't stay longer. It would look like I was eavesdropping. Which I was. Oh well, where there is food, there will be reporters and junior political aides. I strolled toward the buffet table.

The buffet was excellent; the promised background was pretty much a bust. Neither the Senator nor the Bishop said anything we couldn't have guessed for ourselves. The Senator's people were tight-lipped, although I did learn they had cancelled a campaign trip to Iowa so the Senator could visit a military hospital in Arkansas. Interpretation? He's given up on Iowa and hopes he can swing Arkansas off the fence and into the red states' side. Again, nothing I couldn't have guessed for myself.

An hour into the reception, Mel brought me a drink. At first, I demurred.

"Mel, I don't drink before the sun is over the yardarm, in my time zone. Thank you, though."

"Polly . . . may I call you Polly? That's my rule, too, and then only when I know the Senator won't call me for something later in the evening. This is ginger ale."

I laughed. Took a sip, and said, "Don't guess you get many martinis, then."

"Damn few."

We exchanged small talk. He worked me to find out who I was and what I thought. I did the same to him. Neither of us got anywhere. We both knew what we were doing, though, and it was fun.

WhatDrWho Blog

Supreme Court Justice Hugo Black wrote in 1962, " . . . a union of government and religion tends to destroy government and degrade religion." The founding fathers did a good job in the First Amendment to the Constitution of keeping government out of religion. They utterly failed at keeping religion out of government. The move by the One True Christian Church to join itself and the American Freedom First Party is the culmination and condemnation of that failure. It is also an open defiance of the law by the OTCC and Bishop Fallow, and—by accepting the OTCC endorsement—an open defiance of the law by Senator March. March swore to "support and defend the Constitution." That oath of office is prescribed in the Constitution, itself. Add *oath-breaker* to March's list of qualifications.

The goddess Nemesis had responsibility for punishing oath-breakers, and Zeus was fond of punishing those mortals who exhibited *hubris*—too much pride. Where are they when we need them?

This is WhatDrWho.

CHAPTER 10: TIM KARUS

All religions have based morality on obedience . . .
on voluntary slavery. That is why they have always
been more pernicious than any political organization.
For the latter makes use of violence, the former,
of the corruption of the will.
Alexander Herzen 1812-1870 CE

Archbishop Trucido's Office

I met Mr. L'Wazi at the front door, gave his coat to the butler, and escorted the man to Isaac's library where coffee was waiting.

Isaac rose from behind his desk, shook hands, and invited L'Wazi to sit. "Tim, please join us, won't you?" The invitation was for L'Wazi's benefit, not mine. I knew I would attend the meeting. Mr. L'Wazi didn't react, but came—indirectly—to the point.

"Mr. Trucido, I've been led to believe that you have converted your education and experience into new and different channels."

L'Wazi could have found that on the same wiki site where I'd found his bio. It was no secret that Isaac had left the red cap of a Cardinal in the Catholic Church for private life. It was no secret that the departure had not been amicable and that if he had not resigned his position he might have been excommunicated, perhaps jailed. What was secret from all but a few people was his creation of the Council of Twelve, whose members formed the *holding company* that was the One True Christian Church.

Isaac chuckled and then said, "I have found capitalism to be much more challenging and rewarding than being a Prince of the Church."

"It's difficult to be a successful capitalist without also being involved in politics," L'Wazi observed.

"All life is politics," Isaac said. "But not all politics are visible, especially to the uninitiated."

I listened and learned as the two men exchanged what seemed to be banal aphorisms but were attempts to probe one another. *What did L'Wazi know about Isaac? What did Isaac know about L'Wazi? What did they guess about one another?* I tried to put myself in L'Wazi's position, wondering if I would need to protect Isaac from this man. I shouldn't have worried. Isaac was more clever than Mr. L'Wazi. He cut short the conversation and got to business.

"You've traveled quite a way to be here, today," Isaac said. "I'm sure you have something important to say."

Mr. L'wazi nodded. "Many of my people have become disillusioned with the Democratic message. Some members of my organization seek to break with the Democratic Party and to ally with the American Freedom First Party."

L'Wazi paused for a moment. Isaac nodded for him to continue.

"As a very successful capitalist, and one attuned to the religious community . . . " he began.

I felt a chill. *What did he know? What did Councilor Six tell him?*

" . . . you must have some interest in this information." L'Wazi completed his sentence.

"Mr. L'Wazi, you surprise me. I expected a request for funding for your organization; perhaps support for something bogged down in our do-nothing Congress."

Well said! I thought.

Mr. L'Wazi turned over the last of his cards. "Mr. Davis suggested that you might be in contact with Mr. Warwick."

L'Wazi didn't have to say which Mr. Warwick. There was only one, no matter how many were in the telephone directory or on social networking sites. *Richard Warwick*, I thought. *Like Isaac, a dropout from the Catholic Church. Like Isaac, a plutocrat whose real wealth was only speculated. Like Isaac—* Isaac's voice interrupted my thoughts.

"We are acquainted, yes. And our business interests seldom collide." He turned to me as if it were an afterthought. "Tim, do we have a private number for Mr. Warwick?"

I played along, fumbled with my iPad for a moment, and then announced that yes, we had a private number and a note that Mr. Warwick was an avid golfer and skier.

"Mr. Davis suggested that you could arrange for him to accept a call from me." Mr. L'Wazi said. He had just turned up his hole card and thought he had a winning hand.

It took Isaac only an instant to weigh the arguments on both sides of the equation. "Yes, I will tell him you will call, and encourage him to speak with you."

Mr. L'Wazi thanked Isaac, but declined another cup of coffee. That was my cue. I walked him to the front door where we collected his coat.

"Isaac? What was that all about?" I asked when I returned to his office.

"He doesn't want Warwick," Isaac said. "He wants Senator March, rather, he wants Warwick's man in Senator March's office. I will call Warwick. He will give me Mel Appleton's private number. You will call. At the moment, this should be kept between personal assistants and aides. Mr. L'Wazi showed his cards too soon. We will not make that mistake.

"Tim, you heard a name you should not remember. I know you cannot forget it, but you must not let anyone know that you know it."

I knew he meant *Davis*—Councilor Six. I didn't tell Isaac that I knew the names of all the Twelve.

Telecon: Richard Warwick, Archbishop Trucido, and Councilor Three

"What happened in Louisiana?" Warwick asked.

"The Democrat won the Governor's mansion by twelve points. That's a serious loss," Trucido said.

"Our man has already announced he won't run again for the Senate. That's next year. We need to get someone in the race immediately, and we must win at any cost," Warwick said.

"This was a referendum on personality, not the party," Councilor Three objected.

"We can overcome that in the senate race with publicity, and by picking the right man," Trucido said.

"Or woman," Three said.

"Get real. You're not going to get the AFFP and OTCC behind a woman," Warwick said.

"Can we do anything about the governor?" Trucido asked.

"The Lieutenant Governor is our man. Solid Republican. I'm just saying," Three said.

"The governor-elect is a popular figure, military hero, squeaky clean, like that's ever been important in Louisiana politics." That was Warwick. "It won't be easy to remove him. It must be done discretely."

"That can be arranged," Three assured the others. Louisiana was his territory. If anyone could arrange this, he could.

"Let us work with the Lieutenant Governor, first. Make sure of him," Warwick cautioned.

"We are agreed," Trucido said. "Councilor Three will plan the operation. Warwick will contact the Lieutenant Governor and give Councilor Three the go-ahead after he's sure he's firmly in our camp. Councilor Three will vet candidates for the senatorial race. Warwick and I will set up S-PACs to be prepared to support the candidate we agree on."

"Who would replace the Lieutenant Governor should he become the senatorial candidate? Is that a viable scenario?" Isaac asked.

"I have no idea, but I'll get someone on it," Councilor Three said.

~~~~~

Archbishop Trucido's Estate

"Tim, I'm sorry, but you may not attend tomorrow morning's session of the Council of Twelve."

"Yes, sir." I said.

"You are disappointed," Isaac said. "I trust you, Tim. But, these men have dealings that reach beyond the church. They trust no one outside our circle. Not you, not anyone."

"I understand," I said. *I understand more than you know*, I thought. *I know who these men are—I know that they are the heads of the ten most powerful crime families in America and two in Canada. I know what their businesses are. Drugs, prostitution including child prostitution, pornography ditto. I know that they squeeze legitimate businesses for protection, just as their ancestors once squeezed shop owners in the ghettos of New York. I know that they control a lot of unions. I know that they're deep in the business of building and operating prisons-for-profit and have federal contracts to build even more. You really should change the password on your computer, Isaac, although it flatters me. And I love you, too, but I fear for you. I fear for your safety, I fear for your soul—and mine.*

"Would you like to go over the agenda for the afternoon session?" I asked.

"Yes, but first, do you have the menu for lunch?"

That would be easy. Despite the Americanization of their names, these men were a product of their heritage. Antipasto with olives, anchovies, cheese, and capocollo; pasta with tomato gravy; veal; and red wine. Easy-peasy. I wondered if they or Isaac had any idea how revealing that was.

Archbishop Trucido's Library, That Afternoon

"I don't suppose anyone has a comment on Bat Boy's endorsement of Mrs. Kennedy?" Isaac's opening of the afternoon meeting garnered a few chuckles.

"That might be important," Councilor Nine said. "That paper has a bigger circulation than the *New York Afterword*."

Councilor Nine controlled Texas, Kansas, Oklahoma, Nebraska, Colorado, New Mexico, and Arizona. He'd been a college football star. "Boomer" Green—born Guiseppe Verdi, Americanized to Joe Green—was perhaps the most powerful of the councilors.

"Tim?" The Archbishop treated the question about Bat Boy as legitimate.

"Our polls show that the people who read the *World of Weird* are the most unlikely segment of the population to vote. Those who do vote are overwhelmingly fundamentalist, gun owners, and conservative—the 'God and guns' crowd.

"That is," I added after pretending for a moment to think, "they are overwhelmingly likely to vote for conservative candidates. Most of them wouldn't know conservative from liberal if Bat Boy bit them on their noses."

I felt Isaac's approval. I had treated Councilor Green with dignity while turning the Council away from his question.

If religion were the opiate of the masses, as Karl Marx said, and if television were the opiate of the massives, as a dozen authors had said, then our television ads would target the masses of massives who made up the underclass of the US population.

"Are we still going to push Thomas Stanley as the VP nominee?" Councilor Four asked. "He has a solid reputation in Congress and gets good press, but what about his oldest kid—a stepson with Canadian citizenship?"

Isaac looked at me.

Henry Stanly has dual citizenship and was adopted, so he's not a stepson, but there's no need to say that, I thought before answering the question.

"Sir, that was the concern here, as well. We did a snap poll and are running a more in-depth poll. The snap poll showed that the issue is 'not important at all' to 90% of likely voters and, at most, only 'of some importance' to fewer than 5%. It's a non-issue."

"Look," Councilor Three said. "I know that Church members will believe anything you tell them. Well, anything you tell the pastors to tell them. What about people the Church doesn't reach?"

"Sir, the polls cover all demographics. Members of OTCC-affiliated congregations make up only 41% of the demographic, even though they are four times more likely to vote than most people. If anything, the polls are biased against the Church's position."

"Damn clever, Isaac," Four said.

Despite the espresso they'd drunk after lunch, the councilors were lethargic and the afternoon session devolved into gossip, guesses, and groupthink, and adjourned at three o'clock.

~~~~~

National Radio & TV Service
"Breaking news from Louisiana. In a scene reminiscent of the assassination of Huey Long in 1935, the newly elected governor of Louisiana was shot dead on the steps of the state capitol on the way to his inauguration."

Telecon: Warwick and Trucido

"Wait. I want my PA to hear this," Isaac said, and put the call from Mr. Warwick on the speakerphone.

"What the hell happened in Louisiana?" Warwick asked. "Who is responsible? Who will take charge, now?"

Trucido gestured for me to respond.

"Sir, that's hard to say. The state constitution is silent, but we think our people are in position to ensure that the Lieutenant Governor-elect will become the governor."

"He's our man?" Warwick asked.

"Close enough," Trucido replied. "Our contingency plan worked," he added.

Contingency plan? I thought. *If they had a contingency plan it was only because they planned this. And Isaac seems to be okay with it. Mafia and murder. This is not the Isaac I knew when I was a child.*

~~~~~

"Tim, why do you bring tea rather than coffee?" Isaac knew the answer, but wanted to hear me say it.

"This is chamomile. It has no caffeine. Your blood pressure, you know. Anyway, I want you to tell me about tea. The Boston Tea Party." I smiled, and may have chuckled for an instant. Isaac lifted his hand to stroke my cheek.

"I heard your chuckle, Tim. The deeper voice you have earned over the years. When you were a boy, you would giggle. I miss your giggle."

"I miss it too, Isaac. It was something from a happier time, when all I had to worry about was waking in time to dress you for a six o'clock mass."

I poured the tea and sat at Isaac's elbow. "Now," I said. "About the Boston Tea Party."

"You know they take their name from the ruffians who boarded British merchant ships in the Boston Harbor in 1773

64

and dumped barrels of tea into the water. They said it was a protest of taxes imposed by the British Parliament. They called themselves *The Sons of Liberty*, but they were ruffians. Had the British won that war, they would have been denigrated as criminals, but as usual, the victors write history."

"I think I understand," I said. "The Sons of Liberty were the tools of the merchants of Boston to throw off British taxation. Today's Boston Tea Party are tools of the plutocrats. By fighting to reduce taxes on themselves, the BTP people have virtually eliminated taxes on the plutocrats."

"Well said, Tim. But you don't have to worry about the Boston Tea Party. Plans are in the works to deal with their somewhat fragmented leadership."

Like you dealt with the Governor of Louisiana? More murders? I wondered.

CHAPTER 11: BERT RIGHTLY

If the freedom of speech be taken away,
then dumb and silent we may be led
like lambs to the slaughter.
George Washington 1732-1799 CE

Bert Rightly smoothed his pompadour. The talking points for his program were on the screen buried under the Lucite of the desk and on the teleprompters. Three cameras pointed at him. One camera was on his guests. The producer gave the signal, and Bert was on the air.

"My guests tonight include an Imam from a local mosque, a police commissioner from New York, and Senator Edward March. Gentlemen, are you ready for *Take 'Em To The Wire?*" Rightly's audience responded to cue cards and screamed the words of the show's name.

Before the men could reply, Rightly continued, "Imam, one of your colleagues, Ali Abu Ahmad, used his Friday sermon to call for the re-establishment of the Muslim Caliphate and the annihilation of Jews. How does that square with your statement in yesterday's *New York Afterward* that Islam is a religion of peace?"

"Mr. Rightly, the man you refer to is not representative of Muslims, the vast majority of whom are peace-loving—"

"The man spoke from the Dome of the Rock, one of Islam's holy sites. How can you say he's not representative of Muslims?" Rightly interrupted.

"Mr. Rightly, he did not speak from the Qubbat Al-Sakhra, but from public grounds outside the shrine. He was exercising free speech—"

"He was shouting *fire* in a crowded theater," Rightly said. "In a place that is the single most holy site in Judaism. That's an abuse of free speech, Rabbi."

Rightly drowned out the Imam's protest that he was not a Rabbi. "This Imam incited war against enemies of the Caliphate, including America. Which brings up a question for our next guest, Senator Edward March.

"Senator, the Secretary of State announced that the USA will accept 185,000 more refugees, most from Syria, this year, and 300,000 next year. What can you tell us about that?"

"Bert, the current administration is both lax in its screening of refugees, and overly optimistic that they can stop terrorists from the Taliban and Daesh from slipping into this country."

"That's a serious charge, Senator."

"It's a serious threat, Bert. We can expect that most of these refugees will settle in Detroit, which has one of the largest Arab communities outside the Arab world. That great city has enough problems created by years of Democratic, libsymp government. They don't need terrorists fading into the underworld."

"Mr. March," the Imam said. "The bodies of drowned children continue to wash up on the beaches of Greece."

Rightly ignored the Imam, whose microphone had been turned off, anyway. "This raises an important issue for our next guest, the Deputy Commissioner for Communications of the New York Police Department.

"Commissioner, the *American Fire Network* reported this morning that an eighth police officer has been shot and killed in the line of duty in the past six months. The mayor has vowed—and I quote—'to seize every handgun in the city by any means possible.' Second Amendment supporters rallied in front of City Hall, openly carrying assault rifles and handguns. Police defied orders to make arrests. What do you have to say about that? Defying the mayor? What's going on?"

"In simple terms, Bert, the Mayor doesn't make law, and he certainly doesn't make constitutional law. His orders to the police department were clearly illegal under the constitution. I hope you saw the article in *The Tempest Times* in which our Police Commissioner said that if more responsible citizens were armed, criminals would think twice before shooting."

"That is the only thing to come out of this that makes sense," Senator March interjected. "Law-abiding citizens have more than the right to bear arms; the right people have the obligation to do so."

"A bold statement, Senator," Rightly said.

"Perilous times call for bold men, Bert."

CHAPTER 12: THE SCIENCE GUIDE

Science knows no country, because knowledge belongs to
humanity, and is the torch that illuminates the world.
Louis Pasteur 1822-1895 CE

It *Is* Rocket Science *National Television Service*

"Who can tell me some acids found in your home?" Dr. Wallace Anderson, also known as *The Science Guide,* asked. Twenty students from the Friends School of Arlington, Virginia stood around him in the studio.

"Vinegar!" One called out.

"You are right. Common household vinegar has a pH of about 2.4. Remember, anything below 7.0 is an acid. What else?"

"Mayonnaise?"

"A good answer. Most commercial mayonnaise has a pH around 4.5, which makes it not a good host for bacteria."

"Lemon juice," a girl said, confident in her answer.

"Yes, full of citric acid. What about things that are bases?"

"Clorox," called one of the students. "And Drano."

"Good choices," The Science Guide said. "They both are near the top of the list with a pH of almost 14."

"Baking soda," another kid said.

"Another common base, at a pH of about 9. What about sea water?"

"Uh, we don't keep that in the refrigerator," one of the kids said, and giggled.

"Of course you don't," Dr. Anderson said. "But if you did, where do you think it belongs on the scale?"

"They keep talking about *ocean acidification*," George Stanley said. "I guess somewhere around 5 or 6."

"Based on what you've heard, that's a good answer. Actually, seawater is from 7.5 to 8.4. In other words it's . . . " The Science Guide paused.

"It's a base!" the students said.

"Why do people talk about ocean acidification?" George Stanley, bolder than the others, stood with his arms crossed and faced the camera.

"Because saying that the ocean is becoming *less basic* isn't nearly as exciting as saying it's becoming *more acid*," Dr. Anderson said.

So, even the conservationists are using propaganda, George thought. *I thought they meant the ocean was acid . . . carbonic acid created from CO2 absorbed in the water.* The Science Guide's words interrupted that thought.

"It's true that the oceans of the world are getting more acid—meaning, less basic. And it's true that this has a bad effect on a lot of sea life, including corals accustomed to water with a pH around 7.5. The water, especially in the shallows around the continents, is becoming less basic. That's affecting corals and the shells you might find on the beach."

The kids were smart enough to understand *calcium carbonate* and the differences between old shells—thick and strong—compared to modern shells that were thin and weak.

"Acidification is only one problem. On the next program, we'll look at the effect of rising temperatures on the fish that are such an important part of our diet—and our economy."

Not a bad day, Dr. Anderson thought as the children filed out.

House Ignores Science—and Reason

The World Citizen. "'Don't listen to the president; I control the purse strings.' That's the message from Kevin McCarthy, Republican Representative from California, who announced that the US House of Representatives would not support any commitment made by the president to spend any money to fund climate agreements. McCarthy noted that only Congress, and not the president, has the authority to commit funds. Language blocking money to support agreements reached in Paris would be included in *must-pass* legislation currently before the Congress. At least, that's the word from *The Associated Press.*

"Am I the only one who wonders who is pulling the strings of the puppets of the Republican and American Freedom First Parties? Money from *big oil* and *big energy?* Or perhaps money from *big god*—the OTCC? Either way, they're puppets, wooden heads and wooden hearts, unable to think or feel.

"This is Muldoon. Of the much vaunted ten commandments, *Thou shalt not covet* might apply here. But greed seems to be a requirement for membership in the Republican and American Freedom First Parties—and the leadership of the OTCC."

~~~~~

Kiribati, South Pacific Ocean

A storm broke loose an abandoned cargo ship, which breached the seawall. The waves of the king tide washed at least twenty feet above the eight-foot ceilings of the homes along the beach.

The residents had fled before the storm broke. Some found dry land elsewhere on the island; some emigrated to Australia.

Some died.

~~~~~

University of the Witwatersrand, South Africa

"Dr. Dart, here are the data on the Pacific atolls you asked for." The post-doc held a flash drive.

"Sir," she continued, "there's nothing new. The islands are battered by king tides. Sea-level rise coupled with more atmospheric and oceanic energy for storms is wiping them out. What is there left to study?"

"Not study, Dr. Zuma, publicize. I have registered *witwat* with every social networking site on the planet. We will continue to monitor—sea level, storm intensity, ice melts, currents, hectares of land submerged, and deaths. And we will broadcast this to the world.

"We now have links to the German's Antarctic Station, Neumayer, and to the Concordia multi-national research station. We'll echo their broadcasts, too.

"There are people out there who care and who want to do something. I hope we can stir the pot."

CHAPTER 13: THE RED HORSEMAN

The people can always be brought to the bidding of the leaders.
All you have to do is tell them they are being attacked and
denounce the pacifists for lack of patriotism.
Hermann Göring, Nazi military leader 1893-1946

Islamic Center Bombed—KKK Suspected

Mt. Pleasant Clarion, Georgia. Multiple bombs ripped through the Islamic Center early this morning. The building was closed, and there are no known casualties. Fire Marshall Llewellyn says that bombs and the resulting fire completely gutted the building.

Videos and photos of the bombing have gone viral on three social media platforms. The images clearly show the Center and figures in white, hooded robes with red Latin crosses on front and back. Although such robes are often associated with the Ku Klux Klan—the original *hoodlums in hoodies*—the self-proclaimed Grand Wizard of Georgia warns against assuming these figures are members of his organization. "It's more likely they was just a bunch of good old boys out for some fun," he said. "I don't agree with how they done it, but they done us all a big favor."

~~~~~

"Give me your tired, your poor . . .
I lift my lamp beside the golden door!"
Part of the inscription at the base
of the Statue of Liberty

Pause in Refugee Resettlement

New York Afterword. Following the terrorist attacks in
Paris, House Speaker Paul Ryan and Senate Majority Leader
Mitch McConnell both urged a "pause" in resettling Syrian
refugees in the US. They expressed concern that the refugees
were not being adequately screened. They received support in a
statement by Senator Chuck Schumer, third ranking Democrat in
the Senate, who said that a pause might be necessary. President
Obama said this position was offensive. His administration
defends the screening process, characterizes the refugees as
"widows and orphans," and continues to bring 10,000 Syrian
refugees each month into the US.

Refugees Refused

The World Citizen "There you have it, folks. We're back
to the days of witch burning in Europe and New England. We're
no better than villagers with torches and pitchforks storming the
huts of innocents. We're no better than we were during the
1930s when we denied entry to Jewish refugees from Nazi
Germany, and the 1940s when we put American citizens of
Japanese descent in concentration camps. When we are afraid,
both the constitution and compassion take a back seat.

"This is Muldoon paraphrasing Benjamin Franklin:
'Those who would deny the rights of others to find liberty and
safety for themselves, deserve neither liberty nor safety.' Think
about it."

Senator March's Office, Washington, DC

"Muldoon is a loose cannon. He could have done the same thing with different words. His piece has already gone viral and the libsymps are pushing, hard. The problem is not going away; it will not be forgotten before the election. It could cost us several swing states."

March had outlined the problem. "What's the answer?" he added.

"What about Thomas Stanley?" Senator Rivers asked. Stanley was one of the five Congressmen from Rivers's state of Oklahoma.

"What about him?" March said. He needed Rivers, but didn't like him. The need and the dislike were shared by Rivers.

"He sent out a *Dear Colleague* to everyone in the House. He's got connections in Canada. His stepson's father was Canadian. He says we are morally obligated to provide aid. He recommends we ask Canada to take the refugees and pay Canada to do that, at least until the mess settles down or after the election, whichever happens first."

"Mel, why didn't I see that letter?" March asked.

"It's in your red read folder, sir."

March pulled the unclassified note from among the Top Secret briefs that demanded his most urgent attention. He scanned it.

"Mel, get Representative Stanley in here," he ordered. "A bipartisan delegation from the House will visit—"

"Why just the House," Rivers demanded.

"So Stanley can lead it. He's been in office long enough to be thought of as an *elder statesman* but young enough to, well, we'll get to that, later."

~~~~~

Media Posts Traced in Islamic Center Bombing

Mt. Pleasant Clarion, Georgia. Eight county residents were arrested in lightning raids on their homes last night. The

County Sheriff supported by ATF and DHS agents with warrants from a federal judge conducted simultaneous operations at eight homes. A DHS spokesperson said the warrants were based on internet addresses traced to those who posted video and images of the recent bombing of the Islamic Center.

~~~~~

The White House, Oval Office

"Mr. Stanley, I have only five minutes," the president said.

"This won't take that long," Representative Thomas Stanley said. "The Canadians have agreed to be the *port of entry* for all refugees from the Middle East and Africa into the North American continent. The United States will provide support to include funding facilities for housing and feeding the refugees. A bill is in the hopper.

"We are counting on you to ensure that the FBI and Department of Homeland Security send people to work with the Canadian Security Intelligence Service and Interpol to conduct refugee registration and background investigations.

"We will re-settle as many as possible while ensuring the safety and security of both Canada and the United States. We meet our moral responsibility to the refugees and for the safety and security of our citizens."

The president didn't have to ask who Stanley meant by *we*. Stanley's party and the AFFP ruled the current Congress. The president's own party would support this proposal. The funding bill would pass by a veto-proof majority.

Refugees Resettled in Concentration Camps

The World Citizen. "Read between the lines, people. These Canadian refugee resettlement facilities will be the same kind of concentration camps we built to house people of Japanese ancestry during World War II. And you can bet that the *registration* will include biometric identification—DNA, retinal patterns, and fingerprints.

"The president suggested we were afraid of *widows and orphans*. The US strategy is to send our young men to fight in foreign fields, while leaving the women and children at home— to be widowed and orphaned. The Daesh strategy is to send young men to penetrate Western countries and conduct suicide raids, leaving the women and orphans behind to scavenge for food in garbage dumps while trying to avoid slavers and child sex traders.

"This is Muldoon. Have you read the *Alice in Wonderland* stories? Her world is no more topsy-turvy than ours. Think about it."

~~~~~

Bombing Suspects Released

Mt. Pleasant Clarion, Georgia. Eight men arrested in the bombing of the Islamic Center have been ordered released by the District Attorney, who cited lack of evidence to prosecute. "They may have posted those videos, but we can't even prove that they took them."

~~~~~

Terrorism is the continuation of politics
by other means.
Caliph Al-Embic,
Leader of Daesh

Warwick's Estate

"Sales of body armor, including bullet-proof backpacks and jackets for children, are up by 600% since yesterday," Mel Appleton reported to Richard Warwick.

"They're playing into our hand," Warwick replied. "The shooters at San Francisco were Pakistani Muslims, with no known links to ISIS. Still, throw *Pakistani* and *Muslim* in front of people, and they become afraid. The FBI will uncover a link . . . or create one. They know that fear will allow them to increase their budget, and tighten the control of the government on the people."

"What about the non-Muslim terrorists?" Mel asked. "White supremacists and antigovernment fanatics have killed more than twice as many people in this country since 9-11 as have Muslims. What about that child who killed those people in Charleston, for example, and that guy who killed those people at the Family Planning Clinic in Colorado Springs? He looks like he's crazy, but he's white, and not Muslim."

"Not to worry, Mel. Our people will take care of the media, and spin the stories to suit our needs. To control the people, we need an enemy, and the Muslims fill that need quite well. If that gets old, and ceases to excite people, we'll consider bringing up the *white supremacists* and others within the country.

"Actually, that's not a bad idea."

~~~~~

Anti-Terrorism Exercise, Los Angeles, California

Police cars slid to a stop, and officers wearing combat gear—helmets, flack vests, equipment belts laden with ammunition including grenades, and boots, piled out, formed ranks, and inspected their automatic assault rifles with high-capacity magazines. As quickly as they assembled, they prepared to disperse in response to calls from throughout the city. It was a Paris-like terrorist attack on a dozen targets: malls filled with Christmas shoppers, movie theaters packed with kids wowed by the latest *Star Battle* movie, restaurants, bars and a suburban day-care center.

As soon as the calls came in, the commander ordered the troops to stand down.

"Good exercise, folks. You set a record for reaching the assembly point. Your platoon leaders report ninety-eight percent preparedness. Next time, maybe no one will forget their flash grenades, and we'll hit a hundred percent.

"Your leadership, from the Mayor down, knows that you, like the civilians we protect, want to be with your families on Christmas Eve and Christmas Day. You know we've asked for volunteers to take duty at those times—bachelors, Jewish officers, and such. You also know that there aren't enough volunteers, and that some of you will have to be pulled away on those days, and that all of you will be on alert status through the third of January.

"That can't be helped. You knew that when you took your oath."

The commander seemed to realize he had said all he could, and ordered. "Dismissed. Back to patrol. Merry Christmas."

CHAPTER 14: KAREN CLEMENS

Wherever the art of medicine is loved,
there also is a love of humanity.
Hippocrates 460-370 BCE

Próta den kánoun kakó
(First, do no harm.)
Apocryphal words from the Hippocratic Oath

Centers for Disease Control and Prevention, Atlanta, Georgia

The annual meeting of the Director's Advisory Committee was supposed to be a feel-good time for its members and an opportunity for the director to show off the CDC. I didn't have good news, but my three minutes on the podium would be my only chance to make a difference. Another high-school wrestler had died from CA-MRSA—community-associated methicillin-resistant *Staphylococcus aureus.*

The right-wing press, including *God's Word for You,* put their own spin on it: *Despite prayer vigils by his teammates and other boys from God's Christian Army, Mark Walker was lifted into the arms of his Lord at 3:17 AM today.*

Infectious diseases was my field, it was my job to report.

"What's with the wrestlers? Why are they getting it?" the director asked.

"It is spread by skin-to-skin contact, sir," I said. "The schools have the information; they just won't act on it."

"Why not?"

"We don't—"

"Because God will protect His soldiers, and these boys are members of His Army," a doctor of orthopedics interrupted me. He was an MD; I was a PhD. In his eyes and in the director's eyes, every MD outranked me.

"Doctor," I said, "the science is clear. This is an infectious disease, caused by bacteria that have evolved resistance to years of over-prescribed antibiotics. Patients are put on a cocktail of drugs, but that seldom works. I don't see God's hand in that."

"That will be sufficient, Ms. Clemens," the director said.

The next morning, I was summoned to the director's office. My boss and the Deputy Director for Media Relations were already there. I expected to be fired and was surprised when the director asked for more information on CA-MRSA.

"With this last case, the number of CA-MRSA deaths are up by 14% since last month," I said. "The press doesn't have this, yet, but they will as soon as we answer the Freedom of Information requests from *The World Citizen*."

"Can't we stop that, Ms. Clemens?" the director asked.

"As good as," the Deputy Director for Media Relations said before I could answer. "We've claimed patient confidentiality, and redacted all personal information, including hometowns. That leaves them with only raw numbers for the nation. We've been careful to make sure that's put in context with other causes of death among young people: obesity, undiagnosed diabetes, suicide, the whole list. And we're pushing news of other diseases, especially malaria in Africa. That's riling up the black libsymps, and taking attention from this."

"Ms. Clemens, what are we doing about MRSA?"

"Funding research into new antibiotics, trying to speed up new drug trials," I said. "We need to do more. There's a report that bacteria resistant to *colistin*, the antibiotic-of-last-resort, have been found in the United Kingdom. So far, it's only Salmonella and E. coli. The concern is that these bacteria will pass on their resistance to other bacteria."

"Make damn sure that doesn't get to the media," the director said.

How can we encourage research if we keep secrets? I wondered. *Science is supposed to be open.*

The Power of Prayer

The World Citizen. "It's not surprising to this reporter that the only serious, double-blind study of the *power of prayer*, conducted by the Templeton Foundation, showed that people who were prayed for but didn't know it had no better chance of recovery than those who weren't prayed for. Nor was it surprising that those who were prayed for and knew they were being prayed for had a worse chance of recovery than those who weren't prayed for. Yes, worse.

"If one person says he has an imaginary friend, we call him insane. If thirty million people say they have an imaginary friend, we call them religious.

"This is Muldoon. It would be a stretch to think that the prayers of God's Christian Army were responsible for Mark Walker's death, when the real culprit lies hidden in iatrogenic medicine.

"Don't know what that means? Look it up! Educate yourself."

Chapter 15: Justine Lacombe

No Keystone Pipeline

The World Citizen. "The president has rejected a Canadian corporation's application for a permit to complete the Keystone XL pipeline. Unlike his previously stated concerns that the pipeline would contribute to global climate change, the president's rationale simply was that it 'would not serve the national interests of the United States.' I wonder exactly what that means.

"No one seems to care about the president's prevarication and dissembling. It's another example of the American people's ability to forget what is important. Which starlet's marriage to a man—or a woman—five times her age is going to eradicate this debacle from your mind?

"This is Muldoon. Prevarication? Dissembling? Eradicate? Debacle? I'm accused of using big words. If you have big ideas, you need big words. Think about it."

~~~~~

Prime Minister's Cabinet Room, Ottawa, Canada

"We will face energy shortages if not this winter, then next," Justine Lacombe said. The new Canadian Prime Minister was holding his first official cabinet meeting. Withdrawing jets from the anti-ISIS coalition had been an easy decision to make. This was going to be more difficult.

"We've depended on free and open trade with the USA," his Minister of Energy said. "And on their refineries to take tar-sand sludge from us and pump it back as fuel oil and gasoline. We need the additional 200,000 barrels per day we would have gotten as part of the Keystone deal."

"Options?" the PM asked.

"Speed up construction of the remaining nuclear power plants," the Energy Minister offered. "Put more people on the inspection and permitting process. Bring in people from other departments, one or two from each, to help."

"Make sure the Keystone application goes forward after the next USA election," the Foreign Minister said. "The Yankees' *Righteous Right* will win the election. They will be eager to deal."

And eager to ensure the profits of their supporters, the Director of the Security Intelligence Service thought. *Especially at Canada's expense. We need options.*

"Buy those nuclear submarines from the UK," the Minister of Defence said. "We have claim to a large part of the Arctic, and we know there's oil there. The subs are needed for exploration—and, if necessary, defence. But we only need to say *exploration* to justify them."

The men and women in the cabinet room looked at one another in the silence that followed. They were idealists. Many classified themselves as *liberals*. Openness and honesty in government was something in which they believed. On the other hand, enough of them were realists that the plans made their way from the cabinet room to the Parliament and to the Exchequer.

That evening, the Minister of Defence and the Director of the Security Intelligence Service met for drinks, dinner, and discussion.

"Is the Brotherhood prepared?" the Director asked.

"The Brotherhood occupies more than half of the critical positions in the military, and we continue to recruit. The process is slow, of necessity. It is hard to trust someone with your life, and that is what each leader of each cell is doing."

~~~~~

—ringoffire/highflyer earthquakes oklahoma usa what is there query

—highflyer/ringoffire fracking wells wastewater injected lubricates faults

—reddragon/highflyer who is ringoffire query

—highflyer/reddragon confidential source japan how you know about them

—reddragon/highflyer see all know all <grin>

CHAPTER 16: KEN PARNELL

"Onward Christian soldiers!
Marching as to war . . .
Sabine Baring-Gould, 1834-1924 C.E

East Bay Academy, Charlotte, Vermont

Jamie Parnell stared at the blank walls, empty bookshelves, bare desks, and unmade bunk beds in the room that would be his home for the next year. His father, carrying a huge box of bed linen, squeezed through the door.

"Think you've got enough stuff, kiddo?" Ken Parnell asked his son.

"I guess," Jamie said. "I'll have to buy more school uniforms . . . I don't want to wear shorts for the rest of my life! I'm not a little kid—"

"Jamie, we talked about this," his father interrupted. "You promised if you got to pick the school you would . . . " Ken stopped speaking. *What do I say?* he wondered. *I'm abandoning my son, but I can't take care of him. I can't make a home for him when I'm living out of a suitcase, traveling with the vice president. Not this year—maybe next.*

"I know, Dad. I said I'd give it at least a year. When will you come to see me?"

"Jamie, I promise I'll visit every chance I get." Ken didn't say the rest of the words: *but you know what my job is and what my schedule will be like.*

~~~~~

Headquarters, Soldiers of the Cross, Lynchburg, Virginia

The Director General scanned a personnel file. *Navy SEAL, two tours in Afghanistan, hardship discharge when his wife died, son in some private school. Raised in a strict Baptist congregation, an OTCC deacon . . . and assigned to the vice president's detail. Excellent.* "Send in Lieutenant Parnell," he ordered.

"Lieutenant Parnell, when you accepted your commission in the Soldiers of the Cross, what was your oath?"

The Bishop's question was not surprising: the oath began each meeting of the SOC.

"Sir, my oath is *Submission to God; service to the Church; obedience to my leaders; and loyalty to my brothers in the battle against principalities, against powers, against the rulers of the darkness of this world, and against spiritual wickedness in high places.*"

The Bishop nodded. "You know that *God works in mysterious ways, His wonders to perform.* You should know by now that God's soldiers on Earth also work in mysterious—and *secret*—ways."

"Yes, Bishop. Most of my missions were classified. I understand secrecy and the need for secrecy."

"Good. Then here is a secret for you, and you, alone."

Ken Parnell left the Director General and drove back to Washington. He was uncomfortable with some of the things the commander of the Soldiers of the Cross had said, but he could not talk about them with anyone.

CHAPTER 17: A LITTLE CHILD SHALL LEAD THEM

"Would you like to know God's plan for you?
Click here."
Link on the websites of
God's Christian Army
and *The Rebeccas.*

OTCC General Handbook of Instruction for Disciples

2.2.7 Focus on the boys who play football, baseball, basketball, wrestling, track and field. If someone's not man enough to play one of these sports, he won't be man enough to "put on the whole armor of God" and "stand up against the wiles of the devil"

~~~~~

"God's Christian Army will meet in the gymnasium
after school on September 3.
Membership is open to all boys who want to join
varsity or junior varsity sports teams.
Join your fellow Believers and learn God's plan for you."
—Poster similar to that on bulletin boards
of high schools throughout the USA

High School Gymnasium, Mt. Pleasant, Georgia,

The word had been passed: if you wanted to make the team—any team—this year, you would join God's Christian Army. The bleachers in the gymnasium were packed with boys.

Tommy Carron scanned the line of men standing on the gym floor. *Every coach and assistant is here,* he thought.

Football was the most important sport at the school. The football coach was the most important man on staff—and the highest paid. He took the microphone.

"Men, I'm sure that the Lord God is happy to see so large a turnout, today. You make me and your school proud. God's Christian Army is a place for fellowship and mutual support. We are dedicated to using athletics to bring the world to Jesus Christ and to bring Jesus Christ to the world. You will learn more about that during the next year.

"God's Christian Army started in high schools like this one and is expanding to colleges and professional sports. It provides a ladder for your personal and spiritual advancement."

Tommy tuned out the coach. *It's true . . . if you hope to make the team, you've got to join. By the time I'm ready for college, they'll be there, too.*

~~~~

Eden Valley Apartment Complex, Mt. Pleasant, Georgia
Family Fun Day!
Sponsored by Christ's Harvest Church
Bounce House!
Games and prizes for the kids!
Hot dogs, hamburgers for everyone!
Treats for the kids!
September 15 at the playground of the
Eden Valley Apartments, Mt. Pleasant, Georgia
Come and learn God's plan for you!

Patrolman Gary Bloom of the Mt. Pleasant Police Department, the *Resource Officer* assigned to the Eden Valley Apartments, read the notice that had been stuck between the door and the doorframe. As he threw the notice in the trash, he thought, *Harvest Church, bull! Reapers, more than harvesters. And grim reapers, at that. Lure the kids in with sweets and games, and when they are hooked, expose them to original sin, hellfire, and other ugly truths behind that church. Sounds like the MO of a pedophile.*

OTCC General Handbook of Instruction for Disciples
2.3.9 Prepare your teams for war. Recruiting is only the first step. Disciplining and Training is the second. Soldiers must be disciplined, not just discipled. Demand obedience, promptness, cleanliness, alertness. Establish rules for your teams, both on the field and in their lives outside the sport. See Paragraph 5.2.7 for mandatory and recommended rules.

≈≈≈≈≈

Washington Standard Op-Ed Page "A *red zone* used to be a place at the airport where you could not park. Now it's a television channel that advertises camouflage gear decorated with the logos of professional sports teams. Don't tell me it's for hunting; if you go in the woods around here in Cowboys cammo, you might not come out. Saying that football is war is worse than saying that war is a game. We have enough war around the world and in our own cities. We don't need to create more."

≈≈≈≈≈

It *Is* Rocket Science *National Television Service*
The Science Guide faced a room full of scrubbed faces—eighth grade girls and boys from the One True Christian School of Northeast DC.

"Does anyone know what today is?" he asked.

"December 21," a boy replied.

"Yes, that's the date, but what happens today?"

The children stood, silent and still.

"It's the winter solstice," Dr. Anderson said. "The shortest day of the year, and the date of the traditional Winter Solstice, when peoples throughout recorded history and around the world welcomed the return of the sun."

"That's a heathen superstition," a girl said.

Dr. Anderson answered quickly. "I'm not talking about the religious history, but about the science. Since last June 21, the days have been getting shorter. From today, they will get longer, a minute or so every day, until next June 21. This is a reminder of how important the sun is, and how it drives the current global climate change."

"The climate always changes," a boy said. "There's nothing special going on, now."

"You are right," Dr. Anderson said. He was perspiring. "The climate does change, in cycles that last thousands of years. Weather changes, too, in cycles. One thing that drives these changes in this country is El Niño. Who has heard of that?"

"El Niño is the Spanish name of the Christ Child," a girl said. She smiled and looked at her classmates as if seeking their approval.

"El Niño and its counterpart, La Niña, are the names given to changes in ocean currents and temperatures in the southern Pacific Ocean," Dr. Anderson said. "They've been trading places as long as records have been kept. They affect weather far beyond the Southern Pacific, including the United States."

"It's blasphemy to use the Name of the Lord like that!" a boy said. He stepped in front of the cluster of students. "We should not be hearing this!"

Dr. Anderson looked at the television cameras. The only red light was on the camera trained on the boy. Wallace looked at his producer and drew his finger across his throat. The producer nodded.

[FADE TO BLACK]

WhatDrWho Blog

The Science Guide program was interrupted after one of the students accused the host, Dr. Wallace Anderson, of blasphemy for speaking of El Niño as a weather event. NTS said the problem had been traced to a software glitch. Perhaps more cautious than truthful, and more diplomatic than accusing the OTCC School of shortchanging children's education.

Is this important? The current El Niño is rated as at least the third strongest since detailed records have been kept. It is expected to bring wetter weather to the Southern tier of the Continental US, dryer conditions to the Great Plains and Midwest, and hotter than normal temperatures to the Pacific Coast and Northern Tier. Hoped-for moisture in California, Washington, and Oregon is likely to be offset by higher temperatures. No relief in sight there, folks.

The weak-kneed agreements that came out of the Paris Climate Talks can be laid at the feet of the god of greed. Developing countries want; developed countries want to keep. Another sign of our sickciety.

This is WhatDrWho.

~~~~~

"The Rebeccas will meet in the Home Economics classroom
after school on November 3. Membership is open
to all girls and young women of high school age.
Come and learn God's plan for you."
—Poster like that on bulletin boards
of high schools throughout the USA

Home Ec Classroom, Mt. Pleasant, Georgia

Becky popped her gum, ignored the look Susan gave her, and checked once again for messages on her cell phone. Becky was bored.

"Who wants to hang around after school in the home ec classroom, anyway?" she asked. "I want to get to the mall."

It wasn't much of a mall—just a long, winding strip shopping center. At least there was a coffee shop. It was about the only place teens in Mt. Pleasant could hang out.

"I said I would go to the mall with you if you'd come to the meeting," Susan said. Now shush!"

Thirty minutes later, Becky was not just bored, but overwhelmed.

"Are you saying that I can't drive a golf cart?" she interrupted the home ec teacher.

That was unacceptable! Kids in Mt. Pleasant could drive golf carts as soon as they had a state learner's permit. She wasn't supposed to carry friends until she was sixteen and licensed, but parents, eager to escape having to carry kids to school, had made it clear to the police they didn't expect that law to be enforced.

The home ec teacher—who said to call her the *Circle Leader*—had just said that women shouldn't drive. *What a crock!* Becky thought.

"Not that you can't, but you shouldn't. Only if there is no man to drive should you drive," the circle leader equivocated. It was a way of lying without lying, and one that had been taught early to the people who led the Rebeccas and God's Christian Army. Years of ensuring that critical thinking hadn't been taught in the public schools were paying off. None of the children had any idea they were being lied to.

"The Rebeccas are based on biblical authority. The Apostle Paul wrote in First Timothy 5:14, 'I will, therefore, that the younger women shall marry, bear children, guide the house . . . '"

98

And if I want to be a flight attendant? Becky wondered. *Or a Marine?* Her mind filled with fantasy.

~~~~~

"It is an interesting and demonstrable fact
that all children are atheist
and were religion not inculcated
into their minds, they would remain so."
—Ernestine Rose 1810-1892 C.E.

Library Meeting Room, Mt. Pleasant, Georgia

The *Global Explorers* had been created in response to other youth organizations' positions on religion and sexuality. Parents of the boys and girls who were members of the Explorers believed that one could be *good without god.* The parents had taken to heart the Christmas message of *be good for goodness' sake.* Not all of them were comfortable with the notion that kids could be born with sexualities other than *ortho-male* and *ortho-female*, but they were willing to accept the possibility, and to allow their children to associate without prejudice.

On this Sunday afternoon, twenty kids and nearly twice that number of parents were gathered for a program on climate change. The person presenting the program was a science teacher at one of the Mt. Pleasant middle schools.

"Who has heard that global climate change includes *acidification* of the oceans, and that this is killing corals?" he asked.

All the kids raised their hands. A couple of parents, after looking around, did so, too.

"Let's take a look at how that happens," the teacher said.

After explaining litmus paper, and demonstrating his pH meter, he showed a flask whose pH was *just a little* basic. Then, he invited a girl to blow her breath through a straw into the flask. The pH meter slowly moved from base toward acid.

"That's what's happening," the teacher said. "The ocean isn't really becoming acid, just a lot less basic. It's happening through natural processes, mostly at the surface of the water, although currents mix the water.

"Any questions?"

"Why don't we learn this in school?" one of the kids asked.

When he answered, the science teacher looked not at the child, but at the parents standing across the back of the room. "Because our county school board has adopted the federal curriculum, and this is not included in that curriculum."

After the meeting, a parent approached the science teacher. "Why is this not in the curriculum?"

"Mostly because religious fundamentalists in Texas have demanded it be eliminated from their textbooks. Since Texas is the largest single buyer of textbooks in the US what they want dictates what the rest of us get to see and say," the teacher said. "Because the people of this state are too complacent to stand up to a bunch of bigots from Texas."

OTCC General Handbook of Instruction for Disciples

3.3.8 Your Junior Apostles will have walls in their minds, perceptual barriers to the message you will teach. Part of your job is to break down those walls. You will not do that by a frontal attack. Undermine them with bombs of doubt. Do this by asking "Why?" and "What if?" questions.

If a child says, "but my father/mother says . . . " do not tell the child his parent is wrong, but ask, "Why do you think your father would say that?" Ask, "Why would your father believe that?" This encourages the child to question the wrong ideas his parents hold.

Never answer by saying, "We think . . . " or "The Church thinks . . . " Be positive. Say "I know . . . We know . . . The Church knows . . . "

Know your Bible. There is a verse somewhere that answers every question that may be asked.

Your Junior Apostles will have many questions. See Section 9 for frequently asked questions and the approved answers.

CHAPTER 18: THE FIFTH HORSEMAN

Be fruitful, and multiply,
and replenish the earth and subdue it:
and have dominion over every living thing.
Genesis 1:28

Susan Kennedy-Arthur Stewart Campaign Bus

Arthur set aside the sheaf of papers Ruth had given him. It was a summary of topics he and Susan had to know in case a reporter tried to trip them up.

"*The Science Guide*, the program on National TV Service, is focusing on climate," Arthur said. "Neither we nor the opposition have a climate plank in our platforms."

"Bert Rightly will bring in a Canadian scientist and Mel Appleton to talk climate, tonight," Ruth said something that wasn't in the daily summary. No one asked how Ruth might have known that.

"We need one," Susan said. "A climate plank, that is. It's become the Fifth Horseman of the Apocalypse."

Lovely Lena, fishing smack out of St. Andrews, New Brunswick, Canada

Bartoleme opened the net to release a silvery shower of fish into the hold. "About all we can do is sell this catch for fish meal. They can feed it to cats and farm fish," he said. "Not sure they're big enough to call cod."

"It's not right, farming fish," Auguste, his sixteen-year-old son said after sliding the hatch closed. "Farmed salmon never get in water cold enough or deep enough to make the Omega oils that people think they're getting."

"Not much we can do 'bout it," Bartoleme said. "And you can't say we weren't warned. Been over-fishing for years. Don't let 'em grow big enough before we sweep 'em up."

"More than that, Dad," Auguste said. "The waters are warmer than ever. Teacher said that stresses the cod just as they're getting old enough to breed."

I'm glad you're gettin' some schooling, the boy's father thought. *We been fishing for five generations, but I'm the last. There won't be any fish left for you.*

~~~~~

—neumeyer for witwat ross ice shelf collapse continues aerial photos confirm 8 x rate of 2002 larsen b collapse us nasa predicts all will be gone in 5 repeat 5 years potential 5 meter repeat 5 meter rise in sea level

~~~~~

Neumeyer . . . that's the German Antarctic research station. Five meters rise in sea level? That's sixteen, almost sixteen and a half feet, George Stanley thought. *National Airport is only a bit over fifteen feet. Oh, crap!*

~~~~~

Climate Change Collapses Cod Catch

The World Citizen. "One result of global climate change has been warming of the Gulf of Maine. Cod are getting smaller . . . 96% smaller than they were fifty years ago.

"Want more good news? Florida's orange harvest will be the smallest in more than fifty years. The reason is a disease, *citrus greening,* carried by a tiny insect that is killing off the orange trees. The Secretary of Agriculture for Florida said that we are at a tipping point. Some farmers say we've blown past the tipping point.

"This is Muldoon. Just how many more tipping points can pass before civilization collapses? Extremist? Alarmist? Damn right. The truth exists whether you like it or not. Think about it."

~~~~~

Farmers' Market, Mt. Pleasant, Georgia

Marta parked in the handicapped spot in front of the bank and rode the lift from her van to the asphalt. The farmers' market didn't open for an hour, but her favorite people were already setting up: the bakery, the coffee roasters, the woman who had an organic farm a few miles north of Mt. Pleasant. Marta rolled her wheelchair down the aisle where white tents were going up, where folding tables were being unfolded, where people were calling to one another, "Good Market!" and "Need help?" The hour before market began was the liveliest, and Marta found the freshest and best from among the offerings.

"Hi, Linda, were you able to get any peaches?" Marta asked.

"Not for love nor money, Marta," Linda said. "Aren't any Georgia peaches, and there won't be this year."

"Why not?" Marta asked. Her question reflected puzzlement, not blame. Linda understood that.

"Peaches need the cold," Linda said. "Most need at least a thousand hours below 45 degrees during the winter. If they don't get it, they don't make blossoms, and if they don't make blossoms they don't make peaches."

Linda sighed. "Now they're worrying about the Vidalia onions. They're getting' soaked by *El Niño*."

"You gonna be okay, Linda?"

"I hope so. We're south of the cold, north of the rain. We should be okay. And I should have Mountain-dalias next week . . . they're from Vidalia stock, but I can't call them that."

WhatDrWho Blog

The University of Witwatersrand reports more than 1,500 deaths on Kiribati during the last storm. An Australian C-130 aircraft was able to land at Cassidy International Airport but no one has reached the city of London. A US Navy relief convoy from Pearl Harbor is expected to reach the main island tomorrow.

Not all refugees are fleeing conflict in the Middle East. There are tens of thousands of climate refugees who have lost their homes to rising seas and stronger storms.

This is WhatDrWho.

~~~~~

It *Is* Rocket Science *National Television Service*

The show's producer assured The Science Guide that his audience was not from an OTCC school. Dr. Wallace Anderson put on a white lab coat and stepped into the studio.

"What is CO2?" He pointed to the board where he had written CO_2.

"Carbon dioxide."

"And CH_4?" he asked.

"Methane."

"Of course, you know H_2O. What do they have in common?"

The kids stared at the board for a moment. *It's not C, it's not O, and it's not H*, one thought and then experienced an epiphany.

"They're all greenhouse gasses!" she said.

"That is correct, thank you. There is something else they all have in common—they are associated with permafrost that is melting."

Dr. Anderson described permafrost in Alaska, thousands of square miles, tens of thousands of years old, holding tons and tons of organic material and water.

"In Alaska, Canada, Russia, Norway, Finland, and Sweden, permafrost is melting at a rate never seen before.

"When the permafrost melts, the organic material rots. Methane, carbon dioxide, and water vapor are released into the air. These gasses trap the sun's heat, and speed up the melting. It's a positive-feedback loop."

What Dr. Anderson did not say was that if the process continued unabated, the Earth's atmosphere would tip. The planet would become like Venus—with an air temperature of 800 degrees.

UN Raises Ceiling on Greenhouse Gas

The World Citizen. "A report from the United Nations Environment Program says that greenhouse gas—or GHG—emissions may be allowed to rise to 52 billion tons in 2019 and still keep the world from exceeding the two-degrees Centigrade goal. This is a significant increase from past ceilings.

"It is based on assumptions and predictions that emissions in 2030 and beyond will be lower than they thought a year or so ago. In other words, it's more 'smoke and mirrors' from our government.

"One has to wonder: who got to the UN? Are they bowing to pressure from China, which surpassed the United States to become the World's Worst Carbon Polluter? As early as 2015, their emissions were double those of the USA. Are we happy to be in second place?

"Is the UN bowing to pressure from India, which is chasing the World's Worst Polluter title? Are they being fooled by the climate-deniers, including the Denier-In-Chief who sits in the United States Senate? Are they being controlled by him, and his masters?

"This is Muldoon. Remember, the truth is out there and that all politics is lies."

CHAPTER 19: MEL APPLETON

Suppose you were an idiot, and suppose you were
a member of Congress. But I repeat myself.
Mark Twain 1835-1910 CE

Senator March's Office, Washington, DC

"Senator, you have a caucus meeting in thirty minutes."

"Which caucus, Nick? And what's the agenda?"

"The caucus agenda wasn't announced, and it's the Freedom's Torch Caucus." Nick answered Senator March's questions in reverse order. "Called by Senator Rivers."

"Mel, where have you been all morning?" March asked as I walked into the room.

"At American Fire Network, taping Bert Rightly's show for tonight," I said. "Rivers is the Climate Change Denier-in-Chief. The caucus meeting will be about climate."

"What do I need to know?" March asked.

"There's some flap in the news about Antarctic ice melting faster than predicted and someone saying it's slower," Nick said. "Nobody knows for sure. Let me pull up . . . "

"I don't have time for this, Nick."

"But you can score points with the caucus, sir," I said. "Rightly's going to hammer global warming science on AFN, tonight. No one but us knows that. I'll arrange a small press conference after the caucus meeting and give you a few of the points Bert will make tonight. You're the standard-bearer; you will speak first."

"Does Rightly know?" the Senator asked.

"Oh, yes, sir. I scratched his back this morning; he will scratch yours, tonight."

"Good work, Mel."

~~~~~

Fifty-two members of the Freedom's Torch Caucus fidgeted while Oklahoma Senator Rivers, MD, droned about climate models and the elevation of Antarctic bedrock. When he paused to catch his breath, Senator March stood. "Will the Honorable Senator from Oklahoma yield the floor?"

Rivers, surprised, stuttered. "I'm happy to yield to the Honorable Senator from Texas."

"Thank you. Ladies and gentlemen, Senator Rivers has reminded us there is no consensus among scientists that climate change is real. The more they study, the more they argue. What is more important, however, is that climate change is not an issue for voters. The Associated Press will release later this morning a poll showing that while only half of Americans believe in global warming, fewer than fifteen percent are worried about it.

"If they're not worried about it, they won't vote on it.

"I invite the Caucus to consider for a moment the supplemental appropriation requested by the president for military and social programs. Money and taxes, ladies and gentlemen—those are the issues that control the voters.

"On Page 438 of the bill are twenty-two words that would direct unlimited funds from military base construction projects to the Head Start Program. Those words would restore the cuts to Head Start we worked so hard to pass."

Senator March paused for the whispers to die down. "A Democratic staffer on the Appropriations Committee inserted the words. It will take a super-majority to remove them. My staff will send an amendment to all members of this caucus and other members of the American Freedom First Party. Senator Tyrell has agreed to introduce the amendment and take the heat that the self-proclaimed Liberty Party and their libsymp allies in the press will generate. If there are no questions, I suggest we get back to work."

~~~~~

"You got 'em, sir." Mel read the transcript of the caucus meeting. "You said the caucus was aligned with the AFFP and no one barked back."

"It's taken months to reach this point," March said. "It felt like the right time."

~~~~~

Take 'Em To The Wire with Bert Rightly

Bert Rightly perspired, frustrating the makeup artist. A stack of papers with diagrams, charts, and—

"Damn it, Jody, why the hell did you give me equations! Crap. I can't handle word problems, much less equations."

Jody had been Bert's producer for longer than anyone else, ever. She was prepared.

"It allows you to say, yes, you've examined the models. You don't have to know or understand the equations. You might look at the ones I've highlighted. Not the equations, but the author. Mention his name, say his equation is under attack."

"Grumble, grumble, Jody. You're right, again," Bert said, and committed to memory the name, the equation, and the challenge to it. The challenger was an ancient who had no credentials in climatology or modeling. It didn't matter to Bert. The man was a PhD, and that's all that counted.

The audience screamed with Bert as he announced the name of the program and quieted when Bert introduced his guest—a climate scientist from the University of—

"Where?" Bert asked. "And how do you say it again?"

"It's pronounced *gwellf*," his guest, Dr. Coyne, said. "I don't think there's any other word in English that even—"

"And you're some sort of scientist?" Bert interrupted.

"Yes. Earth sciences," Dr. Coyne said. "Geology, oceanology, and climatology. I'm a member of the International Panel—"

"And you think climate change is real?" Bert interrupted, again.

"Yes, Mr. Rightly." Dr. Coyne snapped each word. "Will you allow me the courtesy of explaining?"

Bert looked at the audience who responded to cue cards and yelled, "Yes, yes!"

"Please, Mr. Coyne," Bert said.

Dr. Coyne, Ph.D., Sci.D., stifled his contempt, and said, "The Earth has been warming for some 150 years. It should not be any surprise that the source of warming—the only source—is the sun, and is a result of normal changes in Earth's orbit around the sun."

Bert nodded slowly. This was not what he expected to hear.

"Then all this malarkey about greenhouse gasses is just that? Malarkey?" Bert asked.

"No, Mr. Rightly. And that's the problem. Greenhouse gasses react to the energy received from the sun and exaggerate the warming effect. They are part of what we call *feedback* which takes the normal increase in the sun's energy and trap it on the Earth, raising global temperatures and—"

"I'm sorry, but we have to break for a commercial." Bert turned to the camera. "When we return, Mel Appleton, the hottest political advisor in DC will be here for *Take 'em to the Wire!*"

"Folks," Bert addressed his audience. "Mel Appleton has been a guest before. Shall we *take him to the wire?*" The audience roared.

"Use your cell phones to text a question to the address on the screen," Bert said. "That's for folks here and for folks at home. First question, Mel: What is the position of the American Freedom First Party on climate change?"

"A good question. Bert. I can't speak for the AFFP, but here's a thought. Why should an earthly politician have a say in climate when the Bible says over and over again that Earth will abide, that day and night, winter and summer, seedtime and harvest all will continue?"

"A good answer, Mel." Bert turned to the audience. "What do you think? Was it a good answer?"

Responding to electronic cue cards, the audience applauded.

"Here's another question: Is it true the ocean will soon cover islands in the Pacific?"

"No, Bert. The latest trustworthy data, from our own NASA, is that sea level has risen less than eight inches since the year 1870. Some of those islands are low, but they're all a lot higher than eight inches."

In Arlington, Virginia, George Stanley snapped off the television. *What about the stronger storms that feed on warmer waters? What about the king tides? You won't say anything about those, will you?*

~~~~~

Of the heathen that are around you
shall ye buy bondsmen.
—Leviticus 25:44

Mel Appleton's Office, Washington, DC

Friday the 13th. I hoped it wouldn't be unlucky for me. Warwick had given me the name of Tim Karus. Karus had called and asked me to take a meeting with the chief lobbyist for the NAAPC. The man was on time. His voice was so deep it made ripples in my coffee cup.

"Mr. Appleton, pleasure," he said.

"Good to see you, again, Mr. L'Wazi. Been a while."

"The Press Club, two months ago," L'Wazi said. "Damn good speech the senator gave."

"He is a good speaker, that's for sure," I said.

"You're writing his speeches, now, I suspect?"

"Outlines, only," I said. "The senator always speaks extemporaneously. In fact, he's giving one on the Senate floor at the moment." I pointed to the closed-circuit television.

"Not a problem. It's you I came to see," L'Wazi said.

Danger, Will Robinson! I thought. *This guy is good . . . and he's more than their lobbyist. He's the most powerful man in the NAAPC.*

"Well, sir." That's all I said. He wanted the meeting; he could take the ball and run with it.

"Mr. Appleton, the goals of the American Freedom First Party and those of the NAAPC may not always seem close to one another. However, many of my people share the most fundamental beliefs of the One True Christian Church. Since the AFFP and the OTCC have gotten in bed with one another, a lot of us are in conflict."

My people, he said. And, a lot of *us* are in conflict. He doesn't mean just the NAAPC, either. He's putting himself

114

forward as a spokesperson for every person of color in the country.

"It would be a cliché for me to say anything about *strange bedfellows,*" I said. "You know that there are more things dividing us than joining us." I advanced a pawn and waited for his next move.

"For years, many of my people have voted with the Democratic Party. Some of that is a refusal to vote with the Republicans, which are seen to be the party of the Whites." He chuckled, a deep rumble I felt through the air.

"We have forgotten that Abraham Lincoln was elected by the National Union Party—a cover for the National Republican Party—in the 1864 presidential election," he said.

"We also forget that the history and goals of both parties are so muddled that it's dangerous to depend on history as a guide," I countered. He nodded.

"Some of our loyalty to the Democrats is based on dependence fostered by the Democrats. Dependence nurtured by so many forms of government assistance that a person of color can make more money from welfare than he or she can make at minimum wage jobs—the only jobs offered to most of us."

Most of us, I thought. *And minimum wage. If that's not an Armani suit and a Patek Phillipe watch you are wearing, I'll eat crow—Jim Crow.*

Mr. L continued. "Some of this was created and continues to be fostered by the religion inculcated from the earliest days of slavery—the message that life is hard, and then you die; obey the white master; your reward will be in heaven.

"We have made gains since the early Civil Rights movement. More of us are registered to vote, and more of us do vote. Our middle class is no longer confined to the colored towns of the past, but own homes in middle-class white neighborhoods. We include millionaires, men and women who own nation-wide businesses."

It was his turn to stop. He'd thrown the ball to me. *Religion and protection for the wealthy.* Those were the only two important points in what he said.

"I'm not a theologian," I said. *But I am a quick study.* "I understand that the OTCC no longer openly preaches the Great Chain of Being, on which Blacks are little higher than apes and lower than Whites and Asians. While Church doctrine holds that the Bible—the OTCC version—is the inerrant word of God, and although that Bible still contains some of the odious passages used to support slavery, the Church does not officially preach those verses. There are still churches in the South that might, but it's not widespread. Many of your people would find a home in the OTCC.

"At present, the AFFP has no say in who is a member. Anyone who wishes can declare himself or herself to be a member. There are Klansmen and neo-Nazi skinheads who claim to be part of the AFFP. We try to steer these individuals and groups in the right direction."

Mr. L nodded, so I continued.

"The AFFP supports protection of wealth from inheritance taxes, income taxes, corporate taxes, and capital gains taxes. The AFFP opposes the use of tax money for any purpose not specified in the Constitution. I think that many of your people would find a home in the AFFP."

I had said a lot of nothing. It was what one might find in a shallow high school student's paper . . . a student whose research had not gone past a couple of internet sites. But I had said these things; I had provided the imprimatur Mr. L'Wazi needed. And he understood the message.

The OTCC and the AFFP knew that some people would pervert their message and their position, but Mr. L—and I—also knew that the coalition would someday lay down the law, even to the Klan and the supremacists. The OTCC and the AFFP would accept black middle-class and plutocrats into their ranks—if they would provide financial support. What I didn't say was that the AFFP was prepared to use the KKK and the skinheads as shock troops in the coming war.

We talked for another fifteen minutes, but what needed to be said had been said. The rest was fluff.

As soon as Mr. L'Wazi left, I called Warwick on the secure phone. After providing a summary, I told him, "I've already sent a copy of the recording by secure email. You should see it in your inbox."

Warwick hung up without notice. He always does. Twenty minutes later, he called.

"Well done. When is your next meeting?"

"As soon as he asks for it, sir. Would you like to be here?"

"Unnecessary, and unnecessarily complicated," he said. "You can handle it. Get a photo op with the senator."

Warwick was offering me a great deal of trust, but he was also expecting much. I did not sleep well that night.

~~~~~

Senator March's Office, Washington, DC

"Mel, I'm not sure about this," Senator March said after I told him about the photo op with Mr. L'Wazi.

"Mr. Trucido's people set up the meeting, sir. Mr. Warwick initiated the contact."

"Warwick and Trucido?" the senator pushed his lips into what looked like a child's pout. I knew it meant he was thinking, hard.

"Between the two of them, they have more money than God," he said. "And if the rumors about Trucido's departure from the Vatican Bank are right, that may be literally true. Okay, set it up, but make it brief—and be ready to cut it short."

It seemed to be a photo-op rule that there had to be two chairs, set at a ninety-degree angle to one another, with a small table between them. There was an American flag behind Senator March's chair. The senator and the lobbyist shook hands, exchanged banalities, and sat. I brought in our campaign photographer. His camera was wifi-enabled, and the pictures appeared on a large-screen TV. I was watching the TV. After four shots, I said, "That's a good one. Senator, what do you think?"

"Good. Now, Mr. L'Wazi, what is it we are supposed to be talking about?"

"My endorsement on behalf of the NAAPC, Senator."

"Mel, would you get the photo out, soonest?" That was a clue to leave. I wasn't worried about not being in the room. The microphones would catch everything. Fifteen minutes after I reached my office, the signal light on my desk came on. I knocked and stepped into the senator's office.

"I'm sorry, gentlemen, but there's a call for the Senator. It's the president."

"I'd better take this, Mr. L'Wazi. Mel, please walk Mr. L'Wazi to the lobby." The senator rose and shook hands again with Mr. L'Wazi.

I scanned the transcript of the conversation between the senator and Mr. L'Wazi. The surprise came toward the end, when Mr. L talked about how the World Bank would be the best way to get money to the right places. Neither man said what the right places were. I could guess: secret bank accounts in Caribbean nations.

"As president," Mr. L had said, "you will nominate the next president of the World Bank. That person would have the power to replace the current economist and the staff."

"I think we have an understanding, Mr. L'Wazi," Senator March said.

The senator made a promise to Mr. L, I thought. *I need more background, and I'll need to make sure Mr. L follows through.*

NAAPC Convention, Detroit, Michigan

The carefully orchestrated worship service on Sunday morning put the delegates in a mindlessly loving, forgiving, hand-waving, praising mood. It wasn't enough to prevent fractious arguments that afternoon. The delegates were divided, but not evenly. At 4:00 PM—in time for the evening news on the East Coast—Ms. Nyota Garcia made the announcement. The NAAPC had endorsed Senator Edward March for the presidency. About a third of the delegates had already walked out. The camera operators from *American Fire Network* and *Gods Word for You* were careful not to point toward the rows of empty chairs.

~~~~~

March Takes AFFP Lead

Washington Banner. A Ranogen Poll shows Senator March's lead has risen by seven more percentage points against his closest rival. Burt Rightly's *Take 'Em to the Wire* program on the American Fire Network was the most-watched program last night. After his defense of the death penalty for terrorists, the audience for tonight's show is expected to be even larger.

Mel Appleton

Frank was right. Polly Singer was not only a looker, she was smart and right charming. Frank was too much of a gentleman to say any more about her. I had watched her coverage of the climate brouhaha in Texas a few months ago. There had been some nasty rumors about March taking kickbacks from the oil and gas industry, about applying pressure to award drilling leases to some companies and not to others.

They were just that—rumors, stories created by the Senator's political enemies. Polly had tracked them down. She was firm in her assessment that March was clean, and that his role had been that of peacemaker. I knew better. The Senator hadn't made any money on oil and gas leases, but his son-in-law had. Before he gave me this job, Warwick had given me that information and knowledge of a bank account in Barbados.

"You need to know who you are working for," he had said. "You need to know what might surface to bite him in the butt. You need to be prepared to deny, dispute, and discount."

Frank had made a good decision to confide in Polly. I made sure the Senator knew that. I think he was surprised that I'd say something good about Frank, but I'd promised. I wasn't worried about my job as long as I kept Warwick happy.

~~~~~

—ringoffire/highflyer 7 rep 7 tremors mag < 3.0 oklahoma usa advise net

—highflyer to net confirmed report 7 rep 7 tremors mag < 3.0 oklahoma

—guelphgeolab acknowledges thanks highflyer

CHAPTER 20: SENATOR MARKHAM RIVERS (R-OK)

Everything changes but change, itself.
Heraclitus 535-475 B.C.E.

There is nothing new under the sun.
Ecclesiastes 1:9

Earthquakes in Middle America

The Washington Banner. The United States Geological Service reported seven minor earthquakes in and around Medford, Oklahoma and one near Caldwell, Arkansas. The website of an environmentalist organization, Frack-Follow-Friends, claims to have positive correlation between fracking wastewater injected into deep wells and earthquakes. The *Okie Record* says there is no consensus among scientists, and discounted Frack-Follow's data. The *Okie Record's* science reporter said the report from the 'fracker-cracker' website is bogus.

Senate Office Building, Washington, DC

Senator Markham Rivers made his reputation as Climate-Change-Denier-in-Chief. Now, he was the Cheerleader for Fracking. He had taken money, through S-PACs and under the table, from every oil company in the world. They were pressuring him to deliver.

Boomer Green sipped the Reserve Bourbon the senator had poured for them both. "Too damn many people have discovered the government earthquake website. Can't you stop the geologists from posting an earthquake every time a roughneck in Oklahoma falls off a bar stool? It's frightening the public. That ought to be reason enough."

Boomer had been quarterback of the University of Oklahoma team on which he and Rivers had played. He had been best man at the Senator's wedding, and then a drinking partner after the man's divorce. He wasn't a registered lobbyist, but had an interest in oil and other, less obvious, businesses.

"Markham, the Global board isn't happy," Boomer prodded his friend. "They're talking about cutting subsidies."

Senator Rivers knew what Boomer meant: not only subsidies to scientists at Oklahoma universities and to S-PACs, but also money that went into his accounts in off-shore banks. And Global—Global E-Technic Energy, Ltd.—was the largest energy company in the world.

"You've got to do something about this," Boomer said.

"What do they expect? I pump their position in speeches—including in the *Congressional Record*. I made a speech last month at the Press Club. I introduced seven amendments their lawyers wrote, and got five of them passed. I've held off the people at Interior who wanted to raise the drilling fees. And I broke up the roughnecks' strike."

Old friend, Boomer thought, *you didn't break up the strike. It was my muscle from Kansas City, but it's not something that needs to be said. It's best that everyone thinks it was your golden tongue.*

"I guess they're wondering what you've done for them lately," Boomer said. "What about the government's earthquake website? Can you pressure them to take it down?"

"Cutting funding would be the best way to do that," Rivers said. "The K-Street lobbyists are already messing with the compromise budget. If you can get their lawyers to write

122

something, I'll put it in the hopper . . . or get someone to do it for me."

"Sounds good," Boomer said. "Lunch?"

Conference Committee on the Budget, US Congress

A junior representative from Georgia put the amendment in the hopper. He knew nothing about geology or any science, really. He was home-schooled by fundamentalist parents who believed the Bible contained all the science and history he would ever need to know. His lack of education continued at a private college that prided itself in teaching a *Bible-based understanding of the universe.* Now he was standing before a roomful of senior senators and representatives explaining why they should cut the budget for the US Geological Service. He didn't have a good education, but he had a certain native intelligence.

"I think we all agree," he said—even though he knew not all would agree—"that the government shouldn't be doing things that private industry and universities should be doing. There are lots of companies out there getting free scientific information that's paid for by the taxpayers. That's corporate welfare." *That will not appeal to everyone, but there's a way around it,* he thought.

" 'Sides, if the government needs this information, we can pay these companies to get it. That way, everybody wins. And, we don't have to start paying right away. That can be put off for a while, until people have forgot all this." *And that will get the votes of the AFFP and Republicans.*

Several conferees saw the irony of not giving information to companies, but paying them to retrieve it. They were in the minority, and their objections were voted down. The USGS would take a 30% cut in funding, and would be barred from publishing earthquake data.

~~~~~

—witwat sends storm kiribati beaufort 11 king tides partial evacuation interrupted by storm stop

—reddragon to witwat what witwat

—witwat university witwatersrand south africa

CHAPTER 21: STANLEY AND SONS

I prefer the weapons of dialectic to all other teachings of
philosophy . . . I chose the conflicts of disputation
rather than the trophies of war.
Peter Abelard 1079-1142 C.E.

Stanley Condominium, Arlington, Virginia

George Stanley watched from the balcony as airplanes across the Potomac and Anacostia Rivers lined up to land at the Reagan National Airport. They were visible in the gloaming only by their landing lights. His hand-held scanner carried their radio calls to the tower. He imagined he knew which set of landing lights was Piedmont 3340, American Eagle 2500, Sprint 1970, and a half-dozen others. His thoughts were interrupted by a *whoosh* as the door opened.

"George? You know I don't like you to be on the balcony," his father said. "And, it's getting cold."

"Dad, it's dark! No one can see me. I turned off the living room lights so I wouldn't be silhouetted."

Thomas Stanley sighed. He didn't want to stifle his sons' imagination, their exploration of their world—limited as that was by the need for security. He knew flying fascinated his younger son, and the best view of the airport was from the balcony of their high-rise condominium.

"I will take you to Andrews Joint Base on Saturday if it's not raining. You can watch the planes there."

"But I can't hear them, Dad. They use encrypted UHF radio. All my scanner picks up is civilian VHF."

"Perhaps we can find a way around that," the boy's father said. *There's more than one reason to be on the House Intelligence Committee,* he thought. *The Air Force is always happy to do favors for me. I don't like to take advantage of that, but for the boys . . .*

~~~~~

Friends School, Arlington, Virginia

Henry Stanley laid out his fencing uniform—compression shorts with cup, chest protector, lamé, knickers, gloves, mask, shoes and socks. *Does the list ever end?* he wondered.

George had come into the locker room to help his brother prepare for the match.

"You're wearing more stuff than Father Donovan used to wear," George said. Henry and George had been altar boys at St. Crispin's until this past summer. That was when they'd become disenchanted with the church. George saw that Henry was nervous about the upcoming match, so he babbled. *Maybe it will take his mind off worrying,* he thought.

"I saw Elizabeth Stafford in the stands. I think she's sweet on you."

"She's a nice girl," Henry said. "I took her to a tea dance last week, you know. Zip up the back of my lamé, please."

"How do you have time to do lacrosse and fencing?" George asked.

" 'Cause I'm studying while you're watching airplanes."

"Hey, Big Bro! Flying is a useful thing, and one of these days you'll want a ride and will have to beg me for it."

"Come on, Squirt. I'm dressed. Let's go."

"Do good, Big Bro. When you win, Dad always takes us for pizza."

Stanley Condominium, Arlington, VA

Henry had won his match. After their pizza supper, Thomas Stanley called both boys into his study, but it was Henry whom he addressed. He held a letter.

"Son, you have been accepted at Raleigh Preparatory School. The lacrosse and fencing coaches scouted you last weekend. According to the headmaster, they nearly broke down the door to the administration building they were so anxious to recruit you."

Henry saw George's smile disappear. George looked not at his father or brother, but at the floor.

"Georgie—" Henry began.

"I'm not *Georgie*. I'm *George!* And you're going away!" The younger boy turned to his father. His face twitched as he fought for control. "This is about Henry, not me." Then, his mouth turned down and his voice became bitter. "Dad, may I be excused?"

"No, George. It's about you, too. It's about our family." Thomas knew that would open wounds that had not yet healed, the deep wounds created when the boys' mother had died less than a year ago.

"Boys, you know what my job is and you know why I do it—to make this nation and perhaps the world a good place in which you can grow up—" Thomas didn't finish that thought. Two years ago, he would have said, "—and get married, and give your mother and me grandchildren to spoil." *But George is not likely to have a family and give me grandchildren,* he thought. And changed tack.

"My job has brought you things that millions of kids only dream about. Things like the Friends School and your flying lessons, and someday prep school, then the Air Force Academy, and a chance to chase your own dreams. Henry won his place at Raleigh on the lacrosse field, at fencing matches, and by his grades. But, it was my telephone call that brought the coaches here. You boys will earn your place in the world. Because you are my sons, you will have greater opportunity to explore and find that place.

"George, a door has opened for Henry. It's a door he wants to go through. Doors will open for you, too. I promise.

"Now, will you be happy for your brother?"

Before he fell asleep that night, Thomas Stanley's thoughts churned. *Why do I do it? Really? Am I fooling myself? Can I really make a difference?* He shook off those thoughts. *If not for the country and the world, then for my sons.*

~~~~~

Tempest Times. Henry T. Stanley, son of Representative Thomas Stanley (R-OK) will enter the prestigious Raleigh Academy in Vermont. Younger brother George will remain in the Friends School of Arlington, Virginia. When asked why his sons do not attend public schools, Representative Stanley said that the private schools were better able to accommodate the need for security without the disruption that would be created in a public school.

Raleigh Preparatory School

"Henry, huh? Are you Hank?" The boy who was to be Henry Stanley's roommate didn't wait for an answer.

"I'm Ted. The only one who calls me *Theodore* is my grandmother and she's a hoot—if you can look past her 'old money, old family' façade. In fact, if you Google *old money* you'll find her picture. You'll meet her the next Parents' Day. Oh, that is, I'm Ted Vaughn. From Rhode Island. Where are you from? We'll be on the lacrosse team, together. Do you sail? The school has a sailing program and a dozen Sunfish on Lake Champlain. Maybe this spring—"

"Shhh!" Henry held up his hand, and looked around the room. His eyes were wide. "Do you hear that?" He whispered.

"What?" Ted whispered.

"The silence," Henry said. "The silence in the dark."

Then he smiled. "Ted, you asked me at least three questions. If you don't give me a chance to answer, I'll forget them—"

"The silence in the dark . . . that's from *Dr. Who!* Do you . . . oh, sorry," Ted said.

"First, I'm Henry and don't answer to *Hank* 'cause nobody ever called me that. I'm from . . . well, Oklahoma, but we live in Virginia. Oklahoma isn't well known for sailing, but I would like to learn, and yes, I'm a big *Dr. Who* fan. I've even got the originals on my iPad."

"Why do you live in Virginia?"

"My dad's in Congress."

"Way cool! My dad's running in the next election!"

"Actually, I knew that. That's why we're roommates. Makes security easier," Henry said.

"I should have guessed. At least half the guys in this dorm are sons of politicians, generals, or plutocrats. F-ing guards and babysitters," Ted said. "All my life. Yours too?"

Henry nodded, then listened to Ted's chatter as they unpacked and stowed clothes, books, and electronics.

~~~~~

Raleigh Preparatory School—One Month Later

Henry's philosophy professor was from Germany. He was to be addressed as Herr Doctor Professor. Henry expected to be bored with dark, medieval German philosophers. The professor surprised everyone when he began the semester by relating the salacious story of Peter Abelard and Heloise. Abelard had seduced the girl who was his first cousin and the daughter of his mentor. Her father had castrated Abelard.

When the boys had digested the last part of the story, the professor recited Peter Abelard's contribution to critical thinking:

"Doubt everything. Doubt leads to questioning; questioning leads to truth.

"Distinguish rational proof from propaganda or persuasion.

"Be precise with words and demand precision of others.

"Be wary of error, even in the most sacred texts."

The professor walked down the aisles of desks and handed an envelope to each boy. In the envelope were two cards. Abelard's words were printed on one. On the other was the name of another boy in the class and a proposition. The proposition in Henry's envelope was "Anthropogenic contribution to global warming will prevent achieving the 2C goal." Henry knew what *global warming* meant, and that *anthropogenic* meant human-caused. He had no idea what the *2C goal* was. His partner was to be his roommate.

"You will pair with your assigned partner to create a fifteen-minute presentation on the assigned topic," the professor said. "You will work during this class period and during your study time. The presentation will include arguments for and against the proposition and the conclusion you reach based on these arguments. You are reminded that wiki sites, even the best, are not considered *sacred texts,* although they may help you begin your search."

~~~~~

Raleigh Preparatory School—Three Weeks Later
Henry and Ted stood at lecterns on either side of the screen. The professor had not warned them that they would make their presentation to the entire student body. The boys were glad they'd not been among the first presenters. They'd had

two nights to polish their presentation. Henry pressed his clicker and the first slide appeared.

"The proposition, as stated, contains several unsubstantiated assumptions. The first is that there is an anthropogenic or human-caused contribution to global warming. Based on chemical and radiometric signatures of carbon dioxide, we concluded that humans have contributed to greenhouse gasses—or GHGs—by burning fossil fuels since the industrial revolution began."

Ted put up their second slide, and spoke. "The second element of the proposition was an unspoken assumption that GHGs contribute to global warming. We found sufficient evidence in basic physics to label this assumption, *correct.*"

"The proposition that global warming has occurred has been challenged because of differences in ground-based and satellite-based observations. We examined the science behind those differences," Henry said.

Ted put up the next slide. "We learned that many of the challenges to proponents of global warming have been to the computer models used to predict future global temperatures. We looked at modeling and the science behind the models."

The boys alternated speaking in short, snappy paragraphs, examining each element and showing how they'd reached their conclusions. It was different from what everyone else had done: dry recitations of statements classified as facts or assumptions. When Henry and Ted finished, the student body applauded and cheered. *Bet we get an A for this,* Henry thought. *Wonder what my dad will think, though. He's never said what he thinks, but his party refuses to acknowledge climate change, much less that humans are responsible for it, and certainly not that it will lead to war, famine, disease, and death. That's it! I never thought of it this way, before, but climate change is the Fifth Horseman.*

"A-plus, *Jungen,*" Herr Doctor Professor said. "Your presentation got an entire auditorium excited about learning. The video we made of your presentation will be posted on the school's website if your parents approve. The Academic Dean is already contacting them."

"Herr Doctor Professor seems happy," Ted said after the man had left.

"Yeah, but I wonder what our dads will say," Henry replied.

~~~~~

Raleigh Academy Preparatory School, Lacrosse Field—Two Weeks Later

"Mr. Stanley?" Henry recognized one of the Secret Service agents assigned to the school. "My son, Jamie is here for the game. He asked if you would autograph his program."

"Only if you will call me *Henry*, sir."

Ken Parnell, Secret Service Agent and Soldier of the Cross, grinned. "Okay, Henry, it's a deal."

Henry signed the program and watched the man hand it to a boy who leaned on the railing of the bleachers. Henry spoke to the coach. Then, he walked to the bleachers.

"Jamie? Would you like to sit on the bench with the team?" he asked. "If it's okay with your dad."

Ken Parnell frowned. "Are you sure it's all right?"

"Actually, sir, the coach said he'd rather have Jamie on the bench than you. He was kidding. I think. Maybe."

Ken grinned, and agreed. Henry escorted Jamie to the bench. "Come on, we'll get everyone to sign your program."

"Yes, sir, thank you sir," Jamie spoke for the first time.

"Hey, I'm Henry. Your dad is *sir* 'cause he's an adult. The coach is *coach* or *sir*, but the guys all have first names. Mostly, they go by their last names, though. That's on their jerseys. It's a prep school thing."

"My lacrosse team uses last names, too." Jamie said.

"You play? I should have guessed."

"East Bay Academy," Jamie said.

132

"Okay, men. Warm-up drill." The coach's whistle and call broke up the knot of boys who were signing Jamie's program.

"Come on, Parnell," one of the boys called to Jamie. "Grab an extra stick."

Jamie hesitated until the boy added. "I played for East Bay four years ago. It's the same drill. You'll do okay."

Jamie grinned and joined the drill. He didn't see the coach's eyes on him, or the coach whisper to his assistant.

The coach's whistle stopped the drill and brought the boys back to the bench for a pep talk. The coach reminded them of the other team's known weaknesses. He reminded them of where they were weak and warned them of what the other team was likely to do.

"I know that's a lot to think about, especially during a fast game. But try to keep it in mind—when you're not too busy, that is."

The coach's assistant handed the coach a paper bag.

"Parnell, if you're going to sit on our bench and drill with us, you need a jersey." The coach lifted a souvenir jersey from the bag.

After the game and before Ken Parnell could collect his son, the coach spoke to Jamie. "I watched you during the drills. You're good. You're going to be an outstanding player. Just promise me you won't play for St. Helen!" That was the team Raleigh had narrowly defeated.

"I promise, sir. And, thank you."

Henry Stanley, One Month Later

For the past week men and women with curly wires leading from their collars to their ears had arrived on campus. A score of people in black fatigues spread through the woods surrounding the school grounds. Rumor was that they were on loan from *HaMossad leModi'in ule Tafkdim Meyuhadim*, the Israeli Institute for Intelligence and Special Operations.

The lacrosse team from Brighton Prep walked through metal detectors while guards searched their equipment bags and backpacks. Visitors had to pass through security checkpoints. The Headmaster, Provost, and Deans—*professors emeritus* who had tenure but who were too important to teach, anymore—met parents and invited them to the commons for refreshment.

One of the Deans had escorted Elizabeth Stafford and her mother to my table and brought coffee. Minutes later, the second Dean brought Dad and George to the table.

"I want to see your room," George said even before he greeted me.

"That's part of the tour, Squirt," I said. I saw something in George's face. "Guess I'd better not call you *Squirt*, any more. You must have grown two inches."

"Four. And he's all legs," Dad said.

After showing off my room, and pointing George down the hall to the restroom, I spoke to my father.

"Dad, Ted's father won't sign the release so the school can put our presentation on the internet. He says it's against the party's platform. It's good, Dad, and it's something people need to see. Uh, you know who his dad is, right?"

"Yes, Henry, I do. And he's wrong. The party's platform does not have a climate plank. The greatest opposition to the science of global warming is coming from our own Senator Rivers." I knew who Rivers was, the senior Senator from Oklahoma.

"It's coming from a press that can't spell *anthropogenic*, much less understand it. I'll talk to him, son." He turned back to Mrs. Stafford, smiled, and listened to her gossip.

"Henry," Ken Parnell said quietly. "Jamie is here, and, well . . . I wondered . . . "

I thought quickly. I needed to help dad deal with Ted's father. I needed to gear-up for the game. After the game, I had to dress for the afternoon tea dance and my dinner date with Elizabeth. I really didn't have time for Jamie, but I couldn't say that.

"Hang on, Ken, please," I said, and then walked toward my brother. "George, I need a favor. I have a friend, he's your age, who needs to be shown around and taken to the game. Would you . . . ?"

I had closed the distance between George and myself as I said this, and was able to whisper to George, "He's cute."

George blushed and saw my smile and knew what it meant. "You know?" he asked.

"For a long time, Not-Squirt," I said. "Got a boyfriend, yet?"

George blushed even more. "No, actually, no."

"Will you take responsibility for Jamie?" I asked.

George agreed. His Secret Service detail would cover Jamie; Ken would cover Dad and me. They would get together in the locker room after the game so that George and Jamie could meet the teams for autographs.

~~~~~

Viral Video

The World Citizen. "A video of a school assignment may not be the most exciting thing on the internet. An assignment filled with science and facts is even less exciting. However, a video of the sons of two politicians has gone viral not only on the internet but in the back rooms of Congress.

"Henry Stanley, son of Representative Thomas Stanley of Oklahoma, and Ted Vaughn, son of congressional hopeful Thomas Vaughn of Rhode Island, have stirred the waters with a video that clearly shows that global warming and global climate change are the responsibility of humankind. A certain senator, the nation's Climate-Change-Denier-in-Chief, is said to have been frothing at the mouth. This is Muldoon. Remember, the truth is out there, and these boys seem to have found it."

Press Club Lunch, Washington, DC

People from both sides of the political divide dissected Representative Stanley's speech. It was short, to the point, and well spoken. Stanley defended freedom of speech, the right to disagree without divisiveness, and the right of a son to hold a position different from his father. The more astute observers realized that Stanley had not said what his or his party's position on global climate change was, or whether he agreed or disagreed with his son. Polls in Rhode Island show that Thomas Vaughn had taken a commanding lead in the race for the AFFP nomination for Congress.

Two days later, Stanley received a call on the secure telephone. Usually, that meant someone at the Pentagon, the National Security Agency, the Defense Intelligence Agency, or—more and more often—the Department of Homeland Security—wanted money for something. This call was from Tomas Vaughn, father of Henry's roommate.

"I'm surprised you called on this phone," Stanley asked. "Are the boys okay?"

"Yes, sir. My father is on the board of the company that makes this system. He thought I needed one. Phone, that is. Do you mind?"

"No, although if you're using it I suspect this call is not routine."

"No, sir. You were careful not to say what you believed about what the boys said in the video." Vaughn came to the point.

"Neither the Republican Party nor the AFFP have a climate plank," Stanley said. "Senator Rivers is so far afield that even the Klan is looking to the right to see him. The subject is complex and divisive. It's a hot potato. Let the Church and Senator Rivers and the libsymps fight over it." *Until after the election*, Stanley thought. *And then, we'll need to do something about it.*

There was a long pause. Stanley knew Vaughn was still there. The circuit, although converted from analogue to digital, encrypted, and converted back to analogue and decrypted, was clear.

"Will Rivers give you any trouble?"

"Not likely," Stanley said. "Rivers has lost his leadership in Oklahoma. The national Republican Party is splintering, and the least of my worries is Senator Rivers."

CHAPTER 22: WHATDRWHO

"I keep six honest serving men
(They taught me all I knew);
Their names are What and Why and When
And How and Where and Who."
Rudyard Kipling 1865-1936 CE
The Elephant's Child

Dr. Edward Adams, author of the WhatDrWho blog, scanned headlines from news sources throughout the world. Everyone had something to say about the latest terrorist attacks in London. "Islam is a religion of peace" came from one angle; "All Muslims are terrorists" from another angle. Knee-jerk reaction from US politicians, so focused on the next election they couldn't see the big picture. The Republicans and AFFP suggested prayer; the Democrats, libsymps, and Purples suggested gun control. How strict the control should be wavered between total confiscation and more background checks at gun shows. *Damn Purples! Fence-sitters unable to make a decision or to commit,* Ed thought. *Of course, as polarized as this country is, maybe we need more fence-sitters. Hmmm. May be something to that.* He noted it for a future blog.

Ed raised his head and looked at Kipling's lines framed over his computer terminal, and tackled the keyboard. "'No man is an island,'" he wrote. John Donne said that in 1624. Here's the tag line. "'I am involved in mankind, and therefore never send to know for whom the bell tolls; it tolls for thee.'"

"Today's connectivity, the electronic communication network that blankets the globe, brings stories of murders in London and claims of responsibility by self-styled Muslim terrorists.

"I am not saying we should not be horrified, but we must not be terrified.

"Terrorists scored their first big win with the passage of the American Patriot Act following 9-11. Every time the Act is strengthened, renewed, or enhanced, terrorists score another victory. Every time a TSA agent fondles a child in an airport inspection line, terrorists score another victory.

"You have heard the reactions: on one hand, *pray*. The *Righteous Right* is so busy talking to an imaginary friend they don't have time to think of a rational response. You have heard those who would deny refuge to Muslims or people from largely Muslim countries regardless of their religion.

"You have heard those who blame Islam, and those who profess Islam to be a religion of peace.

"What you have not heard is the still, small voice that says, 'Come on, people, think! They can't all be right.'

"You have not heard the quiet voices that ask, 'What is at the real root of the problem?'

"You have ignored the voices that speak of drought caused by climate change and which led to massive migrations of people from desiccated farmland into the cities of Syria and Lebanon. The privations suffered there created the kegs of explosives that allowed ISIS, Daesh, and their ilk to recruit and strike.

"You have ignored the voices telling you about thousands of children who roam the streets of Syria carrying plastic buckets that they try to fill with food, rotten and diseased, from garbage dumps.

"You have ignored those who tell of the starvation and death that will fall upon tens of thousands of refugees who lack shelter, food, clean water, and who will die by the roadsides of Europe during the coming winter.

"You have ignored the warnings of science that global climate change will create millions more refugees from Pacific Islands, Bangladesh, the Arabian Peninsula, Africa, Central and South America as growing seasons shorten, as insects that pollinate crops die, and as insects that carry diseases thrive.

"In a few days, the more fortunate among you will sit down to a Thanksgiving dinner to be followed by televised football games. Your minds will be on your own situation and whether one particular team's unprecedented winning streak will continue.

"You will not think of things that are really important.

"If you do not listen to the still, small voices, you will die. To add another line from Donne, 'Any man's death diminishes me.' And it diminishes you."

CHAPTER 23: DR. EDWARD ADAMS

History is filled with the sound of
jackboots going up the stairs,
and slippered feet coming down.
After Voltaire 1694-1778 C.E.

I woke to Rudy's screaming. It was a nightmare—his first in months. I rushed to his room. After comforting him, changing the sweat-soaked bedding, putting him back to bed and putting the sheets in the washing machine, I was wide awake. It was 3:00 AM, but I would not get back to sleep. I made a pot of coffee then sat at the computer and checked the headlines. The White House had released a report about "big data," and its dangers to our values. That would make a good blog subject.

The first problem, I thought, *is that they've not defined 'values.' Politicians never do, it seems. Democrat, Republican, AFFP; liberal, conservative. They never tell us what they mean, so we think their values are our values—but they never have to say just what they are or defend them.*

It wasn't long ago that the scion of a southern fast-food chain came out against same-sex marriage because it offended his "biblical family values." I looked up what his Bible said about family values.

Abraham: married his half sister and had a child by her and her maid. That would be incest and either polygamy or adultery. Later, he threw the boy and his mother into the wilderness. Today, he would be charged with child-abandonment and endangerment, or worse.

Isaac: married his second cousin. Incest in most states. Had children by her and his concubines. More adultery or polygamy.

Jacob, later named "Israel," the father of the Jewish nation-race. Married two first-cousins and had children by them and their maids. Incest, and polygamy.

Those were the Fundamentalist Xtians' biblical family values, but they only scratched the ugly surface. There was more.

A pounding on the door interrupted my thoughts.

"Armed police! Open up!"

I pressed F6, and every camera and microphone in the house came on and sent their feeds to a secure server in a salt mine in Kansas. At least, I hoped that the software backup company would capture the data. And, yes, I am paranoid. My articles and blog posts attacking the right-wing radicals—

"Daddy! What's—" My son's voice came through his bedroom door.

"I will find out, Rudy," I said. "Stay in your bed, please."

I opened the front door.

"Can I help—"

"That's him!" a woman said. "He's the one."

Before I could say anything more, two police officers tackled me and threw me onto the floor. They jerked my arms behind me. I felt and heard the click of handcuffs.

"What's going—"

"Find the boy!" the woman interrupted me, again.

"What is the problem?" I asked. "What do you want with Rudy? With me?" *At least I got out a couple of complete sentences—*

"Shut up, pee-do," a male voice growled. Had to be a cop. *What does he—*

144

"Bubba's gonna like you, a lot," another male voice said. I heard several different voices laughing. I understood then what the cop had meant.

"Do you have a warrant?" I asked. Bad decision. Someone kicked me in the ribs.

"Child in imminent danger. Don't need a warrant."

"Who says?"

"I say, you . . . you slime ball." It was the woman's voice. She hissed her esses. "I seen you at the coffee shop, buying that poor boy's affection, and last night, I had a vision. A vision of—"

"Daddy!" It was Rudy's voice, and he was crying so hard he barely got the word out. I turned my head far enough to see him.

He was naked . . . that's the way he slept. Cops held both arms. His legs were wobbly and dragging behind him. Had the cops not held him, he would have collapsed.

A flash lit his face. He blinked and turned away his head. There were more flashes. I heard the whine of a camera's motor drive.

"Wrap the boy up in a sheet or something," the woman said. "And get him to the emergency room. I want a full rape exam. Tell them to find something in his rectum no matter how far up they have to go."

"No! You can't—" I said. A cop kicked me, again, this time, in the head. I saw flashes of light, and then, blackness.

~~~~~

"I'm his attorney." It was the first thing I heard when I woke up. I recognized the voice.

Roger? He's a real estate attorney. And how did he find out, anyway? I opened my eyes. I was in a cell. By myself. No Bubba.

Beyond the bars stood Roger and a cop. I squinted. There were halos around the men's faces and hands, the cop's badge, the lights, anything bright or light-colored.

"I'm his lawyer. I've called a doctor to examine him. You may not prevent me from talking with him; you may not prevent the doctor from examining him."

The cop sneered. "Yeah; maybe. But you gotta fill out papers, first. In there." He pointed to a door. I tried to ask about Rudy, but I saw blackness again.

I woke when someone pulled back my eyelids and shone a penlight in my eyes.

"Concussion." The voice seemed sure. "What happened?"

"Resisted arrest." It was the cop's voice.

Since when is it a crime to resist an illegal arrest? I wondered.

"Where's Rudy?" I asked.

The guy with the flashlight turned loose of my eyelids. I opened them on my own, and asked again. "Where's Rudy?"

"He's being taken care of," the guy with the flashlight said. He was wearing a plastic name badge. The only thing I could make out was "MD." He seemed to understand my concern. "He's okay," he said.

The doctor turned to the cop. "Call for EMS transport to the emergency room. He'll have to be admitted."

"We ain't got no prison wing in the hospital, Doc. He'll have to stay here."

"Officer, if you don't call for EMS transport in thirty seconds, you will be on charges in the next thirty seconds. You, personally. If you have no prison wing, then you'd better send guards, but this man is going to the hospital."

The cop pulled a cell phone from his belt and walked away.

"Rudy?" I asked, again. The doctor seemed to understand what I meant.

146

"He was examined and admitted for observation," the doctor said. "He's in the pediatric wing. I'm afraid you'll not be allowed to see him."

"Why not?" I asked.

"Ms. Sally Johnston from the Department of Human Services has filed a complaint against you. It alleges you kidnapped Rudy two years ago and that you've been abusing him sexually since then."

"But I have papers," I began, "this was all settled." I tried to say more, but was too tired to tell the whole story. Rudy's parents' wills, the powers of attorney, the public records, the push-back from Rudy's aunt and her church, the court's ruling—all the documents in my safe-deposit box . . .

I passed out again.

I woke up a couple of times when the EMS van hit potholes and in the emergency room when they moved me from one gurney to another. I heard the doctor and another voice talking—words about a hairline fracture and sub-cranial hematoma. Someone stuck a needle into the IV line, and I was out, again.

~~~~~

Something had changed. When I woke up, I heard a machine beeping. A nurse came into the room.

"Well, sleepy-head," she said. "You've missed breakfast and are about to miss lunch. How do you feel?"

"Head hurts," I said. I raised my hands and felt bandages. All over my head.

"Here, now, take it easy. They didn't have to do brain surgery, but they did open your skull to relieve pressure. It will be a little tender, and you have a lot of hair to regrow."

"Rudy? How is Rudy?"

The nurse frowned. "They're saying you abused him. The rape nurse said there was no evidence. And he's been asking for you ever since he got here.

"I've said more than I should," she said. "And if I have to, I'll deny it. I hope you understand. The boy's okay, but they're keeping him for observation, and a psychiatrist is to visit him. I shouldn't have told you that, either.

~~~~~

The nurse, the nice one, came in, looked at the machines and made notes on my chart. "Doctor says at least another week to be sure, but they'll not have to open up your head, again. Two fellows are here. They say they are your lawyers. Are you up to seeing them?"

I nodded, winced, tried to cover it up, and said, "Please? I promise to behave."

A sheriff's deputy escorted Roger and someone I didn't recognize. After the deputy left, the second man handed me a business card.

Azisa Beman, JD, LLD
Southern Freedom Law Center

There was an 800 number, an email address, and a website. I looked at the young man. "My home was invaded, my son was dragged naked from his bed and photographed and then subjected to indignities too vile to mention. Policemen who have forgotten what it means *To Serve and Protect* savaged me. I received injuries serious enough to require surgery. I haven't seen Rudy. A self-proclaimed psychiatrist is scheduled to visit him and fill his head with who knows what kind of psychobabble. You need to know this."

"Roger said you were smart," the young man said. "You caught on right away to the psychiatrist. He's the biggest problem at the moment.

"Will you trust me?" he asked.

148

I nodded, regretted having moved my head, and said, "Yes."

"I had to prove to the Sheriff I was really a lawyer and admitted to the Tennessee Bar. He took two days to verify that, which means he knows more than the number on my law license. He knows the SFLC—the Southern Freedom Law Center—is involved in this case. It's not bad. The local people's request for help from the state Attorney General's office will draw publicity.

"And that's our goal. You see . . . "

The tale Mr. Beman spun was horribly believable. A cancer had infested the Department of Human Services. People like Ms. Johnston were the new normal. She cried child abuse, and ripped children from their parents' arms. She cried sex abuse, and jailed people without warrants. And she wasn't the only one with that power.

"You are safe," the young man said. "Rudy is safe. For the moment, anyway. We are watching over you both. But there isn't a child in this state—maybe the entire nation—who is safe as long as Johnston and her ilk are in charge.

"We want you and Rudy to be a test case, to expose her and the coterie of vultures like her."

"Why not a black child?" I asked before I realized how naïve the question was.

Beman didn't seem offended. "Because if a black lawyer were to defend a black family with a black child, the all-white judge and jury would not to see beyond their prejudices. But, breaking a white man and a white child from the clutches of the DHS and the OTCC will bring us the publicity we need to break more children, most of whom are black or mixed race, from the morass of the DHS system."

He stopped talking and seemed to look through me and the wall of the hospital room.

"On the other hand," he said, "there really are predators out there. There really are people, including parents, who abuse kids—emotionally, physically, and sexually. If we weaken the child protective services too much, we open the doors to predation. It's a conundrum."

I wasn't expecting someone as young as he appeared to use words like *predation* and *conundrum*, but I understood that he was older than he seemed.

"Who is this *we* you talk about?"

"Sir, trust is not something to be given or received lightly. Usually, it takes a long time for people to know one another well enough to offer their trust. You have offered me yours; now, I offer you mine.

"We are a movement not limited to Blacks or the SFLC, although the SFLC puts a public face on the movement. We include many people who are appalled at the direction this country is taking. This movement, called by some *Daedalus* after the man who flew to freedom but lost his son in the attempt, is committed to changing the country's direction and defending those who are singled out for persecution. We want you to be a test case."

"You certainly are forthright," I said. "Calling a spade a spa—"

"I'm sorry!" I interrupted myself. "I didn't . . . I mean . . . "

Mr. Beman laughed. It was a soft laugh, and his smile suggested it was a happy laugh.

"Sir, I've been called a lot worse than *spade*, and usually with the f-word as a modifier. I do not take offense."

That broke the ice. Mr. Beman became Azisa, and I learned his last name meant "speaks loudly in thunder-tones." He had adopted it officially after passing his bar exam. Roger agreed to provide an office and admin support for Azisa, and to join him at the defense table. "It's not real estate law," he said. "At least I'm local."

"Defense? I assumed we'd be the plaintiff, and would demand Rudy's return."

"Defense," Roger said, "the district attorney has brought charges against you."

~~~~~

Azisa, Roger, and I were reading copies of the indictment. We were on the second page when the nice nurse interrupted our discussions.

"Mr. Adams, at least four people in this hospital could lose their jobs, perhaps their licenses, over what we are about to do. I no longer pray to god, but if I did, I would ask him to keep all of your mouths shut." She opened the door wider. A different nurse appeared with Rudy. Rudy wore in a hospital gown and blue socks. He saw me, ran to the bed, and buried himself in my side. I wrapped my arm around him and pulled him as close as I could, ignoring the pain from my ribs.

"Daddy, I was afraid," he said.

"I was afraid too, Gizmo," I said. "As soon as I woke up, a nurse told me you were okay . . . as okay as you could be."

Rudy spilled his story. He told me in graphic terms about the exam in the emergency room. He told me Ms. Johnston had demanded he tell her I had raped him, but hadn't believed him when he denied it. He told me he'd pretended to be sick to keep from having to talk to the psychiatrist. "But they're going to make me talk to him, tomorrow. I don't like him. He thinks bad things!"

"Rudy," Azisa said. "The psychiatrist—who is in the pay of DHS—will try to *deconstruct* the bond between you two, the bond behind which hides all the evil sexual things your Daddy has done to you."

"Not!" Rudy said.

"I know," Azisa said. "We know. Rudy? You must go back to your room. The nurses will help us, but we must protect them."

Rudy seemed to understand. He gave me a hug before he and the second nurse left.

≈≈≈≈≈

Dayton, Tennessee, Department of Human Services

They're not going to give me enough time, the man thought. *It will take a lot of time to get him to understand how this man has groomed him to believe the unspeakable things done to him were proper—and to restore his repressed memories of abuse.* The man sighed, smiled at the boy who sat on the edge of the couch, and asked, "Would you like to lie down? Most people find it comfortable."

"No, thank you, sir," Rudy said. "I'm not tired."

He seems polite and tractable. Good, the man thought. "That's okay, Rudy—"

"What is your name, sir?" the boy interrupted.

"I am Doctor Prescott," the man said. "I am your psychiatrist."

"My psychiatrist?" Rudy asked. "How do you mean, *mine*. Did my daddy ask you to talk to me?"

"Well, no Rudy. I was asked to talk to you by Ms. Sally Johnston."

"Then you're her psychiatrist, not mine," Rudy said.

"Well, I suppose you're right, Rudy, but she and I are officers of the court, and we have responsibility for you."

Rudy didn't reply. There was nothing to answer.

The man waited for Rudy to say something. After the boy was silent for a minute or so, the man asked, "Would you tell me about your relationship with Mr. Edward Adams?"

"He's my daddy," Rudy said.

"But your father was," the man looked at his notebook. "Mr. John Martingale."

Rudy sat, quietly, with no expression showing on his face. The doctor hadn't asked a question; no answer was required.

The doctor asked, "Is that correct?"

"Mr. Martingale was my biological father, but he's dead."

"And Mr. Adams?"

Rudy sat silently.

152

"So, Mr. Ed Adams is your uncle," the doctor said.

Again, Rudy remained silent.

"Is Mr. Ed Adams your uncle?" the man asked.

He's catching on, Rudy thought. Inside, he giggled, for the first time since the policemen had taken him away from his daddy.

"No, sir. He's my daddy. And it's *Dr. Edward Adams*—not *Mister Adams*. He was made my daddy more than two years ago."

"I'm sure Mr. Adams's doctorate is on record, somewhere," the psychiatrist began, "but let's—"

"And so is his MD," Rudy interrupted. He had lost some of his control and his face grew red. "He's an MD and a PhD. What are you? I'll bet you're not even an MD."

Now, the psychiatrist turned red. "My qualifications are not the issue, here. What is of issue is how *Mr. Adams* has abused you."

Rudy remained silent for the rest of the session. His daddy's lessons had come back to him. *Use words with precision, and demand precision from others,* was one of those lessons. Rudy realized this psychiatrist wasn't going to obey the rule. Therefore, there was no reason to talk to him.

~~~~~

Dayton, Courtroom

After Judge Webster had invited everyone to be seated and the bailiff had read the docket, the judge spoke.

"This hearing is to determine if the State has enough evidence to charge the defendant with kidnapping and child sexual abuse. The only people who will be allowed in the courtroom are officers of the court and the parties to this case. Witnesses who do not fall into one of these categories will be present only when giving testimony. Officers of the court are cautioned about their responsibilities for secrecy under the rules for juvenile court. Medical personnel will be cautioned they fall under these same rules as well as under the federal Health Information Personal Privacy Laws involving a person's health care records.

"Does any one have any questions about these rules?"

No one spoke. "Good. I am Judge Webster. Of course, the bailiff already told you that. Mr. District Attorney, please introduce yourself and your team."

"Sir, I am Hector Potiphar, JD. Seated with me is Ms. Sally Johnston of the State Department of Human Services, Child Protection Division."

"Thank you. Defense?"

"Sir, I am Roger Smith. With me as lead counsel is Dr. Azisa Beman, and Dr. Edward Adams, father of Rudy—"

"Objection, Your Honor," the DA said. "Whether Mr. Adams is the father is one of the matters we seek to determine."

"Your Honor, that Dr. Adams is Rudy Adams's father was clearly established—" Roger said.

The judge tapped his gavel only long enough to get everyone's attention. "I asked you to introduce your teams, and not to file motions or make introductory statements. Mr. Beman, do you and Dr. Adams understand the charges the state has filed against Dr. Adams?"

"Yes, Your Honor."

"Good. Bailiff? Bring in the child Rudy Adams, and seat him in the jury box."

"Objection, Your Honor!" the DA said. "There will be evidence and testimony not suitable—"

"Mr. Potiphar," the judge interrupted, "the child is a party to the case. Both you and Mr. Beman have him on your witness lists. Further, I understand he received—on the state's orders—an anal rape exam. I doubt if there's anything you can introduce that would shock him. Bailiff, follow my instructions. Mr. Potiphar, your objection is noted and overruled. If you intend to submit graphic evidence or testimony, I will reconsider."

"Yes, Your Honor."

"Then, Mr. Potiphar, you may begin." The judge leaned back in his chair.

"Your Honor," the DA said, "the State will present evidence that Mr. Edward Adams, the defendant, did remove the child Rudy Martingale from the home to which he was legally assigned by Child Protective Services, and did conceal the whereabouts of said child for nearly two years during which time he repeatedly sexually assaulted the child. Frankly, Your Honor, it's open and shut."

"It's my job to decide that, Mr. Potiphar," the judge said. "Mr. Beman?"

Azisa stood. "Your Honor, the Defense will show Dr. Edward Adams was legally awarded custody of Rudy Martingale, that he subsequently adopted this child, that the child's name has been legally changed to Rudy Adams, and rather than attempt to hide Rudy, Dr. Adams enrolled him in public schools, in the local Boys' Club, and in a Little League baseball team. The Defense will show by any standard of proof required that Dr. Adams did not abuse Rudy either sexually or otherwise."

"Thank you, gentlemen—"

"Yes, Rudy?" The judge had seen Rudy stand.

"Sir? May I make an opening statement?"

"Objection!" the DA said.

The judge looked at the defense team and saw no reaction.

"Overruled," the judge said. "Rudy? Do you know the difference between truth and a lie?"

"Oh, yes, sir. Daddy taught me not to lie."

"Objection!" Mr. Potifer said. "Whether Mr. Adams is the child's father—"

"Overruled, Mr. DA. Do not forget this child is a party to these proceedings. He did not identify who had taught him. Rudy, please continue."

"My daddy taught me there's only one way to tell the truth, but there are lots of ways to lie. He taught me the only thing lying does is get you in trouble, because lies will catch up with you."

"A very succinct and mature explanation, Rudy. Please, tell us what we need to hear."

"Yes, sir. Thank you, sir. My mother and father died in a car wreck. Dr. Edward Adams was my father's best friend, and he adopted me."

"Objection, Your Honor," the DA said, "The adoption—"

"Overruled, Mr. Potifer. Do not interrupt this statement, again. Do you understand? You may file objections later, and I will listen. For the moment, do not interrupt."

The DA sat. It was clear from his scowl and crossed arms that he wasn't happy.

The judge gestured to Rudy, who continued. "Aunt Beverly and her church didn't like it, and she told me she would *rescue me* from him. But I don't want to be rescued!"

~~~~~

"I call Rudy Martingale to the stand," the DA announced.

Rudy sat, silently, in his seat in the jury box.

"The child!" the DA pointed to Rudy. "Your Honor . . ."

"Mr. District Attorney, one of the points in contention at this trial is the last name of this young man," the judge said. "Until that is resolved, both sides will refer to him as *Rudy*."

The judge turned to Rudy. "Will that be acceptable to you? And, will you take the witness stand? Please remember our discussion of *truth*."

Rudy nodded, and stepped into the box. The bailiff approached, bible in hand. The judge shook is head. "We've already established that Rudy understands truth from lies. Additional ritual will not be necessary. Your witness, Mr. District Attorney."

Potiphar didn't know how stereotypical he appeared in a three-piece suit, thumbs hooked in his lapels, belly thrust forward, leaning back and looking at the boy from the bottoms of his eyes.

"Your nurses said you often wake up screaming from nightmares," the man said.

Rudy sat, silently.

"Well, answer the question," the DA demanded.

"What question, sir?" Rudy asked.

The DA's eyebrows met over his nose. After a moment, he asked, "Do you often have nightmares?"

"I don't know, sir," Rudy said. "What is *often*?"

At the defense table, Ed Adams found it very hard not to laugh. Rudy was taking his lessons in logic well beyond what he had been taught.

"What?" The DA's face became red. "What do you mean? Are you stupid?"

"Objection!" Azisa called.

"Sustained," the judge replied. "Mr. Potiphar, Rudy is your witness. I should not have to tell you not to badger him."

"Do you have nightmares?" the DA asked.

"I have been told I do," Rudy replied. "But I don't remember any of them."

"What?" Again the DA seemed nonplussed.

"Objection!" Azisa called. He didn't say what he was objecting to, but the judge understood.

"Both of you, approach the bench," the judge ordered.

Azisa and the DA huddled with the judge.

"I have no intention of allowing either of you to turn this court into a circus," the judge said. "Mr. Potiphar, you know as well as I do that dreams and memories of dreams—even nightmares—are not admissible as evidence in this state and I have no intention of making this trial a test case. Unless you can show something more concrete, Mr. Potiphar, I will dismiss this witness. Do you understand?"

The DA, who had hoped for an easy case, was already sweating. "Your Honor, nightmares can be evidence of abuse—"

"Not under this state's rules of evidence, Mr. District Attorney, and therefore, not in my courtroom," the judge said.

~~~~~

I heard what they were saying, even though they were whispering. I knew about the nightmares. They started right after I came to live with Daddy. He let me sleep with him. When I woke, screaming, he would cuddle me and I'd stopped crying. Then, he would ask me about the dreams. I knew he was recording the answers. I knew he would write them down. Later, we would talk about them. He would help me blast away the pictures so they wouldn't hurt me any more.

The dreams had gone away maybe a year ago, until the night Daddy was arrested and they took me to the hospital. I had not remembered the one I had that night until just now. It was the same one I had almost every night in the hospital. It was a dream of my daddy being pulled away from me by a snake with lots of heads. The heads bit him, and I knew he was dead.

~~~~~

"Rudy, do you know what a *private area* is?" the DA asked.

"No, sir."

"It's the area of the body normally covered by a swim suit."

The DA waited.

"Do you understand?" he asked. *He's catching on,* Rudy thought.

"Yes, sir."

"Good. Maybe we're getting somewhere. Has Mr. Adams ever touched your private—"

"Objection, Your Honor. No foundation," Azisa said.

158

"Your Honor, I am attempting to establish foundation," the DA said.

"Overruled, Mr. Beman. Mr. Potiphar, be very careful," the judge said.

"Has Mr. Adams ever touched your private area?"

"Do you mean *Doctor Adams*, my father?" Rudy asked.

"Your Honor, would you instruct the witness to answer the question?" the DA asked.

"His request seemed quite reasonable," the judge said.

"But we've not established—" the DA began.

"Yes, Your Honor," the DA interrupted his own words and turned back to Rudy.

"Has the man sitting at the table—the man in the blue suit—the DA gestured, "ever touched your private area?"

"Dr. Adams, my father, has touched my private area when bathing me," Rudy said. "Is that a problem for you?"

"I am the one asking the questions," the DA said.

"So, you get to say anything you want?" Rudy said. The rising inflection at the end of the sentence turned it into a question, but Potiphar either didn't understand, or didn't take the bait.

Judge Webster successfully hid a smile. *This kid is sharp*, he thought.

"Your Honor, no further questions but I reserve the right of recall."

"Your witness, Mr. Beman," the judge said.

"Thank you, Your Honor," Azisa began. "Rudy, do you believe Dr. Edward Adams is your father?"

"Yes, sir."

"Please tell us why you believe that."

"Objection! Hearsay," Potiphar said.

"Overruled, Rudy, please answer the question."

"My first Daddy told me if anything ever happened to him and Mama, then Dr. Adams would become my father. He gave me a letter saying that. When my first Daddy and Mama died, I had to go to court and tell people I wanted Dr. Adams to be my new Daddy. They said he was."

Letter? Roger slid a note across the table to Ed.

Safe-deposit box, Midtown Bank. Key in top drawer of my desk. You're on the signature card.

~~~~~

Dayton Jail

"The letter's not there," Roger said. "The box is empty."

"But it was there. So was the decree of adoption, Rudy's parents' wills, deed to the house, car title, birth certificates, everything."

Roger and I looked at Azisa. "They got to it," he said. "Somehow, they got to it. This is a bigger problem than I thought. I'll make some calls."

Dayton Courtroom

"The State calls Ms. Sally Johnston."

The DA's questions were brief and revealed little. Ms. Johnston was a twenty-year employee of the DHS. She asserted that Rudy, who she insisted on calling *Rudy Martingale* until the judge warned her a second time, was not legally adopted by Edward Adams, and that Adams had taken sexual liberties with the child. Azisa objected only in the matter of Rudy's name.

"Mr. Beman, your witness." Azisa concealed his smile from the judge.

"Ms. Johnston, you believe the child, Rudy, was subject to sexual predation by his father, Dr.—" Azisa began before he was interrupted by the DA.

"Objection, Your Honor, whether Mr. Adams is the father of the child has not been determined."

"Thank you, Your Honor. I will rephrase," Azisa said. "Ms. Johnston, you said you believe the child, Rudy, was subject to sexual predation by Dr. Edward Adams. What is the basis of your belief?"

160

"I seen him in the coffee shop buying the boy's affections with fancy drinks and sweets."

"Did you ever see Dr. Adams touch the boy, Rudy, in an inappropriate manner?"

"I didn't have to see it to know it was happening," she said. "Seen it in a vision."

Got you! Azisa thought, and moved quickly to the next question.

"When you brought the police to Dr. Adams's home, what did you tell them to secure the warrant?"

"Didn't need no warrant," she replied.

"Ms. Johnston, did you lead the police to Mr. Adams's home without a warrant? Do you believe that the lax interpretation of the Constitution that has been assumed by the Department of Homeland Security also applies to you?"

Ms. Johnston didn't reply, but Azisa didn't expect her to.

"Is there another reason you believe the child should be removed from this household?"

"My job is to place children with families . . ."

"And how do you define *family*?" Azisa inserted into the gap that followed Ms. Johnston's statement.

"The way the Bible does."

Azisa's eyes lit up when he said, "Let's take a look. The first biblical family was Adam and Eve, Cain and Able, is that correct?"

"Yes."

"And Cain murdered his brother, is that correct? That would make the murder rate 25% and higher than it's ever been in any American city. Is that correct?"

No answer.

"Is it correct that Joseph was sold into slavery by his family—his brothers who were jealous of him? Is it true that later he had his brothers arrested for theft after planting false evidence among their possessions?"

No answer.

"Was Lot, who offered his two virgin daughters to a mob of sex-crazed men, later gotten drunk by those same daughters who then had sex with him—the first recorded incident of date rape? And incest, as well."

No answer.

"Are these the biblical families you are emulating?"

Ms. Johnston broke from her daze. "Devil can quote scripture!" she said.

"So can a saint, although I claim to be neither."

The judge pounded his gavel, and whatever the DA was going to say was stifled.

"I have no more questions, Your Honor, but reserve the right of recall," Azisa said.

"The State calls Officer John Cagle of the Dayton Police Department."

Potiphar's questions were *pro forma*, establishing only that the police, augmented by Sheriff's deputies, had arrested one Edward Adams and taken the child, Rudy, to the hospital on instructions from the DHS.

"Your witness, Mr. Beman" the judge said.

Azisa approached the witness box with fire in his eyes.

"Officer Cagle, you were the senior law enforcement officer among those who invaded the home—"

"Objection, prejudicial."

"Sustained."

"You were the senior law enforcement officer among those who broke down the door of the home of Dr. Adams—"

"Objection, prejudicial," Potiphar said.

"Sustained."

"Your Honor, we have shown that the door was broken down—" Azisa began.

"I said *sustained*, Mr. Beman," the judge said.

"I was the chief of the SWAT team, yes," Officer Cagle said.

"And from whom did you obtain the warrant for this home invasion—"

"Objection!"

"Sustained. Mr. Beman, I will not warn you again against the use of inflammatory language."

"Thank you, Your Honor. Officer Cagle, from whom did you obtain the warrant for your actions on the night in question?"

"There wasn't a warrant, sir. Ms. Johnston claimed a child's life was in danger. Under the circumstances, we didn't need a warrant."

"Your Honor, the defense will dispute this at a future time; however, there are still questions for this witness."

The judge nodded, and Azisa continued.

"What did Ms. Johnston tell you that led you to believe the child was in danger?"

"She said she'd seen their behavior at a coffee shop."

"And what did you find when you arrived at the location to confirm a child's life was in danger?"

"The boy was naked."

"He was in his bed until your people removed him from it, is that correct?"

"Yes, sir."

"And a person sleeping naked indicates his or her life is in danger, is that what you believe?"

"No, sir, but Ms. Johnston said—"

"I'm asking you, not Ms. Johnston," Azisa said. "Because a person sleeps naked, is his or her life in danger? Is that what you believe?"

"No, sir, it is not."

"So you saw nothing to indicate the child's life was in danger?"

"No, sir. Not when you put it that way."

"I did put it that way, officer. By the way, Officer Cagle, what do you wear when you sleep?"

"Nothing, sir."

"Thank you."

Azisa looked at his notes, and then asked, "Did Ms. Johnston tell you anything about a *vision* that the child's life—"

"Objection! Based on facts not in evidence," the DA said.

"Your Honor, if we may recall this witness at a later time, I would like to introduce the *facts* that the DA seems to want to deny. Ms. Johnston said under oath she had a vision of abuse. We have sound and video recordings made on the night in question showing Ms. Johnston saying she had a *vision* of abuse as well as brutal treatment—"

"Objection! The state disputes the authenticity of these recordings," the DA said.

"Your Honor, we provided the State a list of expert witnesses who can attest to their authenticity," Azisa said. "The list contains more than a hundred names . . ."

"I for one do not want this matter to last until the next century," the judge said. "Mr. Potiphar?"

"The State accepts the recordings but reserved the right to contest them at a future time."

"A wise decision," the judge said.

Ms. Johnston and the DA both seemed to squirm as Azisa played and replayed the scene in which Ms. Johnston said she'd had a vision.

"One last question, Officer Cagle. Both Dr. Adams and Rudy report that someone with a camera was taking pictures during the entry into Dr. Adams's house and the removal of Rudy. Where are those pictures?"

"I don't know."

"Your Honor, we have requested these pictures during discovery. Neither the police nor the sheriff's department has produced them. We request that you order them to be produced."

The judge took no time at all. "So ordered. Bailiff? Paperwork. Now."

"Your Honor, the defense requests re-cross of Ms. Sally Johnston."

"Objection!" the DA called.

"Overruled, Mr. Potiphar," the judge said, and privately thought, *You made your bed, now sleep in it.*

"Ms. Johnston, what did you mean when you said you *had a vision*?" Azisa asked.

"Objection," the DA called. "You said dreams were not admissible."

"Overruled, Mr. Potiphar. She is your witness. Her statement on the witness stand and on the video recordings is clear. The subject is a *vision*, not a dream. A fine point, I agree. However, you may not object to her testimony in this matter."

"Ms. Johnston? You must answer the question," the judge said.

"It wasn't just any vision," she said. "The Lord God sent me a vision—"

She paused, as if to give Azisa a chance to object. When he didn't do so, she seemed to gain courage, and continued. "The Lord God sent me a vision, like he sent Jacob a vision of angels climbing the ladder to Heaven, and I knew it was a real vision. This was a vision of Mr. Adams abusing the boy.

"The Bible tells of a ladder to heaven, but people always talk about the highway to Hell," she said. "That means there's more people goin' to Hell than to Heaven, and this man—"

"Objection, Your Honor. Not based on facts in evidence; prejudicial," Azisa interrupted.

"Mr. Beman, you may not object to the testimony of your witness. You know better. However, Ms. Johnston, you must answer the questions, but do not editorialize. We seek the truth, not opinion. Do you understand?"

She nodded.

"Do you have any evidence, other than your vision, that Mr. Adams abused the boy? Any evidence at all?" Azisa asked.

"I don't need *evidence*," Ms. Johnston said. "God gave me all the evidence I need."

"By *god*, Ms. Johnston, to whom do you refer?"

"There is only one God!" she said. "The God who sent his Son that we might be saved."

In recorded history, humankind has invented some 2,500 gods. You do not believe in 2,499 of them; I do not believe in 2,500. We're only one god away from complete agreement, Dr. Adams thought. He didn't know that Aziza was thinking the same thing.

"This would be the god described in the Old and New Testaments?" Azisa asked.

"As if a heathen like you—"

Judge Webster didn't wait for Azisa to object. "Ms. Johnston, I warned you not to editorialize. If you continue to do so, I will hold you in contempt. Do you understand?"

"Yes. There is only one God," she said. "He gave us his words in the Bible. You're so smart, you ought to know that."

"Thank you, Ms. Johnston. Would you identify this book?" Azisa handed her a King James Bible.

"It's the Bible," she said.

"It is the source of your understanding and your faith?" Azisa asked.

Ms. Johnston looked a little confused, but said, "Yes."

"Do you believe it is the inerrant word of God?" Azisa asked.

"Yes," she said.

"Would you read the three marked passages, please."

"Matthew 27:46 'And about the ninth hour Jesus cried with a loud voice, saying, "Eli, eli, lama sabachthani?" That is to say, My God, my God, why has thou forsaken me?' "

"Luke 23:46 'And when Jesus had cried with a loud voice, he said, "Father, into thy hands I commend my spirit . . . "' and having said thus, he gave up the ghost.' "

"John 19:30 'When Jesus therefore had received the vinegar, he said, "it is finished . . . " and he bowed his head, and gave up the ghost.' "

"Ms. Johnston, if this is the inerrant word of God, how can there be such contradictions?"

No answer.

"Mr. Beman, I think you've made your point," Judge Webster said. "And we've had enough Bible lessons for one day. Move on, please."

Azisa nodded. "Of what church are you a member, Ms. Johnston?"

"The One True Christian Church," she said.

"Ms. Johnston, is it correct that you brought in a psychiatrist, a Dr. Prescott, to interview Rudy Adams?"

"Mr. Potiphar said not to say anything about him," she said.

"Mr. Potiphar coached you on your testimony?" Azisa said.

Before the DA could think of a reason to object, the woman answered. "He just said what I wasn't supposed to say."

The judge made a note.

"What is Dr. Prescott's specialty?"

"Recovering repressed memories."

Alarms went off in the heads of the defense team.

~~~~~

The psychiatrist was the prosecution's next witness.

"Dr. Prescott, please tell us your professional qualifications," the DA asked.

"I am an MD and a PhD. My PhD is in psychiatry. I am and have been for seven years employed by the Tennessee State Department of Human Resources."

"And did you examine the child, Rudy, following his removal from the home of Edward Adams?"

"I did, sir."

The DA looked at Azisa as if he expected him to object. When Azisa sat, silently, the DA continued.

"And what did you determine?"

"The child has been subjected to grooming to make him tractable and accepting of sexual abuse, and has been traumatized to the point that his memories of abuse have been suppressed. That is likely the source of the nightmares—"

"Objection, Your Honor," Azisa said.

"Sustained. Mr. Potiphar, instruct your witness about the rules of evidence, and refrain from further questioning in this area."

The DA gritted his teeth; then said, "Yes, Your Honor. Dr. Prescott, we may not discuss dreams or nightmares in this court."

Nicely done, Azisa thought. *It leaves open a line for appeal, however.*

"What evidence do you have for abuse and trauma?" the DA asked.

"I'm very much afraid only someone with my extensive training and experience could understand it—"

"Try to explain, won't you?" Judge Webster said. His voice was a steel fist wrapped in a velvet glove.

"Yes, Your Honor. The child exhibited nervousness when asked about sexual contact with his adult caregiver. He refused to meet my eyes when I asked about physical abuse. He flushed and became angry when I talked about Mr. Adams."

"Thank you," Judge Webster said.

"No further questions, Your Honor," the DA said.

Knows how to quit when he's ahead, Azisa thought.

Azisa stood, and approached the witness stand.

"You said you were both an MD and a PhD. From what universities did you receive those degrees?"

"From Wheatly University."

"And what body accredited Wheatly University?"

"I don't know what you mean. It's a church school. I suppose it's accredited by the church."

"And what church would that be?"

"The One True Christian Church."

Azisa turned to the bench. "Your Honor, I have extensive documentation that this university is not accredited by any recognized accreditation body for colleges and universities in the United States of America. I have provided a copy of these documents to the DA, and ask that they be entered into evidence. Since it is difficult, if not impossible to prove a negative, I would ask the State be required to prove accreditation of the university that awarded this man's credentials."

"Objection!" the DA called.

"On what grounds?" the judge asked.

"Withdrawn."

"Please continue, Mr. Beman."

"Dr. Prescott, you said you had a medical degree. Are you a member of the Tennessee State Medical Association, and are you licensed to practice medicine in this state?"

"As an employee of the state, I am not required to have such a license, and I restrict my practice to my duties for the state."

"In other words, no."

"That is correct."

That was one of the corruptions we hoped to expose—and change, Azisa thought. *I'm glad I was able to get it out into the open.*

~~~~~

The state had rested its case, such as it was. It was apparent that the DA expected the judge to rule in favor of the state and hold Adams for trial, and to ensure Rudy remained in custody.

Azisa's first witness was Nurse Susan Plunkett. A sheriff's deputy brought in a woman of about 40. She wore a blue dress, a white pinafore, and a starched, white cap. Her only jewelry was two pins on her lapel. One was a Florence Nightingale lamp; the other, the crest of the university hospital's nursing school.

"Please tell us your professional qualifications, and where you are employed," Azisa asked after she was sworn in.

"I am a Registered Nurse with a Masters of Science in Nursing from the University of Tennessee. I am board certified as a sexual assault examiner, and have performed those duties at the Dayton Hospital Emergency Room for seven years. I am also certified by the Family Court as an expert witness in sexual assault."

"Do you recognize the child sitting in the jury box?"

"I do."

Azisa saw tears form in the corners of the woman's eyes. He paused, looked at his notes, and then asked, "Please tell us, in your own words, how and why you know him."

"Just a moment," Judge Webster said. "Rudy? I suspect what we will hear will be graphic and uncomfortable. Would you like to leave the room?"

Rudy shook his head. "No sir; thank you sir."

"Very well, Nurse Plunkett, you may proceed."

"This young man was dragged into the emergency room at 3:45 AM by police accompanied by Ms. Sally Johnston of the Department of Human Services. I was sitting in reception with the triage nurse. Ms. Johnston demanded the boy be examined for signs of sexual abuse, specifically, forced anal intercourse."

"Forgive me for interrupting," Azisa interrupted. "You said he was *dragged*?"

"One police officer on each arm, his bare feet trailing behind, and what appeared to be a bed sheet falling off his body. Dragged," she said.

"Thank you. Please continue."

170

"I summoned an orderly with a gurney, took the boy from the police officers, and lifted him onto the gurney. By this time, the sheet had come off. He was naked. I covered him with a blanket and with the orderly rolled him toward the examining area. Ms. Johnston tried to follow, as she often did, and I had to remind her, as I often did, that she was not permitted in the examining area.

"Once in the exam room, accompanied by the orderly and a second nurse, I explained to the boy—"

"Ma'am? My name is *Rudy* not *the boy*," Rudy said.

"Of course," the nurse said. "I am sorry, Rudy. I showed Rudy the pediatric sigmoidoscope. I explained I would insert it in his anus, and showed him how the light and camera worked. I said I would be looking for any damage. I explained that a suction tube would be used to draw out fluids.

"By this time, a second nurse had drawn blood and sent it through the pneumatic system to the lab.

"I told Rudy I would apply something to his anus to keep down the pain, but it might hurt, and to grit his teeth, and be brave. As I was saying this, Ms. Johnston burst into the room and demanded I not use anesthetic, because it might, in her words, *mess up the results*. I replied that our lab was quite capable of distinguishing anesthetic from semen and ordered her to leave. She refused. I instructed the orderly to call security.

"By the time security had arrived and removed Ms. Johnston, the results of blood testing had come back; they were negative for the usual suite of STDs; however, tests for both syphilis and HIV would not be available for several hours, and might require further testing including testing of spinal fluid.

"Security removed Ms. Johnston, and I continued with the examination, to include the application of a topical anesthetic."

"And what did you find?" Azisa asked.

"It's what I didn't find," the nurse said. "Rudy's anus was not distended and had normal muscle tonus for someone his age. There were no anal fissures. There was no semen visible; the lab did not find any semen in the fluid sample I sent. The stool in the rectum was not compacted. There was no indication he had ever been subject to anal intercourse, either recent or past."

"Thank you, Nurse Plunkett. Your witness, Mr. Potiphar."

"An impressive statement, Nurse Plunkett. Very well spoken. You said you were certified as an expert witness. Do you know the definition of perjury?" the DA asked.

"I do. Perjury is more than lying. In simple terms, perjury is lying in a way that materially affects a case."

"Your Honor, I offer in evidence the hospital's records of the exam Nurse Plunkett described and ask they and a record of her testimony today be sent to the prosecutor's office to prepare charges of perjury."

"Objection!" Azisa stood. "We subpoenaed those records; the hospital rejected our request, and the District Attorney failed to provide them during discovery."

"Let me see the records," the judge ordered.

After scanning the documents, the judge handed them to the nurse. Potiphar tried to intercept them, but backed off when the judge glared at him.

"Nurse Plunkett? Would you care to comment?" the judge asked.

The nurse scanned the four pages, then looked hard at the top page. "These are not my notes, Your Honor," she said. "They are a rather obvious forgery. I hope neither you nor Mr. Potiphar thinks I would misspell rectum, semen, or sphincter, or would call a sigmoidoscope a speculum." She handed the pages back to the judge.

The judge summoned the bailiff to the bench. After a whispered conversation, the judge signed a form the bailiff handed him. The bailiff left through the door leading to the judge's chambers.

"Do you have any questions for this witness?" the judge asked the DA.

"No, Your Honor."

When convened after lunch, the DA stood. "Your Honor, I learned during the lunch hour that my mother has been placed in hospice care, and is not expected to live more than a few days. I beg of the court a continuance until Wednesday of next week."

"Mr. Beman?"

"The Defense has no objection, Your Honor."

"Very well, we are adjourned until Wednesday at 10:00 AM."

~~~~~

Dayton Jail

"Your *client* ain't here. They took him to the hospital." The deputy seemed smug.

What does he know? Azisa wondered. The answer came when his cell phone buzzed. A text message.

—Adams here for prefrontal lobotomy come quickly

The caller's number was not familiar, but Azisa knew several of the nursing staff had his number. *I have to assume this is from a friend,* he thought. And punched numbers even as he rushed to his car.

The Daedalus people easily overwhelmed the receptionist at the hospital "This is Doctor Smaug from the university. He's been called in to consult. Where is Edward Adams?"

The flustered young man at the desk poked keys. "OR 3—Operating Room 3," he said. "At least he's scheduled in thirty minutes. Right now, he's in Room 317, being prepped. Uh, do you have some ID or something?"

"Kid, Dr. Smaug is the preeminent brain surgeon in Tennessee and you want ID?"

It was easy to overwhelm the prep team, to find a spare gurney on which to load Dr. Adams, and to wheel him from the side entrance to a waiting medical transport ambulance. The ambulance, stolen not an hour before, took the Daedalus team only across the highway to a complex where several doctors had offices, before depositing Adams and the team, who drove away in a van stolen from a medical supply company. The van took them only as far as an industrial park before the team transferred to an SUV. By this time, Dr. Adams was able to sit up, although he was still buzzy from the drugs he'd been given.

Dayton, Willow Elementary School

Rudy had seen Azisa in the courtroom and once, weeks ago, in his father's hospital room. His was a familiar face. Azisa decided to would lead the extraction team. The night before, Azisa had visited Edward Adams.

"Ed, they're not going to release you or Rudy. I tried to contact the judge this afternoon, but he has disappeared. We don't know if he's fled or been eliminated. Nurse Plunkett is missing, too. We've not been able to find out who emptied your safe-deposit box. There's a rot that has spread throughout this community. You offered us your trust when you agreed to be a test case. We got the publicity we wanted, but it's been swamped with propaganda and has placed you and Rudy in danger. I have two requests. First, when our people come for you, will you go with them? Second, do you and Rudy have a safe word?"

Ed Adams's face contorted as one emotion after another flashed through his mind. After several minutes, during which Azisa waited patiently, Ed said. "I give you the life of my son. The safe word is *Alas, Babylon.*"

There were tears in Azisa's eyes when he replied. "Thank you, Ed. I swear on my own life that I, my friends and I, will do all we can to bring you and Rudy to safety."

That was last night. Today, Azisa and two members of Daedalus sat in a van parked behind the elementary school. It was a *field day*, and all the students were engaged in games—competition such as three-legged races and, for the more cerebral, a marathon quiz on popular television programs. Vendors provided hot dogs, hamburgers, crisps, and sodas. The Daedalus van was one among several.

"That's he," Azisa said. He carried a box labeled 'Condiments: Not packaged for resale." Another of his team followed. A third watched from a distance.

"Rudy?" Aziza said when they reached the boy.

"Mister, uh, Mister Beman?" Rudy asked. He concealed his surprise at seeing a lawyer in a delivery uniform.

"*Alas Babylon*," Azisa said. "Your father agreed that we must remove you. Will you come with us?"

It took Rudy no time to decide. *He defended Daddy. He has the safe word, and there's no way anyone could have gotten it from Daddy.*

"Yes, sir. What do I do?"

"Out that door, the white van with the red letters. Go to it. Open the back door. Get in. We will be there as soon as we deliver this to the cafeteria ladies."

Ten minutes later, a white van with lettering declaring it belonged to a national delivery service left the campus, heading south along Highway 27. At Soddy-Daisy, Edward Adams and Rudy were reunited.

"Why south?" Ed asked, after some minutes.

"It will never be expected," one of the Daedalus people said. "There's a driver just outside Chattanooga waiting for precious cargo."

"Precious cargo?" Ed asked.

The man from Daedalus grinned. "Think about it," he said. "From Chattanooga, you'll go east to Interstate 75, then north to Lexington, Kentucky. Not a good place, but you'll go from there to Indiana. We have Friends, there."

Quaker Home, Safe House _____ Indiana

"It's not going to be much of a Christmas, Rudy. I know you wanted a bicycle, but I don't think Santa's going to find us."

"You're very silly, Daddy. I couldn't ride in all this snow, anyway." The current *El Niño* had brought warm, wet weather to the American Southeast, and heavy snow to the Midwest, but no relief to the parched West Coast.

Their hosts, Mr. and Mrs. Young came into the room.

"Indiana may no longer be safe for you," Mr. Young said. "The State Police are cooperating with Tennessee in a search for a dangerous fugitive. Those are their words. There's an Amber Alert out, with Rudy's picture and yours. You are described as a psychopath who has killed, before. Someone reported seeing you at a truck stop in Kentucky."

"A Friend who is a cosmetologist will be here soon to change your appearance as much as possible," Mrs. Young said.

"We're still working on transportation," Mr. Young concluded.

~~~~~

Ed and Rudy had submitted to the cosmetologist. "Not too much of a change," she had said. "Just enough different from the pictures they've posted. Color, and a different hair style, a little gel to hold your part differently."

When she finished, Mr. Young took photographs, and gave them to a man who came and went without being introduced.

The morning after the makeover, Ed and Rudy combed and brushed their hair as they had been shown, and went to breakfast. Waiting for them were an Indiana driver's license for Ed and a school ID card for Rudy. New names, new addresses, and a new school.

"You'll need to memorize this while you eat breakfast. Your wife and sister will pick you up at 8:00 AM. The snow has stopped, the roads are clear. Mrs. Mary Ann Allison is a widow, but she will be your wife for the journey to London, Ontario, where she and her daughter, Jane, plan to visit relatives for the Christmas holiday."

"But Daddy, we have to stay!" Rudy said. "Your work is important."

"Rudy, other than the gossip about Dayton—which is seldom interesting and never useful—all the information I need comes from the internet. And they do have internet in Canada." Ed smiled. "And they have schools, too."

CHAPTER 24: RIDERS OF THE RED HORSE

To be prepared for war is
one of the most effective means of preserving peace.
George Washington 1732-1799 CE

Pentagon, Room M23R7

The Brotherhood of Mithras was based not on rank or age but on knowledge and ability, and on what the membership defined as integrity. Their definition might have seemed bold, but their loyalty was to an ideal, and not to the failed implementation of that ideal. The Brotherhood knew that the rot attacking the body politic had begun years ago. Despite Eisenhower's warnings about the *military-industrial complex*, an unholy alliance forged among military procurement officials, foreign military sales officials, and the corporations that manufactured weapons and delivery systems drove the foreign policy of the United States.

The official leadership of the military—the decorated brass who had not seen combat in decades—and the civilian leadership of the White House and the Congress, none of whom had served at all, had compromised the principles of the Enlightenment and of the Republic in the name of greed. That decision, as it always had and always would, led the nation down the wrong path.

An Army lieutenant opened the meeting. "Our current issue is the expansion of the so-called biometric identification required of all soldiers—including National Guard, Reserves, and retirees—and dependents. The Department of Homeland Security has access to our databases. They can track us, monitor us, deny access to us based on our retinal prints, our DNA, our voices. I say this is intolerable.

"What say you all?"

The discussion examined the issue from many aspects. The conclusion was that if the Brotherhood could keep control of their databases, it would allow them to place their people in positions of responsibility.

"We can control the database. The DHS and their masters in the AFFP and OTCC do not know that, but believe their system is secure. We can put our people and our allies anywhere. We suspect the enemy is trying to take over the Secret Service. Whether to mask their money laundering or to attack the president, we don't know. We need to put our people on the presidential detail. This could open a door." General Fall paused for comment.

If any of the attendees were surprised the Brotherhood included members of the Secret Service, they hid it.

I wonder where else? Lieutenant Sandra Carson thought. *FBI? DHS? I guess my understanding of "soldier" needs to expand.*

"The OTCC relies on personal knowledge of candidates and on what they call *recommends* from local bishops. They'll not be impressed with anything we put in the database." A captain of the signal corps said. She spoke with conviction, and *signal corps* had long meant *intelligence*.

"Does that include both presidential and other details?" An Airman First asked.

The lieutenant thought for a moment. "It appears they are focusing only on the presidential detail. What are you thinking?"

"The most likely AFFP vice presidential candidate is Representative Thomas Stanley, and he has two sons. They already have some Secret Service protection. If nominated, he and they will get dedicated details. Perhaps that's where we need to be. It will give us an opening."

"What about the Democrat, Susan Kennedy?"

There was a long silence before the Airman First spoke. "She has no chance."

"Stanley should be our target," the captain said. "If we are agreed, I'll get on it right away.

"What say you all?"

~~~~~

Headquarters, Soldiers of the Cross, Lynchburg, Virginia

> . . . all armed prophets have conquered,
> and the unarmed ones have been destroyed.
> —Machiavelli, *The Prince*

The conference room was as secure as money and modern technology could make it. The group that met there did not exist. Rather, they were not known to exist except by Archbishop Isaac Tricido, the group's membership, and the members' immediate subordinates. No one had a reason to suspect their existence; no one had a reason to suspect they met in this room; no one had a reason to spy on them.

To the public and the One True Christian Church, the *Soldiers of the Cross* was a social organization, much like the mainstream Protestants' *Men of the Church*. It was the adult version of the boy-athletes' club, *God's Christian Army*. Members of the Soldiers of the Cross gathered weekly for breakfast, networking, and prayer. One weekend a month, they would assemble and perform some civic activity: cleaning up a park, building a playground, or helping a Church member repair a roof.

Only the elect knew that soldiers who passed scrutiny were sworn to secrecy and admitted to an inner circle. The men who met in the conference room on this day were the leaders of the inner circle. The Director General sat at the head of the table.

There was no small talk, no welcome, no invocation, no pledge to the flag. These men knew their roles; they knew what was expected of them. They had no need for ritual, and they were focused on power and purpose, not prayer.

"We have examined and recruited seventy-two more soldiers and scheduled their training," a colonel reported.

"Our man in Army personnel has placed twenty-two military policemen in units guarding armories at key military installations," the next man said.

"We have revised the *Handbook for Investigators* based on the comments from this group as well as those of the psychologists and sociologists on staff. The lead author found the *Handbook for Inquisitors* from the sixteenth century to be a useful source of ideas. It seems people haven't changed much since then."

The men continued to report successes in their individual areas of responsibility. When all had spoken, the Director General rose.

"*No man knoweth the hour*," he said. "However, the wise can be prepared. It is likely the hour will be when the polls close in November. Until we know otherwise, prepare as if that were the hour. Remain cautious, but advance your plans and schedules as much as possible to meet that date."

~~~~~~

Congregational Baptist Church, Atlanta, Georgia

On this evening, the church would be filled for the Wednesday prayer meeting. On this morning, members of the NAAPC filled the pews. They came to hear Mr. Azisa Beman speak. They had been told he was their new leader. Not everyone accepted that.

The opening prayer was subdued, but the voice of the young man who took the pulpit was filled with fire. *We have been betrayed,* were the strongest words of his message. When he finished, all were convinced. *We must stand together* was an expected command, but was overshadowed by his call to action.

"One hundred and seventy years and more ago, good people, mostly white people, mostly Quakers, but others, too, created something called the Underground Railroad. You all know the stories of Harriet Tubman and Frederick Douglas. Some may also know the story of Reverend John Rankin and his wife, Jean—a white couple who dedicated their lives to help slaves reach freedom. How many know Erastus Hussey, a Quaker Abolitionist and Stationmaster—a white man—one of hundreds of white Quakers who were Caretakers and Conductors on the Underground Railroad."

A ragged chorus of *amen* came from the congregation.

"Some of you may trace your ancestry to those who traveled this route to freedom.

"Today, I call upon you to be a part of the re-creation of that Railroad. Recently, a man unjustly accused, was spirited to safety before forces of evil could cut into his brain, yes, in a hospital, cut away parts of his brain to prevent him from speaking out against tyranny.

"This was not in the Middle East, it was not in one of the African or South American dictatorships. It was in the United States. He was not a black man; he was a white man. More important than the color of his skin, he was a man who had spoken out against injustice.

"We will see more of this, and we will see a greater need for people of character, of courage, of conviction to act against tyranny. It is no longer enough to speak truth to power although we must do that. It is no longer enough to stand complacently. It is time to act."

~~~~~~

"A Committee Meeting" Bar, 100 Block, Constitution Avenue, Washington, DC

The wait staff knew their patrons. They were careful to deliver checks to each person at every table. They were a little less careful about how they divided the tab. But a-wink-and-a-nod was traditional in US politics, and the money exchanged between lobbyists and politicians in other venues was far greater than a few dollars on a bar bill.

Boomer Green and Senator Markham Rivers had invited a certain freshman representative from Georgia to join them. The man had cancelled dinner with his wife. She would understand.

"Very good work," Rivers said. "Very well handled. I got two calls from the right people saying how impressed they were." Rivers was not averse to pimping young talent—and offering credit that would someday have to be repaid with interest. The next morning, Green's legal staff filed the paperwork establishing an S-PAC to push the young man's positions to the Georgia electorate. These things, more than anything, were what modern politics was all about.

≈≈≈≈

Iran Demands Israel Be Inspected

Al Jihadi. Iranian Foreign Minister Abdul al-Bakar, speaking before the United Nations General Assembly, has demanded Israel be subject to the same inspections from the International Atomic Energy Agency as is Iran. "It is time the open secret of Israel's nuclear weapons program be acknowledged," he said. "If the world cannot be honest with us, and with itself, we will close our facilities to further inspections."

CHAPTER 25: MEL APPLETON

If you know your enemy and you know yourself,
your victory will not stand in doubt. If you know Heaven
and you know Earth, you may make your victory complete.
Sun Tzu _____-c. 496 BCE

Mel Appleton's Office, Washington, DC

"Mel, what does Senator March think about Representative Stanley?" I had just briefed Mr. Warwick on the senator's schedule. I knew he would have questions.

"Sir, he's expressed concern a Texas-Oklahoma slate will not get the votes he needs elsewhere in the country."

"What have you said to counter this argument?" Mr. Warwick was teaching me even as he spoke.

"Beliefs and commitment are more important than geography, sir," I replied. "But I'm not sure that's enough."

"You're right, Mel. Theory, idealism, belief—those are things for the leadership. Votes are for the masses, and the Democrats. You know Stanley's younger son, George, is thought to be homosexual?"

"I've heard that, sir, yes."

"Relate that to Senator March, but be careful how you phrase your words. The files on Stanley's sons—the files at the NSA, CIA, and the DHS—have been destroyed. You may express mild shock and disbelief that the government would keep such files on *innocents*, but do not get involved in a lengthy discussion."

"Files on innocents, sir?"

I heard Warwick chuckle. "Yes, including you and me. Do not worry. Those files, too, have been purged."

Neither you nor I are innocent, I thought, as Warwick broke the connection.

~~~~~

witwat sends: neumayer reports tremors 2.6 magnitude along north atlantic ridge confirmed here and by ringoffire stop

~~~~~

Storms Batter West

New York Afterword. The weather system that was first forecast to extend the Rocky Mountain ski season has become a nightmare. Heavy, wet snow closed roads and created avalanche conditions throughout Colorado, Wyoming, and Utah. Power lines are down, and the entire city of Boulder is without power.

~~~~~

Take 'Em to the Wire with Bert Rightly

"There you have it, folks. The libsymps keep preaching global warming like it was a new religion while the western USA is buried in snow. Snow is cold stuff, people, not warm stuff. Here to help us understand the facts is Dr. Ernest Jastrow from Wheatly University. Dr. Jastrow, are you ready for *Take 'Em to the Wire?*"

"Mr. Rightly, I'm ready to tell the truth and nothing but the truth. And as long as it's true, I think I'll cross the wire with flying colors."

Bert Rightly chuckled. "You do understand, Doctor. Now, if *global warming* is real, why is it so cold in Colorado?"

"Bert, that's the question of the day, perhaps of the century. If the world is getting warmer, why is so much of it getting colder? There's a simple answer. The world isn't getting warmer. In fact, since 1997, the world temperature has stayed fairly steady. You and your viewers know there have always been bad years and good years. The skiers, especially, know sometimes the snow is good and sometimes it's not. Farmers know some years are good and some are bad. All we are seeing is a natural progression of weather patterns.

"What people are overlooking is God's promise that as long as the earth endures, seedtime and harvest, and cold and heat, and summer and winter shall not cease."

"That sounds like something from the Bible, Dr. Jastrow. Is it your scientific opinion?"

"Bert, it's from Genesis 8:22, and yes, this is one of the proofs that the Book of Science proves the Book of God. This Earth has undergone many changes of weather patterns in the past, including the Great Flood from which God rescued Noah and his family. But the Earth and its people have always persevered and come back from these tribulations. It is the will of God."

"Well folks, we can't argue with the Bible. We send our prayers to the people of Colorado, Wyoming, Nevada, and Arizona, and to the people of the states not yet hit by the storms, knowing that God, in His infinite wisdom, has a purpose and a reason for this crisis. This is Bert Rightly, and this is *Take 'Em to the Wire*."

~~~~~

Stanley Condominium, Arlington, Virginia

"Why do you watch Rightly?" George asked his father.

"Same reason you do, *know your enemy*," Thomas Stanley replied.

"But he's full of shit!"

"George! You may not use that word. Not, at least, until you are eighteen," Thomas Stanley said, and then laughed.

~~~~~

witwat sends: drought levant plus iraq estimated 200 000 repeat 200 000 refugees moving toward baltics, europe stop

~~~~~

Mel Appleton, Senator March's Campaign Plane

"We've got the Georgia vote, sir," I said to the senator. "The Mayor of Atlanta delivered it to us."

"What are you talking about, Mel? He's a libsymp Democrat. Don't tell me he's changed sides."

"No sir, he just ran off his mouth. Muldoon was the first to report it. Seems the first 45,000 refugees from Syria have disappeared into the urban jungles of large cities, including Atlanta. The mayor was frothing at the mouth. Listen, please."

I pressed *play* on the remote. The image of Atlanta's black mayor appeared on the screen. The logo of *God's Word for You* was in the lower right corner.

"They're squatting in homes abandoned by under-water owners, living 20 or more in single-family apartments," the mayor said. "They're camping out in every hospital emergency room in the city. The state constitution requires us to balance our budget and not spend more than we have. That means we have to cut spending on roads, on schools, on police and fire, and on services for our residents, our taxpayers so we can coddle these leaches. This cannot go on!"

I pressed the *stop* button.

"All we need to do is push responsibility on the Democrats. A few words to the press, perhaps a line in your stump speeches."

March smiled. It was a predatory smile. I could see his teeth, clenched through partly opened lips. He spoke without opening his teeth. "Good, Mel. Damn good."

188

~~~~~

Mel Appleton, Senator March's Campaign Plane

"Why do you keep bringing up Stanley? He's not known for anything."

Senator March's voice was under control, meaning he wasn't angry, just puzzled. It also let me know he was open to my suggestion—actually Warwick's suggestion which I was relaying.

"He stood apart from the fight to decide the Republican Speaker of the House, but did stay in the party and national spotlights. He brought a lot of favorable publicity for the party and himself with the refugee deal with Canada. It's working, and so far, it hasn't cost us more than a few million dollars.

"When it came time for the back-room politicians to decide on a vice presidential nominee, his name reached the top of the list to be offered to you. It's not his idea. In fact, he'll require convincing."

"Stanley's what the Brits would call a *back-bencher*. A nobody," March said.

"Exactly, sir," I said. "He's a nobody who will not challenge you, and who will not oppose you in any future election."

"Where does he stand on our ideals?"

"He's a Deacon in the Church. Unblemished reputation. There is a rumor that his younger son is gay."

"Then he is unacceptable," March said.

"It's a closely held secret, sir, and, unacceptable or not and whether true or not, it gives us leverage over him," I said. "And he will be as anxious as we to ensure there is no scandal."

"After the Canadian refugee thing, everyone knows his stepson has dual Canadian-US citizenship," March said.

"His son, sir. Stanley adopted him before his mother died. Henry won't be a liability. He could be a plus. At the moment, Canada is our ally."

March Selects Running Mate

God's Word for You. Senator Edward March (AFFP-TX), the leading candidate for President of the United States, announced this morning that Representative Thomas Stanley has switched allegiance to the American Freedom First Party and accepted March's invitation to be his partner in the campaign as vice presidential candidate. The announcement surprised everyone since Rep. Stanley, until this point, has distanced himself from the spotlight of national politics.

Take 'Em to the Wire with Bert Rightly

"Representative Thomas Stanley from Oklahoma dropped two bombshells on the American People when he declared for the American Freedom First Party and accepted the invitation of Senator March, the candidate who will certainly be the next President of the United States of America, to run with him in the vice presidential slot.

"Representative Stanley is with us tonight, ladies and gentlemen, and together we will *Take Him to the Wire.* Our text address for your questions is on your screen. Let me start with this. Representative Stanley, why did you switch parties?"

"That is an easy question, Bert, and it was an easy decision. What surprised me most was that I hadn't made it earlier. The Republican Party I joined twenty years ago is not the Republican Party of today. The sharp divisions that gridlocked the Congress during recent administrations are not the sign of a healthy political process, but one that is sick and dying. The American Freedom First Party has clear goals, and strong leadership. It is alive and vibrant."

"Pretty powerful words, sir. Here's the next question. Why did you agree to be Senator March's running mate?"

"Another easy question and easy decision. Like you and most Americans, I admire Senator March's leadership. I hope as his Vice President, I can help him implement his plans to make the nation and world a better place for our children."

"Here's a question from a viewer in Enid Oklahoma," Bert said. "We'll use initials only, as always. CG writes, 'What are you going to do about those earthquakes from all the fracking?'"

"A good question, and it's certainly not as easy as the softballs you have pitched, so far." Stanley chuckled. "In the first place, there's no proven link between fracking and earthquakes. However, scientists at Wheatly University and elsewhere are looking for correlations before they can start looking for causes. Senator March's economic platform includes increasing research funds for just this purpose. There are hundreds of little earthquakes around the world, every day. Like the little tremors in Oklahoma and Arkansas, there is usually no damage and no injuries."

~~~~~~

Representative Stanley's Condominium, Arlington, VA

"You were rad, Dad!" George Stanley greeted his father. The boy's enthusiasm was short-lived. "But they're wrong about fracking, you know. And it's not just the earthquakes. They're polluting the water, too."

"George, I've heard all that, but there are so many scientists who say otherwise. There's no consensus."

"Dad, it's the same lie the tobacco companies used to keep people smoking. But we've learned better since then. It's the same lie the chemical industry used to keep CFCs from being regulated for so many years. It's the same lie energy companies are using to mix people up about global climate change, and now, fracking.

"*No scientific consensus?* I'll make a bet with you, Dad. And you can get Eddie to do the search for you. He's the biggest computer geek on your staff. Get him to make a list of scientists with degrees from anywhere except Wheatly or the church colleges who deny fracking is dangerous, and a count of their papers on fracking or earthquakes published in international science journals—not the ones from those colleges—that say the same thing. I'll do the same for scientists who have published papers showing the dangers of fracking. Whoever has the most scientists and papers wins."

"What's the bet?"

"My allowance against an extra hour of flight training."

"That's four-to-one odds, George. I think it's a sucker bet for me, but you're on. Now, bedtime."

~~~~~

Adirondack Mountains, New York

The flatbeds hauling construction equipment, the ready-mix concrete trucks, the pickup trucks carrying ladders and tool boxes, all driven by men and women with hands gnarled by labor and arthritis, attracted no attention. Winter was over, and work crews would repair highways and park facilities damaged by the severe winter and heavy snows. Some of these crews would dig a wine cellar at the estate of Richard Warwick—a very big wine cellar in a very deep hole.

"Coldest winter on record," one of the workmen said to his partner. They had stopped for coffee and sat at the counter of a diner. "I hope them eco-Nazis don't expect anyone around here to believe in global warming."

"Means more work for us," his partner said. He pulled the sports section from the *New York Afterword*, the only paper he could find, and set aside the front page. The first man glanced at the headline, "Scientists Link Global Warming to Severe Storms," and turned to the entertainment section to see if the latest celebrity marriage had tanked.

Richard Warwick confided in no one. His estate was accessible only by helicopter and a forest service fire road that was closed to the public. The wine cellar cover story would stand up to any scrutiny. Backup generators and an air circulation and purification system identical to those on US nuclear submarines were a logical addition. An escape tunnel was explained as a requirement levied by the Fire Marshal, just in case someone were in the wine cellar when there was a fire in the mansion.

It will cost more than twenty million counting the bribes, Warwick thought. *But it will be worth it, and it will take me through any danger from war to insurrection.*

~~~~

Representative Stanley's Condominium, Arlington, VA

"This one's not a scientist, Dad. His degree is journalism," George Stanley said. "Not even journalism, but something called journalism management. And the only thing he's written in years is blogs on the local newspaper, not an academic journal."

"Well, even if you counted him, I would have lost," Representative Stanley said. "I knew that before I got home. I've already called your flight instructor and for bonus points, the Secret Service is primed for pizza. Let's go."

And I need to rethink a lot of thing, Thomas Stanley thought. *And get Eddie to do a lot more research. He'll like that, and with the extra staff the campaign has assigned he'll have time for it.*

~~~~

Kiribati Evacuation Complete

Hong Kong Record. What little is left of the once island-nation of Kiribati is empty save for a weather station staffed by a dozen citizens, and an Australian embassy. The embassy is a ship, anchored in what was St. Stanislas Bay. Only the main atoll remains. No more than 100 hectares of this once island nation is still above water. And even that is at risk of inundation from minor storms.

Of the 2013 population of more than 100,000 people, scarcely 50,000 survived the storms and king tides of the past five years. The majority of those have been relocated to Australia.

~~~~~

Mel Appleton, Senator March's Office

"How much is this Kiribati thing costing us?" The senator asked.

"Not much," I said. "The weather station and embassy are legal fictions to preserve the integrity of the island. They're there to prevent the Chinese from taking control. The Chinese have proven they can build up atolls, add a runway, and claim another 30,000-plus square miles of ocean. Kiribati is only six hours by air from Hawaii, sir."

~~~~~

Follow the Money

The World Citizen. "The economy of the entire Western World, what with hubris we call the *First World*, was built on cheap labor—slave labor in many cases—and cheap raw materials from the so-called *Third World*. It's been that way since the beginning of recorded history and perhaps longer. However, the Third World has wakened and is demanding the things we take for granted—clean water, nutritious food, warm clothing, health care, education, and opportunity to pull themselves from the hardscrabble life of subsistence agriculture. It should surprise no one that *spreading the wealth* has become the theme of the World Humanitarian Summit, the number one topic at the UN General Assembly, and a key part of the reports of the International Panel on Climate Change.

"This is Muldoon. The world doesn't have enough resources to provide seven point four billion people the kind of life we aspire to in the United States. We are close to exceeding the carrying capacity of the planet. Carrying capacity? Look it up; understand it."

~~~~~

Shearwater Mercenaries Encampment, Sierra Leona, Africa

"Why are we fighting them? They're like the Shakers—no sex permitted. No sex, no kids. No kids, the movement dies out."

"*Amra'a Haram* doesn't mean 'no sex.' It just means they'd better not like it."

"That is so wrong!"

"And it doesn't stop them from kidnapping schoolgirls and forcing them into marriage—and sex."

"Anything on the satcom?"

"Yeah, part of the internet went down for nine hours yesterday. No new orders."

~~~~~

Ebola Outbreak in Sierra Leone

The World Citizen. "We all heard the report of zero cases of Ebola in Sierra Leone in the past 42 days. That's supposed to be the incubation period, and was taken to mean the disease had been eradicated. But few of us paid attention to the rest of the story. The first western nurse to survive Ebola had the virus reappear in her as meningitis, months later. Doctors found evidence the virus lies dormant in the testicles of male victims for as much as nine months after they recovered. The Ebola virus is hiding in places where the body's immune system doesn't look, and is still a threat to the health of a recovered victim—and anyone with whom he or she comes in contact.

"This is Muldoon. Pay attention, people. These reports are coming from a country with an overworked and understaffed health care system."

<center>~~~~~</center>

The White House, Cabinet Room

"What do we have on this Ebola outbreak?" the president asked.

Everyone was happy to defer to the head of Health and Human Services, who had brought the Director of the CDC. He was a medical doctor, a pediatrician, and a political appointee who was over his head in virology. But, he had assembled a good staff. He was prepared.

"Sir, the Ebola virus was dormant in many of its survivors. We knew it was possible, but there are not enough laboratory facilities or enough clinicians to test people and follow their cases. The earlier outbreak caused a great deal of fear. Fear kept people from reporting new cases until it was too late to contain it. The international community is sending aid—there's a list on your desk—but it's not going to be enough."

"Why not more?" the president asked.

"It's not just Ebola," the CDC director said. "The cholera outbreak in the Middle East that started two years ago is still going on. There have been at least 200 deaths per month, and those numbers are probably conservative. They do not have the resources to conduct widespread testing, and doctors often report *dehydration from watery diarrhea* instead of cholera as the cause of death. There's evidence some governments are suppressing news of cholera to protect trade and tourism."

"Get me information on what the military can do," the president ordered. "Field hospitals, morgues, whatever. And let us hope we need more hospitals than morgues."

<center>~~~~~</center>

Oklahoma Tremor

Gods Word for You. Oklahoma was hit by an earthquake at 3:43 AM yesterday morning. The epicenter was two miles south of Porum and nearly a mile below ground. The quake was felt as far away as Oklahoma City and Conway, Arkansas. Seismometers at Wheatly University registered the quake, but no one at the school reported having felt it. Damage reports are still coming in, but there are no reports of injuries.

Science or Superstition?

The World Citizen. "GW4U shows once again how trading science for superstition distorts the truth. The epicenter of the Oklahoma earthquake was two miles south of Porum, but not a mile below the surface. An epicenter is defined as the place *on the earth's surface at or below which an earthquake is centered.* The mouthpiece of the OTCC and the Oklahoma oil industry didn't say the magnitude.

"This is Muldoon. In the words of the Reverend Henry Ward Beecher, 'The most dangerous people are the ignorant.' Wonder if he'd be allowed to say that from the pulpit, today."

~~~~~

Mel Appleton, Senator March's Campaign Plane

"Damn good speech you put together, Mel," the senator said.

"Just a few words, ideas, sir," I said. "You got the people to understand, to believe."

Neither the senator nor I were flattering or sucking up. We both knew our strengths. I was the ideas and words guy, he was the delivery guy. We complemented one another, and we both knew it. We'd developed a synergistic relationship that was going to take both of us to greatness.

"What about the Oklahoma earthquakes?" March asked.

Warwick had not given me specific instructions about this, but I remembered something he'd said long ago.

"Senator," I said, "I think Archbishop Trucido and his people will deal with it. Your tack should simply be, 'Let's let the scientists deal with it.' And, perhaps, 'There were more than fifty earthquakes in the world, yesterday. Some were strong enough to cause damage and kill people.' We shouldn't worry about a few little tremors no one felt."

"As always, Mel, you've got the good words." The senator raised his glass of Bourbon signaling the day's work was done. I raised my glass. It was Bourbon, too, although I'd have preferred Scotch.

~~~~~

Seismology Lab, Wheatly University, Oklahoma

"It will be hard to isolate this from the tremors where wastewater from fracking is injected, under pressure, into deep wells."

"They've never proved the quakes in Arkansas and Oklahoma are caused by fracking," a post-doc said.

"They've never proved the world is round, either," Dr. Germain said. "Science never proves anything, but at some point, the weight of the evidence is enough it would be perverse to deny something—that the world is round, that the universe is billions of years old, that fracking causes earthquakes, and that evolution—"

"Enough!" the laboratory chief interrupted. "You're getting close to heresy."

"Yes, sir," Dr. Germain said. *The world is round . . . there's enough evidence. According to the Bible, it must be flat. How else could there be four corners of the earth? How else could Satan have taken Christ onto a mountaintop and show Him all the kingdoms of the Earth? They deny the evidence of their senses!*

"Dr. Germain, you jumped the gun and announced our findings," the lab chief said. "Now, you will prepare our formal news release. But you will not release it until I have approved it. There will be no links between fracking and earthquakes. And no *continental plate* nonsense, either. You will hint at divine causes but hint, only. We must maintain scientific objectivity."

Continental plates? Where did he get that idea? There are no continental plate boundaries under Texas, Oklahoma or Arkansas. The only known thin spot under the USA—except Hawaii—is under Yellowstone, and the hot springs and geysers are well-known evidence, although most people have no understanding of what it means. I should have studied creative writing instead of geology. Dr. Germain thought these things as she stared at the blank page of a word-processor program.

~~~~~

witwat sends: oklahoma 6.5 neumayer confirms 6.5 vic 35.33 -95.27 0943 gmt we were blocked until now switching to squirt &witwat stop

~~~~~

Mel Appleton, Senator March's Office

"Sorry to be late, folks," Senator March said. "What do you have?"

"El Niño continues to cause problems," I said. "Winter in the South East was too warm for peach trees in Georgia and South Carolina. Their economies took a multi-billion dollar hit—and the governors want money. This weather pattern brought some rain to the West Coast but it also brought flooding and mudslides that caused more billions in damages—and the governors want money.

"The El Niño did not, however replenish water in reservoirs and aquifers. California is no longer the *grocery basket of the nation*. Fresh fruits and vegetables are unavailable in many locations except for limited supplies from local farmers' markets and expensive things flown in from Australia, South America, and South Africa."

"What are we going to tell the press?" the senator asked.

"Blaming the water shortages on *greedy companies* worked back in 2015. We'll do it, again. We'll ask people to report neighbors who waste water on lawns or washing cars," I said.

"What pushback will we get from the companies?" the senator asked.

"None, sir. There aren't any companies. They all went out of business or moved to Mexico during the drought of 2015 but we can manipulate the press to make people think they are still in operation."

"What about private swimming pools? Every one of the MacMansions built in the past few years by our friends from the Middle East has a pool . . . or two or three."

"Touchy. How about this. Put a tax on them. The Saudis won't squawk. Make sure people believe the money will go toward building reservoirs and pipelines."

"This is California, people," Senator March said. "Will they go along with this?"

"They're desperate, sir. We can use the federal renegotiation of the Lake Meade water agreement as a hammer."

~~~~~

Coffee Shop, Wheatly, Oklahoma

"Dr. Germain? I'm Dr. Coyne from the University of Guelph. May I join you?"

"You're a long way from home, and please, call me Susan. I'm not sure I want to be known as *doctor* any longer."

"I read your thesis, Susan. And I read the two press releases about the earthquake. I will be pleased to call you *doctor*, when you are ready."

"What do you mean, *when I'm ready*?" Susan asked.

"Even though your doctorate was awarded by Wheatly University, I do not doubt it was earned. The two press releases issued in your name confirmed what I thought. I'm here to recruit you."

~~~~~

Ebola Escapes

World Citizen. "At least a hundred people, some of whom came from Angola, bypassed the Temperature Control Agent of the TSA, pushed through customs and immigration, reached the main terminal at Dulles International Airport, and escaped. The passengers on Flight 4227 had been held for more than an hour after landing, and were not told they would be screened for Ebola.

"TSA had one person with a thermometer. One person to screen more than four hundred passengers. The air conditioning in the plane failed; the jetway, packed with people, had no air conditioning. According to the press release from the Department of Homeland Security, and I quote, 'No one knows what set off the riot.'

"No one knows? An hour delay after a seven-hour international flight? Crowding in temperatures over a hundred degrees? This is Muldoon. It's been over fifty years since John B. Calhoun conducted his experiments on rats living in overcrowded conditions. There were other experiments using primates—chimpanzees as I recall. It wasn't pretty. People are neither rats nor monkeys, but sometimes they act as if they were. Think about it."

Mel Appleton

"If Ebola is loose, and in the Nation's Capital . . . " Senator March began. Then, he looked at me. I fell back on what Warwick had told me.

"Sir, our sources suggest at least a few passengers evaded Immigration and Naturalization and the customs officers.

So far, there seems to be no Ebola outbreaks. Our best bet now is to blame it on the current administration."

Office of the Deputy Director, Department of Homeland Security

This is my opportunity, she thought, even though most of her attention was on the smooth flesh of her principal aide. The young woman lay on a table, face down and naked. *The riot at Dulles is the director's death knell. And I'm the only one in any position to replace him. Sooner than planned, but I will survive.*

She jerked her right arm, and the whip scored the woman on the table.

~~~~~

WhatDrWho Blog

The conventions of the American Freedom First Party and the Democratic Party have turned into non-events. Both the Kennedy-Stewart and March-Stanley-OTCC tickets have swept the primaries. Their lead overwhelmed other candidates who quickly threw in their support.

This is WhatDrWho blogging from exile.

~~~~~

Ebola Patient in NYC Hospital

Tempest Times. Wilson Kwambai from Kenya has been admitted to the University Medical School Hospital in Manhattan with symptoms of Ebola. Mr. Kwambai entered the US illegally after dodging police, customs, and immigration officials at the Dulles airport. He was positively identified from his passport.

A joint statement by the NYC Police, Homeland Security, and the Centers for Disease Control says he does not pose a threat to the people of the city. They encourage people to wash their hands often, cover sneezes, and get a flu shot as soon as they are available.

Flu Shots for Ebola?

The World Citizen streaming online. "There's no doubt Homeland Security was behind the press release that conflated Ebola with the flu. Offer false reassurance and lead the sheep by the nose. In their attempt to quell rumors and reassure the millions who live in New York City, Homeland Security has become the bellwether, the Judas goat leading the nation to complacency—and slaughter.

"They claim they know this guy, but is it just another lie? Do they really know how he got here, how he traveled, how long he's been here, and how many people he may have infected before he collapsed on the floor of the hospital's emergency room.

"This is Muldoon: *Falsus in uno, falsus in omnibus.* Fancy Latin for 'If someone lies about one thing, you should suspect everything he or she says.' Think about it."

~~~~~

Mel Appleton

"Damn it, Mel, this Ebola thing is getting out of hand," Senator March said.

There was a lot behind those few words. I took a minute to think before replying. My boss and mentor, Richard Warwick, had been quiet about Ebola. Meaning I had to think rather than simply issue orders. I thought, and I wasn't happy with some of the things I thought.

"Sir, so far, this is in the lap of the current president, and his Democrat-libsymp supporters. They were in control of the airport, of debarking, immigration scanning, security, and customs. It will be easy to lay the blame at their feet."

"Mel, I'm not looking to assign blame. I want to know if there is a real danger. More important, I want something to be done to make sure there isn't."

"Yes, sir," I said.

As soon as the senator left my office, I called Mr. Warwick. What I didn't know was that Warwick called Trucido, who called someone else.

~~~~~

New York Hospital Bombed

New York Afterword. The New York hospital where Wilson Kwambai was being treated for Ebola was struck by Molotov cocktails and pipe bombs thrown by people who then escaped in speeding cars.

The hospital's sprinkler system put out the fires before they could spread beyond the first floor. Several patients and hospital staff were treated for smoke inhalation.

It is speculated that Mr. Kwambai's presence triggered the attack, which was likely conducted by a right-wing hate group.

Police have recovered two of the cars abandoned a few blocks away. The cars were reported stolen shortly before the bombing was carried out.

Mr. Kwambai succumbed to smoke inhalation. His body will be cremated.

~~~~~

City Council Meeting, Mt. Pleasant, Georgia

Mr. Warwick had asked me to keep an eye on Mt. Pleasant. I knew he'd not forgotten, and that I'd better not forget either. They put their council meetings on the internet. I watched each one.

The most recent meeting began, as always, with the Pledge of Allegiance to the Flag. Before the councilmembers, the staff, and the three citizens who had attended the meeting could take their seats, and as customary, Mayor Redwine spoke. "Please take a moment of silence, before we begin, to organize our thoughts, to think on the challenges we face, and, if you are so inclined, to ask for help and guidance."

After a moment, she lifted her head. "Thank you all for being here. Our first order of business is citizen input. I understand we have only one person who has signed up to speak. Pastor Dorset of the Resurrection Baptist Church, please take the microphone."

"It's now the Resurrection Congregation of the One True Christian Church and I expect you to keep that in mind in the future," the man said without preamble.

"On behalf of the congregations of the One True Christian Church of Mt. Pleasant which includes not only the Resurrection Congregation but also the Mt. Pleasant Christian Congregation, and in the name of the Lord God whom we worship, I demand this council cease this false practice of *silence* and reinstitute the practice of praying to the Lord God for strength and guidance before each meeting. I further demand that the official motto of these United States of America, which is God's Nation upon Earth, *In God We Trust* be displayed in these council chambers so that everyone here knows who is the architect of this city, this nation, and the universe."

The man glared at the council, none of whom seemed prepared for such polemics. The mayor looked from councilperson to councilperson, seeking someone bold enough to respond. Mr. Ivanson caught her eye. She nodded.

"Pastor Dorset," Mr. Ivanson said. "Thank you for your forthright thoughts. I'm sure the council will want to examine them, discuss them, and respond in a timely manner. For myself, however, I would like to note that the Constitution of the United States prohibits any government endorsement of religion. A prayer to any particular god by a government body could be construed to be such an endorsement.

Ivanson continued before the pastor could interrupt. "Mt. Pleasant includes many people who do not worship the same god you do. Indeed, it includes many people who do not worship any god. For this council to endorse a particular god by prayer would separate us from those people.

"I would also like to note that the first motto of this country, *E Pluribus Unum*—"From many, one" is not displayed here. To display 'In god we trust," something adopted in a frenzy of anti-communist fervor some sixty years ago would not, in my opinion, serve any useful purpose. Given the attempts to balkanize this country, attempts by extremes of both the left and right, if we were to display any motto or slogan, I suggest it be *E Pluribus Unum*, and not something divisive.

"No, Pastor Dorset, I cannot support your requests. In fact, I will oppose them with all my strength."

"Heathen! You will be damned—" the pastor began until the mayor's gavel shut him off.

"Pastor Dorset, you have had your time. Mr. Ivanson has responded. We will take your remarks and his under advisement. Thank you. The next agenda item is recognition of the employee of the month. Patrolman Ramsey? Please come forward."

~~~~~

March-Stanley, AFFP Reach 51%

Washington Banner. A Ranogen poll of likely voters shows 51% of all voters would vote for the AFFP ticket in the next election. 38% would vote for the Democratic Party candidates, while 11% remain undecided. The poll has a margin of error of 3.5%.

~~~~~

Mel Appleton

"Fifty-one percent. We've reached the tipping point. A little push in the right places, and this election will be the biggest landslide since Roosevelt beat Alf Landon in 1936." Nick Thackery sounded more like a rooster crowing than a junior member of Senator March's staff when he handed me message.

206

"Don't count your chickens, Nick," I cautioned. "There's still solid opposition in New England and on the west coast. A lot of folks will vote the Kennedy name, even though she's not related to them.

"But, you are right about the tipping point. I don't want to sound like my grandfather, but *success breeds success*. That's an aphorism, and not a law of nature, but there may be a kernel of truth behind it. If we look like winners, we will be winners. That's another aphorism. But we will never say *tipping point*. Never."

Senator March walked down the plane's aisle from the restroom in time to hear me say that.

"Why not, Mel?" I suspected the senator knew the answer, but wanted to hear me say it.

"'Tipping point' has been seized by the climate-changers, sir. They talk about a tipping point when the thermohaline circuit—the Gulf Stream—will tip because of freshwater from Greenland ice melt. They talk about a tipping point when the permafrost will melt and release so much carbon dioxide into the air the atmosphere will tip and we'll have a runaway greenhouse effect that will turn Earth into Venus—with 800-degree temperatures. *Tipping point* has become their code-word for disaster."

"Put that into today's staff memo . . . on the private email server," the senator said. "Given what the New York attorney general is doing to Exxon Mobil, I don't want any official record that we've suppressed climate-change information—no matter how hokey it is."

"Yes, sir," I said. *Even though the scientists are probably right?* I thought. *Even though as soon as you are elected, the Canadian front-company for GETE will re-submit their application and you will approve Keystone XL and bring even more oil into this country to be burned to make more CO2. And it doesn't matter how much you disagree with the Canadian Prime Minister's politics . . . this is business. And money. How*

much money are you going to get out of the deal, and where will
it be hidden?

PART II ELECTION AND TRANSITION

We see as wisdom that which is only knowledge,
and as progress, that which is only change.
—Attributed to Abraham Lincoln, 1809-1865 CE

Democratic Election Watch, Marriott Grand, Washington, DC

The celebration was muted. The Kennedy-Stewart team had not yet acknowledged defeat, but it was clear that the six billion dollars spent by anonymous plutocrats through unregulated S-PACs had bought the election. The American Freedom First Party and the One True Christian Church had swept the nation: the White House, the Senate, the House of Representatives, and all but seventeen states.

Susan embraced Arthur. "We got 32% of the votes. Seventeen percent went to 'none of the above' or to third party candidates. No matter what *American Fire Network* is saying, the election is not a conservative landslide. We have a base of power. We can make a difference."

"You got it, kid. What's next?" Arthur asked.

"What's next? You're going to take a week off and do nothing but hug your wife and kids. I'm going to take a week off to hug my husband. Then, we will come out slugging."

American Freedom First Party Election Celebration, L'Hermitage Hotel, Georgetown, DC

Mel handed the secure cell phone to President-elect March. "It's Mr. Warwick, sir."

March took the phone. "Good evening, sir."

He listened, said *yes sir* a couple of times, and handed the phone back to Mel.

"Mel," he said, "we could not have won without Warwick's money. We might have won without the OTCC endorsement, but it would have been harder. Which reminds me. Who to we have lined up for Schedule-C appointments in the IRS? Don't, don't look it up now. Just be sure to tell them to take the pressure off the OTCC. We're going to change the rule against churches in politics, anyway."

March came back to his earlier point. "We might have won without some of those things but we couldn't have won without you, Mel. Make it official. Announce you will be my Chief of Staff and will head the Transition Team. It will give you a chance to size up your new office in the White House."

"Sir?" I said. "The most critical post is the Director of Homeland Security. What you do, there, will set the tone of your administration."

"The current deputy," March said. "Make it known that she will take the reins. And have the appointment letter ready for me to sign immediately after the inauguration."

"Yes, sir," I said.

~~~~~

Home of James Lesene, Mt. Pleasant, Georgia

James Lesene hung up the phone. "John from *The Clarion* is at the election office. They've declared me Mayor, and you two for the council seats. God has returned to Mt. Pleasant!

"Praise the Lord," Councilman-elect Larimer said. "And pass the hors d'oeuvers," he added.

"The Apostle Paul wrote, 'a little wine is good for the stomach.' At least in the old Bibles. It's too bad he didn't know about champagne," Frank Fabulist said, and popped a cork, and then another and another.

~~~~~

President-Elect March's Office

I expected the call from Mr. L'Wazi—just not so soon. He was one of dozens who had called to express their congratulations—and to make sure March remembered who they were. L'Wazi's call was important enough to be passed to me. After exchanging pleasantries, I forwarded the call to March, but listened to the conversation.

The first few words were fluff. Then, L'Wazi got down to business.

"The current president of the World Bank will turn in his resignation tomorrow. That is known only to a few people. It is critical you contact the board and give me what was promised."

"I am not in a giving vein, today," March said. "Between your begging and my plans, you have become a nuisance." He hung up the phone.

"Mel! Get in here!"

In the few seconds I took to reach his office, March changed his mind.

"Never mind, Mel. I'll handle this. It's not in scope of your duties."

I nodded. That, and wonder, were all I could do.

~~~~~

Hit and Run Takes Prominent Member of NAAPC

The World Citizen. "Mr. Samuel L'Wazi, a Washington lawyer and lobbyist best known for his connection with the NAAPC, was killed last night by a hit-and-run driver. Mr. L'Wazi was crossing the street from a restaurant in Alexandria,

Virginia when he was struck by a vehicle that left the scene of the accident. He was pronounced dead at the scene by EMS.

"The Alexandria police have no suspects but vow to prosecute this case to the best of their abilities.

"And just what does that mean, people? A hit-and-run— or a hit—against a black man with shady political connections? Does anyone really think the police will do anything or find anything?

"This is Muldoon. Whatever happened to *Black Lives Matter*?"

~~~~~

The White House, Transition Team Office

The secure phone on my desk rang. Caller ID was blank. I frowned, but answered.

"Mr. Appleton, this is General Hogg, Deputy Director at NSA. I want to schedule a briefing for you and President March."

"The first thing you can do, General, is unblock your caller ID on all future calls to the March White House. We're not scheduling briefings until next Wednesday. Call back then, please."

"Of course, Mr. Appleton. However, I will call you in five minutes with some time-sensitive information."

I raised an eyebrow. NSA, or this General Hogg, was anxious to make points.

"Five minutes, General."

"General?" I answered the phone that now displayed the caller's name and number.

"Mr. Appleton, you know we sweep the internet and the phone system for metadata, high level summaries we search for terroristic threats. How this works is part of what we'd like to brief you and the president.

"What will not be in the briefing is that occasionally some individual data will fall through the software and land on an analyst's computer screen. The analysts have orders to delete such, immediately. However, sometimes they see things so important they cannot forget them.

"One such message fell out earlier this morning. A text message from Susan Kennedy's aide, Ruth Gordon to her boyfriend, Azisa Beman. The message set up a meet between Kennedy, Gordon, and Beman to, and I quote, *take over the NAAPC.*

"I thought you should know, especially after the death of Mr. L'Wazi."

"I understand, General," I said. "Thank you. What if President March and I showed up on your doorstep Monday about 10:00 AM?"

"Sounds good, Mr. Appleton. Looking forward to meeting you."

I hung up the phone. *Slick bastard. Who is he sucking up to? March? Warwick? Me?*

CHAPTER
26: THOMAS VAUGHN

I am concerned for the security
of out great Nation;
not so much because of
any threat from without, but
because of the insidious forces
working from within.
General Douglas MacArthur 1880-1964 C.E.

Old Eberly Hotel, Washington, DC

Pastors and state party chairmen vetted Freshman Representatives from red states before they were invited to join the Constitutional Caucus. The meeting at the Old Eberly Hotel was reminiscent of a fraternity or sorority rush. It featured an open bar and very heavy hors d'oeuvres. The hotel was a landmark for politicians and their paymasters from K-Street lobbying firms.

The AFFP hosted the meeting with money from an S-PAC funded by the Tractor-Trailer Transport Union, a wholly owned subsidiary of Isaac Trucido's Councilor #1. Soldiers of the Cross provided Security.

Representative, the Reverend Jonas Path (AFFP-AL), Pastor of the Selma, Alabama Path to Heaven Congregation of the One True Christian Church and Chairman of the Caucus greeted Pastor Russell Fallow.

"Good to see you again, Russell. Security tells me everyone we invited is here."

"The press?" Pastor Fallow asked.

"Bert Rightly from *American Fire*, and reporters from the *Banner*, *Tempest Times,* and *Gods Word*," Path replied. "And they know what to say and what not to say."

Fallow nodded. "Let's get to it, then."

Path tapped the microphone, and the crowd quieted. "Welcome, ladies and gentlemen. I hope our newest members are enjoying the hospitality of the American Freedom First Party and our friends from the One True Christian Church.

"Before we continue, Pastor Russell Fallow, Bishop of Washington, has joined us, and will offer an invocation."

Fallow stepped to the microphone.

"Thank you, Reverend Path. Let us pray.

"Almighty and loving God, Creator of the Heavens and Earth and all that dwells therein, Founder and Guardian of this One Nation under God. We, your children who bask in Your love and grace, ask of You that You shed your Heavenly Blessings upon this undertaking and those who will put on the Whole Armor of God, who will Fight the Good Fight, and who will stand up to the Minions of Satan who will oppose this great effort. We ask that You and Your Angels stand by each of us, warn us, protect us, defend us, and sustain our faith in this Great Undertaking.

"We ask this in the Most Holy Name of your Son, our Savior, Jesus Christ. Amen."

A chorus of 'amens' followed.

He actually talks in upper case letters, thought Thomas Vaughn, freshman Representative from Rhode Island and scion of the state's oldest and wealthiest family. *And he speaks of a great undertaking? What is he talking about? What have I gotten myself into?*

Vaughn's election had been a gift from his father. "You will be head of the family," the senior Vaughn had said. "You

216

need experience in how to use people. The best place to learn is in Washington." Thomas's father had then bought the election.

Vaughn brought his attention back to the room. Path had taken the microphone. "Everyone here shares important values—economic freedom, individual liberty, and a strict interpretation of the Constitution, no matter how flawed that document might be."

Path paused to let his last phrase sink in before he continued. "Yes, flawed. Not in the original, but in the flaws introduced by liberal, activist judges who have ruled from their own irrational beliefs and not from the Constitution.

"Rulings and interpretation of the law have come not from the Supreme Court, but from administrative law judges at the lowest level of our courts. Rulings have come from bureaucrats who are not lawyers or judges, but often Schedule-C political appointees of the current president. This has been happening for decades. Sadly, it has occurred even under conservative regimes. It has reached a head in the past few years.

"These judges often include in their rulings that the Congress should clarify, expand, or otherwise clean up the mess the judges, themselves, have created.

"Until now, that has not been possible. You all know Congress has been deadlocked for years. RINOs, the 'Republicans in Name Only'; liberals, libsymps, purple fence-sitters who lack the courage to commit to any position, reeds that blow whichever way the wind blows. These people and others like them have blocked attempts to override these rulings.

"It is the goal of the Constitution Caucus to rectify the damnable, infernal rulings that allow *preverts* and *abominations* to enter restrooms and locker rooms used by our children. It is our goal to firmly establish the rights of gun ownership and to remove restrictions on magazine size, ammunition purchases, and so-called assault weapons that have been passed in states and cities. The Second Amendment applies to the entire nation, and no city or state has the right to opt out.

"It is a goal of this caucus to ensure that no Christian shall be required to perform any act that violates the Inerrant Word of God, regardless of that Christian's job, position, or business.

"It is the goal of this Caucus to return to the fundamentals established by the Founding Fathers."

Applause and cheers filled the room.

This is big, Vaughn thought. *I need to talk to father.*

~~~~~

Vaughn Home, Newport, Rhode Island

Thomas Vaughn's mother had spent most of November supervising the decoration of the mansion—styled a "cottage" by those who could afford such. She was satisfied her home's appearance was just enough better than the neighbors without being "tacky." She had attended a finishing school in Virginia and returned with an understanding that there was nothing worse than tacky.

The Vaughn Christmas party, always held on the 22nd, was especially important this year. The *hoi polloi*—plutocrats, investment bankers, and CEOs of *Fortune 100* companies who were important but lesser than the Vaughns—would come to pay homage to her son.

Thomas and his family had arrived early. The senior Mrs. Vaughn scooped up her grandson Theodore and the junior Mrs. Vaughn and dragged them from room to room to see the decorations. Thomas joined his father in the Smoking Room.

"How was the Freshman Orientation?" Frederick Vaughn asked his son.

"It went well, sir," Thomas said. "I have a better office than I'd expected. Vivian and I have rented a condo in Crystal City with option to buy. There's one thing that disturbs me, though."

Thomas described the party hosted by the Constitutional Caucus. "I expected to be invited to join, but they seem to think

218

all of us who were there automatically became members. I've received position papers, welcome letters from long-time members, and a notice of a mandatory meeting the day before the House convenes in January. I don't know what their agenda is, but I'm not sure I like being dragged into it."

"Have you said anything about this to anyone?" Frederick asked.

"No, sir. Not yet, I wanted—"

"Do not express your doubts to anyone," his father said. "Read the position papers so you understand what is going on. Respond politely but briefly to the welcome letters. Attend the meeting and any other to which you are invited. It took a lot of telephone calls and handshakes to make sure you were included. Don't blow it, son."

You knew about this? No. You orchestrated it, Thomas thought.

"Yes, sir," he said. "But what's going on?"

"What do you know about amending the constitution?" Frederick asked.

"Quite a bit, sir. I have read the position papers. Especially the part about calling a constitutional convention, which seems to be the direction they are headed. Problem is, there are no laws, rules, or procedures for calling a convention, deciding who would represent the states, and how it would be run."

"There would be no questions if there were strong leadership to make it work," Frederick said. "You can be a major force in that leadership. Sol Weizmann—you've met him— knows the constitution better than anyone else. He will work with you over the holidays and will join your staff in January. It will happen; you must be prepared."

I'm not sure this is a good idea, Thomas thought. *Maybe tweaking the Constitution to clarify religious freedom and the second amendment is a good idea, but with amendments. A convention would open the entire constitution to change. Given the power of the AFFP and OTCC, that would be a disaster.*

~~~~

City Hall, Mt. Pleasant, Georgia

The newly elected members of the Mt. Pleasant City Council took their oaths of office on New Year's Day. The city's traffic-court judge administered the oaths. He wore a business suit rather than judicial robes. A few family members, the pastors of the two OTCC congregations, and a reporter from *The Clarion* attended.

" . . . so help me, God."

"Amen," chorused the audience.

Mayor Lesene accepted the gavel from the outgoing mayor and looked at it for a moment before setting it aside.

"Change has reached Mt. Pleasant," he said. "This city is once again in the fold of the Shepherd of this Nation, the Lord God.

"This is not an official meeting of the Council, and no agenda was published. That does not keep me from saying what will happen.

"Meetings will begin with a prayer to the Lord God. I order the staff to post the official motto of these United States, *In God We Trust,* on the wall opposite the council's seats, so we may be always reminded who we serve."

I thought you served the people of this city, the Clarion reporter thought, but he kept recording.

"At our first meeting we will form an Investigating Committee of citizens who shall be empowered to gather information about threats to this city, threats both from without and from within."

"Mr. Mayor, I protest," Councilman Ivanson interjected. "I protest that you would force your religion onto all the people of this city. I protest that you would institute the sort of paranoid

220

committees that served the Inquisition and the witch trials of medieval times. I—"

"That will be quite enough, Mr. Ivanson. This meeting is adjourned." The Mayor turned and left the room followed by all the council members save Mr. Ivanson.

The darkness is falling, Ivanson thought. *What's the expression? 'A voice calling in the wilderness?' I guess I'm it, now.*

~~~~~

United States Capitol Building, Washington, DC

The new Congress convened on the third of January. Members were sworn in. A vote was called to elect the Speaker of the House. There were two nominees—the previous Speaker and Henry Stafford, a seven-term member from Mississippi. Warwick and Trucido had decided to balance a Texas-Oklahoma White House with a Southern Speaker. After all, the South, except for Florida, was solidly conservative, OTCC, and AFFP.

The vote for Stafford was overwhelming. The man who was now two heartbeats from the presidency accepted the gavel from his predecessor and gave a brief and gracious acceptance speech. Then, he said, "Folks, we have a busy legislative session ahead of us, and a lot of committee work before we can get started. If I remember correctly, 'a motion to adjourn is always in order'." His stereo-comical look around the chamber got several laughs, which was what he hoped for.

The motion was made, seconded, and passed. Members went to the watering holes that surrounded the Capitol. Committee meetings could wait until tomorrow.

~~~~~

Telecon: Mel Appleton-Richard Warwick

"Sir, Stafford was elected Speaker," I reported to Warwick.

"Good work, Mel."

"Sir, most of the credit goes to a junior representative, Thomas Vaughn," I said.

"Are you working him?"

"Yes, sir. For some time, now," I responded.

~~~~~

&witwat sends: neumayer relays for concordia massive ice slide ross ice shelf details sketchy stop

~~~~~

&highflyer/&witwat why neumayer reporting for concordia query

&witwat/&highflyer concordia antarctic station comms blocked by usg only link is to us by meteor burst comms sketchy more to follow stop

~~~~~

Special Order 2278, Joint Base Andrews, Maryland. AF 28000 will immediately be flown to Wichita for refurbishment. AF 29000 will remain on alert.

~~~~~

Family Quarters, The White House

"I'm sorry, Mr. President. I know it's tradition that the outgoing president ride home on Air Force One, but one of the planes is down for refit and the other must remain on alert for President March. There is a Gulfstream waiting at Andrews for you and your family, and a motorcade has assembled outside the east entrance."

Lt. Colonel Casey Stewart had the grace to look abashed, even though he understood what had happened. The timing of the refurbishment hadn't been accidental. In fact, it had been moved up by four weeks. Someone got to people at the Pentagon and Andrews.

"I understand, Colonel Stewart. Thank you, and thank you for your service these past months. Now, you'd better get the football to the Oval Office. I think President March is expecting you."

PART III BRAVE NEW WORLD

Dystopian futures are a reflection
of contemporary fears.
—Anonymous

CHAPTER 27: GEORGE STANLEY

"Who controls the past controls the future . . . "
George Orwell, *1984*

Who controls the internet controls the future.
Be afraid. Be very afraid.
Red Dragon

Home of Sugi Close, Falls Church, VA

&grits admin to net homeland will take over internet bury links watch what you say no way to identify you stop

&reddragon/&grits how solid is info

&grits/&reddragon horses mouth

&homeboy/&grits what means grits

&grits/&homeboy guys raised in the south

&homeboy/&grits should be brits bubbas raised in the south

&grits/&homeboy hush your mouf funny though

~~~~~

The White House, Oval Office

Homeland Security presented the plan. "Everyone is in place, Mr. President. We are prepared to take physical control of the internet root computers at government facilities, academic institutions, and private companies."

"Then do it," President March ordered.

A phone call from the Director of Homeland Security before she left the White House put the plan into effect. DHS enforcers swarmed NASA-Houston, the Defense Information Systems Agency in Arlington, the University of California San Diego, the Army's Aberdeen Proving Grounds, corporate server farms in the mountains of Colorado and North Carolina, and six other locations. The operation was completed in less than three hours.

Now, thought the Director of Homeland Security, *we can get to work.* She picked up a secure phone and placed a call to the Director General of the Soldiers of the Cross. "It is done," she said.

I don't like to rely on him, but he can do many things I cannot, she thought. *My people can skim information, correlate it with individuals, and identify them and their locations. We can bring in for questioning anyone we can link to terrorist threats, real or imagined. The Soldiers of the Cross can take care of the perverts, the apostates, the atheists, and other undesirables. There will be enough work to go around.*

~~~~~

Pentagon, Room M23R7, Brotherhood of Mithras

"How does this affect us?" A lieutenant asked.

"At the moment, less than they think. The internet was not invented by Vice President Gore but by us and academic institutions. Although the open links were compromised, our most secure links remain secret. Homeland doesn't know about them. We are not yet in harm's way."

~~~~~

Stanley Condominium, Arlington, VA

George Stanley opened a chat program and turned on the modem.

—red dragon from high flyer with news

—red dragon?

Guess he's not home, George thought. He pointed the Pringles can toward Anacostia.

—maelwen from high flyer where red dragon
—high flyer from maelwen break down now

What? Something's happened! George pressed a function key to wipe certain files, unplugged the modem from the computer and the Pringles can from the modem, cut off the wire he had wrapped around the can, filled the can half-way from a stack of stale chips, stuck the can in his desk drawer, and put the modem on top of his external hard drive. Careful to gather every scrap, he took the shards of copper wire onto the balcony and flung them into the wind. Thirty minutes later, he was sitting at his computer typing an essay when a knock came on his bedroom door.

"George? Homeland has sent a computer security team. They want to make sure your computer is secure."

"Of course it's secure, Dad. I'm on the same server as yours," George said.

"What's the modem for?" One of the agents said, pointing to the device.

"I can't use it any more," George said. I used to be able to connect from the computer to my iPad to transfer stuff. I use a wire, now."

The agent picked up the modem and satisfied himself it wasn't hooked to anything. "Maybe I'd better take this," he said.

"No," Vice President Stanley said. "You will not take anything. George knows not to use the modem."

"Sir, we detected signals from this building, and have raided one apartment. Did you know you had a criminal hacker living here?"

"I thought you people had cleared everyone," Stanley said. "Who screwed up? I want names, and an account of this person's criminal activity. On my desk. By nine AM tomorrow."

"Uh, yes, sir. Sorry to bother you, young man." When the men left Stanley called in his Secret Service detail.

"In future, neither they nor any of their kind are welcome," Stanley said. "The Secret Service provides security for my sons and me. I have complete confidence in you. Neither you nor I need anyone else interfering."

The head of the detail looked at each of his people, got their nod, and agreed.

"George, the modem is usually on the other side of your desk," the boy's father said.

"Yes, sir, and it's usually hooked up, but only to a directional antenna. It can't be intercepted."

Thomas Stanley waited.

"Dad, I use it to talk to people, to get stuff I can't get from the internet, especially through your server. Did you know its filters are even tighter than the ones at school? And I don't mean porn, either."

"What are you trying to reach?"

"News from someone other than *GW4U*, *American Fire*, *The Washington Banner*, and *Wheatly Today*. They're nothing but mouthpieces for the government or the OTCC. And they all say the same thing—and it's all foxprop. I can't get *The World Citizen*, or anything from Canada or the UK. I used to be able to get *Al Jihadi*, but can't any more. They've blocked Australia Met and the Ecuador government, who are the only ones putting out information on the El Niño cycle. And the Japanese university that's putting up earthquake data, and—"

"I understand, son. I'll talk to someone, tomorrow," Stanley said. *And it's not just you they are blocking,* he thought. *As you said, it's my server. I'm being blocked, too. What do they not want me to know?*

~~~~~

Stanley Condominium—Ten Days Later

"The alleged hacker was someone named Michael Cookson who lives in Unit 514," Thomas Stanley said. "He's been blogging under a pseudonym for years. Some of the things he said attracted the attention of the OTCC which reported him to DHS as a subversive."

"What happened to him?" George asked.

"They took him in for questioning and destroyed most of his computer equipment searching for something illegal. They couldn't find anything, and he's back home.

"The White House Communications Agency took all the blocks off our server, except known fraudulent websites and people who go fishing, whatever that means. You must be even more careful not to let anyone know who you are."

"Dad, it's phishing, with a *p h*, not an *f*. And it means trying to steal personal information. The only people I talk to are kids in my study groups at school, Henry, and two others who I trust." *And one of them is Michael Cookson also known as Red Dragon. Now, I know his name. And I need more copper wire.*

~~~~~

—reddragon from high flyer

—hi high u ok not heard

—after u arrested i was raided had 2 destroy chip link u know how long takes 2 unbraid lamp cord

—u no i arrested?

—sorry red i should not have said

—forgotten

—me too

There was a long pause before the next message.

—high can u register squirt darknet use my bitcoin account 45%%gihih##toac register as &highflyer send end to end encrypted as &highflyer/&reddragon stop
—red roger, wilco thank you

I know who you are, George Stanley, Red Dragon thought. *You walk a tightrope. I fear for you, but I admire your courage.*

Chapter 28: Tommy Carron

The most important memories of childhood are the small
conquests, the little victories. It is only when we grow up
that we are expected to win great battles.

Anonymous

Wow-Wow Radio, Mt. Pleasant, Georgia

Tommy Carron listened to the local radio station while
he drove to school. His father had allowed Tommy to take the
Suburban, and Tommy was especially careful. His father's
words rang in his ears. "Tommy, your mother and I love you.
You have never disappointed us, and we know you won't,
tonight. And I don't mean just during the game or on the field.
Do you understand?"

Tommy had nodded. "Yes, sir. I do." Now, his attention
was on the road, on traffic, and on the radio—in that order.

The announcer was excited. "Mt. Pleasant has conquered
its lesser enemies. Tonight the real battle begins. They'll be
using live ammunition, firing bullets and bombs over the middle,
rolling down the field like a tank battalion. It will be kill or be
killed today as Mt. Pleasant and Sharpsville battle for the
Division Championship, and a chance to appear in the Five-A
playoffs. We can count on bombs from Mt. Pleasant's All-State
quarterback and a blitzkrieg offense . . . "

Tommy tuned out the rest of the broadcast. *When did a
game, even one as physical as football, become war?*

Washington Cathedral of the One True Christian Church

"Thou shalt not kill!" Pastor Fallow's voice filled the cathedral. "The Lord God thought it was so important he gave that command to us twice, in both Exodus and Deuteronomy. Thou shalt not kill!

"Throughout this nation, the unborn, gifted with a soul at the moment of conception, the moment the seed of the man and the egg of the woman unite, these unborn are being killed without remorse, without recourse.

"God wants us to have children. 'Be fruitful and multiply, and replenish the earth, and subdue it' He told us in Genesis 1:28.

"Abortion is a direct contravention of the Law of the Lord. It is a slap in the face of the Lord God. Yet abortion is practiced in the open and in secret throughout this nation. Evil has triumphed as atheist liberals fight in the courts and in our state legislatures and in our Congress to keep baby-killers in operation and protected from punishment.

"Psalm 127:3 tells us, 'children are a heritage of the Lord: and the fruit of the womb is His reward.' But abortion denies the Lord that which is His. It is blasphemy, it is anathema."

The sermon continued for another twenty minutes. It was transmitted throughout the nation and displayed on huge televisions mounted in mega-churches, including the Resurrection Congregation of the OTCC in Mt. Pleasant, Georgia. Tommy Carron watched, and wondered, *What about Jephthah, who killed his daughter and gave her as a burnt offering to God because he'd made a deal with God—if God would give him victory over the children of Ammon then Jephthah would offer as a burnt offering the first person who came out of his house upon his return. And that person was his daughter. God thought it was a pretty good thing. What's wrong with this?*

~~~~~~

WhatDrWho Blog

Last Sunday, Pastor Fallow preached that " . . . the unborn are gifted with a soul at the moment of conception, the moment the seed of the man and the egg of the woman unite." That's pulpit propaganda.

Here's the truth—and a question the *intelligent design* people are afraid of. If god designed the human woman's reproductive system, why are about half of all fertilized eggs spontaneously aborted, often without the woman even knowing she was pregnant? Why do 15—20% of women who know they are pregnant have a miscarriage?

The Catholic Church and the OTCC want to shut down abortion clinics. How about shutting down the biggest abortionist—their god? I don't make this stuff up. These numbers come from the National Institutes of Health. Bet they won't be there long after this blog appears.

This is WhatDrWho blogging from exile.

~~~~~

Mt. Pleasant, Georgia Resurrection Congregation, OTCC

Tommy Carron asked his question about Jephthah at the Wednesday meeting of the Mt. Pleasant High School Battalion of God's Christian Army. Pastor Dorset had delivered a sermon about the *whole armor of God*, and then invited questions.

"Sir, last Sunday we saw a sermon on *thou shalt not kill*. But there's lots of places in the Bible God orders people to kill. He tells the Israelites to kill their enemies. And God said it was all right for Jephthah to kill his daughter. I don't understand how both things can be right."

"Since we talked about preparing for battle, that's a good question, Tommy," Dorset said. "But first, what Bible are you reading?"

"Huh? I mean, sir?"

"In what version of the Bible did you read things that cause you to question it?"

"My grandmother's—King James Version," Tommy said. The way the pastor asked the question didn't escape Tommy. Sweat formed on his upper lip.

"That's the problem, Tommy. You know the Bible is the Inerrant Word of God, is that right?"

"Yes, sir."

"It is the Inerrant Word of God in the original manuscript, Tommy. Not every translation is correct. The King James Version was written at a turbulent time of British history. The Reformation was sweeping the world, but Papists remained in England, including a band led by Guy Fawkes who tried to blow up Parliament and the King. England was competing with France, Spain, Holland, and Portugal to colonize the New World. King James the First of England needed a God of war, not a God of peace such as we have found in Jesus Christ.

"Do you understand what I'm saying, Tommy?"

Tommy wasn't stupid. He knew the answer the pastor wanted. "Yes, sir. The translation wasn't accurate."

"That is correct, Tommy. Next Sunday, you will bring that blasphemous book to church and give it to me so that I may destroy it. Bring, as well, sixty dollars, and our bookstore will sell you a copy of the One True Christian Bible, the only Inerrant Bible. You will read the story of Jephthah, and learn that he did not kill his daughter, but that she made and kept a promise of abstinence until she was married. She serves as an example for young women, today."

Sixty dollars? And I can't keep Nana's Bible? And abstinence? I know abstinence pledges don't work, never have.

~~~~~

OTCC General Handbook of Instruction for Disciples

Section 9, Frequently Asked Questions . . .

9.2.17 II Kings 2:23-24 relates that children met the Lord's Prophet Elisha outside their town and teased him because he was bald. At that point, Elisha cursed the children in the

Name of the Lord and two bears came from the woods and killed the children.

When your Junior Apostles ask why The Lord would allow that to happen you will respond that the children disrespected God in the person of his Prophet, and were punished for disrespecting God. If asked by an adult, you will add that the parents did not teach their children to respect God in the person of His Prophet. In both cases, you will be establishing and reinforcing your authority as a representative of the Church.

~~~~~

"And [the men of Israel] took two princes
of the Midianites, Oreb and Zeeb;
and they slew Oreb upon the rock . . .
and Zeeb they slew at the winepress . . .
and brought the heads of Oreb and Zeeb
to Gideon on the other side of Jordan."
Judges 6:25

Mt. Pleasant High School Locker Room

Members of God's Christian Army—boys from all sports teams crowded the locker room. The football team was dressed out for the game.

"Ten minutes, men," the coach announced. "Everybody ready?"

Getting a roar of affirmation from the boys, the coach said, "Then, let us pray.

"Lord God, our Commander, we ask that You look upon Your army of young men. Bless them in their undertaking tonight as they carry the banner of Your love and grace onto the playing field. We ask You to use this game to prepare them for the greater playing field of life. We ask You to smite their enemies as Gideon smote the Midianites, and grant them victory. Like the three hundred who did not bow down to drink, we ask

You to keep these Your soldiers alert and that Thou wilt strengthen their hands."

That doesn't make sense! Tommy Carron thought. *We're playing against the County High School. Half of them go to the same church I do—Resurrection. And I'll bet the other half is churched, too. They're not Midianites! And I'll bet their coach is praying the same prayer to the same God as—*

"Hey, Carron. You waitin' for the rapture? Let's go!" a teammate encouraged. Tommy Carron ran onto the field, surrounded by his team and followed by other boy soldiers of God's Christian Army.

~~~~~

More men go to church than want to.
Mark Twain 1835-1910 C.E.
"Letters from The Earth"

Mt. Pleasant Resurrection Congregation, OTCC

People packed the Social Hour between Sunday School and Service. It wasn't the coffee and donuts. Social Hour was the time to see and be seen. A time to make sure your neighbors knew you went to church, a time to see which neighbors attended—and who didn't attend. Forced smiles and excessive joviality had become the new normal.

"Good game last night, Tommy," Pastor Dorset said.

Tommy Carron accepted the pastor's handshake. "Pastor, before the game, the coach prayed for us to win, and for God to help us smite the other team. The other team's coach prayed the same prayer. You know guys from the County High School team are members of our church. We, uh, we compared notes before Sunday School.

"Why are we praying the same prayer to the same God asking Him to help us beat each other—and asking Him to smite the other team?"

The pastor had seen the prayer. It was in the *General Handbook of Instruction for Disciples*, issued to the lay leadership of the Church—the coaches who led God's Christian Army and the women who supervised the Rebeccas. He easily answered the question.

"Tommy, your coaches prayed for strength and for courage. The Lord can grant those things to both teams without showing favoritism."

That's not right, Tommy thought. *Dennis said he was sure his coach had asked God to smite us, and I know that's what our coach said.*

Pastor Dorset thought for a moment, and then added. "It is good to ask questions, Tommy, but please be sure you have your facts straight." The pastor turned away.

Sharp kid, the pastor thought. *He has too many questions, even though he's probably right about the coaches. The reference to the Midianites in the handbook gave them ideas. I'll report it to the leadership . . . should get me noticed and maybe promoted out of this hick town.*

~~~~~

Mt. Pleasant High School Field House

The next game was Homecoming, and a really big deal. *We're expected to win this one at all costs*, Tommy Carron thought. *Even if it's against one of our toughest opponents. Why don't they ever schedule us against a bunch of wimps, or at least, a team we have a chance of beating?*

"Ten minutes? Everyone ready?" the coach called.

The team and their supporters, crowded into the locker room, roared.

"Because tonight's so special, Pastor Dorset will offer our pre-game prayer. Pastor?"

"Let us pray.

"Lord, we ask Your blessing on this team, on the soldiers of Your young army, on our school, and on our nation. We ask

You to send an angel to cut off our enemies, as You sent an angel to cut off the mighty men of valor, the captains of the King of Assyria, so they shalt return with shame to face their own people. We ask that You send your wrath upon our opponents, even as Your wrath came upon the children of Ephraim, and You did slay them and smote them—"

"No! That's not right!" Tommy Carron's voice echoed from the tiles and metal lockers. "You said to pray for courage and strength, not to harm the other team!"

The silence was broken by the coach's voice. "Carron, you're suspended. Get out of uniform, get out of my locker room, and get away from this game."

"I'll be speaking to your father and the Deaconate tonight," Pastor Dorset added.

OMG . . . Oh, my God. But I can't say that, now, 'cause I can't believe, I can't believe in the god I grew up with. Not if he's like Pastor and Coach say, Tommy thought.

The cheers when the team took the field had died away. Tommy dumped his uniform, pads, and shoes on the floor, put on his blue jeans, trainers, T-shirt, and hoodie, and ran from the locker room. He ran without direction, as long as it was away.

~~~~~

"Son, you can't sleep here." The voice was calm, but firm. I opened my eyes and blinked in the brightness of the flashlight pointed at my face. The voice seemed to understand and pointed the light to the ground. I saw a police officer.

Before I could answer, the officer's radio crackled. "All units. Missing juvenile. Caucasian male age 18, 6-feet, 160 pounds, blond hair, green eyes, name Tommy Carron. Last seen Mt. Pleasant High School at 1930 hours. Assaulted pastor of local OTCC. Hold for Investigating Committee."

My mind couldn't understand. *Assaulted*? No way. *Hold for Investigating Committee*? *If they got hold of me . . . I don't want to think about that.*

240

"Did you assault a preacher?" the cop asked. She didn't ask if I was Tommy Carron. I kinda knew we both knew that.

"No, ma'am. I interrupted his prayer when he asked God to hurt the team from White Ridge High School. That was wrong!"

"Wrong? Right? Not sure what they mean, anymore. All I know is you need to get out of here, and fast. They'll be after you. And the Investigating Committee? They don't need warrants and you'd have no rights."

"Ma'am?"

"You need time and safety to think about things." She pulled out a cell phone and pressed one key. Something on her speed dial.

"Bro? When you leaving on your next run? . . . Still headed for West Lafayette? . . . Got precious cargo for you. Have Denise meet me at the Mecca Donald at the interstate . . . No, I don't owe you. You still owe me so much you'll never pay off." She chuckled and clipped the phone to her belt.

"Kid . . . you're going to Indiana."

"Huh?"

"My brother is a long-haul trucker. He's going to Purdue University to pick up—get this—a load of turf they've created for golf courses. You'll ride with him. He'll get you to a place where you'll have time to think."

"But . . . my parents? And I've got a history test on Monday."

She looked at me like my father sometimes looked at me over his glasses, 'cept she wasn't wearing any. Glasses, that is.

"Pretty stupid, huh?" I said.

"Not really, kid. Your whole life is about to change. Hang on to what you can."

At the university, a professor and his wife put me up for a couple of days before the professor could arrange a way for me to get to Canada. By now, there was a nationwide APB out on me . . . not for being missing, but for assaulting a pastor. And it wasn't the police, but the Investigating Committee that was looking for me.

The professor knew a private pilot who would fly a single-engine plane under the radar into Canada. It was dicey at Toledo, where we had to refuel. Ohio was in the hands of the OTCC, but the pilot spun a tale about remote sensing of the university's test farms. He said I was a student and showed them the infrared cameras installed in pods under the wings. I think they let us go more so they wouldn't have to listen to him than because they thought we weren't libsymps—or worse.

From London (that would be London, Ontario), I was put on a bus to Quebec City, but I'm getting ahead of myself.

CHAPTER 29: POLLY SINGER

Three things cannot be hidden:
the sun, the moon, and the truth.
The Buddha

Old Eberly Hotel, Washington, DC

The dining room was well lit. It was not a place for secrets. It was a place to see and be seen, especially for the up-and-coming, the serfs who rode the surf of the recent election. Neither Mel Appleton nor Polly Singer were serfs. Mel was firmly entrenched as the Chief of Staff for President March; Polly was a prominent journalist for the National Radio and TV Service. The far right and the far left sharing a table raised a lot of eyebrows.

"Polly, thank you for coming. I know you are a very busy woman," Mel said. He had stood when Polly reached the table. The maître d' himself had seated Polly. Several of the other patrons made note of that in their smart phones.

"Mel, thank you for giving me a legitimate excuse to leave the station," Polly said. She laughed quietly. "And congratulations on your win."

Polly did not emphasize the word, *your*, but Mel understood. She knew the score. *Wonder if she knows I work for Warwick? Probably,* he thought.

"It goes both ways, Polly," Mel said. "I've been at my desk 24/7 since the election and have eaten more takeout than a man should. This will be my first real meal in two weeks."

They ordered drinks; the maître d' delivered an *amuse-bouche*. Mel set aside his menu.

"Polly, would you be interested in a government job as principal spokesperson for the Department of Homeland Security?"

Polly was taken aback.

"I don't understand, Mel. How can you offer that?"

"It's a Schedule C position—a presidential appointment subject to congressional approval. With your record, confirmation is guaranteed."

With my record and your president's party's majority, Polly thought. *I lost a chance to make a difference when C-SPAN funds dried up. National Radio Service is under attack . . . pledges and donations are down. DHS will never be defunded. It may not be a 'bully pulpit.' but it will be a pulpit.* It took only instants for these thoughts.

"Sounds like an interesting challenge, Mel," she said. "What's the catch?"

"At the moment, there is no catch. You'll be completely independent," Mel said. "But you know there are a lot of things going on involving the national security, things the president must deal with. Terrorism, threats to the US, disease, war, famine, death, the Four Horsemen of the Apocalypse."

"And climate change, the Fifth Horseman. It's driving the others," Polly said.

Mel pressed his lips together. For a moment, Polly was afraid she'd gone too far.

"And climate change," Mel said. "I understand, and so does President March and Vice President Stanley. They cannot make a big deal of it, yet. You will receive deep background, intelligence briefings. Yes, you will be asked to spin some events, but only if you are convinced that the spin is needed to protect the safety of the nation."

"Mel, I understand *the greater good*. I memorized Kipling's poem about his six honest serving men—who, what, why, when, where, and how. He missed *should this be published? Does this serve the greater good?* Yes, Mel, I want the job."

Polly knew better than to negotiate salary. That was fixed by law for Schedule C jobs. She did get Mel to agree to hire Sugi, though.

~~~~~

Los Angeles Stricken—MERS Suspected

UK Voice World Service. Her Majesty's Consulate in Los Angeles reports hospital emergency rooms in the Los Angeles basin are jammed with people complaining of respiratory distress. The mayor has denied rumors of an outbreak of Middle East Respiratory Syndrome (MERS) brought in by Saudi plutocrats or their servants—some say slaves—fleeing ISIS. Most affected by the outbreak are the elderly and the very young. Our affiliate in Los Angeles has been unable to get accurate numbers, but has learned that more than one hundred are dead at the Central University Health System Hospital.

~~~~~

Stanley Condominium, Arlington, Virginia

George Stanley brought a printout into his father's office.

"Dad? I've checked this with two other sources, one in Japan and one in South Korea. They're usually reliable. The Japanese and South Koreans have consulates in LA. But there's not a peep on any US news source. What's going on?"

Henry Stanley glanced at the headline. "True, but not the entire truth. It's not MERS—the symptoms don't match and the tests don't show the virus. At this morning's briefing, about a hundred thousand had been affected, but only 53 had died.

People in Southern California are in a panic. More people have died in traffic accidents trying to flee the city than from the— whatever it is. Homeland has put an embargo on the news to prevent more panic."

"Embargo. You mean 'censorship,' " George said.

"Yes, I do, but if you've found it, it won't be long before censorship breaks down. Let's hope they find the cause before then."

~~~~~

Dayton, Tennessee, Oak Middle School

"The circumference of a circle is pi times the diameter, and the diameter is two times the radius. Yesterday we learned what pi was. Gary, if I have a circle with radius of five feet, what is the circumference?" Gary was the brightest kid in the class, and the teacher hoped he would be able to put three pieces of information together and reach an answer.

"That's easy, Miss Davis. It's thirty feet."

"Well Gary, that's not quite right. Do you remember we learned that pi equals three point one four?"

"Don't . . . I mean doesn't . . . matter, Miss Davis. It's the same problem that's in the Bible."

As soon as Gary said *Bible*, all but three of the children reached in their backpacks and pulled out Bibles. Gary flipped through his and then announced, "First Kings seven, twenty-three. 'And he made a great basin of metal, circular in shape, ten cubits from the one brim to the other; it was round, and its height was five cubits and its circumference was thirty cubits.' It's the same problem, Miss Davis."

Samantha, one of the students who hadn't reached for a Bible turned in her seat and said, "So the Bible says pi equals three? That is so lame!"

Miss Davis smacked her yardstick on her desk a dozen times before the hubbub subsided."

"Gary, and Samantha, and all of you. The Bible is not a mathematics textbook. This," she said, and held up a book, "is our math text for this class. In it, as we learned yesterday, pi is what is called a *transcendental number*. We use three point one four as an approximation for our problems and homework."

~~~~~

Silence is the greatest adornment of the woman.
Sophocles _____-406 BCE

Dayton School Board

The summons came from the School Board, but the chairman's seat was occupied by someone in clerical garb—black shirt and jacket, white collar, and a perpetually sour expression. Miss Davis set aside her nervousness, and sat in the single chair placed before the dais on which the pastor and board members sat.

The pastor spoke. "You have been reported to this Investigating Committee for examination on the charge that you did question in the classroom the inerrancy of the Word of the Lord God."

Before the man could continue, Miss Davis asked, "Investigating Committee? And who are you, sir?"

The Chairman of the Board answered her. "The School Board has convened as an Investigating Committee under the leadership of Pastor William Sunday of the Dayton Pentecostal Congregation of the One True Christian Church. You will answer his question."

"He didn't ask a question, sir. He made an accusation."

"Be silent, woman!" Pastor Sunday shouted. "Did you or did you not tell your students that the Bible was in error in First Kings seven, Verse twenty-three and declare your textbook to be correct?"

"As near as I remember, I told the class that the value of pi calculated from that verse was not the one we would use in the classroom, but that we would use the one in the math textbook. That textbook, incidentally, is one approved by your church."

The questioning continued, but Miss Davis would not waiver from her statement. She refused to admit that she had blasphemed, and entreated the members of the school board to support her. They sat mute.

By nine forty-five, the Reverend Sunday had exhausted his questions. "You are admonished," he said, "not to disparage the Bible in the future. You are admonished to teach only what is in the approved curriculum and not to interject your own opinions. Is that clear?"

That's what I've been doing all year, Miss Davis thought. "Yes, Reverend.

~~~~~

Ice-Melt Sickness Hits Los Angeles

God's Word for You, American Fire Network, and Tempest Times. The Department of Homeland Security Bureau of Health has determined the recent respiratory difficulties that struck a few Los Angeles residents were caused by melting ice on the bottom of the Santa Catalina Channel. Warm currents melted the ice and stirred up the muck on the ocean bed, releasing non-toxic gasses trapped in the muck. Elderly, children, and persons with compromised immune systems were most affected.

"The ice has melted and the danger is over. This is Polly Singer, for the Department of Homeland Security."

~~~~~

Honesty is the first chapter in the book of wisdom.
Thomas Jefferson 1743-1826 CE

"The only *muck stirred up* is what you put out for DHS," Sugi shouted.

"It was ice melt, all right," he said, a little more quietly. "But it was methane ice, methane clathrates. Frozen methane bound up in water ice. Methane is not toxic but it won't support life. It mixed with the sea breeze and where it was concentrated enough, put people in distress. And there is a lot more of it in the channel, especially where they've used water to pressurize off-shore oil wells. It gives an entirely new meaning to *crystal meth.*"

"Sugi, I . . . I'm sorry. I'm not a chemist," Polly said.

"You're not an airhead, either," Sugi said. "We need to go to my place, use my computer."

"Why?" Polly asked. It was not an indictment; her curiosity showed in a raised eyebrow.

"I have a darknet browser. It's the only place we'll get—"

"Darknet? Criminals? Drug dealers like Silk Road, and conspiracy theorists?" Polly asked.

"And people who want to know more than the government allows on the internet. Come on, trust me?"

Polly was surprised that Sugi's apartment wasn't a man-cave or a left-over-food-everywhere-haven for cockroaches and worse. Clean, neat, and Spartan, until Sugi opened the door to his home office. Two iMac computers, a laptop, and a bunch of boxes whose purpose Polly couldn't guess.

"Impressive," she said. Sugi gestured her to a seat and typed on one of the keyboards.

"Here's the IPCC—the Intergovernmental Panel on Climate Change. If you tried to access it on the internet, you'd be allowed to get to the home page. When you clicked a link to one of their reports, your connect speed would drop to, like zero. After a couple of minutes, you'd get a message that the link had been terminated because the server wasn't responding. The message is a lie, courtesy of DHS—our employer.

"Take a look . . . this is the executive summary, and here's the section on methane clathrates."

Polly read quickly.

"Sugi, how sure are you this is really the IPCC site?"

"See the star on the address bar? It means the site is verified by darknet administrators."

"And who are they?"

Sugi's pause was barely noticeable, but Polly caught it.

"No one knows," he said. "But I've never found them to be wrong."

"Sugi? Can you set up a blog for me on the darknet? Something that can't be traced to you or me? Please?"

"There you go again, saying *please*." Sugi grinned. "Of course I can. What do you want your *nom de plume* to be?"

"Alabama boys speak French?" Polly asked and then chuckled. "How about Mercy Otis Warren?"

"French? Just the essentials . . . how to order wine, read a menu, and find the restroom," Sugi replied while he typed. "Mercy Otis Warren? Good choice."

~~~~~

Methane Clathrates Kill Angelinos

Mercy Otis Warren blog, darknet. Los Angeles deaths, blamed on muck in the channels, were caused by methane, what most of us know as *natural gas*. Natural gas has no smell, so the gas company puts the odor of garlic in their gas to warn people of leaks. This methane, however, didn't come from broken gas lines, so there was no smell to warn anyone. It came from the melt of *methane clathrates*, methane gas trapped for aeons in ice crystals at the bottom of the ocean.

Warm currents in the Santa Barbara and Catalina Channels . . . "

~~~~~

"Good blog, Ms. Singer."

"Sugi, please call me Polly. You're in the driver's seat, now."

"Yes, ma'am, Ms. Polly, but you're still the *talent*. I'm the supporting actor."

CHAPTER 30: TWO MEN NAMED ED

"Order is heaven's first law; and, this confessed,
Some are, and must be, greater than the rest."
Alexander Pope, *Essay on Man,* 1733 C.E.

Mt. Pleasant, Georgia, Ed's Garage

"El Niño, that's some Mexican thang, ain't it? We never used to see so many of them. Mexicans, I mean. They're taking all the construction jobs at that shopping center across the county line. Living in their cars, mostly."

"Yeah, an' the big gas station on the highway? Full of 'em every afternoon. Burritos and malt liquor."

"You know that woman over in Eastside where I was fixin' her roof? She made me show a drivers license to prove I was an American before she'd let me work. Then she called City Hall to see if I was registered! How come all them Mexicans are working on that shopping center? You know half of 'em don't even have green cards."

"Yeah, but somebody's got pull, whoever owns the shopping center or either who owns the construction company."

"Hey, Ralph, get on that fancy phone you're so proud of and goober—or whatever you call it—that construction company. See who owns it."

"I'll *goober* you, you redneck," Ralph replied.

"No, really, find out who it is."

"Somethin' called *Warwick Industries* owns the shopping center. No idea who that is. The construction company's out of Texas."

"No wonder they have all them wetbacks. Texas is more Mexican than white, now."

"Maybe we ought t' do somethin'. That apartment complex down the road, maybe. It's all Section 8."

"There's white folks who live there, too."

"Yeah, but they're Arabs or either white trash." The irony of calling someone else *white trash* didn't resonate with any of the men. Neither did their grammar.

"If they got any sense, they'll stay inside."

"When?"

"Saturday . . . they'll all be likkered up. We'll drag a couple outta their apartments into the parking lot, kick 'em around, burn a cross, and take off."

"Somebody's got to take care of the cops."

"I'll handle the city Po-Pos, and the sheriff's people won't come into the city unless they're called—and, they won't be."

Mt. Pleasant, Georgia, Southside Apartments

The men who conducted the raid were at least as likkered up as any of the men who lived in the complex. Seven pickup trucks, flying the old Confederate Battle Flag, roared into the central parking lot, circled, and stopped. Men who had been riding in the beds of the trucks jumped out. One group passed around torches—rags on sticks—and soaked them in kerosene from a bucket. Flames were quickly passed from person to person.

By this time, people including children, had poured from the apartments.

"What is it? Is it a celebration? Es una celebración? Will there be fireworks? Habrá fuegos artificiales? Will we get candy? Vamos a sacar el caramel?"

254

The children's questions were naïve. Then, reason took over as adults saw the men with the torches, men wearing white robes. Men whose faces were hidden behind white hoods with eyeholes.

"Esto no es bueno! This is not good!" one man said.

"¡Entrar! Ir a vuestros hogares!" another called. "Get inside! Go to your homes!"

Mothers frantically called to children while men stepped between their families and the men with torches.

"What do you want?" one man dared to call.

"We want you and your kind out of here! This is America. It's for Americans and not a bunch of Mexican wetbacks!"

I am from Puerto Rico, the man who had called thought. *I served in the US Army and am a citizen. So are my wife and my sons.* He was smart enough not to reply, but pushed his family toward their apartment.

Three of the invaders had erected a cross wrapped in rags. They sprayed it with kerosene from pumps normally used to spray pesticides. Meanwhile, two of the invaders grabbed the man who had spoken up, and dragged him next to the cross. Either by accident or deliberately, he received some of the kerosene spray. When the cross was lit, the fire reached him, too. The cheers of the invaders drowned his screams.

It was inevitable: one of the apartment residents had a gun. It was inevitable that he would run into his apartment and take the gun from the drawer of his nightstand. It was inevitable that he would step onto the porch of his apartment building. Seeing his neighbor in flames, he aimed and fired.

The sound of a nine-millimeter pistol is unmistakable. The invaders saw one of their members fall, and returned fire. They did not know from where the shot had come, and their bullets flew in many directions. More screams. More people falling. The original shooter was more calm than any of the invaders. He killed three more invaders before a random bullet from the parking lot put an end to his life.

By this time, neither the city police nor the sheriff's department could ignore the calls to the 911-Dispatch Center. Cars with flashing lights in several colors arrived and blocked the escape of the invaders' pickup trucks. Faced with overwhelming firepower, the invaders surrendered. Some tried to pull off their hoods and robes, but there wasn't time.

~~~~~

Dayton, Tennessee, Highway 27 North

Mud from its journey from the road into the ditch spattered the teardrop shaped car. The bullet holes that punctuated both the windows and the two people in the front seat drew most folks' attention.

"Damn electric cars shouldn't be allowed on highways," the deputy said. "Go too slow. Prob'ly pissed off somebody in a pickup. You can see the shots came from higher than the roof. Road rage."

"Sounds good," the sheriff said. "Write it up."

Road rage or some vigilante fundie, wondered the lone reporter who had shown up. He took photos and sent them to a friend who would see they got to the right place.

~~~~~

WhatDrWho Blog

When I was forced to leave Dayton, Tennessee I thought the only thing I would miss would be the local gossip. I didn't think it would be important. I was wrong. I've heard gossip that upon investigation has turned out to be true.

A Primus hybrid car driven by a Dayton High School teacher was found in a ditch outside town. The teacher and her woman companion were killed by a dozen or so of the sixty-seven bullets fired into the car. The official finding was *road rage*, blamed on the car's alleged low speed. There was no investigation. No bullets were removed and saved for ballistic examination. Why?

Sloppy police work? Let me offer another hypothesis based on the facts that have been uncovered, but ignored by the local authorities.

The city's Investigating Committee had examined the teacher. They censured her for teaching science not included in the official curriculum. That would be any science in conflict with the beliefs of the One True Christian Church. Such as the universe is billions of years old, and not 6,000 years old and that pi is a transcendental number, not defined by the Bible. Further, the gossip among the small-minded of Dayton was that the teacher's female companion was more than her housemate.

Finally, there was a bumper sticker on the car— *Blasphemy is a Victimless Crime.* That's politically protected free speech; it's a statement protected by the religious freedom guaranteed in the First Amendment to the Constitution.

A belief in superstition rather than science and a belief that the two women were lesbians was enough to set someone against them. The shooter said that the bumper sticker was the *last straw.* His words were reported by witnesses, a few of whom had not been drinking. His remarks were recorded on a smart phone at a bar near the accident scene.

Whatever the excuse to pull the trigger sixty-seven times, the result was murder. The teacher and her companion deserved better.

If an enraged, mindless redneck can kill with impunity, what hope is there for the rest of us?

This is WhatDrWho blogging from exile.

Rudy Adams, Guelph, Ontario

"Dad, were those two women really murdered for, you know, being lesbians?" I asked.

"That, and because they were *heathens*, according to what the witnesses said."

"Will the killers be arrested?"

"So far, not, and they probably won't be."

"Dad, that's not right! What will their students say? What will the kids think about this?"

Dad pursed his lips and lowered his eyebrows. I knew this meant he was thinking, hard.

"Rudy, that's only one of the things kids need answers to. A lot of things going on affect kids differently from adults. Would you like to blog about that?"

"My own blog?" I asked. "Can I be *tardisboy?*"

Dad chuckled. "You've already thought about this."

"Well, yeah! Can I say anything I want?"

"Rudy, I will never tell you what to say or what not to say—except that you must not libel anyone and you must not use profanity. I might ask questions and make suggestions."

"You've been thinking about this, too," I said. Dad just grinned, then swiveled his chair, and started typing.

CHAPTER 31: TOM KELLEY

I'm a boy born a girl.
I have to prove every day
I'm man enough to face the world.
Anonymous

Clover, Kentucky High School

A dozen members of the Clover High School Battalion of God's Christian Army were hanging out behind the gym. Two of the boys lit and passed around cigarettes. Coach knew what went on but as long as no other teacher found out, he wouldn't say anything.

"You know that Tom Kelly kid?" a boy asked.

"Yeah."

"Well, he's a girl," the first boy said.

"What do you mean?"

"I overheard the coach and the principal talking. The reason he doesn't have to do PT is he's a girl who thinks she's a boy."

"Whoa! He . . . I mean, she uses the boy's restroom—" Matt Angler said.

"And always uses the handicapped stall to pee."

"And has seen us standing at the urinals with our junk hanging out!"

"Oh, gross!"

~~~~~

The door of the Clover High School administrative office banged against the wall. The man who stood in the doorway wore a black suit. His face was so pale his white clerical collar was invisible.

The secretary overcame her shock to ask, "May I help you, sir?"

"I must see the principal. This abomination may not continue!"

"I beg your pardon, sir? What abomination? And may I tell him your name?"

"Know thy place, woman! I am Pastor Angler from the Clover Christian Church, and I must see the principal."

The secretary pressed the lever on the intercom. "Sir, Pastor Angler from the Clover Christian Church is here to see you."

"Invite him in, please."

The secretary stood and opened the door behind her. The pastor was speaking even before he passed through the door.

"Your school harbors an abomination with the connivance, yea, the encouragement, of members of your staff. This is anathema to the Lord God, and must not be allowed to continue."

"Pastor, please . . . what abomination?"

"The girl who dresses as a boy and who uses bathrooms designated for boys."

"Pastor, this person is transgendered, not an abomination. I can't—"

"Deuteronomy 22:5 in the Inerrant Word of the Lord God says, 'The woman shall not wear that which pertaineth unto a man, neither shall a man put on a woman's garment: for all that do so are abomination unto the Lord thy God.' "

Had the pastor's voice been any louder, the windows of the office might have shattered.

In the hallway, Matt Angler and one of his coterie of bullies heard.

"Got him!" Matt said before the boys ran to their next class.

~~~~~

Mr. Barnes had called for an appointment. He would not say the subject, only that he must speak to the principal. When he arrived, he came straight to the point.

"Principal Graham, I understand a girl uses the boys' restroom and that until recently, the boys were unaware of this. They have unwittingly exposed themselves to her. Given the ages of these boys and the girl, the boys can be charged with lewd behavior and branded as sexual deviants for the rest of their lives. They could find themselves in juvenile detention. Some might be charged as adults and jailed. I will ask the court for an injunction to stop this practice if you do not do so."

"Mr. Barnes, discrimination against a transgendered person violates Title 10 of the US Code. Further, allowing this student to use the restroom of the gender with which he identifies is a reasonable accommodation under the Americans with Disabilities Act."

"You spout laws and interpretations of the law as if you were a lawyer. Are you, sir?"

"No, I am not. I rely on information provided by the school board."

"Are you saying the school board members know of this?"

"I . . . I don't know. They must be."

"That will have to be determined. In the meanwhile, you should know that the EEOC and DOE statements you cite are advisory and do not have the force of law. The state laws regarding exposure of private parts of the body to children are considerably more clear than the ramblings of a libsymp in Washington, DC."

"I'm sorry, Mr. Barnes, but until the School Board rules differently the current practice will continue."

"Then, I shall see you in court," Mr. Barns said.

"No doubt," Principal Graham said softly as the door closed behind Mr. Barnes.

~~~~~

"You can't come in here," Matt Angler said. He was leaning against one side of the doorframe; his arm extended across to the other side. Sam Barns stood beside him. Others of their friends clustered nearby.

"I gotta pee," Tom said. "Come on, let me in."

"We know you're a girl. That's why you always sit down to pee. If you can't stand at a urinal, you can't use this restroom."

"I gotta pee," Tom said, again.

"Girl's room down the hall," a boy said.

"Not here, Tranny . . . you can't piss, here," a God's Christian Army member said.

"Yeah, girly-girl, girl's room down the hall," another added.

Matt poked Tom in the chest. The bundle of nerves just below the sternum fired. Tom bent over, gasped for breath, and lost control of his bladder.

"She's wet her pants!" Sam said. The other boys grinned at the growing wetness.

Tom caught his breath and ran.

~~~~~

Matt, Sam, and four other members of God's Christian Army stood in front of the principal's desk. Their faces were sullen. Eyes stared at Mr. Graham. Lips were tightly compressed. They breathed unnecessarily loudly through their noses.

"Boys, I have a complaint that you bullied a student. You called this person names, you refused entry to a restroom, one of you hit this person, and caused an accident . . . um, when the person was unable to use the restroom. What do you have to say for yourselves?"

"Nothing, Mr. Graham. Nothing until my father gets here," Sam said.

"Mine, too," Matt added.

~~~~~

Both Mr. Barnes and Pastor Angler arrived at the principal's office.

"Frankly, Mr. Graham, I don't think you've got a case," Mr. Barns said after listening to Principal Graham. "You have a 'she said, he said' situation in which six boys dispute one girl's story. I told you that if you allow a girl into the boys' restroom, any boy age eighteen and older, or any boy more than two years older than she is, and who exposes himself to her is under the law a sexual predator, a pervert. He can be arrested and charged."

"You cannot fault any of these boys for condemning an abomination! They have committed their lives to the Lord Jesus Christ as members of God's Christian Army," Pastor Angler added.

"Pastor Angler, for the last time, do not call this child an abomination. It is your right to do so from your pulpit. You will not do it in my office."

Behind the gym, Matt and Sam exchanged high-fives with their buddies. "I told you we'd get off," Sam said. I knew my dad would get us off."

"*Our* dads," Matt interrupted.

"Yeah, *our* dads."

~~~~~

There had not been as many people at a school board meeting since the Civil Rights Act of 1968 reached Clover in 1994 and the board had to integrate the schools.

After the Pledge of Allegiance, the chairman opened the meeting to public comments. The first speaker was Pastor Angler whose fire and brimstone was not unexpected.

"You are harboring and encouraging an abomination in the high school. It's bad enough you allow girls to wear trousers, and shamefully expose their midriffs, legs, and br . . . other parts of their anatomy to the lustful gaze of boys. Worse, you are allowing a girl who dresses as a boy to pass as a boy, to use a boy's bathroom, to see the private parts of boys . . . "

The chairman rapped his gavel. "Thank you, Pastor Angler, but your time is up. Please, be seated."

A member of the pastor's flock stood. "May I speak?"

"Yes."

"Then, I yield my time to Pastor Angler."

Before the pastor could resume his diatribe, the chairman said, "That is out of order. We have no such provision. Do you wish to speak?"

"Naw, Pastor's said it."

"Anyone else?"

Following a few seconds of silence, a member of the board spoke. "Mr. Chairman, I move we enter executive session to consider a personnel or legal matter."

"Second."

"Motion made and seconded. All in favor?"

Six members of the board raised their hands.

"Motion passes unanimously. Ladies and gentlemen, please clear the room except for the Board, our lawyer, the recorder, and Principal Graham."

"You will not do this in secret!" Pastor Angler yelled. Mr. Barnes spoke to him and the pastor led his flock out the door.

The board's lawyer spoke. "We were served this afternoon with a temporary injunction that requires us to bar a particular student from using restrooms designated for male students. The student is a biological female who identifies as male, and who has been treated as male until his identity was exposed. The injunction takes effect immediately and we have thirty days to argue why it should not be made permanent."

"What can we do?"

"Tomorrow," Principal Graham said, "we will mark the smallest of the boys' restrooms for use only by this student. We will station a school resource officer at the door to enforce this, and to prevent other students from interfering."

"You know I am opposed to using those police officers to maintain order and discipline in the school," Mrs. Campbell said. "They are there to evict intruders and respond to threats of violence from outside. Don't forget what happened in Spring Valley when the policeman dragged a student from her desk and across the classroom."

"We don't have the teaching staff to do it," another board member added.

"Then we will use the assistant coaches . . . the men, at least," Mr. Graham said. "It will only be until we can appeal and get guidance from the EEOC."

~~~~~

"Have you heard from the EEOC?"

"I'm afraid so, and it's not good. We've received an *ad lidem* letter threatening to sue us in federal court if we do not allow transgendered students to use restrooms and locker rooms of choice . . . the one for the sex with which they identify—and not a *separate but equal* restroom."

"So we're between a rock and . . . I can't believe I was about to say that. What can we do?"

"I don't know, except that Pastor Angler and Mr. Barnes are in Clover, and the person who wrote the letter is in Washington."

~~~~~

The board's lawyer tried to impress upon the principals—including Principal Graham—the key points of the church's argument—the arguments these men would encounter in the Examination.

"The Investigating Committee's charter and authority are unclear," the board's lawyer said. "What is clear is that they represent the will of the majority of the people of Clover. That means little from a legal standpoint. But it does mean they will control the next election. Unless you want to see the board overturned and most of the current school staff out of work, I suggest you accept their order to appear."

There was nothing new at the Examination by the Investigating Committee. Parents and their sons—who were members of God's Christian Army and all congregants of the One True Christian Church—said and re-said the same arguments. Principal Graham's concerns about a federal lawsuit were dismissed, as were his pleas to consider the age and mental health of the transgendered student. After four hours, Pastor Angler called a halt to testimony.

"Immoral behavior has been allowed, even condoned by the school authorities. The abomination is protected by school officials hired to teach, but who have been turned into guards.

"This is an abomination unto the Lord God.

"If the present situation continues, the members of the Clover School Board, Principal Graham, and the staff of Mt. Pleasant High School will be arrested and held for trial."

Pastor Angler banged his gavel.

~~~~~

Tom's Home, That Night
"I'm sorry, Tom, but beginning tomorrow you will have to use the girls' restroom. You may wear pants and boys' shirts. At least they haven't made that illegal—yet," Tom's father said.

"They will . . . if not illegal, it will be against some decree of the Investigating Committee," Tom replied.

A knock interrupted whatever Tom's father might have said.

"Who in the world?"

"Dad, don't answer! It's probably someone from the Committee . . . to arrest us!"

"Nonsense, son. They haven't gone that far—yet. If they had, they'd not knock; they'd break down the door."

Tom's father flipped on the porch light and opened the door. A boy stood on the porch. He was alone.

"Sir, I am Mark Angler. My father will not let this rest. I overheard him on the telephone. He's stirring up the congregation. You and Tom must escape before it is too late."

"This is insane!"

"Insane, sir? So was the so-called hearing you attended today. The world is insane. My parents, they don't know I'm here. They would disown me. They would turn me over to the Investigating Committee if they knew. Please, I'm trying to help."

"Where can we go?" Tom asked.

"Follow the drinking gourd," Mark said.

"I've heard that," Tom said. "The underground railroad from slave times. Go north, to the Big Dipper in the night sky."

"Is there an underground railroad?" Tom's father asked.

"Only bits and pieces . . . some of us are working on it. For now, take what will fit in a suitcase. Leave immediately. Take 60 west; then 231 north. Drive as long and as far as you can and then keep driving. When you reach Jasper, Indiana find the Friends Meeting, the Quakers. Be careful what you say. Ask for *Friends of Daedalus*. There's no guarantee, but most of the Quakers are opposed to the tyranny of the current government, and much of the old underground railroad was run by Quakers."

CHAPTER 32: ANDRÉ BERGERON

"Where ignorance is bliss, 'Tis folly to be wise."
Thomas Gray 1716-1771 CE

GETE Refinery, Fredenberg, Minnesota

A squirt from a bottle labeled "Afreet Nasal Spray" loosened the seals on the recording gauges. André Bergeron, whose Minnesota driver's license, social security card, and Kansas birth certificate read 'Andrew Brown,' peeled away the seals and turned the calibration screws one quarter turn. He had been doing that once a week for ten weeks. When he finished, he reapplied the seals with the same glue used originally. It was in a tube labeled "Athlete's Foot Ointment."

~~~~~

Take 'Em to the Wire with Bert Rightly

American Fire Network. "The eco-freaks are again hoisted by their own stupidity, slogans, and shallow understanding of reality. Their lawsuits could not stop a geothermal power plant in Yellowstone, so they resorted to violence. Department of Homeland Security and Park Police charged at least a hundred with terroristic acts after sit-ins in the highways leading to the site. Meanwhile, drilling for the first geothermal well continues. The libsymps claim they want clean, renewable power. Now, they're trying to protect some microscopic bacteria that live in the hot geysers at Yellowstone? Bacteria are an endangered species? Gimme a break!

"Here to talk about this is Dr. Evan Wilkes from Wheatly University's School of Biological Sciences. Dr. Wilkes, are you ready for *Take 'Em to the Wire?*"

"I'll do my best, Bert."

"First question, what's so special about these bacteria, anyway? They're germs, right?"

"Yes, Bert, they are germs. The only thing special about them is that they live in hot water, something that we use to kill germs. The problem is that some atheist scientists think life originated in warm ponds or around hot vents in the ocean floor, so these bacteria are important to them."

"Wait, are you saying they've found the origin of life in—what do they call it—a primordial soup? Hasn't that scientist in Glenn Rose, Texas, proven that didn't and couldn't happen?"

"No, I'm not saying that. I'm only saying they believe it. The Creation Science Museum in Glenn Rose has duplicated what these scientists claim is the atmosphere of Earth however many millions of years ago. It's been exposed to the same sunlight scientists claim powered the formation of living molecules, but nothing's happened. It's bogus."

"There you have it, folks. Once again, scientists try to pull the wool over our eyes."

~~~~~

WhatDrWho Blog

Leave it to Burt Rightly to twist the truth to serve his beliefs and the ignorance and prejudices of his audience. The bacteria that live and flourish in the hot springs and geysers of Yellowstone are called extremophiles because they thrive in extremes of temperature and chemicals. Learning how they do this is important basic research. It may help us develop antibiotics against the germs that are evolving to be resistant to our best medicines. It may help us understand how life came into being on the Earth. It may help us understand life elsewhere in the universe. It may bring other benefits we cannot predict.

Yellowstone sits on a thin spot in the Earth's crust—thin enough that the molten magma below the crust can heat water and power the geysers and hot springs. The geothermal plant will inject water into a deep well. The water will become steam to drive turbines to produce electricity.

What's unreasonable about that?

This is WhatDrWho blogging from exile.

~~~~~

CHAPTER 33: PRESIDENT MARCH

"I suffer not a woman to teach,
nor to usurp authority over the man,
but to be in silence."
I Timothy 2:11-12

Aircraft Carrier Ronald Reagan

"Captain, this just came in from COMNAVFLTLANT." The radioman's face was white when he brought the message to the bridge.

Executive Office of the President
Executive Order 001
Effective immediately, no woman shall command
any unit, ship, squadron, or other entity
of the United States Armed Forces.
Pending formal personnel actions,
command of every entity shall be assumed
by the most senior male commissioned officer,
warrant officer, or non-commissioned officer of said entity.

Signed: Edward March
President, United States of America
Commander-in-Chief

"Has it been authenticated, verified?" the captain asked.

"Yes, ma'am. It's also on Fleet TV . . . and the comm folks say they're getting scuttlebutt from other ships. What should we do?"

"We follow orders, Mister. The President is the Commander-in-Chief. Please call the XO to the bridge. And have a yeoman pack up my quarters."

~~~~~

Alternet Traffic

&hackattack from mil chatter all women in command us forces must relinquish to males presidential x-order

&sandman confirmed from mil sat usn x-order to all fleet

&highflyer confirmed chatter on aviation frequencies

&reddragon to alternet get this to all stop

&reddragon/&highflyer b careful what u say send to me let me screen u

~~~~~

St. Nicholas Children's Hospital, Arlington, Virginia

"Sarah? Can you feel this?" The doctor drew his finger over the sole of the little girl's foot. Her toes twitched. They had done that before. It was the response of a reflex loop to the spinal cord and back to the foot.

"Yes! It tickles!" she said. That response was new. Until now, severed nerves at L-4 had blocked the nerves' signal to the brain. The medical team had injected stem cells into her spine. They hoped that these undifferentiated cells would learn from adjacent nerve cells, would turn themselves into nerve cells, and would close the gap created in the auto accident.

"She feels it!" the girl's mother said. "It's a miracle! God has answered my prayers!"

God had nothing to do with it, the doctor thought. *It's the result of of ten of thousands of hours of research, of millions of*

dollars spent, of the work of hundreds of doctors, researchers, lab technicians, and others, year after painstaking year.

~~~~~

Office of the Senate Majority Leader

Despite the congressional gridlock during the past decade, Senator James Beasley had won re-election as Senate Majority Leader. He and the Speaker of the House were the two most important men in Congress, and were trying to create a legislative agenda. Their discussion turned to a *Dear Colleague* letter from a freshman representative—Thomas Vaughn of Rhode Island.

"What do you make of it?" Beasley said.

"It's something we've talked about," Stafford replied. "Vaughn either jumped the gun, or did what was needed to get us off our duffs. Mel Appleton has already drafted twelve executive orders. President March will issue them over the next few weeks, perhaps a couple of months, depending on reaction. They're all going to require us to follow up with legislation."

"Our plates are full, and our staffs are already overwhelmed," Beasley said.

"Not necessarily," Stafford said. "We have the entire K-Street crowd to call on. They're chomping at the bit to get access to all the new faces in Congress."

"But they have their own agenda . . . getting legislation to benefit their own paymasters. I've already heard from energy companies, alternate energy companies, for-profit prison companies, pharmaceuticals, you name it, they've all made their *social calls*."

"Tit-for-tat," Stafford said. "We introduce a bill or amendment for them, they craft one for us. Besides, I have the entire law school of Wheatly University primed and ready for internships . . . they're sharp, they're dedicated, and they're free."

"Free? TANSTAAFL—there ain't no such thing as a free lunch," Beasley said.

"You really don't know? The Susana Stafford Foundation is the biggest donor to Wheatly University."

Beasley didn't miss a beat. "What about Vaughn's letter?"

"He's opened Pandora's box. There's no closing it. We need to get in front of him, or we lose leadership. Invite him to a private meeting. He's the scion of a plutocratic family, so wealth won't impress him. But power might," Stafford said. "How about this: you and me, the VEEP, and someone from the president's staff . . . Mel Appleton comes to mind. One of those crab shacks on the Eastern Shore. Butcher paper on the table and buckets of steamed seafood, beer in pint mason jars." Stafford's mind was about six steps ahead of Beasley. *Someone is behind Thomas Vaughn. His father? Most likely.*

~~~~~

The Crabby Shack, Eastern Shore of Maryland

Sol Weizmann spent hours drilling Thomas Vaughn on fine legal points. Thomas's father, Frederick, had flown in, and added his knowledge of the likely participants in the meeting. Thomas was well prepared and confident when he walked across the gravel parking lot, up the wooden steps, and into the clapboard building. The Secret Service detail was sharp—they recognized him immediately. Stafford, Beasley, and Mel Appleton sat at a six-top, round table.

"Thomas—may I call you Tom—welcome," Stafford said. "And please call me Henry. I've never liked *Hank*, and *Harry* just doesn't work. Of course you know Senator Beasley and Mel."

Stafford continued without waiting for an answer. "We got a call from Stanley. He was held up at the bridge, but will be here in a few minutes. You have a driver, I assume? How about a beer?"

Vice President Thomas Stanley arrived about half-a-beer later. Crabs were ordered, and dumped from a steamer basket onto the table. Baskets of hushpuppies and ramekins of melted butter were added. More beer was poured, although little was consumed.

Conversation was light. Schools attended and how their football teams had done in the past season, or were expected to do in the fall. A brief game of "do you know" established links through friends among several of the men, including Thomas Vaughn. *Not surprising*, he thought. *These are among the most powerful men in the country, and father is one of them.*

The polite conversation lasted through most of the crabs . . . until another steamer basket was dumped on the table. It seemed to be a signal.

"Tom, your letter raised a lot of eyebrows," Stafford said.

"The letter may have been unexpected," Vaughn said. "The subject, however, is neither new nor unexpected."

Confident, but not too cocky, Stafford thought. "Not the subject as much as your plan to implement it. The Senate passes the resolution. Then, the House forms itself as a Committee of the Whole to be the convention. It looks good at first glance, but . . . "

The hard questions began. Vaughn's time with Weizmann paid off, as did his father's assessment of these men's personalities. Thomas played them well—well enough they didn't realize they were being played. Before the meeting was over, it had been decided. He would be made chair of a new Committee. It was an honor and position unheard of for a freshman member of the House of Representatives. More than that, it was a committee unheard of in the past: The Select Committee on the Constitution.

St. Nicholas Children's Hospital, Arlington, Virginia

Executive Office of the President
Executive Order 002
Effective immediately, no organization or entity of any nature
that receives funds from the United States Government or any
agency or part thereof, whether through grants, contracts,
payments, awards, or exemption from taxes, shall conduct any
experiments, treatments, research, or other work that involves
stem cells from any source. All stem cells in the possession of
any such organization or entity shall be reported to the Centers
for Disease Control of the Department of Homeland Security,
and shall be surrendered upon demand.
Signed: Edward March
President, United States of America
Commander-in-Chief

The medical team listened as the lead doctor read the order.

"What does this mean for Sarah?"

"Unless the cells we've already injected continue to grow, she will remain a paraplegic. It's unlikely they will do so."

"But we're so close!"

"March issued this order as a sop to the OTCC. It's part of the thirty pieces of silver he must pay them for his election. Sarah's mother is a member of an OTCC church. She believes in miracles. Let her pray. Our hands are tied."

~~~~~

Oval Office, The White House, Washington, DC

President March set aside the fifteenth of the pens he had used to sign the latest executive order and looked up from his desk.

"It is done," he said.

"Rejoice," Pastor Fallow said. "Rejoice in the Lord, those who do His works on this Earth."

Executive Office of the President
Executive Order 003

Effective immediately, no organization or entity of any nature that receives funds from the United States Government or any agency or part thereof, whether through grants, contracts, payments, awards, or exemption from taxes shall perform any kind of abortion of any type at any time during a pregnancy, including the administration of the so-called "morning after" pills, abortion disguised as "dilation and curettage," installation of any intrauterine device, and any other procedure designed in any way to terminate a pregnancy before birth, nor shall birth-control pills be prescribed or dispensed.

Signed: Edward March
President, United States of America
Commander-in-Chief

One witness did not rejoice. Lieutenant Colonel Casey Stewart stood in a corner, holding the "football," a large briefcase, often called a navigator's bag. His mind wasn't on the briefcase, but on what he had seen and heard. *This may be within the letter of the law. He's the chief executive, and the commander-in-chief. He can give the orders he's given. But they contradict law, Supreme Court decisions, and the Constitution. We both swore to protect and defend the Constitution, but he's undermining it.*

<p align="center">~~~~~</p>

Roe vs. Wade Voided

Mercy Otis Warren Blog, darknet. President March has bypassed the Supreme Court and the Congress to outlaw all abortion at any hospital that accepts federal funds. Given the broad reach of Medicare and Medicaid, there's not a hospital in the nation that doesn't get federal funds. Look for rich young women flying to Switzerland and a run on coat hangers in poor neighborhoods.

~~~~~

Pentagon, Room M23R7, Brotherhood of Mithras

"Does anyone wonder why the president signs every executive order as *commander in chief* rather than *president* or *chief executive?*"

"I assume the question is rhetorical," a lieutenant said.

"I agree, but how do you interpret it?" the general asked.

"He plans on declaring martial law, at some point," the lieutenant answered.

"I think you are correct," the general said. "Meanwhile, how do we react to these executive orders?"

"They are a mix of constitutional powers, extra-legal powers, and blatantly illegal assumptions," a captain said.

"As Commander-in-Chief, he has the authority to prohibit women from serving in positions over men, even though this is inconsistent with legislation that permits women to serve in any role in the military."

"He has control of the budgets and activities of executive branch agencies, and can order them not to spend money for abortions or stem-cell research."

"He is planning to issue orders restricting immigration and intake of refugees, and blame it on Ebola."

"Congress has more power than the president to regulate immigrants, but his declaration of a medical emergency and an imminent threat would be difficult to overturn—even if this Congress were interested in challenging him."

"Perhaps we can do a little lobbying of our own.

"What say you all?"

The current health care system
is neither healthy, caring,
nor a system.
Anonymous

White House, Oval Office

"It has been a long battle," President March said as he put down the last of the pens he'd used to sign the bill, "but this is the end of Obama-care. No nation can consider itself great if it cannot provide basic health care for its citizens, and this bill ensures that. It allows everyone a window-of-grace to get insurance from private insurers, without saddling those companies with the requirement to cover pre-existing conditions for those who have deferred buying insurance. It removes the requirements for the healthy to subsidize the sick."

And it eliminates subsidies for those who cannot pay for health insurance. It eliminates the mandate for employers to provide health insurance. It throws millions of people into the Medicaid pot but reduces payments for Medicaid. Lieutenant Colonel Casey Stewart remained still, but inwardly shook his head at the disconnect between what the president said and what the bill said.

~~~~~

Women's and Children's Hospital, _____ County, Texas

"Ms. Davis, I'm sorry, but it's clear. Your baby is a hyper-micro-encephalic. There's no—"

"What'n thunder does that mean?" the girl's father demanded.

"The baby has no brain, and its head is the size of, well, about the size of a tennis ball. The child cannot survive outside of her womb. It may take a breath or two, but it will die within minutes of being born. I'm sorry. I don't know an easier way to say it."

"You gots to get it outta me!" the girl whimpered. "You gotta! It's not my baby!"

"Who is the father?" the doctor asked for perhaps the hundredth time.

The girl looked at her father before answering.

"It's Jethro's."

"You mean the boy from across the holler?" her father asked.

"No, Daddy. I mean your brother."

"Son of a—" the father began. Either he decided not to denigrate his own mother, or was too angry to speak.

"Take it out, doctor. I'll sign the damn paper. Girl-child, you and I will go to hell for this if we don't do a powerful lot of prayin'."

~~~~~

&highflyer/&reddragon raid planned on abortion at womens and childrens hospital _____ county texas can u stop

&reddragon/&highflyer r u sure

&highflyer/&reddragon yes intercept official traffic

&reddragon/&highflyer will notify those who might help

~~~~~

"Everything is ready, doctor," the charge nurse said.

The doctor, the charge nurse, the anesthesiologist, and the girl were the only ones in the operating room. The girl's father was at home, drunk. Her mother hadn't been around for years.

The charge nurse lifted the girl's legs into the stirrups. The doctor stepped into position. Before the anesthesiologist could act, the door of the operating room slammed open.

"Stop what you are doing and step away. Keep your hands where we can see them. You all are under arrest." The four men's uniforms were black. Bloused trousers tucked into boots. Black gloves covered hands. Badges identified them: Department of Homeland Security, National Institutes of Health, Enforcement Division.

They did not have arrest powers, but that did not stop these people, and no one on the hospital staff had the courage to challenge their authority, or their guns.

There were, however, those who did—challenge their authority, that is. The door to the operating room opened again. Silencers muffled a handful of shots. The DHS enforcers dropped.

"Please continue your work, Doctor," a rescuer said. "The room may no longer be sterile, but it is secure."

The doctor nodded. He looked at the anesthesiologist, and received confirmation.

The people who cleaned the operating room that evening were not too surprised at the amount of blood they found, and the pathology department had no difficulty disposing of the bodies.

The coroner ruled the shooting death of Jethro by two shotgun blasts to his chest to be justifiable homicide. In this part of the country, "he done needed killin" was still an acceptable defense.

~~~~~

"We must make laws
to make people good."
—From D. W. Griffith's film, *Intolerance*
1916 C.E.

Sharia Law Hits USA

The World Citizen. "Didn't take long for March to show his true colors. Not waiting for Congress, he issued executive orders to remove women from all command positions in the US military, and to ban any federal funding for any procedure resembling an abortion and for stem cell research. These executive orders were not publicized, but sent only through government and military channels. Hard to keep something like this a secret, though. Wonder what other surprises are in store?

"This is Muldoon: Democracy cannot operate in the dark, and darkness is falling."

~~~~~

The White House, Oval Office

"Birkino Faso? Do they even have an airport?" President March asked.

"Sir, I—" Mel began.

"Never mind. Get this to the Pentagon, FAA, Coast Guard . . . haven't we put them under the Navy, yet? When are we going to? . . . And, Mel, get the press releases going. It's going to hit the fan when people find out about this. Maybe we can beat Muldoon to the punch for once."

Executive Office of the President
Executive Order 004
Effective immediately in order to protect this Nation from the ravages of Ebola no flight, ship, or passenger originating in any of the following countries shall be allowed to land, dock, overfly, or navigate the waters of the United States of America: Liberia, Sierra Leone, Guinea, Nigeria, Mali, Burkino Faso, Ghana.

Signed: Edward March
President, United States of America
Commander-in-Chief

~~~~~

The White House, Oval Office

"Mr. President, the congressional delegation has arrived." Mel Appleton had briefed President March on the likely subject: a constitutional convention. He'd also briefed Warwick, who confirmed his approval.

The delegation looked to Freshman Representative Thomas Vaughn.

"Mr. President, now is the time. You are familiar with the expression, 'in politics what is permissible is limited only by what is possible.' In other words, we are limited only to what we can get away with."

None of the others had ever heard this expressed so clearly, so openly, and so boldly. Even President March was stunned, but only for a moment.

"You and I and the others here understand what you mean," March said. "Please, speak plainly."

"Some of your Executive Orders can be challenged on constitutional grounds," Thomas Vaughn said. "Not only the orders you have issued, but also some you plan to issue."

If anyone had any question about how Thomas Vaughn knew about unreleased executive orders, they remained silent.

"Several potential amendments to the Constitution will have widespread popular support. We and our allies in the OTCC will create support for the others. Clarification of the relationship between church and state including churches' tax exemption, clarification of gun ownership rights, denying automatic citizenship to children of illegals who slip into this country to pop out anchor babies like Pez, and restricting immigration are perhaps the most important of those amendments.

"There are other amendments needed—those relating to income tax, to *Posse Comitatus*, to the presidential succession, to martial law. Those can be passed under the aegis of the first set."

Thomas Vaughn sat silently. He had said what needed to be said. He had said what each of these men wanted, albeit for different reasons. He had done his job. They would have to work out their differences.

Mel Appleton, President March, and Representative Stafford all smiled inwardly. *The boy did well*, each man thought. *And he's mine . . . my creature. No one else could have created this opportunity. The only question is, 'where next'?*

By this time, Lieutenant Colonel Casey Stewart had become, in the eyes of most visitors to the Oval Office, a part of the furniture. They paid him no more attention than they would a chair.

~~~~~

Burglars at the Door

The World Citizen. "The AFFP—the *Always Fund Friends Party*—is digging into the treasury to pay back their campaign supporters and line their own pockets. This morning, the *Washington Banner* reported the Senate approved an amendment to the budget that would strip funding from the United States Geological Survey. The Senate amendment will certainly make it through the reconciliation process.

"The former president's budget for the USGS was $1.1 billion which would have supported research on climate change, the effects of fracking, and earth sciences. Not only is science being defunded, but the money has become a honey pot from which the AFFP can award research grants to pseudo-scientists and energy companies.

"This is Muldoon. God exists only where people believe in him; the truths of science exists whether you believe in them or not. Think about it."

~~~~~

House Dining Room, Washington, DC

Members of the House of Representatives had become accustomed to seeing Henry Stafford, their speaker, and Thomas Vaughn, one of their most junior members, together in the House Dining Room. Although the chefs there did not know the secret of the Senate Dining Room's famous bean soup, the House was proud of its gumbo. Both men at the table had ordered a bowl.

"Gumbo needs thickening," Stafford said.

"My family's chef uses okra," Vaughn replied. "It is easier to get than the *filé* root which is more traditional."

The men's conversation was casual until their entrées were delivered.

"Your notion of a senate-called constitutional convention has passed muster," Stafford said. "The Senate will vote, tomorrow. The results are assured. I will announce your chairmanship. Are you ready for this?"

"Yes, sir. I am."

Thomas Vaughn thanked his host for the meal, but not for the announcement. He offered no obeisance other than the obligatory *sir*. He knew he held the political high ground. Not the moral high ground, but that wasn't important. In fact, it wasn't even relevant.

~~~~~

Market Drop

New York Afterword. The collapse of the health care sector, blamed on the repeal of *Obama Care*, tumbled the entire market today before automated programs shut down trading on the New York exchange. The move is being followed by exchanges worldwide.

~~~~~

> "An important art of politicians
> is to find new names for institutions
> which under old names
> have become odious to the public."
> —Talleyrand 1754—1838 C.E.

What's in a Name?

The World Citizen. "We have word the enforcers from the Department of Homeland Security will get arrest powers and a new job title—*Public Safety Officers.* Mussolini had his brown shirts, and Hitler called his black-shirted goons, the Protection Squadron or *Schutzstaffel* which we know as the *SS.* Remember them? And the *SS-Totenkopfverbande?* You don't have to know a lot of German to know *toten* means dead, and *kopf* means head, and *totenkopf* means skull, which was their symbol, the last thing seen by millions of people on the way to their deaths in the extermination camps operated by the *SS-Totenkopfverbande.*

"This is Muldoon. How did Germany get to that point? Through an insidious erosion of both rights and the rule of law. Look around, people. It's happening to you, too."

~~~~~

Mt. Pleasant, Georgia Public Library

The man in the black trench coat hadn't stood on line with the other patrons, but had marched to the circulation desk. The library employee saw this, but remained polite. "May I help you, sir?"

"I require the checkout records of this person for the past three years," the man said, and handed the woman a piece of paper with a name written on it.

"I'm sorry, sir, but I cannot give you that information," the woman said.

The man showed her a badge and an ID card. *Department of Homeland Security.*

288

"I'm sorry sir, I still cannot give you that information. Please, let me call my super—"

"Young woman, unless you want to be taken for interrogation, you will use that computer behind which you are standing to call up these records."

"Sir, I don't think you've been listening. I didn't say I *would not* give you the information; I said, *I cannot*. The information does not exist. Checkout records are erased once an item is returned. The only information on the computer shows what items are currently checked out."

"I will find out if you are lying, Miss—" the man stared at the woman's nametag. "—Miss Berkshire. If you are, you will be arrested." The man turned and left the library.

~~~~~

"The library will be closed from
February 21 until February 25
for installation of new software."
Announcement posted at
all libraries in the State of Georgia

"They just did a software update in January. What's this for?" Ms. Berkshire asked her supervisor.

"Don't tell anyone where you heard this, but DHS has ordered us to track every book everyone has checked out from the day they got their library card."

"Can they do that? Is it legal?"

"Maybe not, but this comes from the state. The Federal Government sends a lot of money to the state. Of course, it's just our tax money coming back to us after everyone up the line dips into the pot to pay themselves. We never see it at our level."

~~~~~

Mt. Pleasant, Home of Mr. and Mrs. Jason Carter

Mrs. Carter was kneeling in a flowerbed when two neatly dressed young men approached. They had a car, not bicycles. *Not Mormons,* she thought. They stopped a polite distance away.

"Mrs. Carter? Mrs. Jason Carter?" one asked.

"Yes, I am."

"Ma'am, you have a Hispanic woman clean for you."

"Yes, I do. What of it? Who are you?"

"Does she have a green card," the second young man asked, ignoring Mrs. Carter's question.

"Of course not. She's a US citizen."

"Have you seen proof?"

"No. I don't need—"

The first young man interrupted. "You must complete a Form INS-9 at City Hall to include a copy of a green card, an alien registration form, or proof of US citizenship. This will require a birth certificate and a social security card, or a Georgia drivers license."

"Are you going to arrest me if I don't?" Mrs. Carter had gotten angry.

"We're from the Investigating Committee, Mrs. Carter. We do not have arrest powers."

Yet, the second young man thought.

"What's going on here?" It was a man's voice.

"Are you Mr. Jason Carter?"

"Yes, and you two will get off my property instantly and stop harassing my wife!" The man walked down the steps toward the two young men.

"Back off, Mr. Carter," one said. He put his hand on a box on his belt. It looked like a pouch for a cell phone. "If I press this button, my location and a distress call will go to the 911 Center. Police will be here in less than three minutes."

"You can make it easy on yourselves by hiring an American company. One examined and approved by the Investigating Committee. There is a list at City Hall."

The young men left, walking quickly.

"What in blazes was that all about?" Mr. Carter asked his wife. She shook her head.

~~~~~

A New Intifada

The World Citizen. "In a move designed both to garner support for themselves, and to spark the next Intifada, Israeli Zionists have destroyed the Dome of the Rock, the third most sacred site in Islam. The explosion, felt more than twenty miles away, leveled the top of the hill that has become a flash point in Israeli-Islamic relations.

"'We will no longer be prohibited from prayer and ritual at the site of Solomon's Temple, and soon we will rebuild the Temple' said Arvid Messenger, a self-proclaimed spokesperson for an ultra-conservative Zionist movement. 'For too long our so-called leaders have placated those who would destroy us. No more!'

"From Palestine, Intifada has been declared. Some people in Israel are prepared for this, even looking forward to it. This is Muldoon. Who is the puppet, and who is pulling the strings? Think about it."

~~~~~

Mt. Pleasant City Hall

A woman whose hard and care-worn appearance belied her youth stood at the window.

"Can I help you?" the man behind the glass asked.

"Yes, please. I, well, I clean houses for people and I guess I have to register here?"

"Information packet B-17. In the rack beside the window."

"Oh my," the woman said while she flipped through the packet. "This is an awful lot of paper."

"Do I know you?" the man asked. "What church do you attend?"

"There's only One True Christian Church," the woman said.

"Sorry, which congregation?"

"Resurrection, just up the highway."

"Yeah. That's where I seen you. Listen, just get Pastor Dorset to call me with a Recommend, and we can skip all the paperwork except, let's see, this one and this one."

~~~~~

Mt. Pleasant Super-Duper Market

"Are you the manager?"

"Yes, I am," the woman said. "How can I make your shopping a pleasure?"

"On Aisle 13, you display books, including those with lurid covers. I believe they are called *Romance Novels*." The young man and his companion blushed.

"Why, yes, you are correct. How can I help you?"

"We are from the Subcommittee of Rectitude of the Investigating Committee of the One True Christian Church," the young man said. "We require the covers of these books not be visible to children."

"What? You've got to be kidding me. Come on, boys. What's your question?"

"We are not kidding, Mrs."—the boy stared at the woman's name-badge—"Mrs. Clampert. You would be well advised to do as we require. If so, this visit may be kept friendly and unofficial."

The boys turned and marched away from the open-mouthed store manager.

" . . . not I, but the Lord [commands],
let not the husband put away his wife.
Except if the husband is an unbeliever,
in which case he may depart."
—Matthew 19:6

Take 'Em to the Wire with Bert Rightly

There was only one guest on Bert Rightly's *Take 'Em to the Wire* program, but he was the new political icon, especially for the younger voters. Rhode Island Representative Thomas Vaughn sat comfortably while Bert started the program and then cut to the hot topic of the day.

"Treason is no longer the only crime defined in the Constitution. Delegates from several southern states have convinced the Constitutional Committee that sodomy statutes need to be included. A compromise was reaches when adultery was included as a crime, and civil divorce was prohibited except for fornication."

"Mr. Vaughn, I think we all can agree the government should prohibit the perversions defined by the sodomy laws and should prohibit adultery, but what's the deal on divorce?"

"Bert, when marriage was a rite of the church, spelled *r-i-t-e*, then marriage and divorce were church matters. However, nowadays, the government grants certain rights, spelled *r-i-g-h-t-s* and levies certain obligations on married couples. Marriage is now a contract sanctioned by the government. One cannot break a contract on a whim; therefore, divorce must also pass the muster of the state."

~~~~~

WhatDrWho Blog

People whose superstitions rule their minds are capable of twists of illogic that stupefy the enlightened.

Representative Vaughn claims when marriage was a r-i-t-e of the church, the church could call the shots, but when the government stepped in, and granted r-i-g-h-t-s and levied obligations on married couples, the government had a say in marriage and divorce.

Let's look at this closely. As long as marriage was a rite of the church, the church could say who could be married and who couldn't. When the government got involved, then under the equal protection clause of the constitution, the government could no longer deny the right to marry to same-sex couples. That's how the Supreme Court ruled in 2015.

The good people of Kentucky plan to require a note from a man's wife before he can buy Viagra. Now, the AFFP and their puppet-masters in the OTCC plan to be in your bedroom by putting anti-sodomy provisions in the constitution. That's a reversal of the Supreme Court. How long before they think to reverse other Supreme Court decisions?

This is WhatDrWho blogging from exile.

~~~~~

Office of the Director, Department of Homeland Security

"What should we do about this *Science Guide*? After we cut off the earthquake data from Japan and South Africa, he got a bunch of kids fired up again, and they're making waves."

"You will do nothing." The voice on the speakerphone was anonymous, but everyone knew it held power. The voice continued.

"We have traced the internet addresses of the children who raised this issue. From there, we have found thirteen teachers who are teaching from their own beliefs, and not from the approved *No Child* curriculum. Nine were arrested and examined by local Investigating Committees; the others will be treated likewise. We will find more who have been drawn in by our plans. You will take no action."

The line cut off. The Director looked at her staff. "You heard," she said.

~~~~~

The White House, Cabinet Room

"We must have greater control of the internet," Mel said. He didn't say who *we* were. *Let them think they are included*, he thought.

His orders came from Richard Warwick, who was chafing at the traffic criticizing the March administration. Mel knew that *we* included Warwick. *And the OTCC?* Mel wondered. *No, Trucido knows the importance of Fallow's broadcasts, and Fallow probably doesn't understand the internet beyond what it does for him. President March may think he's in control, but it will really be Warwick.*

Mel had prepared the president for this topic. The president picked up the ball.

"We need one chief. Now, there are at least five: Defense, your Information Systems people; NSA, you have your tentacles deep in the whole communications infrastructure; NASA, you're tying comm satellites together; and FCC has oversight over commercial networks. How did the previous administrations allow critical nodes at libsymp universities, like those California schools? Don't answer. I know the reason—the internet was a joint effort between Defense and universities. But it's grown up, now. It's a critical component of national security.

"I want one chief, and I want plans to ensure complete control. Do not release this to anyone.

"The chief will be the Director of Homeland Security. I will transfer control of NSA and its budget to Homeland. Legislation to transfer the FCC and NASA will be introduced tomorrow. We'll find a other way to handle the universities."

Mel looked around the room and saw shock and awe.

Shock and awe, Mel thought. *Buzz words from Bush II's lying campaign in the Middle East. George W had to prove a particular part of his anatomy was bigger than his father's. Didn't work, but who remembers that, now? And who cares? March doesn't.*

〜〜〜〜〜

Mt. Pleasant, Georgia, Parson Family Drug Store

"You must remove those things from open display." After he said that, the young man's lips tightened.

"You mean the condoms?" the pharmacist asked.

"They are an abomination unto the Lord," the young man said.

"They also prevent STDs—sexually transmitted diseases," the druggist said. *And unwanted pregnancies,* he thought. *But I suspect you don't want to hear that.*

"You shall remove them from view. You may continue to sell them to persons age twenty-one or greater. Anyone who purchases condoms must sign a registry. You will provide a copy of the registry to the Investigating Committee."

The pharmacist was accustomed to government regulations, not only for the more serious drugs he provided, but also for things like pseudoephedrine—precursor of *hillbilly crack.* But condoms? The order the young man handed the pharmacist was clear. And it was signed by the mayor.

Can't see the truth if it were in front of them, the pharmacist thought. *Georgia is 8ᵗʰ in the USA in the number of people who claim to be Protestant Christians, but it's also sixth in HIV, third in syphilis, and sixth in gonorrhea according to the Gallup Poll people and the Centers for Disease Control. And these people want to ban condoms.* He shook his head, and began to pull down the display.

OTCC General Handbook of Instruction for Disciples

6.4.3 The Sin of Onan (Genesis 38:9) displeased the Lord, and the Lord slew Onan. Onan sinned in three ways. The first was masturbation. He spilled his seed on the ground rather than engage in normal intercourse. Masturbation is an abomination in the sight of the Lord. Onan's second sin was engaging in a sexual activity other than normal intercourse for the purpose of procreation. That too is an abomination. Finally, he was disobedient to the Lord's command that he father a child upon his widowed sister-in-law.

When presenting this topic or answering questions on it, you shall emphasize the first two points. If boys ask questions about nocturnal emissions, you will answer that they are the result of evil thoughts, and that the boy must pray for forgiveness and strength to avoid them.

Rudy Adams, Guelph, Ontario

Dad handed me the Handbook. "Rudy, would you read this paragraph and tell me what you think about it?

I read the first three sentences before saying, "Dad! I shouldn't be reading stuff like this!"

"Come on Rudy, I'm the one who does the laundry around here."

I was blushing and so embarrassed I couldn't say anything.

"Rudy, do we need to talk about this, again?"

"Um, no Dad. You said it was normal."

"Then will you read the paragraph, and perhaps write something about it?"

tardisboy Blog: The Sin of Onan

In the King James Bible, Onan's sin was not masturbation, but failing in his duty to father a child for his widowed sister-in-law. The OTCC has rewritten Genesis 38:7-10 to suit their own views: that masturbation is evil. I wonder if they're enforcing Leviticus15:16-17 that says if a guy has a wet dream, he has to bathe but is still unclean until nightfall. They sure don't say anything about that in their handbook.

The OTCC's Handbook for Propagandizing Children is pretty clear that they believe masturbation is not only evil, but an abomination and a sin.

Is the Sin of Onan a Sin? The DHS hasn't deleted this information from the old CDC website, yet, so you can check it out for yourself.

Every man's ejaculation includes as many as 200 million sperm cells.

Even if—and that's a big if—one of those sperm finds its way into an egg, then 199,999,999 sperm die. How does that square with the sin of Onan?

If anyone is a sinner, it is god. According to the creationists, he is responsible for making sure that fewer than one in two hundred million of his children might survive.

If the creationists can make claims without any facts, then I can, too. Here's the final word: God wanted boys to masturbate, so he gave them opposable thumbs.

This is tardisboy, blogging from exile.

~~~~~

"I order therefore . . . that women
adorn themselves in modest apparel, . . .
not with braided hair, or gold, or pearls, or costly array;
but that which becometh women
professing godliness . . . "
I Timothy 2:8-9

Mt. Pleasant, Georgia Home of Mr. and Mrs. Bainard

Mrs. Bainard opened the door, expecting to see one of her neighbors. Instead, a young man and a young woman greeted her. They wore what Mrs. Bainard thought of as *Sunday-go-to-meeting* clothes, although the woman's looked old fashioned, even dowdy. She frowned. The neighborhood had a phone tree to warn one another of Mormon and Seventh Day Adventist missionaries. Someone should have called.

"I didn't think you could, what do you call it, *proselytize* any more," she said.

"Good morning, Mrs. Bainard," the young man said. That was odd. The missionaries didn't usually know her name.

"I am Elder Sampson," he continued. "And we are not proselytizing. We are from the Committee of Rectitude of the Investigating Committee of the One True Christian Church of Mt. Pleasant. You are the mother of Becky Bainard."

Mrs. Bainard put her hand to her mouth. The young man's words became jumbled in her mind.

"Has something happened to Becky? She's at school. What's happened!" she said.

"Your daughter is in violation of the school dress code. She is held by the Director of Rectitude. She has been covered with a robe from the school choir until you can remove her."

"You're not making sense! What are you saying?"

"Your daughter's clothes were inappropriate and immodest and displayed too much of her flesh and lower limbs." The young man stuttered, but then spoke more firmly. "She was in violation of the standards of decency established by the dress code."

Mrs. Bainard's mind slowly organized the jumble of information and correlated it with what her friend Regina had said a few weeks ago. Mt. Pleasant Christian and Resurrection Baptist—the two largest fundamentalist churches in Mt. Pleasant—had merged under the banner of the One True Christian Church. Members of older and more mainstream congregations were abandoning their churches and flocking to the two mega-churches. Both had expanded their schedules, and each offered three services on Sunday.

"What have you got to do with the school? What ever happened to separation of church and state?" Mrs. Bainard asked.

The young man was well prepared. He had memorized the answer. "The Bureau of Education of the Department of Homeland Security has mandated that communities take greater responsibility for their children's education. Local school boards have contracted the Church to enforce policies of the School Board including the dress code and other matters of behavior and discipline. When acting in this capacity, we are agents of the government—the School Board. There is no conflict between Church and State."

"Oh." Mrs. Bainard said. "Oh." She couldn't think of anything else to say.

"Mrs. Bainard, you or your husband must remove Becky Bainard from the school immediately and return her dressed in compliance with the dress code. The Office of Rectitude can explain the code to you. Do you understand, and will you comply?"

"Uh, yes, of course. Right away."

~~~~~

" . . . know ye not that your body is the temple of the
Holy Ghost which is in you . . . ?"
I Corinthians 6:19

House Chambers, Constitutional Convention

"Desecration of those who have passed to their Heavenly Reward must cease. Autopsies, removal of organs and tissue for experimentation and transplantation. These are anathema." Representative Pyle's argument was fervid to the point of being fevered. However, it was fear of the power he represented, the power of the One True Christian Church that swayed the Constitutional Convention.

~~~~~

New Dark Ages

The World Citizen. "The Dark Ages began when Christians burned the pagan Library of Alexandria. In Europe, during the Dark Ages, prayer, incantations, potions made from

300

excrement, and hopes for miracles were the only form of medicine available. Medical research, including dissection of cadavers, was prohibited.

"If Representative Pyle has his way, what is left of the American health care system after the collapse earlier this year will descend into superstition and darkness.

"This is Muldoon, stocking up on aspirin before it is outlawed."

~~~~~

"The power to tax
[is] the power to destroy."
Chief Justice John Marshall
1819 C.E.

Mt. Pleasant, Georgia Office of *The Clarion*

"Didn't take them long to fire back," Junior Mabry said. He folded the single sheet of paper into an airplane, and sailed it toward his partner, who was also his wife.

The woman snagged the plane from the air, unfolded it, and frowned. "It's just the County's annual tax assess—

"Oh, my gerbils!" she interrupted her own words. "It's gone from three hundred thousand to seventy million dollars? This dump? Sorry Junior, but you know it is a dump."

"I know, and the assessment is bogus. We'll spend time and money appealing. We'll lose."

~~~~~

Buckhead Mall, Atlanta, Georgia

The salesman moved to the next display. "This model has a longer battery life. That's important for school kids who don't always have a place to plug in. It has the same parental control software, and a better wifi receiver."

"What's different about the wifi?" the customer asked.

"Greater, what they call Q-value. Able to distinguish between multiple signals in a crowded place—like an apartment complex or a classroom. And receives more frequencies. And it's only $299 more than the other model."

"Sold," the man said, and pulled out a credit card.

"I'll need to see a Georgia driver's license, too," the salesman said.

"Sure . . . can't be too careful with credit cards, even with the new chip."

"It's not that, sir. Computer serial number and identifier have to be registered with Homeland Security . . . can't have terrorists using computers, can we?" The salesman was nervous. So far, no one had objected to this requirement, but he knew there would be a first time, and he would lose a sale. The customer frowned, but handed over his driver's license.

~~~~~

Editorial

Mt. Pleasant Clarion, Georgia. In their rush to destroy *The Clarion*, the City of Mt. Pleasant has condemned our office building in favor of a developer who promises to build yet another fast-chicken joint and add a handful of minimum wage jobs and more congestion to the traffic that already stalls movement on the thoroughfare.

The city and the county have not played well together for years. Now it seems they're not even talking to one another. The county has assessed the property at $70,000,000. We accept the city's offer to purchase the property at the county's assessed value.

Junior Mabry, Owner and Editor

~~~~~

House Chambers, Constitutional Convention

"Folks, the flap about the value of pi has made it from Dayton, Tennessee to the national media. Let me assure you, that the story that the Tennessee State Legislature tried by law to change the value of pi to three is not true." The speaker was a senior representative from Tennessee.

"What is true is that courts in Tennessee, Louisiana, and elsewhere in this nation have ruled that Creation Science may not be taught in our schools, but that the *theory* of evolution must be taught. We've heard scientists defend theories, but when it boils down, they're only theories.

"I hereby introduce a clause in the new Constitution of these United States of America that requires all competing explanations for the origin of the universe and the origin of life to be taught alongside one another in our schools."

The clause was approved by a vote of 430 to five.

~~~~~

It's Only a Theory

World Citizen. "When someone says that evolution is only a theory, it should be clear that they don't understand what is meant by *theory*. For science, a theory is the best possible explanation for observations and facts. The theory of evolution has been tested repeatedly, and so far, there have been no factual challenges that have stood up to examination.

"The alternatives proposed by Xtian fundamentalists include creationism (sometimes called by the oxymoron, 'creation science') and intelligent design. There are no facts that support either of these. However evolution, as the most logical explanation for life on Earth, is supported by the sciences of physics, chemistry, biology, embryology, paleontology, geology and half-a-dozen other –ologies.

"This is Muldoon. Before you comment on science, be sure you know what you're talking about."

Theme Park Closed by Riot Police

The World Citizen. "The so-called 'gay day' at the largest theme park in Orlando, Florida was halted today. Riot police and agents from the Department of Homeland Security, Bureau of Rectitude, backed up by US Army forces in armored personnel carriers, crashed the gates and began indiscriminately rounding up people, shackling them in plastic tie-ties, and tossing them in the back of paddy wagons. The DHS claims there was a 'credible terrorist threat' against the park, and the terrorists included, in their words, 'US citizens who have become radicalized.'

"This is Muldoon. Remember, *people driven by fear choose stability over freedom.* I wish I'd said it first. Think about it."

~~~~~

Appointments of Note

Army Bugle. General Robert Brackenbury has been named Commander of Carlisle Barracks, Pennsylvania. General Brackenbury's great-great-grandfather was a sergeant at Carlisle Arsenal in 1860. He served with Lt. Roger Jones, noted for setting fire to the Federal Arsenal at Harper's Ferry on April 19, 1861, to keep it from Confederate forces.

~~~~~

Mt. Pleasant, Georgia, Library

"There are four hundred books missing. I don't understand. We expect some *shrinkage* from people who simply fail to check out books and some from outright theft, but four hundred in the past month. It doesn't make sense."

"May I see the list?" the Adult Services Librarian said. She scanned the list and felt a sick sensation in her stomach. *Books about science, evolution, cosmology, geology, paleontology. And Sam Harris's 'Letter to a Christian Nation,'*

Mark Twain's 'Letters from Planet Earth,' Ambrose Bierce, 'Fahrenheit 451,' 'To Kill a Mockingbird.' I guess I can understand Lenny Bruce, but I still don't like it. Banned books. Books that challenge the fundamentalists' beliefs. Banned by theft—the coward's version of book burning. The Nazis have returned, only now they're hiding behind the Bible.

Ray Bradbury's 'Fahrenheit 451 was named for the temperature at which paper burns. If the fundies have their way, we're headed for an 800-degree Earth, the Venus syndrome. Do they really think they can stop that by stealing books?

~~~~~

Headquarters, Soldiers of the Cross, Lynchburg, Virginia

The Director General's question caught the staff by surprise. "What do we know about this Brackenbury?"

Two members of the staff looked around the table, hoping the other would speak first. Finally, one of them spoke.

"Sir, old-line military family. Father, grandfather, uncles served. West Point graduate."

"Church member?" the Director General asked.

"Don't know, sir. I'll find out."

"Why do you know him?"

"Served under him in Afghanistan, sir. He seemed to be an effective leader."

"Keep an eye on him. Carlisle has been strategic since the French and Indian Wars. The northeast is volatile."

"Yes, sir." The major nodded. Others on the staff wondered what the Director General's concern was, but no one dared to ask.

~~~~~

Mt. Pleasant, Georgia High School Auditorium

No one said anything about the new uniforms of the cheerleaders. The girls were wearing long skirts that reached their ankles. Under the skirts were long leggings to conceal their legs when they twirled. Their blouses were loose, and long-sleeved. The only visible parts of their bodies were their faces and their hands.

The cheers were the same, but the student body's enthusiasm seemed muted.

~~~~~

An educated and informed public
is the crooked politician's worst enemy.
—Anonymous

House Chamber, Constitutional Convention

"School teachers unions and libsymps have used the First Amendment to suppress school vouchers to allow parents to take control of their children's education. The teachers are simply trying to protect their jobs; the libsymps want to drag education down to the level of the lowest achiever." The speech of the Congresswoman from Alabama was impassioned. Although Alabama schools were among the worst in the nation, she was a Congresswoman; therefore, what she said was deemed correct.

A provision to require governments at all levels to funnel seventy-five percent of schools' budgets to parents as vouchers became part of the new constitution.

Public Schools' Death Knell

The World Citizen. "The Unconstitutional Convention has guaranteed the destruction of the public school system by requiring that 75% of school funding be paid in vouchers issued to parents. The math is simple: public schools will have their funding cut to 25% of the current levels. The vouchers are not enough to pay a child's tuition. Only parents with disposable income will be able to send their kids to the private academies and magnet schools that will receive most of the education dollars. Students of poor parents will be relegated to schools that will implode from lack of funding.

"The first public school in this Nation was the Boston Latin School, which was open to boys from all socio-economic backgrounds. The school was started by the Puritans in part to keep these young men occupied and out of trouble. The irony of the Nation's public school system now being destroyed in the name of religion is lost on today's OTCC and their lackeys in the Congress.

"This is Muldoon. 'Education is a weapon whose effect depends on who holds it in his hands . . . ' Joseph Stalin said that. The voucher program is a weapon aimed at the hearts and minds of this nation. Think about it."

~~~~~

&highflyer/&reddragon why otcc getting away with all this

&reddragon/&highflyer people would rather believe pleasant lie than uncomfortable truth that why so many people in church

~~~~~

Permafrost Melt Increases

UK Voice World Service. The joint British-Norwegian expedition to reindeer country has returned with disturbing news. Permafrost across the top of the world is melting faster than ever. The melt exposes tonnes of organic matter that decays, releasing carbon dioxide into the atmosphere, increasing the level of that greenhouse gas. Reports from Canada and Alaska provide similar information. Russia is silent, and has refused to allow western scientists to visit, claiming they would be spying on Russia's oil and gas exploration.

The lead investigator says that the added carbon dioxide will trap more heat and encourage additional melting. This positive feedback would create a run-away greenhouse effect and an 800-degree atmosphere, the Venus-syndrome.

~~~~~

Mt. Pleasant, Georgia City Council Meeting

"The next agenda item is a proposal to change the name of this city from 'Mt. Pleasant' to 'Mt. Zion.' What does the staff have to say?"

"Mr. Mayor, the name change is not a difficult thing. A resolution by the council will begin a process to be undertaken by the staff. It will involve filings with the state legislature and the Secretary of State for corporations." The voice of the City Manager droned. After five minutes, there was no one save himself who had any idea what he was saying.

"Any questions?" he concluded twenty minutes later.

"The cost?" One councilmember was still awake.

"Less than a few thousand dollars, mostly to reprint stationary and change a few signs," the city Manager said.

The motion passed 4-0. Had Councilman Ivanson been present, it would have been 4-1, but Mr. Ivanson was no longer on the council. In fact, he was no longer. Period. Everyone agreed his death at the hands of a "person or persons unknown" during a home invasion was a great tragedy, a loss to the community. His position on the council would be filled at a special election in a few months. The only candidate was a member of the AFFP and the OTCC.

~~~~~

The White House, Oval Office

"My fellow Americans, as you know when I became your president, I inherited a world in turmoil created by my predecessors' failed foreign and domestic policies. Under the previous president's leadership, an untold number of terrorists entered this country under the guise of refugee resettlement.

These terrorists have disappeared into the ghettos of major cities. Despite the heroic efforts of the Department of Homeland Security to root them out, many remain. Leaders of their so-called religion preach hatred, and seek to radicalize not only their own kind but also weak-kneed Americans, libsymps, purples, and worse.

"In order to ensure the safety and security of this Great Nation, I have taken several steps.

"First, effective immediately, the draft is re-instituted. Able-bodied young men will receive notices to report for induction into the Armed Services of the United States of America. Any male age of eighteen or older but who has not registered must do so in the next six weeks. Then, the grace period will expire.

"Legislation has been introduced under the *Posse Comitatus Act*. This will allow the Department of Homeland Security to use the Armed Forces of the United States to enforce laws and regulations under the purview of that Department.

"We have strengthened our borders with radar and other sensors. I have ordered Coast Guard command be shifted to the Navy to increase our patrol capabilities on the Great Lakes and in coastal waters. We will stop and detain anyone crossing at any point other than an authorized port of entry, and we will stop and detain anyone whose credentials our agents question. We will stop this clear and immediate danger to the United States of America.

"I do not take these steps lightly. This situation is temporary but must be faced head-on."

The light on the television camera went dark. Technicians unplugged and removed microphones and cameras. Only when that had been done and the Oval Office cleared of all but the vice president, Speaker Stafford, Senator Beasley, and Mel Appleton did President March speak.

"How many people believe this is a temporary measure?"

"Enough, Mr. President," Mel said. He sounded confident. The president raised an eyebrow.

"You and the Congress have been leading them to these decisions," Mel said. "We have controlled news from the Constitutional Convention. Everything you said today has been justified in our news outlets."

President March was the only one who knew what the next step would be. Eventually, he would have the excuse he needed to declare martial law. The only question was whether he would do that before the mid-term election or would wait until before the general election.

~~~~~

Mel Appleton walked the few steps from the Oval Office to his own office. It had been the president's private office, a workspace under previous administrations. President March hadn't wanted it. When he assigned it to Mel, he had sent a mixed message. *I want you close, but I also want you to do all the work.* That thought surfaced in Mel's mind, as well as one generated by the meeting he'd just attended. *And what work will he want, now? What is he planning? And what is Stafford planning?*

Vice President Stanley had a longer walk to his office in the Old Executive Office Building and longer time to think.

I've received a dozen invitations to Thanksgiving dinner. All from people who want to score points. The celebration would turn into a political meeting. That's not what I want for Henry and George. The staff of the VP's mansion will cater. They're drawing full salary, and I don't ask much of them. Maybe the boys would like to invite a friend or two.

Thomas Stanley had refused to move from his condo in Arlington to the vice presidential mansion on the grounds of the US Naval Observatory. It would have meant a twice-a-day commute to the Friends School for George. The Secret Service had protested. The mansion staff, afraid they would lose their jobs, protested, but less loudly. Stanley won the argument and took for himself the daily commute from Crystal City to the Old Executive Office Building or the Capitol. Stanley's neighbors hadn't complained about the background investigations, not after they saw the extra security, the emergency generators, and the value of their condos triple.

Stanley pushed aside this distraction and reviewed the president's TV appearance, and the remarks that followed. *He's up to something. What's the next logical step? Martial law? No. Too extreme. Suspend 'Habeas corpus'? Possible. The camarilla headed by Vaughn is already trying to work that into a new constitution. And Stafford has something up his sleeve, too. I wish I knew . . .*

CHAPTER 34: BIG BROTHER II

And he causes all to receive a mark:
the number of the beast.
Revelation 13:16-17

Speaker Stafford's Office, US Capitol

Biometrics money had bought an audience with the Speaker of the House. Jim and Leonard had rehearsed what they would say in the seven minutes allotted to them. As soon as they said *implantable biometric chips,* Stafford raised his hand, picked up his phone, and said to someone, "Cancel my appointments for the rest of the day."

Stafford looked at Jim and Leonard, founders and sole proprietors of Biometrics, LLC.

"Gentlemen, I want to hear more, and I want my experts in on this conversation. I trust you don't mind?"

No way your experts can to reverse engineer the chips, Jim thought. *Even if you squeeze our Chinese suppliers. It's not the chips; it's the software.*

"No, sir. No problem."

The recipients of the first shipment of implantable chips were sexual predators, released from prison after serving their sentences. Arizona was the first state to pass a law requiring parolees to receive the chip, and the state's order of five hundred Biometrics, Inc., readers and detectors was followed by thousands, as parents demanded that every school be equipped at every entrance.

~~~~~~

DHS Director's Conference Room

Polly Singer, like everyone else, set her smart phone on the conference table next to yellow pads, cheap government-issue ball point pens, and coffee cups. The difference was that Polly's phone was set to record voice input.

"The principals from Biometrics met with Speaker Stafford yesterday. He's interested in their implantable bio-identification chips. Arizona is already implanting chips in sexual predators, and putting detectors at every school in the state," an aide reported.

"Actually," the director said. "That's a good thing. The states take the lead, we come in through the back door and get access to their data bases."

"And it's just like the *stop smoking* campaign," another aide said. "We painted smokers and big tobacco as the bad guys. We start with people everyone can hate, perverts, rapists, and pedophiles. Then, we expand."

"And how far will we expand?" Polly Singer interjected. She was there to collect information for press releases, but this conversation begged a *law of unintended consequences* input.

"What's your point, Ms. Singer?" the director asked.

"Only that every action has a reaction. We must acknowledge that so that I can prepare for the reaction."

"Good point, Ms. Singer. What's the upside?"

"The upside?" Polly said. "If you put a frog in boiling water, it will try to escape. If you put a frog in lukewarm water and slowly heat the water to boiling, the frog, a cold-blooded creature, will happily remain in the water until it dies.

"The lesson is that if change is small and gradual people are more likely to accept it than if it is large and abrupt. Slow and gradual change is often the way the new normal is created.

"If DHS is to take the lead in this, DHS needs to know more about the chips and the detectors, especially their limitations. And I need to know what is planned so I can prepare for the pushback—and, if possible, anticipate it."

"Ms. Singer is correct," the director said. "The Bureau of Security has the lead, but you will keep her in the loop. The press can be our best ally, especially if we let her play them."

The White House, Oval Office

"Mr. President, this order to implant these chips in our soldiers will not be taken well." The Chairman of the Joint Chiefs stood with his legs apart for stability, and because he thought it made him seem more imposing. "Our medical people have serious concerns about infection . . . something about pushing bacteria through the skin and into the bone. They say it would be nearly impossible to control. They say they have no information on the outcome of the Arizona program. Sir, the Joint Chiefs believe this is premature."

"Sir, the FBI agrees," the director said. "These things have had far less testing than any implantable medical device in history."

The Director of Homeland Security sat calmly while the men spoke, and then she said, "I will implant the chips in more than a hundred thousand of my Public Safety Officers. I would not recommend it for them and for your people unless I thought it was safe."

"Based on what?" the Chairman asked.

"Enough, people." The president picked up a pen and signed his 129th Executive Order. "We've hashed this out before. Doctors from the DHS Bureau of Health have given their approval."

Yes, it will speed soldiers and law enforcement past security checkpoints. It will also make the job of the military's graves registration people a lot easier. But where will it go, next? Mel Appleton wondered while making copies of the executive order on acid-free paper. The original was destined for what would become the March Presidential Library.

Pentagon, Room M23R7, Brotherhood of Mithras

"Chip implants have begun. Our orders are to reach one-hundred percent in 90 days, including National Guard and Reserve units."

"Do we know the detectors' locations?"

"No, sir. DHS has convinced the president that they, alone, should decide locations. We can look, we can watch, but we don't have the resources to catch them all."

"Is there a way to disable the chip?"

"A trusted source has said that there is. The chip is powered by a radio frequency wave emitted by the detectors. Like the base of a rechargeable toothbrush. We know the frequency. A strong enough signal should burn out the chip."

"What would be the effect on the soldier?"

"A sharp pain, sir. Some heat would be generated."

"Can you reveal the source of your information?"

"Private message on the alternet—Mercy Owen Warren. Checked and rated at 98-percent."

"We are working on a chip of our own to replace the DHS chip. It would be programmed to resemble the DHS chip until we needed to change it."

"As soon as you are ready, test it on me," the general offered. "If it works, and doesn't kill me . . . well, we'll see what happens next.

"What say you all?"

≈≈≈≈

"Sugi, I can't believe what they are planning," Polly said. She had played back the recording of a meeting, which had been preserved in the cloud as a rock-and-roll song by a dead artist from Memphis.

"Eventually, they're going to put those chips in everyone, not just sexual predators, not just criminals, but everyone! And there will be detectors everywhere . . . schools, airports, train stations, shopping malls . . . national parks, probably."

"You gonna put this out?" Sugi asked.

"I already have," Polly said. "To some restricted addresses. Now, it's time for the rest of the world to know."

The Real Mark of the Beast?

Mercy Otis Warren blog, darknet. The OTCC tells us some people will receive the mark of the beast, and shall be cast into eternal fire and damnation. Odd, coming from the same church that professes *love thy neighbor*. Contradictions never seem to bother them. According to the Bible, the *number of the beast* is *666*, which shall mark the unsaved. It's from the *Revelation of John*, one of the most difficult books of the Bible to understand.

Understanding has gone out the window. The AFFP and the OTCC have decided that sinners—which means anyone they disagree with—will not be marked with a number but with a computer chip. How long before everyone, sinners or not, will be marked? Does anyone believe the OTCC and their allies in the AFFP will stop after implanting chips in criminals?

If you put a frog in boiling water, it will try to escape. If you put a frog in lukewarm water and slowly heat the water to boiling, the frog, a cold-blooded creature, will stay in the water until it dies. Please do not try this at home. It is apocryphal—it is not true. It is a parable, a story made up to teach a lesson.

The lesson is that if change is small and gradual we are more likely to accept it than if it is large and abrupt. Slow and gradual change is often how the new normal is created.

Our government is making those small changes, and we are sitting in the pot while the water gets hotter and hotter.

This is Mercy Otis Warren. Don't know who I am? Try looking me up on the internet. You won't find an answer. I've been deleted—by order of Homeland Security.

~~~~~

DHS Command Bunker, Outside Washington, DC

"Ms. Singer? We have orders to search everyone leaving the bunker." The guard was polite, but there was no question in Polly's mind he was serious.

"Of course," she said. "Purse. I'll empty my pockets on the table, if that's okay?"

"Yes, ma'am."

"Um, ma'am, this is a flash drive. They're prohibited. I'll have to ask you—"

"Sorry. It holds only the stories that have been released . . . you can check against the record . . . "

"Ma'am, I don't know anything about that. I'm gonna have to call Central Security."

"I understand. May I sit while I wait?"

"Ms. Singer, we've found the flash drive contains only press releases that have been authorized. Why do you have them?"

"If I am going to rewrite the present, I need to remember the past. If you don't understand, please ask the Director. I work for her."

~~~~~

Telecon: Mel Appleton and Polly Singer

"Christ, Mel, they're blocking all of Kennedy's statements." Polly's voice was low and calm, but there was no mistaking the steel in what she said.

"Not all, just some."

"It might as well be all of them. And who is doing this? It's an off-year election. Every Freedom Party seat is safe, including that idiot senator who still believes storms and earthquakes are *god's will*. Why does the AFFP need to censor the libsymps' postings?"

"There are some swing states where blogs, especially the ones by Mercy Otis Warren, are making a difference."

Sugi's Apartment

"Mel spoke specifically of the Mercy Otis Warren blog. They've got a hook into the darknet. The DHS will target us. Sugi, you must break any connection between you and me."

"Not a chance, Miss Singer!"

A knock at the door interrupted whatever else Sugi planned to say.

"Armed Police. Open the door!"

Sugi turned the knob. Two *Protectors* in black flack armor rammed the door open. They threw Sugi to the floor.

"Stay down! Stay down! Let me see your hands! Lady! On the floor! Let me see your hands!"

"I'm Polly Singer, I work—"

"Don't care who you are. On the floor!"

The men handcuffed Sugi and Polly and ransacked the apartment.

"Hey, she's DHS brass," the man who rooted through Polly's purse said. "Singer."

"Heard the name. You sure it's her?"

"Ms. Singer, we're sorry, but the brief was that a dangerous subversive was operating out of this place, and that he was armed."

"You found no weapons," Polly said.

"If you don't count the nail file in your purse," the man said. "No, ma'am."

"And subversives? Both Sugi and I work for DHS. He's my sound man. We were planning . . . " Polly decided she'd said enough.

"No, ma'am. We will have to take the computers. Standard procedure."

Polly hoped the sudden decrease in blood to her face would either not be noticed or be attributed to the stress of the situation.

"No problem," Sugi said. "Um, any idea when I'll get my stuff back? I use it to edit Ms. Singer's audio and video."

"Can't say, sir. Ma'am. We're just doing our jobs—just following orders. You understand."

I understand too well, Sugi thought. *People who were 'just following orders' gassed my grandparents.*

CHAPTER 35: SHEARWATER

Nemo relinquo
Leave no comrade behind.
Ancient military command.

Shearwater Encampment, Sierra Leone, Africa

"Anything on the satcom?"

"Yeah, text message coming in from my sister. Wait . . . Wait . . . Oh, crap!" The comm officer handed the satellite phone to his commander.

—ebola ur loc get out while u can marty mcfly

"Marty McFly?"

"Family code. Means it's her."

"Assemble everyone, including the wounded. We need to plan."

Why didn't we get this through channels? the commander wondered. "Keep on the comm link and let me know when command sends orders."

~~~~~

"Nothing from command, sir. They're on the air . . . I'm copying messages to units in Liberia and Guinea on lobes of the satcom signal. Situation normal there," the commo said.

"You heard that, folks. And you heard the message from his family. We've scanned what we can. *UK Voice World Service* has carried the Ebola story, and they've always been a good source. The only thing from command has been *hunker down* and *stand by*. And you know what that means. We've been left hanging. We sure as hell can't walk up to a ticket counter and buy thirty-two tickets to the US. Where are we most likely to find a long-range aircraft?"

"We're closer to Kenema, but we won't find a trans-oceanic aircraft anywhere but Lungi."

"What's the route to Lungi look like?"

"Amra'a Haram has been reinforced by Daesh-wannabes. They're guarding bridges here, here, and here. We won't be able to avoid firefights."

It took less than an hour to break camp, load the wounded into SUVs, and mount the 50-caliber machine guns on pickup trucks. To the untrained eye, these men looked like any Daesh unit. They were prepared to break out the black flag of ISIS or any of several other flags. And they were prepared to take out anyone they might meet.

The preparations were unneeded. The unit's size and arms intimidated the amateurs of Amra'a Haram, the Daesh allies, and others—hoodlums using the banner of Islam to rob, rape, and murder. The convoy passed unimpeded, and took refuge in an unoccupied warehouse just southwest of the Lungi airport.

"There's a goddamn Spartan on the apron," the spotter reported.

"Whose?"

"Chad bought some, but this one has UN markings."

"Bet they brought in medics for the Ebola thing."

"Range?"

"Not long enough."

"Anything else?"

The recon leader shook his head. "I have one man watching. He has a secure radio."

The mercs had settled for the night when the roar of thrust reversers woke them. "What?" the commander asked.

"Boeing triple-seven," the spotter reported. "Transoceanic range. Taxiing to the service docks, not the terminal. Refueling."

"Gar-un-damn-tee it's here to remove US diplomats," the commander said. "They'll probably load just after dawn. We've got only a little time. Looks like the crew is going to the terminal."

"How do you want to play this?"

"When they finish refueling, we'll seize the aircraft and load our people. We'll take the crew and anyone else who shows up as hostages. Captain Kline will fly us into the US. Depending on where the flight plan brings us over land, we'll divert, land, destroy comms, and make a getaway."

"Risky, but it looks like our best option."

"For years, we've fought for the CIA. We've never questioned what we were fighting for. Each of you was once a solider, sailor, or airman of the United States of America. The United States of before the takeover, before the tyranny we're hearing about. We all swore to preserve and protect that United States, not the one we are returning to.

"What say you all?"

~~~~~

The runway at Staunton, Virginia was about two thousand feet too short for a Boeing 777. Experts from the company and the government determined the plane had been flown with flaps fully extended, well below the rated stall speed. There had been six feet of runway left after it rolled to a stop.

"It wasn't me, sir," the original pilot told the DHS interrogators. "It was one of the mercenaries. And frankly, sir, I'd fly right-seat to her any day. She's one hell of a pilot."

~~~~~

Heroic Pilot Makes Safe Landing

God's Word for You. The heroic pilot of a chartered airliner made an incredible, safe landing in Staunton, Virginia after the plane's navigation systems failed. "We were flying on fumes," a member of the flight crew said. "There was no way we could have made it to a bigger airport."

The plane, a Model 777, sits in a parking place at the Staunton airport while experts decide how to fly it out of an airport that is much, much too small for it.

~~~~~

Mercenaries Return to USA

Mercy Otis Warren blog, darknet. A group of American mercenaries, once employees of the CIA, abandoned by their employer and their country, hijacked an airplane and flew from Africa to Staunton, Virginia. They've disappeared into the forests of the Shenandoah Mountains. Maybe. By now, they could be anywhere.

They were fighting Amra'a Haram in Sierra Leone, Africa. Were they exposed to the Ebola outbreak in that country? Have they brought the virus into the USA? More important, they're armed. Heavily armed. What are their intentions?

The official reports are that the airplane was carrying tourists from Miami to Richmond when it lost its way in weather. The official reports are lies.

~~~~~

&shearwaterpatriots/&martymcfly all 32 be home none sick gone to ground rupert rupert

Chapter 36: Tomorrow's Headlines

It is not the stars that hold our destinies,
but ourselves.
William Shakespeare 1582-1616 CE

Cold Snap Destroys Citrus Crop

Mt. Pleasant Clarion. The word from Florida growers is grim. The latest cold snap has destroyed next year's crop of oranges. Downed power lines meant no power for the blowers and sprayers normally used to protect the trees. Smudge pots, carried into the groves and lit by hand, were of little use in temperatures below freezing for hours at a time. The Chicago Exchange has halted trading in FCOJ—Frozen Concentrated Orange Juice.

Closer to home, roads and schools remain closed as winter storms dump more snow on the county than we've seen in more than a hundred years—combined. We're lucky, in a way. The storms here haven't snapped power lines like they've done elsewhere and we don't have hills high enough to create avalanches like those that have closed interstate highways in Washington, Oregon, and California.

~~~~~

Tommy Carron, Quebec, Canada

Quebec City was a real kick. First of all, I stayed in a student dormitory that was party central. Either I was old enough, or I looked old enough, to drink beer, and Canadian beer is awesome! The guys made sure I didn't get more than a little buzzed. After the first time, that is.

I wrote a letter to my parents. It had to be reviewed by someone before it was sent. "We will carry it to the States and mail it in an envelope from a legitimate company. We cannot guarantee delivery, and there's no way to get a message back from them. I'm sorry." Jacques, my official host, said.

Jacques and his family included me in their Christmas, but I missed my parents.

The day after Christmas, Jacques put me on a bus for Saint-Jean-sur-Richelieu. It was the home of the Royal Military College. I wouldn't be going there, but to the Cégep de Saint-Jean-sur-Richelieu, a kind of high-school-junior-college-boarding-school combined. I would have to learn French. Oh, and ice hockey. There was no football, not like I knew it. And I would get a *stipend,* which is like an allowance. I asked Jacques about the money. He said people in the US were paying, but he didn't know who.

~~~~~

House Chambers, Constitutional Convention

"The issue is clear," Thomas Vaughn said. "Unlimited money is poured into political campaigns by organizations through tax-exempt S-PACs. Yet, we gag churches that would exercise the Freedom of Speech guaranteed in the Bill of Rights.

"The proposal to allow churches to participate in the body politic while retaining their tax-exempt status is rational and reasonable. I call for a vote on this provision."

The electronic tally-board filled with *aye* votes. Vaughn smiled. *Another provision incorporated, and only seventeen to go.*

"Mr. Chairman?" the speaker was a representative from Kentucky.

Vaughn recognized her.

326

"Mr. Chairman and Delegates. You know that for years the government has been subsidizing the National Radio and Television Service. We have been successful in eliminating government funding for this left-wing, libsymp, fellow-traveling propaganda organization. What you may not know is that the National Radio and Television Service still has tax-exempt status as a federally chartered 501(c)3 corporation. Meaning, donations to this blue outfit may be tax-deductible.

"I propose we revoke their tax-exempt status." The woman looked to Vaughn.

"The Honorable Representative from Kentucky is correct," Vaughn said. "The tax-exempt status of the National Radio and Television Service must be revoked. While this is not a matter for the Constitutional Convention, it is a matter for this House of Representatives. May I ask for a vote on a resolution to refer this matter to the House when it meets in plenary session?"

Nicely done, Stafford said, and turned off the television feed from the House Chambers.

~~~~~

Baywatch Yacht Club, Detroit, Michigan

The boat could not qualify as a yacht, but the owner's father was a member, so the boy was allowed to dock at the Baywatch Yacht Club.

"Who are those people?" Mrs. Snodgrass asked her husband. The Snodgrasses were at the adjacent slip, watching the crew prepare their boat for sailing.

"No telling," her husband said around his highball. "The boy's just not like us." The couple watched a handful of people carrying backpacks and rucksacks board the go-fast boat.

"He's a hoodlum," Mrs. Snodgrass said.

"Hurry up!" Mr. Snodgrass said to his crew. "It's almost dark."

"Do you think Lake St Clair will be iced over this winter?" Mrs. Snodgrass asked.

"Nonsense!" her husband replied. "It's a rumor spread by those eco-freaks from the university. I don't know why we're required to support such organizations."

The Snodgrass yacht left the slip just as the go-fast boat fired its engines. The converted Navy SEAL training boat slid into the Detroit River minutes ahead of a DHS platoon.

~~~~~

Stanley Condominium, Arlington, Virginia

Ring of Fire shows seven earthquakes in Oklahoma in the past twenty-four hours. Nothing more than a 4.6. And a 5.7 in Japan. Japan's not surprising. The whole country is on the edge of tectonic plates. One volcano is acting up in Iceland. That must be why the UK press is worried about air travel.

George Stanley read the summary from the Japanese university. He pulled data from what was left of the USGS intranet. DHS hadn't found the dedicated circuits linking universities and laboratories. Automated seismometers, powered by solar cells, scattered throughout the world, were still reporting by obscure satellite links. The German's Antarctic Station Neumayer still reported through witwat, the University at Witwatersrand, South Africa. Scientists at universities who still had access to the data were analyzing and posting. George had hacked into the servers of a university in Fairfax, Virginia.

George condensed the information and passed it to Red Dragon. Three hours later, it reached scientists at the University of Guelph.

"Where does this come from, eh?" Dr. Susan Germain asked. "And how does he or she get the information? The US has shut down all earthquake reporting on the internet. And they've done their damnedest to block Canada, too."

"Don't know, Susan," the lab chief said. "Is it accurate?"

"So far, everything we get from this source has matched what we've gotten from our own seismometers," Susan replied.

"I say *run with it*. We'll put it back into the alternet to protect our source, eh?"

~~~~~

Stanley Condominium, Thanksgiving Day

"Thank you for inviting Jamie," Ken Parnell said as he ushered his suit-clad son into the condo.

"The invitation was to you, also, Ken," Vice President Stanley said. "Please join us at table. And you are off duty according to Agent-In-Charge Chatsworth. Will you join me for an aperitif?"

Ken watched as Stanley closed the door to his study and poured two fingers of liquor into each of two old-fashion glasses. "*Canadian Prime*," Stanley said. "Thirty year old single malt. It can't be called *Scotch Whiskey* only because of European Union rules. Still, it is filtered through peat."

After toasting and sipping, both men sat.

"Ken, the invitation to Jamie came from my son, George. It is a closely guarded secret that George is gay. Are you comfortable with that?"

If Ken were shocked at how Thomas Stanley opened the conversation, he gave no sign. "Sir, I know you best through your son, Henry, with whom you have trusted me. He is a fine young man. I cannot imagine that your other son, George, is any less than his brother. I trust him but more important, I trust my son. And, sir? If I may be blunt, neither you nor I need say anything more unless the boys ask."

Stanley had been sitting on the edge of his seat. Now, he leaned back in the chair. "Thank you, Ken, not only for what you said, but also for your trust. And I agree. I trust my sons, too."

Agent Chatsworth knocked and entered. "Sir? Your elder son's date and her family have arrived."

Henry had already greeted Elizabeth and her parents and seated them in the living room. The staff had served drinks. Stanley greeted Stafford and exchanged *air-kisses* with Mrs. Stafford.

I hate that particular cultural meme—that cliché, he thought. *But it's her way, and I need to keep close to Stafford. What's the saying? 'Keep your friends close, but your enemies closer.' Why do I think of him as an enemy?*

~~~~~

The White House, Mel Appleton's Office

"No, Mr. Appleton," Thomas Stanley said. "Those chips will not be implanted in my sons or me. You've seen the numbers from the military. Over ten thousand soldiers have had reactions, nearly all involving antibiotic-resistant bacteria. More than ninety percent of those have died. Nine thousand, one hundred seven dead soldiers—more than we have lost since 2001 in the Iraq and Afghanistan wars. No sir, the risk is unacceptable."

"Mr. Vice President," Mel Appleton said. "Please understand that extraordinary measures would be taken to ensure your safety and theirs. The chips would help the Secret Service better protect them and you. Further, you would serve as an example—"

"An example I will not be," Stanley said. "Nor will my sons. This discussion is over."

~~~~~

DHS Director's Office

"What do you have on Singer and her soundman?"

"His computers are clean, Mistress. Just video clips, sound bytes, assembled stuff cleared for release. She's never put out anything that hasn't been approved."

"Nothing we know of. But someone's leaking to the Mercy Owen blog."

"You think Singer is the leak, Mistress?"

"She's the only one on the core staff who I didn't hire. She is Mel Appleton's creature. She has a Class A secure cell phone. No way to know who she talks to on it."

Appleton, the president, shadow men and women who are so high up in the government they are anonymous. No one who isn't firmly in the right camp—the far right camp. Are you worried, or are you jealous? The Director's aide wondered.

"What do you want me to do, Mistress?" the aide asked.

"Destroy her. Except for nuclear weapons, I have more power than the president. It's time to use it."

The Director stroked the cheek of her aide then slapped her, leaving a bright red handprint on the woman's cheek. "Don't let me down."

"No, Mistress."

~~~~~

Old Eberly Grill

The waiter was discreet. "I'm sorry, Ms. Singer, but your credit card was declined."

"What? Oh, here, use this one."

Polly turned to her lunch companion. "I'm sorry, Frank. Must have demagnetized the strip or the chip. Can the chips be demagnetized?"

"This is still secret, but there's evidence that the DHS biochip readers can short out credit card chips," Frank Hopkins said.

"I'm sorry, ma'am. This one was declined, too." The waiter was more nervous than Polly.

"Polly, let me . . . " Frank began.

"Nonsense, Frank." Polly dug in her purse and found enough cash to pay the bill.

"Enrique, there won't be much left for you, but I'll make it up to you, next time."

A check of her account on-line showed nothing more than *account closed by consumer*. Polly called the bank.

"I'm sorry, ma'am," the customer service drone said. "I have no more information than you see on line."

"Was it identity theft?" Polly asked. "It must have been. I didn't close the account. Did someone open another account in my name? Can you re-open this one? Can you issue a new card?"

"Ma'am, I wouldn't know if you were subject to identity theft, and I cannot answer questions about other accounts over the telephone. I cannot re-open this account or open a new one and issue a new card over the telephone. You'll have to visit one of our banking offices. If you'll tell me you zip code I can suggest some local addresses."

Polly's questions about the second card yielded the same results.

"No, ma'am. I cannot open a new account. Your credit score has dropped to zero, and the IRS has frozen your checking account."

It took seven minutes to listen and respond to the voice menu at the IRS phone number. Then, Polly waited another thirty minutes before a human answered and cut off the blistering hip-hop elevator music. Then, she spent ten minutes answering the same questions for six different people before the sixth said, "I'm sorry, Ms. Singer, but I cannot give you that information over the telephone. Our records show we sent a letter explaining the circumstances nearly two weeks ago. If you like, I can have another copy sent."

"Yes, please," Polly said. *Too damn bad I can't hang up a cell phone by slamming the receiver on the hook.*

PART IV SIGNS AND WONDERS

He worketh signs and wonders
in the heavens and on earth.
Daniel 6-27

guelph sends 0315 gmt iceland volcanism reduced to tremors < 2.0 ditto japan chile 5.6 and 4.3 past day oklahoma usa fifteen frack related tremors same period

~~~~~

Senator Rivers' Office, Russell Senate Office Building

"The Canadians are saying the shaking in Oklahoma is caused by fracking," Senator Rivers said. "I'm getting a lot of frack—I mean flack. I've done what I can, but even Homeland hasn't been able to shut down this rebel internet thing. Can't you do something?"

"How about a *diplomatic message* to the Canadians?" Boomer asked.

"We've lost any diplomatic edge we might have had, and the president's not yet willing to declare war on Canada," Rivers replied. "We need the Alberta tar-sand oil."

Could we take out a university? Boomer thought. *Maybe we won't have to. Maybe just a couple of professors.*

~~~~~

guelph sends 5 Mar 0017 gmt iceland volcanism remains < 2.0 ditto japan stop concern pressure building iceland sends reports of expansion lava domes coordinates follow ecuador 4.2. oklahoma 7 frack related 2.2-3.4

~~~~~

Office of the Speaker of the House

Speaker Stafford looked at the image. Then he looked at the Pastor who had been sent by Gordon Fallow, the Bishop of Washington and spiritual head of the OTCC.

"It is much too soon for this," Stafford said. "Yes, Congress has the authority to determine the design of the flag, but to replace the stars with a Latin Cross? Please tell Bishop Fallow that politically, it is much too early and we have many more important things on our agenda . . . including the church-state relationship."

Idiot. Fallow must think he's really in charge. There is no way his boss could have known about this.

The telephone call from Archbishop Trucido's Councilor Six changed Stafford's mind quickly, and the bill was introduced the following day.

House Chamber, Constitutional Convention

The delegates from Virginia were adamant that *Lee-Jackson Day* be celebrated in their state. Mississippi, supported by the Carolinas, Alabama, Tennessee, and Georgia demanded that *Decoration Day*, commemorating the Civil War dead, remain on their calendars.

"This may be the only *states-rights* issue left," Thomas Vaughn joked with Stafford. "And, it was a useful compromise. We eliminated all Federal Holidays except Epiphany, Good Friday, Easter, Pentecost, Memorial Day, 4th of July, Veterans Day, Thanksgiving, and Christmas."

"Presidents' Day? The King holiday?" Stafford asked.

"Gone," Vaughn said. "And the Church will eliminate Halloween at the local level."

~~~~~

guelph sends: 31 Mar 0600 gmt oklahoma usa fifteen frack related tremors < 4.0 iceland, jp quiet ecuador 4.6 coordinates follow puerto rico 6.5 coords follow

~~~~~~~

WhatDrWho Blog

The death knell sounded for the First Amendment to the Constitution, today. Southern states were allowed to keep holidays celebrating the slaughter of the Civil War. Elsewhere, the delegates to the illegal constitutional convention rewrote the calendar to eliminate all federal holidays save six Christian holidays and three patriotic holidays. This is the same mind-set that co-opted patriotism and the flag and turned both into tools of religious propaganda.

This is WhatDrWho blogging from exile.

~~~~~~~

&highflyer/&reddragon anyone have contact guelph?

&reddragon/&highflyer will ask

&reddragon anyone contact with guelph?

&tardisboy guelph main node down explosion seismology building 3 dead

&reddragon/&tardisboy you kin whatdrwho query

&tardisboy/&reddragon of course he my dad

~~~~~~~

Theme Parks Closed

Gods Word for You. The Department of Homeland Security has ordered the entire Orlando complex of theme parks closed due to multiple credible terroristic threats.

~~~~~~~

&tardisboy/&reddragon guelph lab working from music building keep secret send data to me

&reddragon/&tardisboy wilco who dead query

&tardisboy/&reddragon senior prof two graduate now dr from wheatly in charge anyone have spare seismometers query

&highflyer/&reddragon tardisboy request legitimate can we help query

&reddragon/&highflyer you plugged into seismometer net you handle

George got busy on the net. Three weeks later, a truck loaded with bananas stopped at Rensselaer Polytechnic Institute, and turned west to Interstate 87, reaching Montreal after three days on the road.

&tardisboy/&highflyer guelph up and running thank you yanks

&highflyer/&tardisboy who you call yanks you yank <grin>

~~~~~

No Fun for Anyone

World Citizen. "Unable to stop the annual 'Gay Day' at one of the nation's preeminent theme parks, DHS played the terrorism card and shut down the livelihood of an entire city. Look for a huge jump in jobless claims, and a mass exodus of workers. If the shutdown goes past July 4, there won't be enough people left to reopen the parks. Meanwhile, a *creationism* theme park that defies both science and sense remains in operation just a few miles outside Orlando, guarded by both the DHS and the SOC. Prejudice and ignorance, more than politics, makes strange bedfellows. This is Muldoon paraphrasing H. L. Menken. 'No one ever went broke underestimating the intelligence of the American people.'"

~~~~~

&highflyer/&reddragon ringoffire reports earthquake mag > 9.0 > 9.0 vicinity greenland today 0721 gmt confirmed witwat, sydney, guelph

&reddragon to net massive earthquake vicinity greenland 0721 gmt flow control atlantic europe links report

    &newsboy contact lost with europe via atlantic cable

    &foxylady i have link ny to England

    &bangersnmash link london to holland ok

    &dikedyke netherlands to helvetia ok

~~~~~

The White House 5:34 AM, Mel Appleton

"What's so important you've got to wake the president at five thirty in the morning?" I asked, even as I pressed the button on my phone to do just that. The Marine Lieutenant who had the night watch seemed calm, but he had pounded on my door and then entered, flipping on the light as he did so.

"Sir, we have reports from military installations in Newfoundland, Greenland, and Europe, and ships at sea in the North Atlantic of hearing an explosion. All at about the same time. Satellite data is being examined. Something big has happened but it's not nuclear. There is no sign Russian or Chinese forces are at heightened alert."

What the hell? I thought. I had heard the key words, *not nuclear*. We couldn't get a goddamn weather satellite up—not since Senator Rivers got that program defunded because he thought it encouraged climate activists—but the military kept their orbital sensors polished.

I tried to remember my fifth grade geography lessons. Could the North Atlantic Rift have opened? By then, President March had answered his phone. I compressed the report. "Sir, explosion somewhere in the North Atlantic. Really big but probably not nuclear. I'll have more information when you reach the situation room. No immediate danger."

While I dressed, I gave orders to the lieutenant. "Call Andrews, and have Air Force One and airborne command post crews alerted. And get a Marine Air One flight ready for immediate evacuation of the president."

"Do you want the helos here?"

I thought for a minute. We couldn't hide three huge helicopters from view, and their presence would raise too many questions.

"No, but after you make those calls, alert the Secret Service to have a convoy ready to depart for Andrews—or to rendezvous with the helos at Bolling."

After a quick, *yes, sir*, the lieutenant disappeared.

I called Mr. Warwick on the special cell phone, and briefed him as I dressed and walked through the halls. I beat the president to the situation room by less than a minute. Someone at the Pentagon had plotted the time the explosion was heard at various places and used the speed of sound to determine the probable origin of the explosion. The map showed the North Atlantic, North America, and Western Europe. In the center of the map was Iceland. A red circle surrounded it. As soon as the president sat, a Navy mess steward brought coffee for him and then for me. The Air Force officer who carried the *football* declined coffee.

A video link from the Pentagon opened. The briefer was an Army brigadier. He was brief, if that's not a tautology. "Mr. President, an explosion was heard and reported from bases in Newfoundland, Greenland, and the United Kingdom."

As he spoke, red dots illuminated.

"We also have reports from ships at sea." More dots lit, and he explained how the location had been plotted.

"One ship, a Coast Guard research vessel, was passing west if Iceland at the time of the event, but has not responded to our calls. It is presumed lost."

Coast Guard research vessel, I thought. *Code-words for a spy ship. Probably headed for the Arctic to monitor Russian and Canadian oil exploration. It would have had the best communication suite available. If we couldn't contact it, it was lost.*

"We had no satellite in position but one will be within range of Iceland in . . . " the general glanced to his left. " . . . in twenty-two minutes."

He did not say what the satellite might or might not show.

"We've ordered one of our boomers—ballistic missile submarines—to depart _____, and have launched reconnaissance aircraft from _____." He named two bases at which the US didn't officially have any forces. "The aircraft should reach Iceland in 90 minutes. We should be the first on station, and the first to know what happened, sir."

President March picked up his coffee cup. Unseen by anyone else, he signaled me to speak.

"Is there any danger to the president?" I asked the question he could not.

"We do not believe so, sir. Iceland is volcanic, and very active. Evidence suggests a natural disaster."

"Anything from the earthquake people? The universities? What about the pirate site in Canada?"

"A team at the Pentagon is making calls, now, sir. The Canadian site went dark two weeks ago. We'll notify you as soon as we hear."

The universities . . . but not from the USGS. That had been one of the first cuts. The Canadian university site is dark and a blogger reported an explosion in their seismology lab. It's too late to wonder about that, now, Mel thought.

Selma, Alabama, Path to Heaven Congregation, OTCC

> "Then said Jesus unto him,
> Except ye see signs and wonders,
> ye will not believe."
> John 4:48

"God has promised us signs and wonders, and behold, He has delivered!" The Reverend Jonas Path managed to stretch the first word of that sentence into three syllables. He was on a roll, and would have the congregation rolling in the aisles and speaking in tongues before his sermon ended. One of Path's staffers in Washington, a woman who had a friend in the Pentagon, had called to confirm the destruction of Iceland by fire and earthquake.

He also warned us of false prophets, thought Aaron Nichols as he squirmed in the pew.

~~~~~

Tommy Carron, Saint-Jean-sur-Richelieu, Quebec

I've learned French and how to play ice hockey and soccer, which they call football or *footie*, but I'll never be as good as the boys who grew up with both. They don't mind, though, and are good sports about my French with a Yankee accent. I keep telling them I'm from Georgia, and not a Yankee, but they just laugh and keep calling me a Yankee. I have a lot of friends at the boarding school and at the military school, 'cause we scrimmage against them in sports a lot. I send letters to my parents once a month, but of course, I never hear from them.

Recruit-Corporal Liam MacLauren, Saint-Jean-sur-Richelieu, Quebec

A senior non-commissioned officer delivered the envelope addressed to Recruit-Corporal MacLauren. Liam stuttered his thanks, and opened the envelope. It contained a formal invitation, written by hand, to dinner in a private dining room of the college. The invitation did not say who his host would be, but specified dress uniform.

Liam entered the room to find the Lieutenant General of the Army who had been on the board that vetted Liam and given him a place at St. Jean. The School Commandant, the Tactical Officer of Liam's Element, several instructors, and a handful of officers, enlisted personnel, and cadets filled the room.

Liam was allowed a beer and sat at a table with people he knew to be powerful, but who treated him as one of them. The courtesy, the casual conversation, the way they paid attention to what Liam said, the way he was encouraged to participate in informality among his seniors were something he'd dreamed of for years. After dinner dishes had been cleared, the General stood and related to all the story of Mithras. Then, he looked directly at Liam.

"Recruit-Corporal MacLauren, you once told me you could kill in the defense of the Canadian Confederation. Are you prepared to die in the service of your country and the Canadian people? Are you prepared to swear on your life you will never reveal what is about to be told to you tonight?"

Liam stood. He did not hesitate. These people had offered their trust. They had rescued him. "Yes, General. I swear."

Liam absorbed the information about the Brotherhood of Mithras. "It crosses not only service boundaries," a woman Air Force officer said, "but international boundaries. You will find the Brotherhood in the Yanks' military, in the UK, and elsewhere. Do you have any questions?"

"No, ma'am. I guess I'll learn more when it's needful."

Liam knew he had sworn a blood oath, although no blood had been spilled.

~~~~~

Russell Senate Office Building, Senator Rivers's Office

"Boiling water?" the Senator asked.

"Yes, sir. The Navy reports there's not much more than a cauldron of boiling water where Iceland used to be. Steam is rising to the stratosphere. The entire population of the country, at least 330,000 people, are dead. There were forty-five on the US Coast—"

"Boiling water," the senator repeated. "That should shut up the climate-Nazis who are worried that cold water from melting glaciers will shut down the Gulf Stream. This should heat it up plenty."

"Sir, it's not the cold water they're worried about. It's the fresh water. Cold water is good, because it sinks to the bottom and—"

"Enough!" the senator said. "You know I'm not interested in techno-babble."

"Yes sir." The senator's PA waited while the senator read his daily news briefing—on paper because he found a computer screen 'hard on his eyes.'

And it's not just the Gulf Stream, the aide thought. *It's the entire thermohaline circuit, the Atlantic component, anyway. Cold water sinks in the north, flows south and is warmed by the sun, then back north in the Gulf Stream. If it weren't for the Gulf Stream, England and a lot of Europe would be a lot colder than they are.*

~~~~~

Aaron Nichols, Selma, Alabama

I tried to find out what was going on, but a lot of the internet didn't seem to be there. No matter what I put in the search engines, I got only one thing: official announcements by the Department of Homeland Security Bureau of Natural Sciences.

According to the government, there had been a volcanic eruption in Iceland. According to the government, relief was on the way. According to the government—

As soon as I tried to get international news, or something not from the USG, a popup blew past my popup blocker:

QUERY NOT AUTHORIZED.
RESTRICT QUERIES TO
AUTHORIZED SITES
BY ORDERS OF THE
DEPARTMENT OF HOMELAND SECURITY.

WTF? Was all I could think. I brought in my friends.

"Guys," I began, only to be interrupted by Stephanie

"And gals," Stephanie said. "But you'd better not say that. 'Boys and girls' is okay; 'men and women' is better; maybe 'people' would be best."

"Thanks, Stephanie," I said. "I know you're all more than boys, and . . . well, some of the girls, including you, scare the heck out of me. When I say *guys*, I really mean all of you. Guess I need another word, huh?"

"How about *folks*," one of the girls said.

"Or *patriots*," another added. The room fell silent.

"Patriots," I said. "We're faced with some bad stuff. The internet has been taken over by the DHS. They have to keep it going—too much depends on it. The entire banking system, stock market, a lot of the phone system, most of the US electrical power system. But they're blocking and—" I paused long enough to get their attention— "and they're probably tracking, too."

The stunned silence that followed gave me space to insert my real agenda. "We are going to re-create the internet without the government."

There was a lot of pushback, mostly geeky and not political. In other words, not why we should do it, but how.

Aaron trembled a little. His friends said they'd linked to an underground, an alternet. But since this was his idea, they expected him to go first.

woodenboy sends who there

&reddragon/woodenboy welcome to alternet don't be surprised if we don't trust you at first

woodenboy/&reddragon no problem we b 15 friends want 2 help

&reddragon: monitor; send info; when u r verified we send too

wb wilco

~~~~~

The White House, East Wing July 4

Three television cameras fed the press pool. Two others operated by President March's staff documented the event for the Presidential Library. Behind the president stood Vice President Stanley, Speaker Stafford, Senator Beasley, the Director of Homeland Security Director, and five multi-star generals. The freshman representative from Rhode Island, Thomas Vaughn, stood at the president's right hand. Behind these adults, on risers brought in for the occasion, stood 45 children—members of *God's Christian Army* and the *Rebeccas* from the One True Christian Church School of Northeast DC. Each of the children had a small American flag—the new flag in which a Latin cross replaced the stars that had been in the union. The children had been given strict instructions to hold their flags up, but not, under any circumstances, to wave them. Nothing must be allowed to detract from the president.

Rather than standing behind a lectern, the president sat at a desk—also brought in for the occasion. The only ornaments on the desk were an inkwell and pen, a small American flag and a presidential flag in a brass base, and a pint-sized replica of the Liberty Bell.

The producer gave the countdown, the red light on the center camera came on, and President March spoke.

"Two hundred and forty two years ago this Great Nation declared its independence from the tyranny of King George of Great Britain. It took time to win the war that followed, and more time to hammer out the first Constitution of these United States of America. We have lived under that Constitution for some two hundred and thirty years.

"Meanwhile, the world has changed. Patriots on both sides of the aisle have worked diligently to make the Constitution keep up with those changes. Their efforts have often been blocked by those who hold on to antique beliefs. Their efforts have often been blocked by activist judges, who believe they, and not the People of the United States are the best voice for the law.

"Thomas Jefferson wrote more than two hundred years ago that 'The time for fixing every essential right on a legal basis is while our rulers are honest and ourselves united.'

"In the years since, we have seen this Great Country change from a United States to a fractious, divided nation. It has only been in the past two years that we have once again become united under the banner of the American Freedom First Party and the One True Christian Church.

"Under that banner, and with the mandate given at the last election, your representatives have re-created the Constitution of the United States of America. All the questions that might divide us have been answered. All the protections from fear, from foreign invasion whether insidious or armed, and from activists have been incorporated. There is no longer any question that while anyone may practice any religion they choose, this Great Nation is a Christian Nation, *One nation under God.*

"I am humbled that the Committee on the Constitution, so ably chaired by Representative Thomas Vaughn of Rhode

Island, has asked me to be the first to sign this historic document."

The president took the pen and signed his name to the scroll that had been unfurled on the desk. Then, he handed the pen to Vaughn.

Thomas Vaughn had the grace or the presence of mind to look surprised before he, too, signed the document. The president pushed back from the desk as the pen was passed from hand to hand. Commentators identified each signer. The commentator's voices were hushed, even though they were in studios miles from the White House.

~~~~~

&eli1990: new constitution unconstitutional

&umjd: ditto unconstitutional

&harvardlaw8801: late to the table but both are right

&woodenboy: i pledge allegiance to the first constitution of the united states of america and to its bill of rights. i promise to be independent of thought. i promise to educate myself so i can make my own judgments. i promise to question everything. i promise to stand for what is right stop patriots pledge stop

&brooklynpizza: u da man woodenboy

&woodenboy: pledge from steph shez girl but wants everyone to know, believe

&brooklynpizza: she da woman

~~~~~

WhatDrWho Blog

Baron Montesquieu, a messenger of the Enlightenment, said, "We attribute to God those traits we most value. If triangles had a god, he would have three sides."

The values of the OTCC were forced upon us through Presidential Executive Orders and laws. Now, the AFFP and OTCC have conspired to create an illegal constitution to enshrine their beliefs.

You can be sure you've found the right god to worship when your god hates the same people you hate.

This is WhatDrWho blogging from exile.

US Navy Atlantic Fleet Command Center

"Sir, it's confirmed. The Atlantic gyre has tipped. The thermohaline circuit has stopped. There are still currents but not where we expect. We have no idea where it will settle down." A Lieutenant who had been monitoring Fleet Coms reported. *If it ever does settle down*, she thought.

The captain reacted quickly. "Lieutenant, get COMLANT on the secure phone and brief him. Tell him we're preparing FLASH traffic for the Pentagon. Include your best guess on the potential impact on navigation. Yeoman? Coffee, please."

"Captain, I'm not supposed to brief COMLANT. It's considered *teaching,* and women aren't allowed to teach. The gyre will not affect navigation," the lieutenant said. "It's climate. The United Kingdom, Ireland, Central Europe, the Low Countries will have a cold winter, and maybe no spring at all. It will be worse than 'the year without a summer.'"

~~~~~

Mall Riot Claims Twenty

New York Afterward. Police are calling the events at the Brooklyn Mall a riot created by rival drug gangs. Witnesses say it was armed government forces that began shooting without provocation. This newspaper has been flooded with cell phone photos, recordings, and videos that seem to confirm that. So far, we've not been able to say what or who caused the riot. All we have so far is that more than 200 people were injured, many by bullets, and that forty-seven are dead.

DHS Command Bunker

"The weapons fitted with Biometrics readers failed to distinguish between our forces and the insurgents," the Chief of Counter-Terrorism reported.

"Our people relied on those chips. They fired at anyone who seemed to be involved in the fracas and expected the guns wouldn't fire at people wearing our chips. It didn't work. Their targets included thirty of our own people. Seventeen are dead."

"Is there any chance our people were mistaken?"

"No, ma'am. It's the chips."

"My God!" the director said. "Where does that leave us? Those chips are . . . damn near everywhere."

"Mistress? Two people are responsible for the chips' programming," the aide said. She stood silent and naked, vulnerable but hopeful.

The Director of Homeland had removed the woman's padded handcuffs and released her from the contraption that held her, arms aloft, toes barely touching the floor, flesh exposed. The Director smiled, caressed the woman's skin where the marks of the whip were fading.

"Have we been able to reverse-engineer the code?"

"Yes, Mistress."

"You have a new mission."

"Yes, Mistress."

Two thousand eight hundred sixty-three miles to the west, an executive jet landed at the San Jose airport. A woman in black leather leading others in similar clothes, deplaned. Less than an hour later, they boarded for their return to Washington Dulles Airport. In Cupertino, two men who once hoped to be part of the one-percent lay in pools of their own blood.

~~~~~

348

GW4U, All Media Channels

Responding to what they call credible threats, the Soldiers of the Cross will provide security for all OTCC churches on Christmas Day. Only one door to each church will be open to permit easier screening of the congregation. Congregants without bio-chips may be denied entry.

~~~~~

Tommy Carron, Saint-Jean-sur-Richelieu, Quebec

I can't believe it! Andre grabbed me after class and took me to the electronics lab. He had helped me try to send an email to my parents using what Andre called the alternet. And, he had gotten an answer—an email from my parents! It was short, but they are okay. They had gotten my letters and know I am safe.

"We cannot do this often," Andre said. "The alternet is, how you say, *spotty* and the US authorities always try to locate our nodes. Every message carries risk. I'm sorry."

"*Merci beaucoup, Andre. Ce est le meilleur cadeau de Noël jamais,*" I said. And it was—the best Christmas present ever.

~~~~~

Coldest Winter Since 1816

UK Voice. The Hadley Center has published the numbers, and it's official. November was the coldest November on record since 1816, the *Year Without a Summer*, and so far, December looks as if it will beat even that record. The Home Office reports shipments of fuel oil have been delayed. Pirate activity in the North Sea has resulted in two oil tankers being hijacked. Despite modern satellite surveillance and the best efforts of the Royal Navy, the ships have not been located. Parliament continues to debate re-opening some of the old collieries at Newcastle. Suspected sabotage at two nuclear power plants has resulted in their shutdown and rolling blackouts have been instituted throughout the United Kingdom.

~~~~~

&highflyer/&reddragon uk met office coldest winter on record oil tankers hijacked 2 nuc plants sabotaged rolling blackouts in uk

&reddragon/&highflyer rolling blackouts here too thank secret service for generator keeps us going will get this to net

&highflyer/&reddragon who knows ss not me <grin>

"God gave Noah the rainbow sign,
No more water, fire next time."
Words of an old spiritual

National Cathedral, One True Christian Church

"And when they were come into the house,
they saw the young child . . .
and fell down, and worshipped him . . . "
Matthew 2: 11

"Today is the date of Epiphany, and throughout this Nation, Messengers of the One True Christian Church are preaching, for the first time in centuries, the Newly Revealed Truth.

"The so-called *Three Kings of Orient-are,* the *three wise men,* were not from Cathay, China, India, or Iran. They were not gentiles or heathens, but Jewish rabbis, following the prophecies of the Old Testament, prophecies from Daniel and Isaiah, prophecies of the Messiah!

"The message of salvation through Our Lord Jesus Christ is not for the heathens or the preverts, but only for the chosen— the people of this Nation who have made God the Supreme Leader and the Supreme Power."

What was left of the internet didn't have enough bandwidth to broadcast Pastor Fallow's sermon. It wasn't until Tuesday that the text of his message from the Washington Cathedral of the OTCC reached Windsor, Ontario.

That's not right! Tom Kelly thought. *Have they removed 'love thy neighbor' from their new Bible? Of course, I'm one of the 'preverts' they hate.*

Tom opened his shirt and looked at himself in the mirror. His top surgery had been successful, and the scars on his chest were barely visible. His bottom surgery had been scheduled, and he felt fear mixed with wonder.

~~~~~

&kievgatekeeper russian tanks on darnytskyi bridge

~~~~~

Silver Diner, Waldon, Georgia

The Mayor had an office, in a small building that served as City Hall and as a garage for road maintenance equipment. He held office hours in a diner. Today, the booth held only the Mayor and the Pastor of the Waldon Christian Church of the OTCC.

"Mayor, you are expected to sit tomorrow as a member of the Investigating Committee in the Examination of Harold Baker."

"Dog-gone it, Pastor, the only reason we're a town is so we can get state money to fix our roads! And the only reason I'm mayor is 'cause nobody else wanted to run. I ain't gonna make Waldon and you and me the poster childs for your Investigating Committee. Heck, Harold's a member of the church!"

"Harold professed his faith as a child, and was accepted in membership of the Waldon Christian Church. But that was years ago. The Church has grown. It has become so much more since then. But Harold has not accepted that. He has become anathema for encouraging Blacks to register to vote, and for demanding your precious road-paving money be used in Colored Town. His arguments before the County School Board against the policies of the Bureau of Education amount to treason, Treason is a crime of such enormity that the antiquated laws of legal procedure—*habeas corpus*, the right of council, and others, must be suspended.

"I expect to see you there, tomorrow after service."

The mayor and Harold had been friends for a long time. As soon as he got home, the mayor called Harold.

"The pastor's talkin' treason, Harold. He's gonna railroad you . . . tar and feather you. He warned me if I tried to defend you, I'd be Examined, too. Harold, you gotta get out of here."

~~~~~

&wartberg government overthrown neonazis in control radio tv prime minister missing

CHAPTER 37: KAREN CLEMENS

Ignorance and bigotry are diseases of the mind.
Anonymous

"Pigs?" the Director of the CDC asked.

"Sir, it's something we've known, but it's not been important. Denmark reported it years ago. Another variation of methicillin-resistant *Staphylococcus aureus*. The Danes had thirteen case-patients who reported exposure to pigs," I said.

"Clonal complex 398," one of the doctors at the conference table said. I knew all he wanted to do was hear himself talk, maybe make a few points with the director. "A variant of MRSA transmitted from pigs to pig farmers in Arizona."

The Director looked at the map displayed on the big screen. "And what's the red dot on New York?"

"We received a call from a hospital in New York. They have a case of Ebola—confirmed. The patient is in quarantine," I said. "So are thirteen hospital staff and an ambulance crew who came in contact with him."

"And—what is that? Jackson, Mississippi?" The Director pointed to the map.

"Malaria, sir. Seven cases."

"So what?" a different doctor asked. "We have more than two thousand cases in the country every year."

"The Mississippi cases are a new variety—treatment with standard drugs has failed," another doctor who wanted to hear his own voice retorted.

"More than a new variety," I corrected. "It's a mutation of the *Plasmodium* parasite. It's swept Cambodia, Laos, Viet Nam since 2008. The British have developed a new treatment using a drug developed to kill parasitic worms. They've agreed to fly a batch in. It should arrive later today."

"It's not been approved for use in the US," a doctor said.

"And it's off-label, anyway," another chimed in.

"Have we notified the FDA?" another asked.

"You mean the *Bureau of Food and Drugs*? Homeland took them over a month ago." The director said. *They lasted only a little longer than we did*, he thought.

"I'll get a waiver, sir. Through a friend in the White House. We'll get the approval before we get the drug," another career-climber said.

I kept my words short and snappy, hoping to shut down the constant interruptions. "The orange dot in Brazil is another outbreak of Zika fever. We've seen it, before. Causes micro-encephalopathy and Guillain-Barre Syndrome. Imported from Africa. Carried by the *Aedes aegypti* mosquito. The first US cases were reported in 2016 in Arkansas, Virginia, and Texas. It's spreading."

"What's behind all this?" the director asked. "Ebola, MRSA, malaria? Is it some communist plot or something?"

"No sir," I said. "They're anthropogenic—human caused. We have warmed the Earth, releasing new parasites and vectors from the newly created tropics. We've demanded cheap bacon, which means raising pigs in factory conditions where diseases spread. We've over-prescribed antibiotics—for ourselves and those penned-up pigs. We've refused to use drastic measures to isolate disease outbreaks in third-world countries on the grounds of political correctness. We've sent only token support to countries in Africa and South East Asia with outbreaks of Ebola and the mutated polio virus. Those things are coming back to roost."

"What's your name?" the Director asked.

I've been on your staff for more than four years, briefing you at least once a week and you don't know my name?

"Karen Clemens," I said. "RN, MSN, PhD—Infectious Diseases. I know what I'm talking about."

Something seemed to register with the director.

"Fred?" he addressed his PA. "Get her on the White House access list, get the Gulfstream ready for immediate takeoff, and get us an appointment with the president ASAP."

He knew it would irritate the mostly male medical doctors in the room, but the director said, "Dr. Clemens, would you put together a five-minute PowerPoint for the president? Can you do it on a laptop while airborne?"

"Yes, sir."

~~~~~

&dardanus russian fleet westbound through hellespont

CHAPTER 38: THE BLACK HORSEMAN

Inter arma einim silent leges.
In times of war, the laws fall silent.
Cicero 107—43 BCE

Refugees Flee Atlanta

Wow-Wow Radio Mt. Pleasant, Georgia. "Interstate highways are clogged with traffic as citizens of Atlanta flee cold, hunger, and rioting that have swept the city. The Highway Patrol is helpless to respond to accidents often described as road rage run amok. However, there seems to be no shortage of volunteers to push disabled and burned-out vehicles off the roadway. Still, traffic crawls.

"Units of vigilantes, calling themselves a *Home Militia,* established barricades on the roads leading to the two major towns in this county. There are rumors that shooting has broken out between these vigilantes and refugees.

"The governor has declared a state of emergency and activated the National Guard, but only a few units are not already deployed to support the Department of Homeland Security.

"We have little news from the rest of the Nation, but it appears this is not a local phenomenon. There are reports of looting in abandoned areas of major cities."

&lkklad/&usamithras russian boomer nevelskoy strait southbound possible destination japan sea stop

&usamithras/&reddragon anything else on russian submarines query

&reddragon/&usamithras no on subs but partial message said deployment mobile missile launchers Kamchatka details follow

~~~~

&dikedyke water wolf loose thousands dead links uk helvetia at risk

~~~~

Mel Appleton, The White House, Oval Office

"My fellow Americans," President March mouthed the familiar but tired, greeting. "Once again we see the results of the failed policies of the previous administrations and of the liberals who would turn the Government into a grab bag of riches for those who are unwilling to work, unwilling to labor to provide food and shelter for themselves and their families.

"Their greed, plus corruption of local governments still under libsymp control, led to food shortages in a few neighborhoods. Rather than wait for the daily supply trucks from warehouses throughout the nation, these parasites looted grocery stores. In their haste, they often destroyed more than they stole, worsening the situation for themselves and for everyone.

"Faced with a breakdown in law and order, many people fled cities, seeking shelter in smaller towns. In some cases, they met armed resistance from patriots protecting their families and homes.

"A quick response by Public Safety Officers of the Department of Homeland Security, reinforced by citizen soldiers of our Armed Forces and National Guard, turned back the lemmings who would flee their cities, and put a stop to the free-for-all battles on the highways and byways of this Great Nation.

"Food deliveries have resumed. There may be occasional spot shortages, and your kids may not always find their favorite cereal or snack on the shelves. This, too, will be remedied. Please, be patient.

"To those who would take the law into their own hands, I have this message. *Habeas corpus* has been suspended. You will be caught and locked up until you can appear before a federal magistrate. You will receive the sternest punishment allowed under the law.

"To those who have held up the standards of this Great Nation, and who have persevered in these times of adversity, I have this message. You are the true Americans, the true Patriots, and you will be rewarded."

As usual, President March waited until all the television equipment had been disconnected and removed before speaking to his kitchen cabinet.

"Mel, do we have enough jails to hold them all?" the president asked.

"Yes sir," I said. "Do you remember those conspiracy theorists who were sure the government was converting old Wal-Mart stores into jails and FEMA was building concentration camps?"

"Don't tell me . . . " the president began.

"They weren't far off, sir." I filled in the silence. "Bare bones barracks and messing facilities on military installations, including some closed since the end of World War II. Hidden in the military construction budget. Rather than spend money on family housing, we built prisons."

And left military families in run-down buildings that didn't meet fire code, and in cheap trailer parks on the edges of military reservations, I thought.

"And food deliveries?" March asked.

"Every Army and National Guard transportation unit has been mobilized. We've sent DHS Agents—Bureau of Drug Enforcement—to guard them and to make sure our Mexican suppliers fulfill their contracts. We increased guards at seaports and airports and came down hard on the Longshoreman's Union."

That confirmed my suspicion—Warwick has a hook into the Mafia, I thought.

"We've invaded Mexico?"

"Not really, sir. Just a few hundred DHS agents making sure the food trucks aren't messed with by the drug cartels. Some of the *cárteles* have figured out they can make more money smuggling tomatoes or Argentine beef than cocaine."

~~~~~

&hackattack omaha base high alert locked down tight

&reddragon/&hackattack no broadcast us forces status send direct &usamithras not net

&hackattack/&reddragon wilco sorry

&reddragon/&hackattack okay you didnt know you good source

~~~~~

Pentagon Room M23R7, Brotherhood of Mithras

"Lieutenant Carson, what do you have for us?" General Kline asked. Although the Brotherhood of Mithras was a meritocracy, military custom was hard to put aside, and the general chaired the meeting.

"Sir, following the riots and flight from several major cities, the president has ordered military transportation units, including the National Guard, to transport groceries from Mexico and from ports on the east and west coasts. Two problems: they're leaving some of our units without adequate transportation or rations and they are burning up military fuel supplies. Here is the list of units; the second column shows how long they can last without resupply. Here is a list of military fuel depots, with an estimate of when they will be emptied."

"We're seeing similar problems with fleet oilers and normal resupply of bases and ships," a Navy Commander added.

"What are we doing about it?"

"A Canadian brother has diverted bunker oil, vehicle fuel, and jet fuel from refineries to our bases. The mechanics and nature of the diversion are closely held secrets," an Army Spec4 said.

"If the Brotherhood agrees, the Army will seize the old FEMA warehouses. They're untouched and probably not even known to DHS or the White House," Lt. Carson added.

"The FEMA warehouses contain nothing but MREs and some disgusting 'survival food' sold by a televangelist who had a connection with someone in FEMA. Do we have numbers?"

Lt. Carson put up her third chart. "Warehouse locations, keyed to specific units of the military, and estimates of how long the warehouses could feed the specified units."

She looked around the room.

"What say you all?"

~~~~~

FEMA Warehouse, Lexington, Kentucky

"We have orders to pull MREs and other rations from this warehouse," the Army Sergeant told the guard.

"Yeah, heard that. You're expected. Uh, if a few were to fall off the back of your trucks, we could feed our families, at least until things get back to normal."

"You haven't . . . ?" the Sergeant began.

"No, we took an oath, just like you. We have a duty, just like you. But it's getting right hard . . . and our families are hungry. We're at the end of the supply chain, here."

~~~~~

President March Takes on Looters

God's Word for You, American Fire Network, Washington Banner, and *Wheatly Today.* Rioting has intensified in New York and Chicago, and has broken out in Detroit, Atlanta, and other large cities following the hijacking of food delivery trucks and the looting of key food warehouses. The looting and hijackings are the work of libsymps, criminals who are bent on destroying the fabric of this Nation.

In order to combat this rebellion, President March at 6:00 AM today, declared Martial Law throughout the nation. Here is the president's statement.

"My fellow Americans, it is with a heavy heart I respond to this new and developing threat. A group of criminals who call themselves *Liberty Partisans* in some parts of the country, and *Minutemen* in others, seized upon the lifeblood of the nation: its commerce and in particular, food.

"Warehouses and trans-shipment points were looted; the eighteen-wheelers which deliver food to your local grocery stores were hijacked. Their drivers were cruelly murdered.

"Your government and the Public Safety Officers of the Department of Homeland Security responded quickly, and you will find food in your grocery stores. However, some elements of our society seized upon this news as an excuse to loot neighborhood grocery stores. The artificial shortages they created have led to worry, fear, and riots.

"This is a clear and present danger to the United States of America.

"A coordinated effort is needed to quell all aspects of this situation. This means the seamless cooperation of local police departments, state police, highway patrol, units of the Armed Forces, and Public Safety Officers of the Department of Homeland Security. The only way to ensure complete cooperation and coordination is to put all responders under the control of a single organization. The only way to do that is to declare martial law.

"Therefore, I have done so.

"Those who serve and protect, those who willingly place themselves in the path of real and present danger, who may sacrifice themselves to protect this nation and its citizens have already been alerted; plans have been made; and, yes, operations have begun."

~~~~~

&chicagocub no food riots here one grocery store looted but that a normal saturday night

&garyingary just back from otr to chi no problems there
&flowergirl otr?
&garyingary over the road long haul trucker
&phoenixfreddy why whole country we calm
&converseone fat dumb happy in hub city friend in atl says aok there
&modernbard rotten in denmark and dc

~~~~~

Martial Law

The World Citizen. "You've heard the official story. You've heard the Criminal-in-Chief. According to him, because of food riots in the cities of New York, Detroit, Atlanta, and Chicago, he has declared martial law across the country. The whole country. What you didn't hear is that he has also ordered the activation of all military units, including the National Guard and Reserves.

"He told us, 'operations have begun.' Translation: fighting has broken out between US troops and local militias, and between DHS goons and mobs of angry citizens. You didn't get that from the White-Wash House, did you?

"This is Muldoon. Who are you going to believe?"

~~~~~

&sunsinyi/&usamithras us forces returning home from korea dprk aware massing on dmz

~~~~~

Tim Karus, Archbishop Trucido's Estate

"A message from General Hamilton to the Director General of the Soldiers of the Cross was intercepted." I reported. "According to custom, he was taken on a guided tour of the gold repository at Fort Knox. They showed him some of the defenses, and took him into one vault. He demanded to see others. The custodians refused. He had them executed before he inspected the other vaults.

"Isaac, Fort Knox is empty. Even the one vault is a sham. A few gold bars, then gilded lead bars." *Councilor Ten has responsibility for that part of the country* I thought. *Amazing that he could pull this off. More amazing, I don't think he told Isaac, and he didn't pay Isaac his share.*

"Tim, take a message for Councilor Ten. Invite him to visit. Say nothing about Fort Knox. Do you understand?"

"Yes, Isaac," I said. *I understand more than you know. Councilor Ten is responsible for looting the US gold reserve. You planned to put your man there, but it was too late. Someone got there before you. You're getting old, Isaac. You're getting sloppy.*

~~~~~

Hurricane Hillary Hits Hard

The World Citizen. The hurricane that destroyed so much in Miami had a broader effect. Electrical substations damaged by previous hurricanes, including Katrina, which passed over Florida on the way to destroy the Mississippi Gulf Coast, were rebuilt only to *pre-hurricane standards.* That's all FEMA would pay for, and as much as the utilities' customers were willing to pay. Meaning that these electrical facilities were vulnerable to

366

Hurricane Hillary. Power outages extend from the Florida Keys to Cape Canaveral and west to Tampa. The Department of Homeland Security, in FEMA uniforms, is promising help to rebuild—to *pre-Andrew* standards—meaning just as vulnerable as before.

~~~~~

&couzan hillary cat 5 grand isle landfall

&highflyer/&reddragon aus met sets hillary track to pass over kenner cat 5 and cat 4 at baton rouge

&tardisboy/&reddragon my friends launched weather satellite polar orbit confirm cat 5 at new orleans

~~~~~

Hillary Makes Second Landfall

The World Citizen. "Winds over 150 miles per hour reported when the eye passed over Kenner, west of New Orleans. Australian Met and a new Canadian site are tracking the storm, but there is no word on death and destruction. Hillary continues on a north-by-northwest path. Brief messages from oilrigs in Gulf suggest all shut down, but not all evacuated in time to escape the storm. This is Muldoon. This storm is Katrina with PMS. We didn't learn from Katrina and we'll not learn from Hillary."

~~~~~

The White House, Oval Office

"Any good news, Mel?" President March rubbed his eyes, then took a large sip of his coffee.

"It's a stretch to call it good news, sir. The polls still show you are seen as the leader who can take us out of the current mess. Most of the news is about the mess."

"Let's have it, Mel."

"Rioters from the western DC suburbs attacked the homes of some of our friends in Middleburg. Two Saudi princes are confirmed dead. Their mansions were looted. It's not surprising what was taken was food, liquor, and cigarettes. Most of the art, furniture, and rugs that once might have fetched millions of dollars at auction were either untouched or destroyed."

"What kind of reaction are we getting from the Saudis?" President March asked.

"Noncommittal, sir. They're dealing with larger problems, mostly raids from Yemen. It looks like they cannot protect themselves."

"That's good news, Mel. Got any more like it?"

"Hurricane Hillary damage reports from first landfall are in. The storm not only wiped out much of Miami, but also the so-called *Millionaires' Mile*—the mansions of the rich and notorious. The hurricane has made a second landfall on the Mississippi delta south of New Orleans. No reports from there, yet. The Director of Homeland Security put on a FEMA jacket for a press conference, promising aid to rebuild."

"Where are we going to get the money?" March snapped.

"Your press conference is scheduled for 1:00 this afternoon. We'll break into the soap operas. Should give us a huge audience. I recommend you put the onus on the Congress to come up with the money. You're in the cat-bird's seat on this one."

"More good news, Mel. Keep going."

"North Korean troops have crossed the DMZ. The South Koreans have responded with force and appear to be holding the line. Russia has warned China not to get involved.

"You asked for updates on military command changes. There was one big one: the general commanding Fort Knox has been replaced by a General G. G. Hamilton."

"Neither good nor bad news, Mel, but please get me General Hamilton's file—not the Army one, the one Homeland has. Anything else?"

"No, sir. The Cabinet is waiting in the meeting room."

The White House, Cabinet Room

"Mr. President, we have traced a major node of the so-called *alternet* to Indianapolis. It's being carried on a broad-band system owned and operated by the city with the knowledge of city officials." The man from the Bureau of Communications, Department of Homeland Security knew to keep his remarks short.

The president looked at the Director of Homeland Security. She was the only woman in his cabinet and probably the most powerful woman in the country. She was good at what she did, however.

Like Mel, she's Warwick's creature, March thought. *Why? What does she have on him?*

"Why can't we shut down this alternet?" President March asked.

"Two reasons, sir. They're embedded in the internet, and we can't shut down alternet without shutting off our own communications. Second, they're also operating outside the internet on links we have trouble finding. Highly directional, low-power radio signals, for example."

"How important is Indianapolis to them?"

"Sir, it's only one of their nodes. If we shut it down, they would switch to others."

"It would send a message, though. Especially if we caught a bunch of them in the city," the president said. "And we need to send a message." He turned to the Chairman of the Joint Chiefs. "General Harris? Create a plan to take out that node and its operators; brief me in two days. With luck, the hurricane will distract everyone's attention."

"Sir, even with the changes to the *Posse Comitatus* act and the new Constitution, we will need something to justify direct military involvement."

"Let me worry about that, General. You create the plan."

"Mel, spin the food shortages into more riots created by the disaffected. That will justify our next step."

~~~~~

GETE Refinery, Fredenberg, Minnesota

Andrew Brown looked at the new control system. Solid state, redundant computers; dedicated links separate from the internet, large high-definition displays, and the system administrator password. He had control of every refinery and the entire petroleum pipeline system in the United States and Canada. His orders from the Brotherhood were clear.

~~~~~

Clover, Kentucky, God's Love Congregation, OTCC

" . . . he that hath no sword,
let him sell his garment,
and buy one."
—Jesus to his disciples, Luke 22:36

"The Disciples of Satan mass to our north! What was once a part of this United States of America has fallen to libsymps, to haters of God, to those who pervert the Justice of the Lord by spiriting away through their underground railroad those who we call before His tribunal. Having flouted God's law, they turn against mankind as well to covet and then to steal, to kill.

"We will not be able to see Pastor Fallow's sermon from the Washington Cathedral today because all communication circuits are dedicated to controlling the riots in Atlanta, New

370

York, Detroit and Chicago. We did receive a message from Pastor Fallow early this morning that Public Safety Officers from Homeland Security, as well as Soldiers of the Cross, are being moved to those cities and elsewhere to enforce the Law of the Land and the Law of the Lord."

~~~~~

&garyingary troops amphibious landing gary moving south i90

&buckeyeboy convoy westbound i74 passed oldenburg

&maelwen/&buckeyeboy army or dhs troops or soldiers of cross

&buckeyeboy army dhs soc all same apcs ak47s attitude

&daytondude ditto i70 west through vandalia 22 apcs 8 large trucks

&hoosierdad ditto i65 northbound crothersville apcs truks

&reddragon target likely indianapolis send convoy details and timing where possible flow control flow control indianapolis convoys and hurricane hillary only

~~~~~

The White House, Situation Room

He that lives by the sword
shall die by the sword.
Revelation 13:10

"What happened, General Harris?" The president bit off each word, clenched his teeth, and stared at the Chairman of the Joint Chiefs.

"Information got to the wrong people, Mr. President. Operational security was compromised. You will recall the Joint

Chiefs advised against including amateurs from the Soldiers of the Cross in this campaign."

"You may not blame them!" the Director General said. "They are led by the Lord God and they march under His banner. Their—"

"Enough!" The president interrupted the Director General. "We are discussing a military operation and not theology." He turned to the Chairman of the Joint Chiefs.

"Nor are we assigning blame, General Harris. What happened?"

"We approached Indianapolis from the north and south, and with two convoys from the east. Reconnaissance showed the interstate highways to be clear and all bridges in place. Intelligence confirmed no possibility of resistance until we reached I-465, the Indianapolis ring road. We had air assets prepared to strike targets as needed when our convoys converged on Indianapolis.

"All four convoys were ambushed well before reaching the ring road. The insurgents—"

"Call them *traitors*," the president said. "*Insurgents* lends them a legitimacy I do not want them to have."

"Yes, Mr. President. The traitors were well armed and well disciplined. They attacked from hiding with anti-tank weapons that disabled over seventy percent of the convoy vehicles with their first strike."

"Were the four convoys not in touch with one another? Could they not warn each other?"

"No, sir. We know the traitors can monitor military communications. The convoys were under strict orders to maintain radio silence. Vehicles with long-range communications were the first targeted. The traitors knew what they were doing. There is little doubt they included American military personnel."

"Survivors?"

"Uninjured and ambulatory were loaded on busses or trucks and driven to Rantoul, Illinois where they were dumped at the old Chanute Air Force Base. The trucks and busses were disabled and abandoned. We do not know how the drivers escaped.

"Military intelligence intercepted a message to *God's Word For You* from the Indiana University Hospital that they were treating a number of individuals who were, in their words, 'injured in multiple vehicle accidents near the city,' and that their morgue and the city coroner were processing more than three hundred dead."

"General Harris, this is a disaster. Mel? I assume GW4U is sitting on this for now?"

"Yes, sir," Mel Appleton answered. "But if GW4U has it, Muldoon will have it, too. We haven't heard from him, but we will. And so will everyone else."

"Can you spin it for *Gods Word* before Muldoon—"

"Already on it, sir." Mel interrupted the president, something he rarely did. *Spin it, already working, already calling them 'traitors' and worse names. These 'traitors,' stopped an invasion of a major population center. If those fanatics from the Soldiers of the Cross had reached Indianapolis, any resistance would have been met with air strikes—justified in the minds of these people. The insurgents may have killed 300, but they probably saved thousands of lives.*

~~~~~

Guerilla Warfare in Indiana

The World Citizen. "Criminal-in-Chief March sent DHS goons and soldiers to Indianapolis to shut down a not-so-secret node of the alternet supposed to be there.

"For the first time, armed civilians from the OTCC army, the SOC—Soldiers of the Cross—were along for the ride, and the killing. Whatever happened to *turn the other cheek?* Patriots from units of the Liberty Partisans and the Minutemen intercepted this invasion force, destroying many vehicles and capturing others. Messages from hospitals in and around Indianapolis put the number of dead at 300. There were no Patriot casualties. This is Muldoon. The church did not invent martyrdom, but it seems to thrive on it. Despite the carnage, this may have been a win for the OTCC. Think about it."

~~~~~

Those who can make us believe absurdities
can make us commit atrocities.
—After Voltaire 1694-1788 C. E.

Relief Convoy Disaster

God's Word for You. Convoys from churches in Ohio, Indiana, and Kentucky, carrying food for their brethren in Chicago, encountered heavy fog in Indiana and were caught in multiple chain-reaction accidents along the interstate highway. At least thirty volunteers, including children from God's Christian Army and the Rebeccas were killed. The survivors heroically helped rescue civilians caught in the pileup. Members of the One True Christian Church in states close to the cities whose food supplies were interrupted by terrorists have vowed to send new relief convoys.

~~~~~

The White House, Oval Office

"Goddamnit, Mel! How did Muldoon manage to scoop *GW4U*? What took *GW4U* so long to get out their bull-crap story?" Warwick demanded.

"Sir, *GW4U* had our version of the story in time for the seven o'clock news, but their local studio was hit by a power failure, and was dark until nearly four AM. They—"

"Sabotage?"

"Does not appear to be, sir. Underground substation in Georgetown hadn't been maintained in years. Explosion in a transformer knocked out the entire substation."

"And GW4U doesn't have backup generators?"

"No, sir. I've got someone on it, but generators of that capacity just aren't available. DHS has priority, and they've scooped up—"

"Mel? DHS works for the president. Fix this." Warwick hung up.

Sir, I continued the conversation in my imagination. *I've already thought about that. The president has told the Director to get generators to GW4U. But by making DHS so large, you and March have confounded internal communication lines so much that no one knows who to pressure to get this done. I've sent Frank Hopkins to DHS to work the problem. Sir.*

I hung up my imaginary phone.

~~~~~

&redstick disaster baton rouge 90 percent destroyed send help water medics food tents

~~~~~

New Orleans is Gone

The World Citizen. "With the help of many on the alternet, and squirts from all over the south, we've been able to piece together the devastation from Hurricane Hillary. You'll not see this from GW4U or the DHS, but our sources check out 100 percent.

"Deaths: more than 220,000 so far, most in New Orleans which was completely flooded, and Baton Rouge. Neither city is likely to recover from this blow.

"This is Muldoon. New Orleans was rebuilt after the Unnamed Hurricane of 1947 and Hurricanes Betsy, Camille, Georges, and Katrina—five of the most destructive hurricanes in recorded history. Isn't the definition of insanity doing the same thing over and over and expecting a different result? Think about it."

~~~~~

GETE Refinery, Fredenberg, Minnesota

André Bergeron put a map of the Gulf of Mexico on one screen and a list of drilling and production platforms on another. On a third, a map of refineries.

The platforms in the Gulf are toast, he thought. *Forty-five were damaged beyond repair. And 6 of those are leaking into the Gulf at a rate at least double the infamous 2010 spill. It will be months or more before the damage is contained and at least a year before any of them are back in production.*

At least twenty refineries were damaged to some extent. People are catching on, he thought. *Already gas prices have spiked. The average price of a gallon of regular gasoline in the US is $14.50 with a DHS ration book, and more than $50 on the black market.*

Where to begin? He wondered, and turned to the master control where every press of a key opened or closed a valve in a pipeline somewhere in the USA or Canada.

~~~~~

&falconone food prices Atlanta doubled in one week

&strongman mega corps ship usa food to europe better prices

&falconone how you know

&strongman stevedore port of savannah

~~~~~

Food Prices Skyrocket

The World Citizen. "Stories of high food prices and shortages of basics like cereal and bread are confirmed nationwide. Reports that wheat and other grains are being shipped to Europe are also confirmed—not that your government wants you to know.

"This is Muldoon. Do you know that Mr. Kellogg invented corn flakes to keep people from eating meat and then becoming ravaging sexual animals? Rest in peace. Mr. K. There is no way you could have predicted or prevented today."

CHAPTER 39: THE FIFTH HORSEMAN

Climate change does not respect borders; it does not respect who you are—rich or poor, small or large. Therefore, it is what we call a global challenge which requires global solidarity.
Ban Ki-Moon 1944-_____ CE

Cold Times in the Old Town, Tonight

World Citizen. "You won't hear it from your government, but Australia Met has predicted severe storms over the northern half of the US and southern Canada. In California, we've already seen high winds and heavy snow loads on trees, dead or stressed by the past eight years of drought. Trees have fallen onto electrical substations and power lines, leaving over fourteen million people without power. Calectric has said they cannot get crews out to make repairs until the storm subsides.

"Failure to maintain power lines and remove trees has been a recurring theme for the past twenty years. This is Muldoon. It is a flawed species that cannot learn from its past mistakes. Think about it."

~~~~~

Canadian Prime Minister's Cabinet Room

"The New England Electric Consortium is asking for a ten percent increase in power from us," the Minister of Energy reported. "They're experiencing a shortage of heating oil."

"Our man reports there's a surplus of heating oil at ports on the southeast coast of the US," the head of the Security Intelligence Service said.

"Yes, but it can only be transported to New England in US-flagged ships," the Home Secretary said. "An ancient law—the Jones Act—requires all shipping between US ports be on ships built in the US and crewed by US personnel."

"Even in this situation?"

"There have never been enough US ships to meet demand, and tankers flagged in other countries find it more profitable to ship US petroleum products to Europe."

"What are the consequences if we don't send the electricity?"

"Deaths. Hundreds, perhaps thousands."

"And the effect on Canada if we do?"

"Rolling blackouts in Quebec, Ontario, Newfoundland, and the Maritimes. Perhaps an hour each day in any given location."

"Do it, then. But keep a close eye on the effect. The Yanks don't seem to understand the Law of Unintended Consequences—like that Jones Act thing. I don't want to see this come back to haunt us."

~~~~~

WhatDrWho Blog

A severe Pacific winter storm is moving eastward. Oregon, Washington, Idaho, Montana, and British Columbia are blacked out with over 7000 known dead. UK Met Hadley Centre predicts the storm will grow in intensity as it is swept by the so-called polar vortex into the Midwest and Northeast. DHS Bureau of Weather is not saying. Meanwhile, heavy rains soak the south while rare winter tornadoes sweep Oklahoma, Texas, Arkansas, Tennessee, and Mississippi.

This is WhatDrWho blogging from exile.

Rolling Blackouts Nationwide

The World Citizen. "Always a dollar short and a day late, years of talk and political posturing and environmental enthusiasm have not kept up with the need for alternate power sources. The Watts Bar 2 nuclear power plant came on line in 2016. The last one built before that was in 1996. One reactor in twenty years? That's a poor record, people.

"Strong winter storms, linked by science to global climate change, have wreaked havoc with wind farms across the nation, and fewer than half of the turbines are still functioning. Not that there were ever enough of them to make a significant contribution to the grid.

"You'll not see reports of rolling blackouts in the pathetic puppet press, but they're happening, and you're feeling them. What excuse is your local power company offering? Whatever it is, it's a lie.

"This is Muldoon. Zip up those parkas, people. The proper collective noun for a large group of baboons is a 'congress.' Seems to explain a lot, doesn't it?"

~~~~

Hearing Room, Congressional Committee on Energy

The scientist from what had been the Department of Energy, now the Bureau of Power, Department of Homeland Security, was unapologetic.

"There are many reasons besides the storm that power is failing across the nation. Deregulation of the electrical power industry which was sold by lobbyists as a way to create competition and lower prices only created middle-men whose rake-offs increased the cost of electricity.

"The so-called Enron crisis, which was artificial and avoidable, wasn't the alarm it should have been. Greed and bribes have nearly killed the system. There is no money to be made in new transmission lines, and at least 30% of the generated power was lost getting it to places like California which have for years refused to allow any new power plants to be built within its borders."

The Junior Senator from Kentucky jumped in. "When you add the libsymp's politically motivated attack on clean coal power, would you say we face a crisis of our own doing?"

"Senator, I cannot speak to the reasons behind what you call an attack on coal, except to point out that coal is the dirtiest of all fossil fuels, and there is no such thing as clean coal. However, I support your supposition that the crisis was self-inflicted. And your party's war on science is certainly a contributor."

The chairman's gavel broke before he could silence the shouts between the two men.

~~~~~

Pravda: truth
Izvestia: news

There is no *Pravda* in *Izvestia*
and no *Izvestia* in *Pravda*.
—Russian aphorism from the
Communist era

Samizdat

The World Citizen. "This is my last article or broadcast on the internet. The Department of Homeland Security has shut down our servers in Washington and New York. We're operating from a temporary node in the mountains of— I'd better not say. But they're sure to find it and shut it down, too.

"During the Communist regime in the former Soviet Union, the only real news was passed from person to person through *samizdat*: pages typed on manual typewriters with multiple sheets of carbon paper. Does anyone besides me remember carbon paper—or manual typewriters?

"*The World Citizen* is as of today a modern *samizdat*. We'll be producing flash drives with our message. We'll be sending bits and pieces, whatever will fit, on the *Squirt* system and the alternet. At least, they've not been able to shut that down. It will be difficult for you to know what comes from us and what's posted by the propagandists of DHS, the OTCC, and the AFFP. The Bureau of Rectitude has already sent out information claiming to be from us, but which is not. You know what we stand for. Pay attention to what you hear; think about it. Find the truth for yourself. This is Muldoon with a message for the AFFP and the OTCC: 'Just because you've silenced someone doesn't mean you have converted him.'"

~~~~~

Del Bonita, Alberta, Canada

Despite the best efforts of the DHS, the border between the USA and Canada was porous. The Canadian commander stared through his binoculars at the white flag.

"Surrender or truce?" he mused.

"They're Yankees," his aide replied. "Can we trust them, sir?"

The commander thought for a few moments. "Will you and the others trust me long enough to assume it's a flag of truce?" he asked.

The aide had the grace to blush. "And longer," she said.

The Canadian commander recognized the gesture that identified the Yank as a brother in Mithras; the American commander nodded at the countersign, and relaxed.

"We are 4,000 soldiers—regular army," he said. "We have transport for all—APCs and trucks. Our fuel tankers are depleted. No wounded. We seek refuge with our brothers until we can return to victory."

"As soon as you can be vetted," the Canadian officer replied, "we will return your weapons and ensure you are well supplied. Are you willing to allow us to take the lead?"

~~~~~

&delriocommand/&usamithras 4108 regular army safe and billeted

&usamithras/&delriocommand please hold in place and thank you

&usamithras/&tomsdad mission briefing at del rio arrive soonest report canforces command

&tomsdad/&usamithras wilco

~~~~~

Tom Kelley, Windsor, Ontario

"Like what you see, Tom?"

The mirror showed Tom Kelly and his dad, standing behind him."

"Yes, Dad. This is me. This is the me I've wanted since I was, like, seven years old."

"Are you ready to pay the bill?"

Tom tucked his penis in his underwear and pulled up his pants. "Yes, Dad. I'm ready."

"We will leave for Del Bonita, tomorrow. There's an American military unit encamped there. They need intelligence; they need a courier to contact their allies still in the States. It will be dangerous, Tom."

"I know, Dad. You've always encouraged me to do what I believed in . . . like knowing that I was a boy. Are you okay with all of this?"

"Yes, Tom. I'm happy for you, and happy you have the courage to act on your beliefs." *No matter where that may take you*, the man thought, but did not say.

~~~~~

Refugee Crisis Reaches USA

The World Citizen Samizdat. "Refugees from Europe are joining those from the Middle East, Africa, and Central-South America to stream into the USA through Mexican and Canadian borders. In a policy reminiscent of the *Exodus*, a ship carrying Jewish refugees from Europe to the Mandate in 1947, modern ships carrying refugees have been intercepted by the US Navy and escorted back to their ports of departure. There are rumors that at least two ships defied Navy orders, and were sunk.

"Dulles International Airport has run out of room to park the influx of private jets, including at least one Boeing 747, which have brought a different class of refugee into the country. The Department of Homeland Security has begun moving the planes to military bases in South Carolina."

~~~~~

Tom Kelley, Del Bonita, Alberta, Canada

"Tom, at sixteen you're too young to be a regular soldier, but you're old enough to be a member of a militia. That will be your cover . . . and it will be real. The people who you've been staying with are members of a militia called the Soldiers of 1776. They've been outlawed by the USG, and you will be arrested if the feds discover the link. You know the names and hometowns of members of other militias. Your job is to smuggle SIM chips for iPhones to as many of those people as possible. You must be sure they're the right people. Those SIMs have the encryption keys for the net we'll be using when we return to the US. When we return, we want to be met with allies, not ambushes."

We? Tom wondered, and then realized: *Dad is part of this, too.*

~~~~~

Pentagon, Room M23R7, Brotherhood of Mithras

"Russia and China are facing off over the war in Korea," an Army captain began the meeting. "Both are at heightened alert."

"Anything threatening us?"

"Not since the president pulled out our troops."

"Anything nuclear?"

"Both countries have put some of their boomers to sea, but our brothers tell us there's no indication they'll go nuclear. We've sent that information through appropriate channels."

"And at home?" an Army Spec-Four asked.

"There are two flows of refugees. Those heading north into Canada include the military units we have sent, and some organizations styling themselves *Patriots* and *Modern Minutemen*. There are also reports that bands of survivalists from the northwest are moving to Canada.

"The second flow is from the northern tier of the Midwest—Illinois, Indiana, Ohio, Michigan—toward the warmer south. We have used this as justification to move military units from New York and New England. We gave this information to our contacts in Canada. They are massing forces in Quebec."

The briefer, an Air Force lieutenant, paused for questions.

"I think we should encourage our contacts in Homeland to deploy as many of their forces as possible to the Midwest," an Army captain said.

"What say you all?"

~~~~~

Whitefish, Montana

The minstrel boy to the war is gone,
In the ranks of death you will find him;
His father's sword he has girded on,
And his wild harp slung behind him.
Traditional

"It's a boy. He's been shot. Medic!

"Stay with me, son . . . stay with me! Medic! What's your name, son?"

"Tom Kelley . . . father at Del Bonito . . . tell him, please. Tell him his son died for his country . . . and that he was happy."

The boy's breath stopped, his eyes glazed.

Tom Kelley, Del Bonito, the soldier memorized.

~~~~~

Pentagon, Room M23R7, Brotherhood of Mithras

"The Army has lost contact with the Rocky Mountain Brigade. They were chasing survivalist *rebels*, and the Army fears the worst—that they were overcome by hostile forces. We have word they have reached Canada and established a camp near Aetna. They report 89% strength. Wounded are being transported to various hospitals in the area."

CHAPTER 40: THE PALE HORSEMAN

I am sick and tired or war.
Its glory is all moonshine . . .
War is hell.
William Tecumseh Sherman 1820-1891 CE

The White House, Situation Room 3:00 AM

"Mr. President, the Sino-Soviet faceoff over North Korea continues. The Russians and Chinese have increased their readiness. The Russians deployed sixty-four mobile missile launchers. We are unable to track them through the taiga forests of northern Russia. Do you have any questions, sir?"

President March shook his head, and the televised link from the Pentagon went dark. The president, the aide who carried the football, the president's senior military aide, and Mel were the only ones in the situation room.

"Mel, it's time to get out of Washington," President March said. "What can we do?"

"General Fall," Mel addressed the senior military aide. "Have Air Force One prepared for immediate takeoff. And scramble the Marine helos."

"What's the story for the press?" March asked.

"The UN is relocating to Brasília," Mel replied. He was on his own, without Warwick's advice and orders. "Fear of Ebola in New York, mostly, but we don't need to say that. Attacks on delegates who are foreign-looking is another reason, but we don't need to say that, either. Delegates to the Security Council departed last week. You are flying to Brasília to address the Security Council and a rump session of the General Assembly. You're the *peacemaker*, sir."

"As long as our *Peacekeepers* are on high alert," March said. Mel knew he meant the US fleet of nuclear-armed ballistic missiles and bombers.

Brazil's a good choice, March said. *And it may be a long visit. As soon as I get to a computer, I can transfer accounts from Barbados, South Africa, and Australia to banks in Brazil. Hell, I can do that from Air Force One.*

As soon as the meeting broke up, Mel hurried to his office and called Warwick.

"Mel, yours was the best response. You will remain. I will need you in DC."

"Yes, sir."

~~~~~

Vice President Stanley's Condominium

"Mr. Vice President, the president will leave the country for Brazil, where he will address the United Nations. The Rules of Succession dictate we remove you to a secure location. Can you be ready in an hour?"

"Yes, of course. What about George and Henry?"

"It would be best if your sons were to continue their routine. If we removed them people might make the wrong assumption. We will supplement their details, but there's no reason to believe they would be in any danger."

The secret service agent saw the vice president's frown. "Sorry, sir. I mean *in any increased danger.*"

"Will anyone else be relocated?" Stanley asked while putting out clothes to be packed.

"The Chief Justice and the first two other members of the Supreme Court we can reach and a handful of Congresspersons. It's just precautionary, sir."

"Supreme Court? Congress? This is more than protecting succession. What's going on?"

"That's all I was told, sir. I'll tell you if I learn any more."

Thomas Stanley wakened George to say goodbye. "We'll be in touch. They assure me there's secure communications where I will be, and you know how to use the secure phone in my den. Your detail will take care of you . . . and make sure you do your homework. Please listen to them; do what they ask. This won't be long—only until the president returns from Brazil."

"Yes, sir. May I tell Henry?" George asked.

"You may call him after school today."

~~~~~

Air Force One, Over the Atlantic Ocean

"Sir, the Russians have deployed more mobile missile launchers," General Fall hung up the secure phone and reported."

"We should strike first," President March said.

"Mr. President, the mobile launchers are intermediate-range missiles," General Fall protested. "They cannot reach American territory. Intelligence sources confirm the warheads are conventional explosives, and the most likely target is North Korea."

"And if the launchers hold ICBMs? And if they're nuclear?" March asked.

"Defense would notify you if the Russians transmitted launch codes, and would provide warning of any launches," General Fall said.

"Not good enough. We must strike, first. Stewart, open the football," March ordered.

The air pressure in the room seemed to drop as everyone except March inhaled at the same time. The American strategy had been for years *retaliation*, and not *first strike*. Lt. Colonel Casey Stewart looked at General Fall.

"Sir, that is unnecessary," General Fall said. "Our deepest intelligence sources assure us this is between the Chinese and the Russians."

"General, you are out of order. Stewart, open the football."

General Fall nodded. "I verify code 'Mark Anthony.'" The General used one of the two access phrases he and Casey had memorized.

No one saw the look the two soldiers exchanged, or the determination in Casey's eyes. "Yes, sir."

Casey pressed the code sequence. As he did so, he thought of the lines he had memorized, "Friends, Romans, countrymen, lend me your ears. I have come to bury Caesar, not to praise him."

Rather than opening to reveal the nuclear launch codes, the twenty-five pounds of C4-S explosive in the briefcase detonated. Air Force One was shielded and protected from many external threats, but no one had imagined an explosion of this magnitude in the president's quarters. The entire starboard side of the fore cabin blew into space. Walls between the quarters and the aft section collapsed. The escort tankers, fighters, and NEACP aircraft watched the death of the majestic Boeing 747 called *Air Force One*.

The flight crew in the cockpit was isolated from the rest of the aircraft. They survived the original explosion but not the 125-mph impact with the water of the South Atlantic Ocean.

Raleigh Academy, Classroom 107

The boys looked at the door when it opened and bounced off the doorstop before being halted by the hand of the man who stood there. Secret Service Agent Ken Parnell waited only long enough to spot Henry Stanley. "Henry, we must go, now. Leave your books but bring your backpack. This won't take long."

Henry whispered to Parnell as the man urged him to hurry. "You're not supposed to be in the classrooms."

"Do you have your cell phone?" Parnell asked.

Henry nodded.

"Give it to me."

Henry did not hesitate. He handed Parnell the phone. Parnell removed the battery. They entered a service hallway. Parnell threw the battery and phone against the cinderblock wall, smashing them.

"What?" Henry said. He would have stopped, except Parnell's hand on his shoulder pushed him toward an exit door.

"Your cell phone can be tracked. Even when powered off. A broken phone will suggest you were attacked." The man ripped the radio from inside his jacket, pulled the curly wire from his ear and the microphone from his wrist. He threw them against the wall.

"Another red herring. So they can't track my radio. They will know pretty quickly we're both off the grid. They'll start looking for us."

"Ken, what's going on? Who will be looking for us?" Henry asked. That he'd used Parnell's first name was a sign of his fear.

"Out the door; in the truck. I'll fill you in. We have to move," Ken responded.

~~~~~

Washington, DC, House Office Building

Two men and a woman entered Representative Thomas Vaughn's office. They flashed badges that meant nothing to Thomas.

"Sir, the president is dead. The Congress is being dispersed to ensure continuity of government. Please, come with us."

"What about my son, Ted? My wife? My—"

"Sir, this is precautionary. Your family's details will be increased. It is important the American people know you are safe."

~~~~~

Friends School, Arlington, VA

The removal of George Stanley from his school had gone smoothly. His Secret Service detail were loyal members of the Soldiers of the Cross. None questioned the orders nor hesitated to follow them.

They whisked George into a black SUV with heavily tinted windows. The SUV became one of five identical vehicles in a convoy on Interstate 66 West. Traffic thinned after Centreville, and they turned off the red and blue lights and sirens. At Interstate 81, they turned south and then took state and county roads west, deep into the Allegheny Mountains.

~~~~~

Department of Homeland Security Alternate Command Center

"Mr. Vice President, the president is dead. Air Force One blew up over the Atlantic Ocean. There is no possibility of survivors. Chief Justice Thomas is waiting to swear you in."

"Where are my sons? What caused the explosion? Were they attacked? Are we at war?" Stanley asked.

"Your sons are being taken to safe locations. We are not at war. Our forces are on heightened alert. So are the Russians and Chinese, but that's over North Korea, not us. The cause of the explosion is not known, except that it was internal to the plane and not the result of a missile.

"We have a video conference set up in the Situation Room, sir."

Thomas Stanley took the oath of office, witnessed by three members of the Supreme Court, seven members of Congress, and a dozen Secret Service agents. The recording went to US news agencies and parts of the internet that were still functioning.

"Make sure it gets the widest coverage," ordered Mel Appleton. "And get the president back to the White House as soon as possible."

Office of the Speaker of the House

Speaker Henry Stafford had politely but firmly refused to be relocated. His Secret Service Detail outnumbered and outgunned those sent to remove him.

"I will be safe in Washington, DC at the heart of this Nation, or I will die with it," Stafford said. He knew one of his aides was videotaping the confrontation. "That is the end of it, and that is final."

As soon as the DHS people left, Stafford spoke to his staff and Senator Beasley. As Speaker Pro Tem of the Senate, Beasley would be Stafford's successor as president should something happen to both Stanley and Stafford.

"I want the entire House of Representatives dispersed to military bases throughout the nation. We are in a crisis, and we must protect our ability to govern. This means ensuring the survivability of our Congress. Senator Beasley, I recommend you do the same with the Senate."

"Shouldn't we name a new vice president, first?" Beasley asked.

"And how long do you think that would take? Days? Weeks? We cannot delay, Senator."

"Of course, Henry. Right away." Beasley turned to leave.

Henry, he says. I am now only one heartbeat from the Presidency and still he calls me 'Henry.' Presumptuous fool!

~~~~~

&reddragon for net president march dead stanley now president

~~~~~

Henry Stanley

Ken Parnell drove a pickup truck—something the groundskeeper used. Tools—wheelbarrow, rakes, shovels—filled the bed. He drove off the campus through a back gate. I didn't see the face of the person who closed it behind us. He?—She?—wasn't in uniform or the long overcoats the Secret Service wore. The sky was overcast, but the sun peeked through. I looked at my watch and the sun. We were headed north.

"Ken? What's going on? Where are Dad and George?" I figured if anyone would know, Ken would.

"President March is dead," Ken said. "You know that means your father is president. He's in a hidden command post, taken there as soon as the late president took off in Air Force One earlier today. There are people who don't like some of the things your father believes in, but they can't kill him, yet. They took George hostage for your father's good behavior. They won't harm him; they need him.

"I was ordered to take you hostage, too. Henry, I won't do that. There's something rotten in America, and I won't be part of it. This isn't a kidnap. It's a rescue."

George Stanley

One of the Secret Service agents checked the bathroom before letting me in. The man stayed in the doorway, and then took me to a booth at the back of the truck-stop diner.

"Order what you want, but please be quick. We're more vulnerable here than on the road," the man said.

"Where's my dad?" I asked the question I'd wanted to ask since we had left Friends School. "And Henry? And where are we going?"

"Your father and Henry are safe. We are taking you to a place where you will be safe. Only the driver of the lead vehicle knows. It's better that way."

I saw impatience in the man's speech and in the way his eyes rested on each person who entered the diner before moving on. I ate quickly, but didn't drink much of my soda. *Don't know when they'll stop, again,* I thought. *Don't know when I'll be able to pee.*

~~~~~

New President

The World Citizen Samizdat. "A White House spokesman said that President March died when Air Force One crashed into the Atlantic Ocean, but gave no details or explanation. Our sources tell us the plane exploded in mid-air before falling into the sea.

"The nation has a new president. Vice President Thomas Stanley, former Representative from Oklahoma, was sworn in surrounded by a Secret Service detachment. He is at a secret location. We've been promised he will return to Washington, DC, soon.

"Who is next in line? By law, the House of Representatives must select a new vice president. Until then, the Speaker of the House, followed by the President Pro Tem of the Senate, are next. But Speaker Stafford has ordered the House to be dispersed throughout the country . . . there will be no quorum of the House as long as his order is in effect.

"This leaves us with Stafford and 'Weasely Beasley.' Stafford is buried so deeply in his, um, ambitions, he can't see daylight. Beasley is afraid of his own shadow and more afraid of Stafford. This is Muldoon. In the beginning was the word, in the end only the cliché. We're between a rock and a hard place, between the devil and the deep blue sea, between Scylla and Charybdis. How did we get here? Where are we going? Think about it."

Mel Appleton, The White House

"Mel, President March relied on your organizational skills and your advice," President Stanley said. "Would you keep the chief-of-staff job and the office?"

"Yes, sir. I will. Thank you."

"Thank you, Mel. Now, what's important?"

I spent an hour alone with the president, listing and describing the most critical tasks and decisions facing him.

"But before you can tackle this list," I concluded, "you should make a televised appearance from the Oval Office. May I bring in a makeup tech, and have the crew set up the cameras?"

"Certainly, Mel."

～～～～

Henry Stanley

Henry hid in a small compartment under bananas on their way from Honduras to Canada. The truck stopped. A young man opened the compartment.

"*Bienvenue au Québec*; welcome to Quebec," he said. "I am Remi, and I will be your conductor for the next part of your journey. But first, you piss, I think? Are you hungry?"

"Yes, but I don't think I'll ever eat another banana," Henry said. He laughed, but it was a false laugh. "What's going to happen to my father?" he asked. "And George?"

"Your father is safe; we don't know yet about your brother."

～～～～

Warwick's Estate

"The younger son is in protective custody, but the older boy has disappeared."

"What do you mean, disappeared?" Warwick demanded.

"Our man in the Secret Service removed him from his classroom but they were attacked before they left the school. We suspect he's been kidnapped by someone, but we have no idea who. No demands have been made.

"They dumped the Secret Service agent by the side of a road. He had been beaten pretty badly, but gave a description of the attackers and their vehicle."

~~~~~

Somewhere in Province Quebec, Canada

Remi made two calls, and then put aside the cell phone. He talked while Henry ate. "Henri, your father is now the President of the United States. President March is dead. His plane exploded over the Atlantic Ocean off the coast of French Guiana. Your father's position is secure and his safety is assured, at least for the moment. Known forces seek to control him. If they cannot control him, they will remove him. They kidnapped George and hold him hostage for your father's good behavior. George is safe. We are working to remove him."

Henry absorbed the threat to his father and brother. *Ken Parnell had help. Remi was expecting me.* "Remi, who are you? Who is the *we* you speak of?"

"Henri, all I can say is that we are friends. If you will trust me, I will take you to someone who will answer all your questions."

~~~~~

George Stanley

I spent the night in a barracks of an unnamed military base. I had breakfast before they took me to a helipad where a V-22 Osprey sat. *Marine Corps, I'll bet*, I thought, although the craft was unmarked.

There was only one person in the cockpit.

"May I ride in the copilot's seat?" I asked.

The pilot looked at the Secret Service agent, who shrugged. "No reason why not." The man's instructions were clear. *Keep the boy happy; do nothing to suggest this is anything more than a rescue to ensure his safety. Promise him anything.*

The Osprey was the coolest non-jet aircraft in the US inventory. I watched everything the pilot did and memorized the instrument readings during vertical flight and transition to horizontal flight. When I heard the pilot sign off with air traffic control, I pressed the intercom button and asked, "How about a little stick time?"

The pilot jerked his head to the left and stared at me.

"I've got a student ticket and two-hundred-fifty hours ASEL and sixty-one hours in helos," I said. "And twenty hours in a glider in Switzerland. Oh, and seven hours in a hot-air balloon. They're all legal and logged hours." *If they don't lose my logbook!* I thought.

"Sure . . . just be gentle," the pilot said. He grinned. "I don't want you to shake up the guys in the back. Put your hands on the controls. I'll make a couple of maneuvers. You follow. They you can try. Okay?"

"Sure, that's how my aerobatics instructor does things," I said.

"Aerobatics, too? I'd better watch out—you may get my job." The man laughed, but I don't think he was laughing at me.

"This is going to be a six hour flight. How about I take a nap?" the pilot asked after a sequence of maneuvers.

I grinned. "I don't think so, but thanks for the offer. Uh, may I see the flight plan?"

The pilot showed me the route to our destination. "We're going to some hot-shot's estate in the Adirondacks. About the only way to get there is VTOL."

When we were thirty minutes from our destination, the radio interrupted our conversation. "Romeo Foxtrot Seven Seven squawk ident."

"Would you do that, George?" the pilot asked.

I pressed the button on the transponder.

"Romeo Fox cleared through approach corridor. Contact destination on 257.8 Sierra."

I switched the number one radio to the new frequency.

"257.8 *Sierra*?" I asked.

"Secure frequency, encoded. Same system Apple implemented once . . . before DHS threatened to shut them down, completely. Only sender and receiver can decrypt."

Same system the alternet uses, I realized. *I wonder if I'll be able to connect when we get to wherever we're going.*

Collège Militaire Royal de Saint-Jean, Quebec, Canada

"Mr. Stanley, I am Justine Lacombe. Welcome to the Royal Military College of Saint-Jean."

"I know who you are, sir. You're the Prime Minister of Canada," Henry replied.

"Not many of your countrymen know Canada has a Prime Minister," Mr. Lacombe said. "Even fewer would recognize his name."

"Actually, sir, your name has been vilified in American media since the day you won the election, and promised to withdraw Canadian fighter jets from the coalition fighting ISIS."

"Perhaps you should catch up on the news from America," the Prime Minister said. "We will talk more tomorrow, please."

~~~~~

George Stanley

Not only was my room nicer than the one in the barracks the night before, but there were pajamas and clothes in my size. A lot of clothes. *How long will I be here?* I wondered. *And where are Dad and Henry?*

"My name is Richard Warwick," the man who joined me at breakfast said. "I will be your host for a while, at your father's request. Your father is safe. He was taken to a secure location when President March left the country for a conference in Brazil. Unfortunately, President March never arrived. He is dead and your father is now President. We also took steps to protect you and Henry."

At my father's request? If it was at my father's request, you would say one of our safe words. I shouldn't have to ask. You should say it. But you didn't. Something's wrong!

"Your father will return to Washington later today or tomorrow and will address the nation from the Oval Office. He's made one address by video conference from his safe location, but the symbolism is important, don't you agree?"

All I agree is you're one smooth son of a b—, I thought, but responded with a "Yes, sir, that makes sense. When may I speak to him? And Henry?"

"You may speak to your father and brother as soon as the Secret Service can install a secure phone. Because of our location, that will take several days."

You can have a secure satellite phone flown here in less than six hours. That's a disconnect; is it a lie? You are more guard than guardian, I think. I kept my face carefully expressionless when I said, "Thank you sir, I understand."

Tractable, toward, trusting. Those are the words for today.

Tim Karus

"Warwick got ahead of us," Isaac said. "He's kidnapped George Stanley and is holding him at his estate in New York. I want that boy, Tim. And I want the heads of the SOC men who sold out to Warwick."

Trucido's iMac screen showed a photo of George Stanley, a photo of George in a swimsuit, standing on a diving board.

Why do you want him, Isaac? He's older than I was, but I know the look in your eye.

~~~~~

&maudi/&reddragon stanley younger son captive at warwick estate adirondacks can you notify right people stop

&reddragon/&maudi who are you how do you know stop

&maudi/&reddragon my life in your hands trucido aide tim karus tell president stop

&reddragon/&maudi u safe with me stop

~~~~~

Tommy Carron, Saint-Jean-sur-Richelieu, Quebec

Remi, who had become more than my host, but also a good friend, woke me up at 6:00 AM.

"We have a new guest. He's a Yankee—well, at least, he's an American. He's a refugee, like you. He speaks no French. They thought if you would be his host and translator, at least for a while, he would be more comfortable. Will you do this?"

I was a little surprised. Everyone at my school and the military school was bilingual. Most of them spoke English better than I spoke French, but I agreed. I was dressing while we talked.

"What 'they' thought I should be there?" I asked.

Remi grinned. "You will meet them, at breakfast."

The Yankee turned out to be from Oklahoma by way of Virginia and Vermont. He was Henry Stanley, the son of the new American president. He had a New England Yankee accent. *His French is going to be something,* I thought, and nearly giggled before they came to the table.

They turned out to be the Prime Minister of Canada and two of his cabinet members—Defence and Intelligence—who ate breakfast with Henry, Remi, and me. Mr. Lacombe talked about the need to organize the flood of American expatriates and refugees.

"We are running out of resources to care for them," the Prime Minister said. "We want to help but we cannot. The unseasonable winter has strained our food supplies and we fear for the next wheat crop. We cannot import food from Europe—they have food shortages, too. I do not know what to do except reject future refugees and return many of those who have already arrived. I do not want to do that."

"Many will be imprisoned, perhaps executed, if they return," Henry said.

"Not if they return as an army," the Prime Minister said. He looked hard at Henry. The man's lips were compressed, his eyes narrowed.

"Many arrived armed. They call themselves patriots. Entire military units have defected, and are living in barracks or tent cities. It is a closely held secret that they are here and that we have not confiscated their weapons. Together, the patriots and military constitute an army. An army that could successfully return to the US—if you were to lead it."

We sat in a bubble of silence amid the chatter of the cadets in the dining hall. Then, Henry answered.

"Sir, I accept. What is your timeline? How large an army do you anticipate? Will Canadian forces join us? Will Canada provide air cover? You said *lead* and not *command*. Big difference. We need to talk about it. I'm sure I will have more questions, but those are all I can think of now."

The Prime Minister folded his hands on the table. "I have a question for you. What do you know of your father?" he asked.

"Only that he has become president and will—"

"Your biological father," the Prime Minister interrupted.

"He was Canadian," Henry said. "He died before I was a year old. I may not say any more, sir."

"Do you know why?" Lacombe asked.

Lacombe waited for Henry's answer.

"He was assassinated by Canadian republicans because he was an earl," Henry said. "But I think you already know that."

"Many Canadians are fiercely independent of the United Kingdom, although we remain a member of the Commonwealth and the Queen is our monarch," Mr. Lacombe said. "Many other Canadians are fierce Royalists. You inherited your father's title. On balance, I think it is time to acknowledge that."

~~~~~

Mel Appleton's report to Warwick was brief, but it created a firestorm. Warwick immediately called Trucido.

"President Stanley will repeal most of March's executive orders."

"Why is that a problem?" Trucido asked. "They are enshrined in the new constitution."

"But they are all enforced by agencies of the executive branch, and Stanley is now the chief executive. He has worded his order to prohibit enforcement. It's the same trick March used. The Golden Rule: he who has the gold, rules."

"What are you going to do about it?"

"It is time to play our trump card."

Our trump card . . . the Stanley boy, Trucido thought, and reluctantly agreed.

~~~~~

The investiture of Henry Tudor Stanley as Earl of Richmond was held in the chapel of the school. The Governor General, as the Queen's representative, presided. Afterwards, over tea and biscuits, he described Henry's genealogy.

"Your father's line is noble, but your mothers' perhaps more so. She is descended from Katherine, daughter of Charles VI of France. In fact, if the French still had a monarch, you'd have the best claim to the French throne."

"Your knowledge of genealogy is amazing, sir," the Prime Minister said.

"Justine, I have few duties and a large staff. I'm allowed only one political office: to remove the Prime Minister if warranted. I am rather glad that's not been the case. Otherwise, it's speeches at academic colloquiums, charity fundraising, and university graduation exercises. Lots of time to pursue my hobby."

~~~~~

The White House, Mel Appleton's Office

The call was on the special cell phone. *Warwick*, I knew.

"Yes, sir."

"Mel, I'm glad you weren't on that plane. You're the best I have."

I'm the best you have, I thought. *I'm your creature, and you never intended me to rise beyond this position. Certainly not as long as you think you can use me.*

"George Stanley is franked up, safe at my estate," Warwick said. "Tell President Stanley that George is hostage to his good behavior, and that he must not interfere in any way with the original orders and the plans of the AFFP and OTCC. Let him draw what conclusions he will."

"Yes, sir," I said, and thought, *You're threatening the life of a child! You crossed the line, Richard Warwick. You crossed the line.*

~~~~~

The White House, Oval Office 11:00 AM

President Stanley addressed the nation. "A number of the late President March's executive orders were unconstitutional when they were issued. Despite the adoption of a revised constitution, I question their validity. Therefore, the following Executive Orders issued by the late president are hereby rescinded: 001 regarding women in command positions in US military units; 002 regarding stem cell research; 003, regarding abortion and other women's medical procedures; and Number 129 regarding implantation of computer chips.

"The orders will not be enforced by any Executive Branch Agency.

"Other Executive Orders issued by President March are undergoing review. Some have merit, and I will issue amended orders in the near future."

President Stanley put down the single pen he had used to sign his Executive Order Number One.

"I know this will be unpopular with some people in this country," he said. "I know this places the lives of my sons in jeopardy."

In response to gasps and quizzical looks, he added, "The government of the United States had been infiltrated by people with their own agenda, and their own goals. I hereby serve notice that those are neither the agenda nor the goals of this administration.

"As deeply as it pains me to do so, I must put the life of this nation ahead of the lives of my sons."

~~~~~

Warwick's Estate 11:00 AM

Ken Parnell was the only passenger in the AH-1Z helicopter inbound to a secret location in the Adirondack mountains. His orders were to join the Secret Service detachment protecting a person of interest. Ken's sources had given him the details. The person of interest was Jamie's friend, George Stanley, and he was a prisoner.

"What are your orders?" he asked the pilot.

"Drop you off, refuel, and return to base, sir," the pilot answered.

"Any problem waiting until I get my feet on the ground?" Ken asked. "I may need you to relay info to HQ . . . things I can't put even on secure comms."

"No problem, sir. Happy to help," the pilot responded.

"George, I was sent to guard you. I'm really here to rescue you. I helped your brother on his way to sanctuary in

Canada. He asked me to find you and told me to say 'Golden Compass.'"

One of our safe words, George thought. *Safe words Warwick didn't have. Can I trust this man?*

"You wonder if you can trust me," Ken said. "You know me . . . you know my son, Jamie. You know how much your brother and you mean to him. In the end, it's not safe words and it's not politics, it's people and relationships. That's all I can say. The rest is up to you."

"I trust you, sir," George said. "What's the plan?"

"The safest place for you is with Henry in Canada. The helo I came in is being refueled. It will get us halfway there. We'll have to refuel somewhere. And I'll have a gun to the head of the pilot the whole time. It's not a great plan, but it's the only one I have."

"You can forget the pilot," George said. "I can fly the helo. But what about Jamie? They're going to find out you are behind this. What will happen to him?"

"Think the worst, and you'll be half right," Ken said.

"Then, we'll have to get him out, too," George said.

"Unacceptable risk to you."

"Sir, you and whoever you are really working for want something from me. I trust you, but if you expect anything from me you'd better find a way to rescue Jamie."

~~~~~

George monitored the radios, but heard nothing.

"They've got to know about us," Ken said.

"Yes," George replied. "They know what frequencies we can monitor. They'll be operating on others. We should be all right as long as they don't send fighters after us. But we need to refuel. Any ideas?"

Ken pointed to an airport on the map. "Small, but it says they have the right fuel. I can't find an alternate."

George nodded, and tweaked his heading a few degrees. "Got a credit card?" he asked, and laughed.

"Don't think I've ever sold fuel to a Marine helo, especially one piloted by a kid," the man who ran the Fixed Base Operation said.

"You got a well?" George asked. "I sure could use a big dipper of water." *Follow the drinking gourd*, he thought.

The FBO operator stared at the boy. "Yeah. Yeah, I've got gourds full of water."

Then he said, "Um, who you runnin' from, if you don't mind me asking?"

"To start with, my name is George Stanley," the boy said.

"Olie-Molie," the man said. He turned to his ground crew. "Top off the tanks and make it fast.

"Your dad's going to take us out of this mess," he said to George. "You need anything else?"

"Only your trust," George said. "We've even got a credit card to pay for the gas."

"Better not use it," the man said. "A lot of the internet is blocked, but they've had to keep it open. They can track transactions. Keep your card in your pocket."

Charlotte, Vermont, East Bay Academy

George landed the helo on the school's front lawn. Ken jumped out, knowing he was trusting the boy with his life and his son's. He ran toward the building and flashed his credentials at the resource officer. "Official business," he said. "Will you help me find student Jamie Parnell? He's a friend of the president's son. I need to remove him so he does not create a threat to the other children."

The words, *official, president, threat* echoed in the resource officer's mind. "Yes, sir! Follow me," he said, and ran ahead of Ken toward the school's office.

Minutes later, Jamie was in the helo. Ken saw surprise on Jamie's face when he realized George was at the controls. Surprise, and something else. Ken tucked that thought away.

George raised the collective. When they were above the fence that surrounded the school, he pushed forward on the cyclic. The helo resumed its flight to the north.

Telecon Warwick and Trucido

"Have they found him?" Trucido demanded.

"It's a goddamn goat-rope!" Warwick said. "Either they've landed, or the kid is flying through the trees. Radar can't see them. Homeland has scrambled fighters and the Air Force is trying to get an AWACS with look-down radar, but the closest is—"

"He's got to be found," Trucido said, and slammed down the phone.

"You sanctimonious jerk," Warwick said to the dead line.

Collège Militaire Royal de Saint-Jean, Quebec, Canada

"Nice wheels," Henry said when George showed him the helo. "I had to leave the car Dad gave me, but you managed a helo. Slick."

The mention of their father was enough to sober both boys.

"Dad's already making waves," George said.

"I know. He's cancelled a bunch of March's executive orders and is challenging the new constitution. That's going to piss off a lot of people."

~~~~~

With the help of technicians from the Security Intelligence Service, including a young woman not older than fourteen but who wore the uniform of a Leading Aircraftsman, George reached the alternet.

410

&highflyer/&reddragon golden compass and yukon safe in canada red queen red queen stop

&reddragon/&oldpatriot stanley sons safe in canada confirmed red queen can you notify father stop

&oldpatriot/&reddragon wilco

~~~~~

"Golden Compass and Yukon safe. Red Queen." President Stanley looked at the slip of paper he found under his napkin. Careful not to be seen, he crushed it in his hand.

~~~~~

The White House, Mel Appleton's Office

Warwick's anger came through the tiny speaker of the secure cell phone.

"The younger Stanley boy escaped aided by the same Secret Service agent who supposedly was assaulted when the older brother was supposedly kidnapped. It's pretty clear he was a traitor the whole time. How did someone find out the boy was here?"

"Already on it, sir. NSA cracked a message on the alternet that George Stanley was at your estate. The message came from somewhere in Virginia, but that's as far as they could track it. Who knew about—"

"Other than people at my location? Only Trucido, you, and the two pilots. No such message ever came from here. Where are the pilots?"

"Dead, sir."

"That leaves Trucido. I'll contact him."

Tim Karus

"Tim, you didn't tell anyone where the younger Stanley boy was, did you?" Isaac asked.

"No, Isaac. Of course not." I forwent the obvious question, *Why are you asking me?*

"The boy was removed, rescued. There were messages on the internet. One from Virginia."

I called upon every iota of the control I had learned as Trucido's acolyte and catamite.

"Do you want me to investigate, sir?"

"No, Appleton has the NSA tracing messages. They'll find where they originated."

~~~~~

WhatDrWho Blog

The French deep-sea research vessel *Nautilus* has reached and recovered portions of the wreckage of Air Force One. Their analysis confirms an explosion occurred in the forward, starboard cabin that houses the president's quarters. What is surprising is that they found chemical traces of an explosive, suggesting the explosion was the result of a bomb. How a bomb got aboard remains a mystery.

The US Department of Homeland Security Bureau of the Secret Service disputes the French findings, claiming there is no way such a bomb could escape their screening. A spokesperson said the French are once again trying to stir up dissention in this Nation.

Meanwhile, the Congress, charged to select a new vice president, remains isolated and sequestered on the orders of Speaker of the House, Henry Stafford. As long as there's no new vice president, Stafford is next in line to become president. I don't believe in coincidences. Stafford's up to something.

This is WhatDrWho blogging from exile.

~~~~~

Tim Karus

The conference table, large enough for the Council, held only three people. Although Warwick had objected, Trucido had insisted Warwick fly to Virginia, and that I be present for their meeting.

"Gentlemen," I said, "Washington is in turmoil over President Stanley's saying the government has been infiltrated. Stanley has asked for the resignation of the Director of Homeland Security. There is talk he will cancel martial law and convene Congress. When that happens, they will select a new vice president who would supplant Stafford, and who may not be in your control.

"There are reports classed as 'likely correct' by intelligence that Henry Stanley is forming an army in eastern Canada and plans to invade the United States.

"Food riots and other civil unrest continue throughout the United States."

"We have got to get control of the situation," Warwick said.

"And here is how we will do that," Trucido replied.

~~~~~

&maudi/&reddragon village elders will keep congress from meeting know of henry army in quebec president in danger may trace my messages stop

~~~~~

The White House, Oval Office

A man wearing a curly wire from his collar to his ear, burst into the Oval Office.

"Mr. President, we have a credible report of an airborne threat to the White House. We need to evacuate you, immediately." A second man followed the first, then a third.

"You're not my regular detail," President Stanley said. "Where are they?"

413

"In the convoy, sir. Please, you need to leave now."

Stanley followed the men and ducked into the black SUV. The convoy moved through nearly empty streets. By the time it reached the Walter Reed National Military Medical Center, President Stanley had been injected with a powerful narcotic and was unconscious.

~~~~~

Office of the Speaker of the House

"Sir, President Stanley has been taken unconscious to Walter Reed. Indications are he suffered a brain embolism. It's unlikely he will regain consciousness. Where would you like to be sworn in?"

"Make sure he stays alive," Stafford ordered. "The ceremony will be in the Oval Office. You have time to get television set up. Let's roll."

The White House, Oval Office

Bert Rightly's normally acerbic voice was a somber whisper. "President Stanley fainted at his desk, and was taken to Walter Reed. The doctors say he's suffered a massive cerebral hemorrhage and is not expected to regain consciousness. Under the laws governing succession, and because the Congress has not elected a new vice president, the Speaker of the House, The Honorable Henry Stafford, will be sworn in as president.

"Just a moment . . . yes, yes . . . we have word that the presidential motorcade has arrived. The swearing-in will happen momentarily."

The White House, Mel Appleton's Office

Mel left the door between his office and the Oval Office open as Presidents March and Stanley had wanted. He was working at the computer when he heard the president's telephone ring.

"Stafford. Who . . . Yes, sir."

Warwick or Trucido, Mel thought. *The only people he would call 'sir.'*

"I've learned that they're using propofol . . . Yes, it's the same stuff that killed that pop star. Stanley's being monitored constantly . . . I know how it happened. They'll keep him alive. On the upside, we'll make sure his son knows where his daddy is. Walter Reed is fortified and surrounded by our troops. If the kid shows up, he and his daddy are toast."

Son-of-a-bitch, Mel thought. *They staged this! Warwick and Trucido. And they did it because they think Stafford will follow their instructions. He's taking advantage of it, but I wonder if they really know him.*

~~~~~

Headquarters, Soldiers of the Cross, Lynchburg, Virginia

"The younger Stanley boy escaped with the aid of one of our own."

"Do we know where they are? And what of the traitor? What about his family?"

"The Stanley boy flew the helicopter. Our pilot tried to stop them, but was killed. They refueled at a small airport. The fixed base operator was interrogated. He knew who Stanley was, but didn't know where they were going. He was executed.

"They rescued the traitor's son, his only family member, from a school in Vermont. They are likely in Canada."

~~~~~

Collège Militaire Royal de Saint-Jean, Quebec

George and Jamie, Remi and Tommy, Henry, and the Prime Minister filed into the room. Cadet Sergeant MacLauren, assigned to Henry's security detail, carried a TAVOR X-95 carbine and stood where he had a clear line-of-fire to the door.

"I have two choices," Henry said. "I can abandon the invasion, in which case they'll keep Dad in a coma until he dies—and he will die if they keep pumping drugs into him. I can invade. If I invade, there are two likely outcomes: they'll ambush us if we try to rescue Dad, or they'll kill him before we get to him. There are no easy choices."

"Henry, you've got to lead the invasion," George said. "Do you remember when Dad said he had to put the life of the country before the lives of his sons? He didn't know then we were safe."

No one else offered an opinion; this was a decision for the two Stanley boys.

Henry nodded. "You're right, of course, George. Mr. Lacombe, we will continue with our plans."

~~~~~

The White House, Oval Office

"Mr. President." Thomas Vaughn stepped into the Oval Office. "What can I do?"

Smooth, Stafford thought. *Just the right balance of obsequiousness and strength. Something to be said for being raised by old money.*

"Thomas, come in, please sit down."

"Mel, close your door, please."

"Thomas, there are some things you need to know. One is that some very powerful people were not happy with the brief administration of President Stanley. They put him in the hospital."

"Do you mean . . . ?"

"Yes, his coma was induced. If these people can get to one sitting president, they can get to another. I want to be damn sure that doesn't happen. And you are going to help me."

Help you, or else, Vaughn thought. "Yes, sir; of course. What can I do?"

"Start sounding out Congress. We can't keep them scattered all over the country much longer. We need to make sure whoever they name vice president and the next speaker are not aligned with the far right—religious or political. We'll call them compromise candidates. If the godfathers think my replacement will be another libsymp like March, they'll be reluctant to remove me.

"I want you working the phones 24/7, and meeting with me each day with the results. As soon as you think you've got a respectable majority and a viable candidate, we'll call them all back to DC."

"Yes, sir. I understand." *I understand you want me to do more of your dirty work. It wasn't enough to pervert the Constitution? To kiss up to those bigots, those tools of the so-called Christian Church?*

~~~~~

&highflyer/&usamithras henry stanley will return 1 december 1 december

&usamithras/&highflyer copy first december

~~~~~

Pentagon, Room M23R7, Brotherhood of Mithras

"Henry Stanley's army will enter the US at zero hours the first of December. We have deployed military forces away from the invasion routes. *Agents provocateur* have stirred up trouble in the Midwest and South, drawing DHS forces into those states. There is still much to do.

"If you are agreed, we will assemble the Brotherhood, take control of the War Room at zero two hundred local time tomorrow, and execute Plan Patriot.

"What say you all?"

~~~~~

Collège Militaire Royal de Saint-Jean, PQ

Henry Tudor Stanley faced his key staff. He wore a khaki uniform without insignia except for the escutcheon of the Earl of Richmond on a breast pocket and the former American flag—the stars and bars—on his right shoulder.

"We have three objectives: knock out the Department of Homeland Security Bunker under CIA headquarters; take control of Washington, DC; and rescue President Stanley and return him to office.

"Sun Tzu said the supreme act of war is to subdue the enemy without battle. We are facing a force that can be a hundred times larger and more powerful than we are. The more we can subdue without battle, the more likely we will reach our goals. We must take advantage of every opportunity to win without conflict.

"Our strategy will be to move swiftly while gathering support from Minuteman and Patriot units as we press toward Washington.

"Our main forces will cross on every available bridge and ferry from Niagara Falls to Montreal. They will form the Western and Center Columns. Some of the Center Column will pass close to Fort Drum, home of the 10th Mountain Division of the US Army. That unit has been deployed to Memphis, Tennessee to maintain civil order. No resistance is expected.

"Other units, primarily American military forces augmented by irregulars, will cross into North Dakota, Montana, Idaho, and Washington. They will be small, and will operate clandestinely to stir up trouble to draw US forces toward them. Their secondary objective is to capture US military installations.

"Smaller units will cross at Three Rivers—I'm sorry my French is not good enough to give that city its proper name—and Quebec City. They will sweep through Maine, Vermont, New Hampshire, and Massachusetts. These units will form the third column, pass well west of New York City, toward Philadelphia, and into Maryland. We have already sent agents to those states to contact Minuteman and Patriot units.

"The people of the USA are accustomed to seeing military convoys. That will work in our favor. They are unlikely to report something so familiar.

"We have allies who will monitor radio, telephone, and internet traffic. They may not be able to stop it, but they can warn us.

"G-2, what have I overlooked?"

"Sir, we cannot leave Carlisle Barracks at our backs. It may be the *Bunker Hill* of this war," the Chief of Intelligence said.

"Do we have any contacts in the area?"

"We have sent two men to recon," the G-2 said. "A contact was vetted. They'll approach the contact and try to get access to the post."

Pentagon, War Room

The guards at the War Room had no reason to deny entry to the soldiers who presented credentials. They all passed the biometric scans. Shift change had been four hours ago, but the guards were accustomed to people assembling for exercises and crises. At least one of the soldiers approached each person already on duty. A signal on their subvocal radios, and they drew their side arms.

"You are under arrest. Come quietly and you will not be harmed."

The second wave of the Brotherhood entered; the original watch staff was outnumbered three-to-one—odds too great even for a hero. One woman managed to hit the duress alarm under her desk, but the security command post had been secured five minutes earlier.

Two HUM-Vs drove through the gates of the Washington Naval Yard; two more through the gates of Fort

Meyer; one drove onto Bolling Joint Forces Base. The credentials of the people in the vehicles passed muster, and the arrests of the Joint Chiefs of Staff and their Chairman went easily.

Pentagon, Conference Room, Brotherhood of Mithras

"I had a dog that loved to chase cars. My boy couldn't keep him in check. Once, when the dog broke the leash, the car he was chasing stopped. My kid hollered, 'You caught it, what are you going to do with it?'

"That's the question, folks. We have control of the War Room and we have the Chiefs on ice. The excrement is going to hit the rotating airfoils in about fifty-six hours when Henry's army starts crossing bridges. We may have a few hours grace. Are we prepared to play this charade for three days, possibly more?"

"Yes, sir. The cover story is holding. A 'succession of command' exercise. The Chiefs are observing from a secret location. The shift we relieved has been vetted; those who are members of the Brotherhood will continue to fill their places. The next shifts will be treated similarly as they show up. Those who are not members will be dismissed. Since they've been working twelve-on and twelve-off for the past three months, they'll not likely complain. They'll also be told this is a secret operation."

"We have fifty-six hours to move more troops out of harm's way, and out of Henry's way.

"What say you all?"

~~~~~

"Shoot if you must,
this old gray head,
But spare your country's flag,"
she said.
—*Barbara Frietchie* by
John Greenleaf Whittier
1807-1892 C.E.

Carlisle, Pennsylvania

"Barbara Frietchie?" the man asked. The woman's appearance—short skirt, high leather boots, short jacket with fur at the collar and wrists, platinum blonde hair, and heavy makeup—did not evoke the image of Barbara Frietchie but of a prostitute. But the man continued, "I'm Mithras Rider; this is Camelback."

"I'm Frietchie, also Mithras Tall Drink," she completed the exchange of recognition words. "My car . . . the commander expects us.

"General Brackenbury?"

"That's the one," she said.

The woman did not drive to the headquarters building but to the General's home. It was a huge natural stone edifice that the men might have mistaken for the Officers Club had she not explained. The two guards snapped to attention when the woman got out of the car.

A man in fatigues, with three stars on his collars, met them.

"Gentlemen, welcome. I see you've met my G-2, Colonel Darla Patterson. She's usually in camo, but that would have drawn the wrong kind of attention downtown."

"Gentlemen, you are in danger here, but your commander needs this information. I'll be brief. The Brotherhood is in control of Carlisle Barracks. The entire complement of the post will join your forces. Please keep

Colonel Patterson apprised of your movements. If she's not available, I am Mithras Able Boy. Questions?"

"No sir."

"Thank you, sir."

"See you in Washington," Brackenbury said.

Colonel Patterson took the men to the car they had left in a shopping center.

"Thank you. See you in Washington," one man said.

"I'll be here . . . monitoring comms and providing intel," she replied. "Good luck to you."

~~~~~

Mauritania, West Africa

The *Klaatu Maru*, a freighter converted into a passenger ship, left Casablanca on a southwesterly course. It would turn and follow the coast of Africa to Johannesburg. The passengers had paid well for their passage although their accommodations were Spartan. Water was rationed, and a bath in anything other than seawater was impossible. The crew was concerned about pirates and kept water between the ship and the African coast.

"GPS shows we are 170 km west of Luanda," the watch officer reported to his relief. The new watch officer shook sleep from his eyes—it was three o'clock in the morning, and he'd not yet had tea.

"Any chatter that might be pirates?" he asked the radioman.

"No sir. I heard a piece of a distress call. I thought it might be pirates, trying to lure someone to their position, but it cut off before giving coordinates."

"Very well, keep a sharp ear on your scanner."

A waning gibbous moon lit the sea well enough for the watch officer to see thatthe water ahead of the ship was unusually rough. He glanced at the weather instruments. The wind was broad on the starboard bow at seven knots—hardly enough to stir the water. He did not consider slowing.

The Equatorial Counter Current once flowed from near Mauritania on Africa's west coast toward Cape Verde, before swinging south and east toward Guinea. When it met the Guinea Current, it was pushed eastward to join the South Equatorial and the Gulf Stream. Now, this water, warmed by the summer sun, flowed south along the African coast where it met the cold waters of the Benguela Current. The two great rivers of water collided off the coast of Angola where a temperature inversion occurred—the warmer waters flowed under the colder water. At the bottom of the ocean, warm water bathed ice-bound chunks of methane—*methane clathrates*—that had not seen temperatures greater than minus thirty degrees in millennia. Slowly at first, then more quickly, the clathrates melted.

As the melting became greater, the water's capacity to absorb the gas was exceeded, and gas bubbled to the surface.

The *Klaatu Maru* sailed into the cloud bubbling from the bottom of the sea. Without oxygen, the passengers and crew suffocated. The ship, guided by automatic systems, sailed south until it ran aground on the breakwater north of Tombua Bay.

~~~~~

&maudi/&reddragon otcc mission caluquembe angola reported ship klaatu maru ran aground tombua 300 dead cause unknown

~~~~~

Trucido's Estate

"Tim, does anyone know what our missionary in Angola means by this message about the ship?"

"The best guess is one of those fast-acting diseases that are springing up in Africa."

"How are our relocation plans coming?" Isaac asked a more important question.

"Eighty percent of the gold, platinum, and diamonds have been sent in small batches in diplomatic bags to our man in the embassy in Brasilia then placed in your vaults," I said. "The vaults were closed. They can only be opened with your passcode." *Which I know*, I thought. *You were careless again, Isaac.*

"The rest is being shipped over the next few days as Bibles and religious materials to our people in the cathedral. Your home is ready, staffed and guarded. The Bishop of Brazil has expressed some concern that not all of the right people have been bribed, but he's confident that will be solved."

"I'm not happy about that, Tim. Send another platoon of the Soldiers of the Cross and provide quarters for them. Bachelors . . . I don't want to worry about family loyalties. They can find enough whores to keep them happy. You will leave this afternoon and take charge of things in Brazil. I will remain here until the new year."

"Yes, sir."

&maudi/&reddragon target list follows

~~~~~

Major Troop Deployment

The World Citizen Samizdat. "There are more riots than the goons from DHS can handle, and they've called in the heavy artillery and tanks. There's a major redeployment of military units in the entire northeast. They're moving toward the Midwest—Ohio, Indiana, Illinois, Tennessee, Kentucky.

"Batten down the hatches if you live in those states. This is Muldoon. Sometimes, the boy who cries wolf is right, and the wolf is at the door. Think about it."

~~~~~

&highflyer/&reddragon army on the move stop when becomes public please ask for intel pass to &usamithras they are coordinating

&reddragon/&highflyer wilco

&reddragon to net burn bad guys repeat burn bad guys

Bad guys meant anyone not known to be on the side of Red Dragon and High Flyer. The orders were unambiguous: *burn them* meant destroy them. Signals to hidden programs downloaded long ago were sent. Hard disks crashed, flash memory vanished, and e-proms cooked. The internet and the alternet were in the hands of the good guys.

∼∼∼∼∼

Trois-Rivières, Quebec

December 1, 0001 Hours. Two columns of vehicles—APCs and civilian SUVs painted army drab—approached the bridge that spanned *La Fleuve Saint-Laurent*. They were followed by trucks carrying both soldiers and supplies. At the rear of the column were field ambulances, mostly civilian EMT vehicles painted drab, but with large white circles and red crosses on sides and top.

From *Parc Labiolette* came the martial sounds of drums and brass instruments. Despite the hour and the cold, The Cadets of Shawinigan had demanded to be part of the effort. Too young to fight, they were not too young to salute their elders.

∼∼∼∼∼

Headquarters, Soldiers of the Cross, Lynchburg, Virginia

"They will try to rescue their father. They will probably use a helicopter to remove him. Remember, the younger boy is a pilot."

"What have you done to prevent that?"

"Three teams of two men, each. Armed with Stingers—shoulder-mounted SAMs—surface-to-air-missiles. They can home in on the infrared of the helicopter exhaust. They will be in position in ten hours."

CHAPTER 41: FINIS

And the fourth angel poured out his vial upon the sun,
and power was given to him to scorch men with fire.
And men were scorched with great heat.
Revelation 16:8-9

DHS Bunker

"I'm sorry, Ms. Singer, your ID is no longer valid. Please wait here." The guard was polite but brusque. Thirty minutes later, a woman arrived with papers in her hand.

"Ms. Singer, your employment with the Department of Homeland Security has been terminated. I have instructions to retrieve from you all government property in your possession, including your cell phone. You will be required to sign this paper acknowledging your termination for cause, meaning you will not be eligible for unemployment compensation. These documents affirm your security oath to include a prohibition against working for any media company, organization, or outlet for the next ten years."

"You can't have the cell phone. It was given to me by the White House," Polly said.

The young woman's mouth hardened. "Guard!"

~~~~~

&lakerfan catalina channel bubbling ice melt sickness freeways jammed with refugees

Pentagon, War Room

"What do we have on the DHS bunker?"

"The worst of cold war paranoia with the best money could buy. Deep, reinforced, self-contained." The captain put a diagram on the screen.

"Fuel-air bomb won't do it. A B-2 with conventional bunker busters might, but even that's not certain."

"Tactical nuclear? Tomahawk, maybe? Precision guidance," someone asked.

"I'm opposed to going nuclear," an Air Force Lieutenant Colonel said. "There's no doubt in my mind that General Fall and Colonel Casey agreed."

Silence followed. Everyone knew Air Force One had suffered an internal explosion in the president's quarters. Many surmised the cause. This was the first time it had been spoken of. The speaker had once been a member of the White House detail. The others acknowledged his experience and understanding. It was agreed—conventional bunker busters, but no tactical nuclear weapons.

~~~~~

The Eastern Column of the invading army met resistance at Greenbelt, Maryland. Members of the Soldiers of the Cross had set up a defense at Good Luck Road. They faced the oncoming army, but were unprepared for the attack by Patriot units from their rear.

~~~~~

Interstate highways, the commuter routes of US Highways 1, 50, and 29, and the grand avenues of Washington provided easy access to key targets. The invading army met little resistance.

~~~~~

&steeldrummer   hundreds   dead   scarborough   tobago suffocation gas from sea

~~~~~

The White House, Oval Office

Mel's office door was cracked open.

Stafford addressed Representative Vaughn. "Thomas, Stanley must be killed before this invading army gets any closer. If they get him off the drugs, he'll be president. That must not happen—"

Stafford broke off when Mel entered the room.

"Perhaps Representative Vaughn and I should take care of this for you, sir," Mel said. He thought he saw a glint of something in Stafford's expression. *Triumph? He thinks I'm his creature, too?*

Mel dismissed the Secret Service detail. He and Thomas Vaughn, the junior representative from Rhode Island, drove toward Walter Reed.

"Thomas, your son is a friend of George and Henry Stanley, isn't he?"

"Well, yes. Ted and Henry were roommates at Raleigh Academy."

"Would your son like to see his friends' father assassinated? Would he like to know you had a hand in that?"

Vaughn heard a threat in what Mel said.

"Where is my son? What have you done with him?"

"Thomas, as far as I know, your son is safe. For the moment. You know Stafford's allies held Stanley's youngest boy hostage for Stanley's good behavior, don't you? What makes you think he and his coterie of vultures won't do the same to Ted?

"Thomas, we're almost there. You have little time to make a decision. We've been ordered to eliminate President

Stanley. I plan to ensure he's alive when Henry's army reaches Walter Reed. Are you with me?"

Vaughn needed less time than was available to decide. "You are right. I was wrong. What do I need to do?"

"Follow my lead," Mel said.

When Mel and Thomas reached Walter Reed, Mel removed a revolver from an ankle holster and handed it to Vaughn. "I'm sorry, that's the best I can do."

"Not a problem, Mel. I'll just have to make it count."

The Secret Service guards recognized Mel and Thomas, and they understood the power structure: these were important men, close to the president. That gave Mel and Thomas the time they needed. They fired. Men fell. An agent had time to draw his Glock. He raised the pistol and fired. The bullet struck Mel in the left shoulder. Mel dropped.

The Secret Service agent turned the pistol toward Thomas Vaughn whose five-shot Beretta was empty. Before the agent could fire, there was a report, and a blotch of red appeared on his chest. He fell to the ground. Thomas Vaughn spun around to see the young man in khakis who stood behind him, pistol in hand.

"Mr. Vaughn, will you surrender?" Henry Stanley asked.

"Surrender? Henry, I've been expecting you," Vaughn said. "Stafford sent us to assassinate your father; Mel turned it into a rescue mission."

Henry grasped the situation. "We need to get out of here before Stafford's forces regroup. Please, help me with my father and Mr. Appleton."

Henry spoke into a two-way radio. "Yukon to Golden Compass, *My kingdom for a horse.*"

George was less than a quarter-mile away. He stifled a giggle before he keyed the microphone. "Horse on the way. Three minutes. Rooftop."

He opened wide the throttle of the UH-1H.

Before the skids hit the roof of the hospital, Cadet Sergeant MacLauren, wearing a flak jacket and carrying a serious assault rifle, jumped from the side door of the helo. "Load! Load! Now, now, now!" he yelled.

"Liam! You've been watching too much American TV!" George made sure the intercom switch was set to *private* and left it on long enough to hear Liam's laugh.

Tommy Carron, wearing a medic's armband, helped load the unconscious men onto the floor of the helicopter.

~~~~~

&oldpatriot/&reddragon white house secured by friendlies stafford suicide most blood cleaned up

~~~~~

"Horse squawk ident."

George pressed the button and crossed his fingers that the code was a good one. His breath stopped when two Army Blackhawk helicopters popped up beside him. He began breathing again when one moved into position ahead of him and he heard, "Horse from Bosworth, follow me."

~~~~~

&frerejacques paris brule tremblements de terre effondrement ville tout est perdu

&pqprime brother john reports paris is burning earthquakes have collapsed the city all is lost

~~~~~

"Horse from Bosworth. SAM launch! They've locked on! Evade! Evade!"

~~~~~

Pentagon, War Room

"The Brotherhood is in agreement. We will cut off the heads of the hydra that has seized this nation."

"We have air assets in New York and Virginia ready to destroy the three key targets."

"We have identified and are tracking twenty secondary targets. There may be collateral."

"In an acceptable range?"

"Yes, ma'am."

"I say we execute the plan.

"What say you all?"

~~~~~

WhatDrWho Blog

Hamas-Daesh has vowed revenge on Israel for an air attack in the Syrian province of Quneitra that killed a several fighters and a key leader of the Daesh organization. Speaking for Daesh, Muhammad Hashem said, "When Israel attacks anywhere they want in whatever way they choose and at any time they elect, then we have the right to make a similar response at a place and time, and in a way of our own choosing."

There's no one who questions what this means: their target will be the USA.

This is WhatDrWho blogging from exile.

~~~~~

&guyanagal georgetown guyana sea beyond offings burning

&shearwaterpatriots1/&usamithras soldiers of cross hq lynchburg captured no survivors

&shendoah33/&usamithras mithrasair intercepted fired on steered into target massive explosion stop

&shearwaterpatriots2/&usamithras mopping up at shenandoah target no survivors stop

~~~~~

At a walled and gated estate in Brazil, Tim Karus stood on a balcony. He held a rum punch and the hand of a Brazilian boy with dazzling teeth and dark eyes.

~~~~~

&mithrasair22 adirondack target destroyed bunkerbuster awesome stop

&meadeee hack attack hoover dam gates wide open turbines blown no electricity from here lake draining warn downstream stop

&windycitygirl city blacked out no electricity one hour left on generator will lose chitown satcom link stop

&mithras1776 homeland hq bunker surrounded but fortified we outnumbered but accept challenge stop

&whatdrwho reports of nuclear explosions jerusalem baghdad riyadh stop credible source stop

&longjohnsilver usn destroyer found adrift caribbean all dead doc says gas/suffocation stop

&reddragon any ideas anyone any link klaatu maru, tobago, gyuana, usn destroyer stop

&witwat atlantic gyre restored warm currents where not before methane clathrates melting gas killing exploding stop if enough methane melts atmosphere will tip runaway greenhouse venus-effect 800 degrees stop

CHARACTERS

Adams, Rudy [tardisboy] and **Adams, Edward, PhD [WhatDrWho]**, his father. Dayton, Tennessee and Guelph, Ontario.

Al-Embic, Caliph: Leader of ISIS/ISIL/Daesh.

Allison, Mary Ann and daughter Jane: Quakers, members of the Underground Railroad.

Anderson, Wallace, PhD, SciD: The Science Guide, *National Television Service.*

Angler, Ernest: Pastor of God's Love Congregation—OTCC, Clover, KY and Presiding Officer of the town's Investigating Committee. Sons **Matthew** and **Mark**.

Appleton, Mel: Political advisor and speechwriter to Senator (later President) Edward March after assignment by Richard Warwick. Becomes confidant of President Stanley.

Baker, Harold: Waldon, Alabama "libsymp." Warned to leave town just before being brought before an Investigating Committee.

Bat Boy: Chiropteran whose life and exploits were reported in the *World of Weird*.

Beasley, James: (AFFP-NV) Senate Majority Leader.

Beman, Azisa: (speaks loudly in thunder-tones). Lawyer for Southern Freedom Law Center; boyfriend of Ruth Gordon.

Bergeron, André AKA Andrew Brown: Canadian intelligence operative and senior GETE refinery operator, Fredenberg, MN.

Brackenbury, General. Commander, Carlisle Barracks, Pennsylvania.

Carron, Tommy: Mt. Pleasant, Georgia. Flees false charge of assaulting a Pastor. Becomes part of Henry Stanley's inner circle.

Carson, Sandra: Lieutenant, US Army; West Point graduate. Member, Brotherhood of Mithras.

Clemens, Karen: RN, MSN, PhD; horse-holder at CDC, Atlanta.

Close, Sugi: Warm-blooded Alabama boy, alternet administrator, sound man for Polly Singer.

Clover, Kentucky: Mr. Barnes, lawyer; son Sam Barns; Principal Glenn; School Board member, Mrs. Campbell.

Cookson, Michael: Internet savvy blogger and hacker. Pen name "Tom Paine"; hacker name "Red Dragon." Arlington, VA.

Coyne, _____, Dr.: Polymath on faculty of University of Guelph, Canada.

Dart, _____: Dr. at University of Witwatersrand, South Africa.

Davis, _____: Councilor #6 to Archbishop Trucido. Territory: US east coast from Maryland to Florida; Caribbean.

Deputy Director, Department of Homeland Security: Career civil servant; promoted to Director under March administration.

Director General of the Soldiers of the Cross. Unnamed figure who reports directly to Archbishop Trucido (q.v.). Commands the Soldiers of the Cross, including those who are members of the Secret Service. Probable head of intelligence for Trucido. Staff members include disciples within the ranks of the army and others who handle raids, arrests, torture, etc. Headquarters, Lynchburg, VA.

Fabulist, Frank: OTCC member, elected to Mt. Pleasant City Council.

Fall, General: USAF; member of the Brotherhood of Mithras. Instructor, USAF Academy; faculty member, Squadron Officers School; Commander of White House military detail.

Fallow, Russell: Pastor; Bishop of Washington and public head of the One True Christian Church (OTCC).

Garcia, Nyota: Chair of the NAAPC National Convention.

Germain, Susan, PhD: Wheatley University. Post-doc working in seismology lab. Recruited to University of Guelph, Ontario.

Gordon, Ruth: Staffer for Susan Kennedy. Girlfriend of Azisa Beman.

Graham, _____: Principal, Mt. Pleasant, GA, High School.

Green, "Boomer" College football friend of Sen. Rivers. Unregistered lobbyist for Global E-Technic Energy (GETE), Ltd. Archbishop Trucido's Councilor Number Nine and head of Kansas City Mafia.

Hackers and Hashtags (where known):
bangersnmash (alternet link UK to Holland)
buckeyeboy (presumed resident of Ohio)
brooklynpizza
chicagocub
converseone (presumed resident of Spartanburg, SC)
couzan (presumed resident of south Louisiana)
darkknight (hacker, gamer; associate of reddragon)
daytondude (presumed resident of Dayton, Ohio)
dikedyke (alternet link Holland to Switzerland)
eli1990 (presumed Harvard Law graduate)
falconone (presumed resident of Atlanta)
flowergirl
foxylady (alternet link US to UK)
frerejacques (presumed resident of France, perhaps Paris)
garyingary (presumed resident of Gary, Indiana)
grits (Sugi Close, net admin)

guyanagal (presumed resident of Georgetown, Guyana)

hackattack (Kevin Stewart, Omaha)

harvardlaw8801 (presumed Harvard Law graduate)

highflyer (George Stanley)

hoosierdad (presumed resident Crothersville, Indiana)

kievgatekeeper (presumed location, Kiev, Ukraine)

iddoc (Karen Clemens)

lkklad (presumed Mithras member, Cape Lazarev, Russia)

longjohnsilver (unknown observer, in Caribbean)

maelwen ("stained maiden" net admin)

maudi (mouse, as in churchmouse) Tim Karus

meadeee (presumed electrical engineer, Lake Meade/Hoover Dam)

mercyotiswarren (Polly Singer blob, pseudonym)

mithrasair22 and 33 (aircraft flown by members of Brotherhood of Mithras)

mithras1776 (command element, ground unit, Brotherhood of Mithras)

modernbard

newsboy

oldpatriot (contact on White House staff)

phoenixfreddy

pqprime (presumed resident of Province [du] Québec)

realityrocks

reddragon (Michael Cookson, net admin)

redstick (presumed resident Baton Rouge which is French for "red stick")

ringoffire (Japanese university? student?)

sandman

shearwaterpatriots (Shearwater mercenary company)

shenandoah33 (presumed spotter, observer in Shenandoah Mountains)

steeldrummer (presumed resident, island of Tobago)

strongman (stevedore, Port of Savannah)

sunsinyi (presumed South Korean soldier; Mithras?)

tardisboy (Rudy Adams, son of Dr. Ed Adams)
tomsdad (father of Tom Kelly)

umjd (presumed doctor of law University of Maryland? Montana?)
usamithras (command element, Brotherhood of Mithras in the USA)
wartberg (verified German contact)
whatdrwho (Dr. Ed Adams)
windycitygirl (presumed resident of Chicago)
witwat (University of the Witwatersrand, South Africa)
woodenboy/wb (Aaron Nichols, Selma, Alabama)

Hamilton, G. G.: General, USA. Takes command of Ft. Knox September 2020. Member, Soldiers of the Cross.

Harris, General: Chairman, Joint Chiefs of Staff under President March.

Hogg, General: Deputy Director, NSA.

Hopkins, Frank: Personal Assistant to Senator March then head of Dallas district office. Later on March's White House Staff. Boyfriend of Polly Singer.

Ivanson, _____: Member, Mt. Pleasant, GA city council (later murdered).

Johnston, Sally: Department of Human Services employee, Dayton, TN.

Karus, Tim: Former altar boy to Archbishop Trucido, later, aide.

Kelley, Theresa/Tom: Transgendered (born female, identifies male) teen, Clover, KY.

Kennedy, Susan: Two-term governor of Oregon, running for President in 2016 on the Democrat ticket.

Kline, General: ranking member, Pentagon branch, Brotherhood of Mithras.

L'Wazi, Mr. Samuel ("one with the knowledge"). Chief Lobbyist for NAAPC.

Lacombe, Justine: Prime Minister of Canada.

Larimer, _____: OTCC member, elected Mt. Pleasant, GA City Council, 2016.

Lesene, James: Mayor-elect of Mt. Pleasant, GA.

Llewellyn, _____: Fire Marshall, Mt. Pleasant, GA.

Mabry, Junior: Editor/Owner, *Mt. Pleasant Clarion*. Partner/wife, unnamed.

MacLauren, Liam: Royal Canadian Air Cadet, later Cadet Sergeant, Canadian Army assigned to Henry Stanley's security detail.

March, Senator Edward: R/AFFP-Texas. Later President of the United States.

Mt. Pleasant, GA: Pastor Dorset (Resurrection Baptist); Susan _____; Becky Bainard and parents; Elder Sampson and woman, Investigating Committee.

Muldoon: Commentator for *The World Citizen*.

Nichols, Aaron: Teen member of Jonas Path's congregation, Selma, Alabama. Geek/hacker; joins alternet hashtag: woodenboy.

Paine, Tom: Pen name of blogger [see Michael Cookson] visited by government agents after doing research on Bitcoin.

Parnell, Ken: Secret Service, chief of Henry Stanley's detail. Son **Jamie** friend of Henry and George Stanley.

Path, Jonas, Reverend: US House of Representatives, (AFFP-AL). Pastor, Selma Fundamental Baptist Church, which becomes Path to Heaven Congregation, OTCC.

Patterson, Darla: Lt. Col., intelligence officer at Carlisle Barracks; member, Brotherhood of Mithras.

Potiphar, Hector JD: District Attorney, Dayton, Tennessee. Prosecutor in trial of Dr. Ed Adams.

Prescott, _____ Dr.: Psychiatrist in league with Sally Johnston.

Pyle, _____: Representative, US Congress.

Red Dragon: See Michael Cookson.

Redwine, _____: One-time Mayor, Mt. Pleasant, GA.

Remi _____: Host, friend of Tommy Carron and Henry Stanley at St. Jean.

Rightly, Bert: Talking head on *American Fire Network*, evening program, *Take 'Em to the Wire*.

Rivers, Markham: MD, (R-OK). Chair, Energy Committee. Climate change denier-in-chief; fracking earthquake denier-in-chief. In the pay of GETE and perhaps others.

Science Guide AKA **Dr. Wallace Anderson**: Host of kids science program on the National Television Service.

Secret Service not listed separately: Chatsworth (Senior Agent in Charge, Thomas Stanley detail).

Singer, Polly: National Radio Service, National TV Service; former intern C-SPAN. Later spokesperson for DHS.

Smith, _____: Victim of incestuous rape, _____ County, TX.

Smith, Roger: Dayton, Tennessee real estate attorney, friend of Ed Adams.

Stafford, Elizabeth: Daughter of Henry Stafford (q.v.). Long-time girlfriend of Henry Stanley.

Stafford, Henry: (AFFP-MS) Seven-term Representative. Plutocrat, elected Speaker of the House. Philanthropic donor to Wheatley University.

Stanley, George: Younger son of Rep. Stanley. Hacker name: High Flyer.

Stanley, Henry T.: Adopted son of Rep. Thomas Stanley. Father (deceased) Canadian; mother then married Thomas Stanley, who adopted Henry.

Stanley, Thomas: US Representative (R/AFFP-OK), on Intelligence Committee; later Vice President under March; later President. Widower. Father of George and Henry.

Stewart, Arthur: Vice-Presidential candidate, Democratic ticket.

Stewart, Casey: Lt. Col.. USAF. Holder of "football" containing nuclear launch codes.

Thackery, Nicholas: PA/aide to Senator/President Edward March.

Trucido, Archbishop Isaac. Former Cardinal and head of Vatican Bank; leader of One True Christian Church and a council which consists of the heads of the 12 Mafia Families in the US and Canada. That he is leader of the OTCC is known only to Tim Karus and the Councilors. Estate in Shenandoah, Virginia.

Councilors where known (Americanized names)

#1 Capp, Abe: NJ. Transportation, waste removal unions.

#2 Unknown: presumed Canadian.

#3 Boudreaux, Louisiana and Mississippi.

#4 Emmet: Chicago and vicinity.

#5 Unknown: CA, WA, OR, AK.

#6 Davis: MD, DC, VA. Interface with Black Mafia in DC, elsewhere. Ordained. In charge of penetration of the Secret Service.

#7 Earnhart: NC, SC.

#9 Green, Boomer: TX, KS, NE, OK, and likely other western states.

#10 Harris: WV, KY, TN.

#11 Edwards: NY.

#12 Unknown: presumed Canadian.

Vaughn, Thomas: Representative (AFFP-RI). Son **Theodore (Ted)**. Father **Frederick**. Wife **Vivian**.

Walker, Mark: High school wrestler and member, God's Christian Army who dies of CA-MRSA.

Warren, Mercy Otis: Heroine of the American Revolution; name used by Polly Singer on underground blog.

Warwick, Richard: The "king maker." Capitalist, plutocrat with worldwide (although hidden) interests. His (fortified) estate is located in a remote section of the Adirondack Mountains.

Wilkes, Dr. Evan: Wheatley U biology; guest on Bert Rightly's show.

Webster, _____: Judge, Dayton, TN. Trial of Ed Adams.

Weizmann, Sol: Constitutional law expert, joined staff of Thomas Vaughn.

Young, Mr. and Mrs.: Indiana Quakers, part of Underground Railroad.

Zuma, _____: Post-Doc at the University of Witwatersrand, South Africa

_____, Bartoleme: Captain of Canadian fishing boat. Father of Auguste.

_____, Dennis: Player on County High School, team and member of Tommy Carron's church.

_____, Dr.: Head of the Centers for Disease Control

_____, Eddie: on Stanley's staff, computer geek.

_____: Freshman representative, Georgia; allied with Senator Rivers and Boomer Green.

_____, Haley: former employer of Mel Appleton

_____: Head of Canadian Security Intelligence Service

_____, Piyush: former employer of Frank Hopkins

_____, Regina: friend of Mrs. Bainard.

_____, Sam (Samantha): Head of Features for Dallas NRS.

GLOSSARY

2C Goal: Two degrees centigrade rise in average global temperature, predicted to be the upper limit of increase before significant disaster overtakes the environment. This has been translated into limitations on greenhouse gas production thought to keep temperature rise at or below 2C.

Ad lidem **letter**: A letter notifying someone of a potential lawsuit against them.

Aerostat: Tethered balloon. As used here, a platform for radar monitoring the border for planes carrying illegal drugs. Also used to detect low-flying aircraft and cruise missiles.

Al Jihadi: Arabic language internet news source.

Alternet: Reconstituted internet using shared computers, wifi signals transmitted from home to home using potato chip can antennas and FM radio (RDS—Radio Data System, the digital signal that carries the name of the artist and song that is playing, and similar information); from city-to-city and nation-to-nation by obscure links including the long-forgotten copper wires buried in undersea cables, and hijacked satellite links such as the ones used by stores to maintain inventory.

Amra'a Haram: Fundamental Islamic jihadists. The name loosely translates as "women are taboo."

American Fire Network (AFN): Right-leaning cable TV news network; home of Bert Rightly's "Take 'Em to the Wire" evening program.

Anycast: Software that allows the internet's root name computers to operate from multiple servers at multiple geographic locations.

APB: All Points Bulletin issued by police for others to be on the lookout for a fugitive.

APC: Armored Personnel Carrier.

Army Bugle: Unofficial publication of the US Army.

ASAP: As Soon As Possible.

ASEL: Aircraft, single-engine, land.

ATC: Air Traffic Control.

ATF: (Bureau of) Alcohol, Tobacco, and Firearms. Shorthand for the government agency with responsibility for regulating those items.

AWACS: Airborne Warning and Control System. Aircraft with heavy-duty radar on top and a mini-command post inside.

BCE/B.C.E.: Before the Common Era.

Beaufort Wind Scale: Commonly accepted scale used to describe wind speed. See:
http://www.spc.noaa.gov/faq/tornado/beaufort.html

Blue States: States with a large liberal population and generally liberal governments at state and local levels.

Border States: States uncommitted to the left or the right.

Boston Tea Party: Right-wing, loosely organized people who oppose taxation for themselves. In doing so, they manage to eliminate most taxation for the plutocrats who are their puppet-masters.

Burner: Term applied to cell phones and tablet or laptop computers bought with cash and often untraceable to the user. May also apply to laptops borrowed at internet cafés. The term was popularized in HBO's *The Wire* program in which burner phones were often used by drug dealers.

C-SPAN: Cable-Satellite Public Affairs Network funded not by the government, but by the cable television industry and its subscribers.

CA-MRSA: Community-associated methicillin-resistant *Staphylococcus aureus*.

CE/C.E.: In the year of the Common Era.

CDC: Centers for Disease Control and Prevention.

CFCs: Chlorofluorocarbons. Chemicals whose molecules contain carbon, chlorine, and fluorine, used as propellants for aerosol sprays, making packing foam, and as refrigerants. Freon (a brand name of DuPont) is perhaps the best known. They were shown to have contributed to the destruction of ozone in the upper atmosphere, and their manufacture has been phased out. See the Wikipedia article, and then follow the external links. See also information on the US EPA website.

CIA: US Central Intelligence Agency.

Commo: Communications Officer.

Concordia: Antarctic research station, operated by several countries in cooperation. (*Concord* is from the Latin meaning, "harmony.")

Constitutional Caucus: Caucus of the US House of Representatives. Goals include rewriting the constitution to guarantee economic freedom, individual liberty, and [their] interpretation of the constitution. They are behind the call for a constitutional convention.

Counter-prop: Official government sources that offer information that conflicts with that posted by anti-government sources such as *The World Citizen*.

Cryptocurrency: An artificial currency, such as Bitcoin, used to pay for goods and services often on the darknet side of the internet to avoid sales and services being tracked by governments.

Daesh: The alliterative and loose acronymic name, from the Arabic, for the self-proclaimed "Islamic State of Iraq and Syria," also called ISIS and ISIL. al-**D**awla **a**l-Islamiya al-Iraq al-**Sh**am). The name is similar in Arabic to words for *Dahes* (one who sows discord) as well as some words with vulgar connotations or denotations.

dailykos (www.dailykos.com): Internet news source.

Daily Mail: UK news organization.

Department of Defense (DoD): US government organization.

DFW: Aviation code for Dallas-Fort Worth airport.

DHS: Department of Homeland Security. Subordinate organizations include the Bureau of Communication (was the National Security Agency and the FCC); Bureau of Education; Bureau of Environment (was the Environmental Protection Agency); Bureau of Health (was the National Institutes of Health [NIH]), NIH Enforcement Division; Centers for Disease Control (CDC); Bureau of Natural Sciences (was United States Geological Services, parts of the National Aeronautics and Space Administration, and the President's Scientific Advisory Board); Bureau of Power (was Department of Energy); Bureau of Recovery (was Federal Emergency Management Agency); Bureau of Rectitude (closely linked with Investigative Committees, q.v.); Federal Bureau of Investigation; Central Intelligence Agency; and others.

DMZ: Demilitarized Zone separating North and South Korea.

DPRK: Democratic People's Republic of Korea, more commonly, North Korea.

E. coli: *Escherichia coli*. A bacterium found in the environment, foods, and the intestines of humans and animals. Some strains may cause illness and death. http://www.webmd.com/a-to-z-guides/e-coli-infection-topic-overview

E-prom: Erasable programmable read-only memory. Computer chip, usually a critical part of a computer.

EMS: Emergency Medical Service(s).

Fascist: A person who believes in/supports an authoritarian, nationalistic, conservative, right-wing government and society. See also OTCC, AFFP.

FISA: Foreign Intelligence Surveillance Act. Law passed in 1978 and strengthened following Islamist terrorist attacks on New York and the Pentagon on September 9, 2011.

FOI: Freedom of Information; a process by which individuals, especially journalists, request records and information from government agencies.

Foxprop: Disparaging term for political propaganda. From the *kitsune,* a fox of Japanese legend—a shape shifter—and the legends of the Quechua, a fox of the Andes—a scoundrel.

FrackFollowFriends, often just FrackFollow:
Conservation group working to show dangers of fracking (e.g., earthquakes, water pollution).

Free States (blue): Name applied to states whose people/governments were not aligned with the OTCC/AFFP takeover of the USA. Include Maine, New Hampshire, Vermont, Massachusetts, New York, Pennsylvania, Michigan, Connecticut, Indiana, Florida, California, Oregon, and Washington.

Freedom's Torch Caucus: A Caucus of the US Senate; membership includes all senators from red states—whether they like it, or not.

Froward: From "to-ward" and "fro-ward." See also "toward" and *Richard III*, Act III, Scene i. A froward child is intractable.

Fundie: Religious fundamentalist usually of the Christian or Muslim persuasion. See also *mindless fundie*.

G-2: The intelligence section or officer of a military staff.

GETE: Global E-Technic Energy, Ltd. Major multinational energy company. Controlled by Kansas City, USA, Mafia. Major figure: "Boomer" Giavano.

GHG, Greenhouse Gas: Gasses in Earth's atmosphere that "trap" heat from the sun, e.g., carbon dioxide ($CO2$), Methane ($Ch4OH$), and water vapor ($H2O$).

Global Explorers: Boys and girls group formed by secular humanists in response to the Boy Scouts' positions on religion and sexuality.

GMT: Greenwich Mean Time (five hours ahead of Eastern Standard Time).

God's Christian Army (GCA): Male only organization of high school and college athletes; echoes elders patriarchal and fundamentalist beliefs. Recruiting tool of the One True Christian Church. See also Rebeccas, Soldiers of the Cross.

God's Word for You, GW4U: Religious cable TV channel, newspaper, internet site. Studios in Georgetown, DC and elsewhere.

Golden Compass: Safe word and nickname for George Stanley.

Handbook of Instruction for Disciples: One True Christian Church (OTCC) guide for lay leadership including Sunday School teachers, adult leaders/coaches of God's Christian Army (q.v.), and Rebeccas (q.v.).

Handbook for Investigators: One True Christian Church guide for members of Investigating Committees and their agents.

Hellespont: Also known as the Dardanelles; strait separating European Turkey from Asian Turkey; connects the Sea of Marmara (and thus the Black Sea) to the Aegean Sea (and thus the Mediterranean).

Helvetia: Switzerland.

Interpol: International police organization.

Investigating Committees: Groups of citizens, usually chartered by local congregations of the OTCC with the cooperation of secular authorities. Like the committees that conducted the Inquisition or the Salem Witch Trials. May include subcommittees on Rectitude. May be contracted by local school boards to enforce dress codes, discipline, and comportment in the schools.

IV: Intravenous.

Je sui l'information: French newspaper ("I Am the News").

K-Street: Euphemism for lobbyists based on the location of many offices of the paid flacks who write legislation to benefit their corporate bosses rather than the American people.

L'Internationale: Socialist newspaper published in France.

Liberal: A person who is open to new opinions and information and who supports a government and society based on individual rights and freedoms.

Liberty Partisans: Loose association of armed resistance fighters.

Libsymp: Derogatory term used by the far right to label people whose beliefs are anathema to the far right. Includes free-thinkers, atheists, agnostics, and all non-Christians.

Lungi: Capital of Sierra Leone.

Marty McFly: Safe word.

Meningitis: A disease characterized by inflammation of the membranes covering the brain and spinal cord. It is usually caused by a bacterial or virus infection. It can be caused by several different viruses including herpes. At least one case has been attributed to the Ebola virus.
www.cec.gov/meningitis/index.html

Merc/Mercs: Mercenary, mercenaries.

MERS: Middle East Respiratory Syndrome.

Meteor Burst Communications: Also meteor trail or meteor scatter. Communications system that bounces signals off the ionized trails of meteors in the upper atmosphere. Google "meteor burst comms" and check the Wikipedia article and the .pdf from the National Security Agency.

Methane: Natural gas. See:
http://dwb.unl.edu/teacher/nsf/c09/c09links/www.casahome.org/methane.htm

Mindless fundie: Fundamentalist (e.g., Christian or Muslim) whose thinking has been taken over by propaganda from the pulpit, and who is therefore unable to think for himself or herself.

Minutemen: Association of resistance fighters, mostly ex-military.

MO: *Modus operandi;* method of operation, usually of a criminal.

Mt. Pleasant Clarion: Newspaper, centrist and non-aligned.

NAAPC: National Association for the Advancement of People of Color. The organization as depicted herein exists only this narrative, and its representation there is intended not to resemble any extant organization.

NEACP: National Emergency Airborne Command Post. Boeing 747 aircraft.

Neumayer: German Antarctic research station.

New York Afterword: Left-leaning newspaper with national circulation and internet site.

NPR: National Public Radio and television service.

NRS: National Radio and television Service.

Offing: the most distant part of the sea visible from land.

Oh My Higgs . . . The Higgs boson was dubbed "the God particle" by people who had no sense. Period. The expression, "Oh my Higgs and little Piceans" is a parody of "Oh, ye gods and little fishes."

Okie Record: Right-leaning newspaper and internet news site, Oklahoma.

OTOH: On the Other Hand. Text message shorthand.

One True Christian Church (OTCC): A coalition of evangelical, pentecostal, and fundamentalist Xtian churches led by a "conference" with a "moderator," but in reality, controlled by Archbishop Isaac Trucido and his people. Their goals include control of the American Freedom First Party (AFFP) that includes the plutocrats who own or control ninety-nine percent of the wealth of America.

PA: Personal Assistant.

PBS: Public Broadcasting System.

PM: Prime Minister.

PMS: Post-menstrual syndrome. Allusion to women's state of mind around the time of monthly menstruation.

Po-Po: Police.

Posse Comitatus: The common-law or statute law authority of a county sheriff, or other law officer, to conscript any able-bodied man to assist him in keeping the peace or enforcing the law.

POTUS: President of the United States

PQ: Province [du] Québec.

Purple: A state or a person that is neither "red" nor "blue." A fence-sitter. Someone who is unable to commit to a position. (Definition from *OTCC Handbook for Investigators*.)

Ranogen: National polling organization whose only clients are the American Freedom First Party and the One True Christian Church. [After **Ran**dom Number **Gen**erator]

Rebeccas: A social organization for young women of high-school age who are propagandized by the One True Christian Church (OTCC) to believe in abstinence-only birth control, that marriage is mandatory, and that submission to their husbands is required. Activities include quilting and homemaking. Led by Circle Leaders from the OTCC.

RDS: Radio Data Service. Portions of the radio spectrum used to provide information such as song title and artist's name to radios so equipped.

Red Queen: Code phrase to identify George Stanley to Red Dragon.

Red States: States with an effective majority of AFFP/OTCC members.

Ring of Fire: Nickname for Japanese geological service or university web site that reports earthquakes and volcanoes worldwide. Blocked by DHS from users in USA and Canada but accessible to George Stanley after September 2018.

Rupert: Safe word.

S-PAC: Umbrella term for certain Political Action Committees, including non-connected PACs, super-PACs, and hybrid PACs. As used here, specifically applies to those who do not have to report the names of donors. Sometimes called "dark money" PACs. They are supposed to support issues and not candidates; however, this is often a thin fiction. See, for example, http://www.fec.gov/ans/answers_pac.shtml.

Satcom: Satellite communications.

SCOTUS: Supreme Court of the United States.

Security Intelligence Service: Canadian semi-equivalent to the US FBI.

Soldiers of the Cross (SOC): Men's social organization at congregations of the One True Christian Church. Becomes an armed force following the Righteous Right's takeover of the USA. Their missions include penetrating the Secret Service and carrying out military actions on behalf of OTCC leadership.

Southern Freedom Law Center: Ultra-liberal organization that tracks hate crimes and hate groups, and provides counsel to persons accused or treated unjustly by any government organization.

STD: Sexually Transmitted Disease.

Tempest Times: New York, right-leaning newspaper; perhaps internet news site.

Tonne: 1,000 kilograms. Each kilogram equals 2.2 pounds, making a "tonne" equal to 2,200 pounds.

Toward (TOO ward): Archaic. After "to-ward" and "fro-ward." A toward child is tractable and trusting, easily influenced.

TSA: Transportation Security Administration.

UHF: Ultra High Frequency (radio)

UK: United Kingdom.

UK Voice, UK Voice World Service: United Kingdom mainstream newspaper, HF radio, satellite, and internet.

USG: United States Government.

USGS: United States Geological Survey. All material attributed to the USGS herein is real. Their mission and 2015 proposed budget numbers are real.

VEEP: Vice President.

VHF: Very High Frequency (radio).

vic: Vicinity; in the vicinity of.

VTOL: Vertical takeoff and landing as a helicopter or Osprey aircraft.

Washington Banner: DC, right-leaning newspaper.

Washington Standard: DC, left-leaning newspaper.

Water Wolf: Dutch nickname for their ancient enemy, the sea.

Wheatley Today: Internet newspaper from Wheatley University.

WitWat: University of the Witwatersrand, South Africa.

Wow-Wow Radio: AM radio station, Mt. Pleasant, Georgia.

World Citizen: Left-leaning newspaper/internet streamed, forced off the internet and underground by the US government; became samizdat. Home of Muldoon.

World of Weird: US tabloid newspaper primarily sold in convenience stores and at supermarket checkout lines.

WTF: What the Heck? Text message shorthand.

XO: Executive Officer; second in command.

Yukon: Safe word and nickname for Henry Stanley.

BIBLIOGRAPHY: REFERENCES AND READING LIST

Internet links were current when copied. Links to wiki sites were authenticated from other sources. The reader is encouraged to follow links and references.

Alaskan permafrost: http://www.alaskacenters.gov/permafrost.cfm

Antarctic Ice Melt: *Al Jazeera*, 2 November 2015. Google "Ross Ice Shelf NASA" and read the entry at Wikipedia, slate.com, and NASA's Visible Earth other entries from NASA, for example.

Antibiotic Apocalypse: *BBC.com/news* December 21, 2015.

Aquifer recharge:
http://waterinthewest.stanford.edu/groundwater/recharge/

Arsenic in drinking water: Wikipedia.

Barbara Frietchie: Perhaps best known from John Greenleaf Whittier's poem by that name. Read it at
http://www.poetryfoundation.org/poem/174751.

Biometric Identification *USAF Afterburner*, Spring-Summer 2015. The *then* system did not include DNA or retinal scans.

Boiling Frog anecdote: Start with
https://en.wikipedia.org/wiki/Boiling_frog and follow some of the references. See also http://conservationmagazine.org/2011/03/frog-fable-brought-to-boil/

Calhoun, John B.: (Rats in overcrowded conditions) See Wikipedia and follow the links at the end of the article. See also Sagan, Carl, Shadows of Forgotten Ancestors.

Canadian jets withdrawn from anti-Isis coalition: *The Telegraph*, www.telegraph.co.uk, November 5, 2015.

Cholera in the Middle East: NPR November 6, 2015.

Climate change: The two principal sites, both of which posit that change is occurring and that it's anthropogenic, are the International

Panel on Climate Change (IPCC) at www.ipcc.ch and Skeptical Science at www.skepticalscience.com. I have not found a legitimate site (e.g., one ending in .edu or .gov) that shows any proof that (1) climate is not changing or (2) that it's not anthropogenic. If you find one, please post to my blog at www.Stuff-of-Life.org.

Climate change collapses cod catch: *Washington Post*, October 29, 2015.

Clonal complex 398 methicillin resistant Staphylococcus aureus (MRSA) and association with pigs and other livestock: http://wwwnc.cdc.gov/eid/article/14/9/07-1576_article; http://umash.umn.edu/resources/pdf/pigs-mrsa-112013.pdf

Creation Museum, Kentucky: https://en.wikipedia.org/wiki/Creation_Museum (and follow links)

Creationism Theme Park, Florida: http://www.pensapedia.com/wiki/Dinosaur_Adventure_Land

Creation Evidence Museum of Texas: www.creationevidence.org/

Deaths, American Military, Iraq/Afghanistan: Wikipedia; extrapolated.

Drug-resistant malaria in South East Asia: BBC News, 20 October 2015 (www.bbc.news.com) citing "Nature Communications" and "Lancet Infectious Diseases."

Earthquake data (global): earthquake.usgs.gov

Ebola Virus in Sierra Leone: NPR, November 7, 2015.

Florida citrus greening: *NPR* December 1, 2015.

Fracking and Wastewater Injection, Earthquakes: https://pubs.er.usgs.gov/publication/ofr20161035 [download entire report at the Links to Document Report 31.0 MB pdf] See also the *Washington Post* article of July 3, 2014.

German Antarctic Station Neumayer: (a very cool place in more ways than one) https://www.awi.de/en/expedition/stations/neumayer-station-iii.html

God Works in Mysterious Ways: This does not appear in the Bible, and may have first appeared in a 19th century hymn by William Cowper. See also Romans 11:33.

Industry Lies/Scientific Consensus: See Merchants of Doubt by Naomi Oreskes and Erik Conway. There is a documentary film available.

Islamic Preacher Calls for Caliphate: *Israel International News* October 28, 2015.

Ivermectin, antihelmenthic, may work on malaria: *BBC News*, 27 October 2015 http://www.bbc.com/news/health-34649016

Jones Act:
https://en.wikipedia.org/wiki/Merchant_Marine_Act_of_1920

Los Angeles, CA, Anti-Terrorism Exercise December 21, 2015, based on report by Martin Kaste, *NPR*, December 22, 2015.

Malaria in SEA Creates New Refugee Crisis *BBC News*, 20 February 2015.

Malaria in USA: http://www.cdc.gov/malaria/about/facts.html

Medical research during Europe's Dark Ages: Sagan, Carl. *The Demon Haunted World*. Kindle edition.

Mercy Otis Warren: Political writer and propagandist of the American Revolution. Find her on Wikipedia, and explore the links.

Methane clathrates: Wikipedia and elsewhere.

Moratorium on Stem Cell Funding: *NPR* November 6, 2015.

New Orleans Hurricanes:
http://web.mit.edu/12.000/www/m2010/teams/neworleans1/hurricane%20history.htm

Nuclear Power Plants in the US: https://www.eia.gov

NY Attorney General Investigates Big Oil for Possible Climate Change Lies *New York Times*, November 5, 2015.

Ocean Acidification: $H_2O+CO_2 = H_2CO_3$. Water plus carbon dioxide equals carbonic acid. This is a simplistic look at what is a larger and more complex process. See, for example https://theotherco2problem.wordpress.com/what-happens-chemically/

Pause in Refugee Resettlement: *AP*, November 17, 2015.

Polio Emergency in Ukraine: *NPR* December 3, 2015.

Polio Vaccine Can Go 'Feral': *NPR* November 10, 2015.

Power of Prayer to Heal (or Not): Look it up on the Templeton Foundation web site.

Rats Overcrowded: See Calhoun, John B. in Wikipedia, and explore the links.

Red Zone: *The Washington Post*, September 8, 2012. Tracee Hamilton.

Ross Ice Shelf: See Antarctic Ice Melt.

Russian Minister on Bitcoin: www.cryptocoinsnews.com 28 October 2015.

Strategic Petroleum Reserve:
https://en.wikipedia.org/wiki/Strategic_Petroleum_Reserve

Transgendered students' rights and restrictions (South Dakota):
http://www.cnn.com/2016/02/17/politics/south-dakota-school-restrooms-transgender-bill/

UK Met Hadley Center: Headquarters of the United Kingdom meteorology operation. Look up "Hadley cells" in Wikipedia.

UN Raises Ceiling on GHG: *New York Times*, November 6, 2015.

Underground Railroad: freedomcenter.org

US House Won't Pay for Climate Deal: *AP,* November 30, 2015.

US to Take Refugees: *AP* September 21, 2015; *NPR*, September 22, 2015.

Viagra, Kentucky bill would require note from a man's wife:
http://america.aljazeera.com/articles/2016/2/15/ky-bill-would-require-men-seeking-viagra-to-get-note-from-wives.html

War on Drugs Targeted Blacks:
http://www.cnn.com/2016/03/23/politics/john-ehrlichman-richard-nixon-drug-war-blacks-hippie/index.html and
http://www.nydailynews.com/news/politics/nixon-aide-war-drugs-tool-target-black-people-article-1.2573832

Zika Fever/Birth Defects: *BBC News on line* November 29, 2015. **In Arkansas**: WSBTV.com, January 27, 2016. **In Virginia**: WTKR.com, January 27, 2016. **International Health Emergency** *Al Jazeera* February 1, 2016. **Higher temperatures speed up spread of Zika**: *AP* February 3, 2016 (Seth Borenstein). **History, etiology** *Huffington Post*, February 1, 2016 (Vincent Ricaniello).

DISCLAIMERS

This narrative takes place in a reality like our own, but which is not our own. Events attributed to our-world news sources are correct as written. All were verified from multiple sources; however, usually only the primary source is cited. Other events occur only in the reality in which this narrative occurs.

It is intended that people and institutions in this narrative not be construed to represent people or institutions, their beliefs, or their actions in our reality. I have the greatest respect for the University of Witwatersrand, in South Africa and have tried to portray them in a supportive and sympathetic light. Dr. Dart, of course, has an analogue in the late Dr. Raymond Dart. In the words of Muldoon, "Don't know who he is? Look him up!"

I think I'm a fair dinkum speaker of English, but I relied on Google Translate for other languages.

Quotations from the Bible are from the King James Version and are in the public domain. Some were redacted without, however, changing their meanings.

"Politics makes strange bedfellows" is credited to Charles Dudley Warner *My Summer in a Garden*, 1870 and is in the public domain.

Trademarks used herein, including American Eagle, Armani, Band-Aid, Beretta, Boeing and their aircraft, Clorox, Drano, Forbes, Fortune 100, Glock, Google, Gulfstream, iMac, iPhone, iPad, Lucite, Patek Philippe, Pez, Piedmont, PowerPoint, Pringles, Sprint, Starbucks, Suburban, TAVOR X-95, Velveeta,

Vidalia, and any others are the property of their owners in all realities.

The words of Peter Abelard, French theologian and scholar (1079—1142 CE), while translated and paraphrased, are an accurate representation of his philosophy.

Henry Tudor Stanley's genealogy is that of the man who became King Henry VII of England, after defeating King Richard III. But you've figured that out, already, right?

AUTHOR'S AFTERWORD

This novel began on November 1, 2015 in response to the NaNoWriMo challenge to write a 50,000-word novel during the month of November. By November 30, I had reached 70,000 words. After investing that time and effort, I decided to continue writing and expanded the narrative to 110,000 words. In early January 2016 I sent the manuscript to Brendan, a long-time friend, reader, contributor, and commenter on my writing.

Brendan replied politely but firmly and pointed out significant problems with the narrative.

After reading Brendan's comments, I spent the first three months of 2016 cutting, reordering, and revising. What you have is the result.

By definition, a dystopian novel doesn't have a happy ending. In fact, like *On the Beach*, *Childhood's End,* and one less well known, *Level Seven*, it ends with the end of the world.

To produce such a novel, one takes a few current events, notions, and trends; projects them into the future with exaggeration that should not become adynaton; mixes them well and adds a plot and some characters. That is what I tried to do.

One such current notion, perhaps the most egregious, is the attack on science by some Christian fundamentalists, most notably the "young earth creationists" and people who believe that creationism should be taught alongside science. According to a Pew Research poll, reported on 2014-09-14, more than half of Americans think creationism should be taught in school along with evolution. If creationism were to be taught, it should be in a class that featured Aesop and other fables. It is not a science and there's nothing scientific about it.

Another is the denial of global climate change by those who believe their god would not let it happen or that he has said that humankind is too puny to affect his creation in that way, even though he gave them dominion over the earth. It is perverse to deny global warming, to deny that it has adversely affected climate and that it will likely continue to do so, and to deny that there is an anthropogenic component. It is as perverse as denying that the planets orbit the sun and that the earth is a sphere. Well, a "tri-axial oblate spheroid."

Other concepts used in this narrative include the push by certain Christian fundamentalists in the United States toward a theocracy. The trend of right-wing politicians to embrace, cater to, and kowtow to Christian fundamentalists and the inability of other politicians to stand up to this should be obvious to even the casual observer. This may be more dangerous than their attack on science.

Another notion incorporated was the pseudo-science of "recovering memories." I commend to you Carl Sagan's book, "The Demon Haunted World" for more on this subject.

Modern neuroscience has shown conclusively that we create barriers in our minds, and that those barriers block information—no matter how well presented—that conflicts with our initial beliefs. In fact, it has been suggested that information that conflicts with our initial beliefs may raise the existing barriers and strengthen them. This narrative is an attempt to assault some of those barriers with a force strong enough to cause at least some readers to question, to ask, "What if?"